THE WEIRD CAT

The Weird Cat

an anthology

edited by

Katherine Kerestman and S. T. Joshi

WordCrafts

Published by WordCrafts Press
Cody, Wyoming 82414
www.wordcrafts.net

"Those who'll play with cats must expect to be scratched."
~Don Quixote de la Mancha

Contents

Introduction
Katherine Kerestman and S. T. Joshi

A well-told horror story has much in common with your own cherished puss. To begin with, a person cannot rudely and without ceremony take up either book or cat and indulge himself in it; rather, if a suppliant will permit the story or the cat to *come to him* gradually, then either will allow him to succumb to its power by degrees, until the petitioner no longer commands his own will. Furthermore, one must approach book or cat in a proper frame of mind; for either cat or book will, at first, tolerate but a gentle stroking of its fur, and then, only later, will it allow the devotee to knead its musculature and sinews; by this means, book or cat will subtly insinuate itself into the aspirant's own reality, so that the end result of the interaction is a communion of consciousnesses. Kitty jumps upon your lap and purrs, and you turn the page of your book.

Pray, take heed! Some dire thing is afoot! On your lap, Kitty stirs, her ears lifting into two small velvet tents. She raises her chin, stares expectantly into the gloom beyond the aura of the reading lamp, gazes at something which you cannot see! Her silken hairs begin to fluff, signaling her unease. Swiftly, Kitty moves from your lap onto the arm of your chair, where, channeling Bastet, she strikes an Egyptian-cat pose, her expectant stance and twitching whiskers communicating unseen peril.

The hairs on your neck begin to rise in sympathy. As you doggedly continue reading your book, you cast frequent glances at your cat: Kitty provides you with a sixth sense which you lack, a window into the unseen and the uncanny. You are mindful that cats dwell in a larger world than our own, the gulfs and abysses of which we can obtain but a shadowy glimpse, through their eyes.

Kitty arches her back and opens her mouth just a little, showing her teeth—and your book is forgotten as you peer hard into the distance, striving to see what she sees. As the threat looms closer . . . *she hisses!* And, because you cannot see what she sees, you begin to feel fear, though you may not admit it.

The several splendid and unique qualities of the feline race recommend them to weavers of tales of terror and mystery, who often employ our friends as a literary device. Quiet creatures, cats do not always reveal their thoughts to us, even though (when you love them) you can learn some of their secret language. Sometimes they lavish their affection (and demand reciprocity), and some-times they do not, baffling our kind. Being noiseless, cats are often unobserved, so that, when a person—all of a sudden—notices that there is a cat in a room, she may be startled. Swift as well as quiet, cats are able to appear and disappear at will, as well as creep, skulk, and stalk, especially when hunting.

Unfortunately, some of our species are frightened by cats. Having been domesticated, the cat has long been associated with other fearsome domestic animals—the housewife, the wise woman, or the enchantress. Like the woman, the cat is not always as domes-ticated as she is generally supposed to be—and when she is not, she strikes fear in the confounded observer. Being solitary and disdaining the herd, a cat walks alone, a preference that engenders misgivings in the minds of more tribally- or community-minded animals. Being a night-thing, the cat knows a world that is for-bidden to most of us in our hours of repose.

Relatively helpless in their smallness, their softness (which is a lack of protective exoskeletal armor), and the diminutive pro-portions of their teeth and claws, cats must perpetually be wary, existing always in some state of fear, lest they be ambushed. When threatened, our little friends bristle their tails, caterwaul, and hiss that terrible *hisssss*—and when these weapons are ineffective, they must leap and tear with small, but sharp, teeth and claws. The transformation of your beastie from soft lap-cuddler to razor-sharp projectile is a sight that is terrible to behold. Sometimes your cat undergoes this transmutation in defense of self, sometimes to protect her young ones or her humans.

Beautiful, lovable, and enigmatic entities who straddle the world in which humans dwell and another beyond our ken, cats have, since antiquity, been recognized as a different order of being. The ancients conceived of them as gods who protected home and hearth—and as inscrutable Sphinxes who withheld from human-kind their eldritch and unearthly knowledge—while, in another era, Inquisitors condemned them as familiars of Satan, for their independence and their close association with the daughters of Eve, whose magic conjured cheese out of milk, clothing out of plants, and children out of carnality.

That the myriad and wondrous attributes of the Feline can incite befuddlement and strike fear into the hearts of some people—and yet arouse the gentler emotions of sympathy and affection in others—is a strange paradox of the cosmos that is often employed by writers to enrich the development of an unsettling mood which is appropriate and necessary to the weird tale.

In this volume the editors have gathered a wide array of tales, essays, poems, and even extracts from letters that exhibit the myriad ways in which cats and weirdness are inexorably linked.

Rudyard Kipling in "The Cat Who Walked by Himself" provides a wistful anthropology of the cat and its grudging domestication within the framework of human life. His tale may perhaps reflect his era's stereotypical view of the role of the human female in society, but it nonetheless underscores the cat's intelligence and independence. Fables about cats have always been popular with writers and readers, and Lafcadio Hearn found a Japanese fable ("The Boy Who Drew Cats") when he emigrated to that island nation and absorbed its culture. Lewis Carroll created a fable of his own with his tale of the Cheshire cat, as do Katherine Kerestman in "The Witch of the Dark Woods" and Manuel Pérez-Campos in "Talmir and Threstenios."

The disturbingly close relation of the little housecat with the big cats of the forest and the veldt is underscored in Sir Arthur Conan Doyle's "The Brazilian Cat" and Sax Rohmer's "In the Valley of the Sorceress." That latter tale also plays with the notion of metempsychosis—the transformation of the human into animal. E. Nesbit, in one of her children's books, incorporated this idea in a more genial fashion ("The Cat-hood of Maurice") as a way of emphasizing the need to eschew cruelty to animals.

The close association of cats with the supernatural realm—and their unique ability to battle with the baleful entities from that realm—is the focus of a number of tales ranging from Algernon Blackwood's "The Attic" to Jason C. Eckhardt's "Ghost Bats" to Stephen Mark Rainey's "Nimbus." Ghostly cats themselves are featured in Ramsey Campbell's "Cat and Mouse," while Hank Schwaeble's long and complex story "Nine" tells of a battle between cats and other evil entities that may have stretched back to the dawn of recorded history, while Alan Dean Foster's "Le Chat Noir, La Femme Vieille" exhibits a cohort of stray cats in Paris who have more on their minds than mere personal survival.

H. P. Lovecraft was one of the great ailurophiles (cat lovers) in human history, and an entire volume of his writings on cats (*The H. P. Lovecraft Cat Book*) has appeared. His own owlish fable, "The Cats of Ulthar" (1920), is very well known (as are such tales as "The Rats in the Walls" and *The Dream-Quest of Unknown Kadath*, where cats play a critical role). We have chosen to include lesser-known writings by Lovecraft, among them a letter in which he discusses a preternaturally aged cat of his own acquaintance in Providence, R.I. Lovecraft's influence extends to other tales in this book, including Caitlín R. Kiernan's "The Cats of River Street" (which melds cats with the hybrid sea creatures of

Lovecraft's "The Shadow over Innsmouth") and Tony LaMalfa's "The Crimson Curse."

Ambrose Bierce was a ferocious hater of dogs, but that attitude did not automatically translate into a love of cats. But that he found a compelling fascination with the species is evident in his well-known tale "The Eyes of the Panther." We have chosen a more unfamiliar tale, the early humorous sketch "A Cargo of Cats." Darrell Schweitzer follows Bierce in a comic treatment of cats and the supernatural in "The Adventure of the Hanoverian Vampires."

It is unsurprising that the weirdness associated with the cat has been the subject of poetry. From William Blake to Rainer Maria Rilke to Robert W. Service, cats have inspired some of the greatest poets in literary history. Lord Dunsany, a master of the prose poem, links the cat with the Sphinx in "The Sphinx at Gizeh."

H. P. Lovecraft's "The Cats" (1925) was written in the depths of his despair in the teeming megalopolis of New York, and it evokes both the terror of that unnatural landscape and the terror inherent in the feline species. Contemporary poets of all sorts have teased out the fearsomeness that lies just under the surface of even the cuddliest kitten.

As Brandon R. Grafius notes in his essay in this volume, the subject of cats and the weird is all but inexhaustible. We hope that this sampling of some of the rich literature on this motif will entice you to look at felines in ways you haven't done before, and to ponder what worlds of wonder and mystery they look upon through their enigmatic eyes.

The Tyger

William Blake

Tyger! Tyger! burning bright
In the forests of the night,
What immortal hand or eye
Could frame thy fearful symmetry?

In what distant deeps or skies
Burnt the fire of thine eyes?
On what wings dare he aspire?
What the hand, dare seize the fire?

And what shoulder, & what art,
Could twist the sinews of thy heart?
And when thy heart began to beat,
What dread hand? & what dread feet?

What the hammer? what the chain?
In what furnace was thy brain?
What the anvil? what dread grasp
Dare its deadly terrors clasp?

When the stars threw down their spears,
And water'd heaven with their tears,
Did he smile his work to see?
Did he who made the Lamb make thee?

Tyger! Tyger! burning bright
In the forests of the night,
What immortal hand or eye
Dare frame thy fearful symmetry?

The Cat Who Walked by Himself
Rudyard Kipling

Hear and attend and listen; for this befell and behappened and became and was, O my Best Beloved, when the Tame animals were wild. The Dog was wild, and the Horse was wild, and the Cow was wild, and the Sheep was wild, and the Pig was wild—as wild as wild could be—and they walked in the Wet Wild Woods by their wild lones. But the wildest of all the wild animals was the Cat. He walked by himself, and all places were alike to him.

Of course the Man was wild too. He was dreadfully wild. He didn't even begin to be tame till he met the Woman, and she told him that she did not like living in his wild ways. She picked out a nice dry Cave, instead of a heap of wet leaves, to lie down in; and she strewed clean sand on the floor; and she lit a nice fire of wood at the back of the Cave; and she hung a dried wild-horse skin, tail-down, across the opening of the Cave; and she said, "Wipe you feet, dear, when you come in, and now we'll keep house."

That night, Best Beloved, they ate wild sheep roasted on the hot stones, and flavoured with wild garlic and wild pepper; and wild duck stuffed with wild rice and wild fenugreek and wild coriander; and marrow-bones of wild oxen; and wild cherries, and wild grenadillas. Then the Man went to sleep in front of the fire ever so happy; but the Woman sat up, combing her hair. She took the bone of the shoulder of mutton—the big fat blade-bone—and she looked at the wonderful marks on it, and she threw more wood on the fire, and she made a Magic. She made the First Singing Magic in the world.

Out in the Wet Wild Woods all the wild animals gathered together where they could see the light of the fire a long way off, and they wondered what it meant.

Then Wild Horse stamped with his wild foot and said, "O my Friends and O my Enemies, why have the Man and the Woman made that great light in that great Cave, and what harm will it do us?"

Wild Dog lifted up his wild nose and smelled the smell of roast mutton, and said, "I will go up and see and look, and say; for I think it is good. Cat, come with me."

"Nenni!" said the Cat. "I am the Cat who walks by himself, and all places are alike to me. I will not come."

"Then we can never be friends again," said Wild Dog, and he trotted off to the Cave. But when he had gone a little way the Cat said to himself, "All places are alike to me. Why should I not go too and see and look and come away at my own liking." So he slipped after Wild Dog softly, very softly, and hid himself where he could hear everything.

When Wild Dog reached the mouth of the Cave he lifted up the dried horse-skin with his nose and sniffed the beautiful smell of the roast mutton, and the Woman, looking at the blade-bone, heard him, and laughed, and said, "Here comes the first. Wild Thing out of the Wild Woods, what do you want?"

Wild Dog said, "O my Enemy and Wife of my Enemy, what is this that smells so good in the Wild Woods?"

Then the Woman picked up a roasted mutton-bone and threw it to Wild Dog, and said, "Wild Thing out of the Wild Woods, taste and try." Wild Dog gnawed the bone, and it was more delicious than anything he had ever tasted, and he said, "O my Enemy and Wife of my Enemy, give me another."

The Woman said, "Wild Thing out of the Wild Woods, help my Man to hunt through the day and guard this Cave at night, and I will give you as many roast bones as you need."

"Ah!" said the Cat, listening. "This is a very wise Woman, but she is not so wise as I am."

Wild Dog crawled into the Cave and laid his head on the Woman's lap, and said, "O my Friend and Wife of my Friend, I will help your Man to hunt through the day, and at night I will guard your Cave."

"Ah!" said the Cat, listening. "That is a very foolish Dog." And he went back through the Wet Wild Woods waving his wild tail, and walking by his wild lone. But he never told anybody.

When the Man waked up he said, "What is Wild Dog doing here?" And the Woman said, "His name is not Wild Dog any more, but the First Friend, because he will be our friend for always and always and always. Take him with you when you go hunting."

Next night the Woman cut great green armfuls of fresh grass from the water-meadows, and dried it before the fire, so that it smelt like new-mown hay, and she sat at the mouth of the Cave and plaited a halter out of horse-hide, and she looked at the shoulder of mutton-bone—at the big broad blade-bone—and she made a Magic. She made the Second Singing Magic in the world.

Out in the Wild Woods all the wild animals wondered what had happened to Wild Dog, and at last Wild Horse stamped with his foot and said, "I will go and see and say why Wild Dog has not returned. Cat, come with me."

"Nenni!" said the Cat. "I am the Cat who walks by himself, and all places are alike to me. I will not come." But all the same he followed Wild Horse softly, very softly, and hid himself where he could hear everything.

When the Woman heard Wild Horse tripping and stumbling on his long mane, she laughed and said, "Here comes the second. Wild Thing out of the Wild Woods, what do you want?"

Wild Horse said, "O my Enemy and Wife of my Enemy, where is Wild Dog?"

The Woman laughed, and picked up the blade-bone and looked at it, and said, "Wild Thing out of the Wild Woods, you did not come here for Wild Dog, but for the sake of this good grass."

And Wild Horse, tripping and stumbling on his long mane, said, "That is true; give it me to eat."

The Woman said, "Wild Thing out of the Wild Woods, bend your wild head and wear what I give you, and you shall eat the wonderful grass three times a day."

"Ah," said the Cat, listening, "this is a clever Woman, but she is not so clever as I am."

Wild Horse bent his wild head, and the Woman slipped the plaited hide halter over it, and Wild Horse breathed on the Woman's feet and said, "O my Mistress, and Wife of my Master, I will be your servant for the sake of the wonderful grass."

"Ah," said the Cat, listening, "that is a very foolish Horse." And he went back through the Wet Wild Woods, waving his wild tail and walking by his wild lone. But he never told anybody.

When the Man and the Dog came back from hunting, the Man said, "What is Wild Horse doing here?" And the Woman said, "His name is not Wild Horse any more, but the First Servant, because he will carry us from place to place for always and always and always. Ride on his back when you go hunting."

Next day, holding her wild head high that her wild horns should not catch in the wild trees, Wild Cow came up to the Cave, and the Cat followed, and hid himself just the same as before; and everything happened just the same as before; and the Cat said the same things as before, and when Wild Cow had promised to give her milk to the Woman every day in exchange for the wonderful grass, the Cat went back through the Wet Wild Woods waving his wild tail and walking by his wild lone, just the same as before. But he never told anybody. And when the Man and the Horse and the Dog came home from hunting and asked the same questions same as before, the Woman said, "Her name is not Wild Cow any more, but the Giver of Good Food. She will give us the warm white milk for always and always and always, and I will take care of her while you and the First Friend and the First Servant go hunting."

Next day the Cat waited to see if any other Wild thing would go up to the Cave, but no one moved in the Wet Wild Woods, so the Cat walked there by himself; and he saw the Woman milking the Cow, and he saw the light of the fire in the Cave, and he smelt the smell of the warm white milk.

Cat said, "O my Enemy and Wife of my Enemy, where did Wild Cow go?"

The Woman laughed and said, "Wild Thing out of the Wild Woods, go back to the Woods again, for I have braided up my hair, and I have put away the magic blade-bone, and we have no more need of either friends or servants in our Cave."

Cat said, "I am not a friend, and I am not a servant. I am the Cat who walks by himself, and I wish to come into your cave."

Woman said, "Then why did you not come with First Friend on the first night?"

Cat grew very angry and said, "Has Wild Dog told tales of me?"

Then the Woman laughed and said, "You are the Cat who walks by himself, and all places are alike to you. Your are neither a friend nor a servant. You have said it yourself. Go away and walk by yourself in all places alike."

Then Cat pretended to be sorry and said, "Must I never come into the Cave? Must I never sit by the warm fire? Must I never drink the warm white milk? You are very wise and very beautiful. You should not be cruel even to a Cat."

Woman said, "I knew I was wise, but I did not know I was beautiful. So I will make a bargain with you. If ever I say one word in your praise you may come into the Cave."

"And if you say two words in my praise?" said the Cat.

"I never shall," said the Woman, "but if I say two words in your praise, you may sit by the fire in the Cave."

"And if you say three words?" said the Cat.

"I never shall," said the Woman, "but if I say three words in your praise, you may drink the warm white milk three times a day for always and always and always."

Then the Cat arched his back and said, "Now let the Curtain at the mouth of the Cave, and the Fire at the back of the Cave, and the Milk-pots that stand beside the Fire, remember what my Enemy and the Wife of my Enemy has said." And he went away through the Wet Wild Woods waving his wild tail and walking by his wild lone.

That night when the Man and the Horse and the Dog came home from hunting, the Woman did not tell them of the bargain that she had made with the Cat, because she was afraid that they might not like it.

Cat went far and far away and hid himself in the Wet Wild Woods by his wild lone for a long time till the Woman forgot all about him. Only the Bat—the little upside-down Bat—that hung inside the Cave, knew where Cat hid; and every evening Bat would fly to Cat with news of what was happening.

One evening Bat said, "There is a Baby in the Cave. He is new and pink and fat and small, and the Woman is very fond of him."

"Ah," said the Cat, listening, "but what is the Baby fond of?"

"He is fond of things that are soft and tickle," said the Bat. "He is fond of warm things to hold in his arms when he goes to sleep. He is fond of being played with. He is fond of all those things."

"Ah," said the Cat, listening, "then my time has come."

Next night Cat walked through the Wet Wild Woods and hid very near the Cave till morning-time, and Man and Dog and Horse went hunting. The Woman was busy cooking that morning, and the Baby cried and interrupted. So she carried him outside the Cave and gave him a handful of pebbles to play with. But still the Baby cried.

Then the Cat put out his paddy paw and patted the Baby on the cheek, and it cooed; and the Cat rubbed against its fat knees and tickled it under its fat chin with his tail. And the Baby laughed; and the Woman heard him and smiled.

Then the Bat—the little upside-down bat—that hung in the

mouth of the Cave said, "O my Hostess and Wife of my Host and Mother of my Host's Son, a Wild Thing from the Wild Woods is most beautifully playing with your Baby."

"A blessing on that Wild Thing whoever he may be," said the Woman, straightening her back, "for I was a busy woman this morning and he has done me a service."

That very minute and second, Best Beloved, the dried horse-skin Curtain that was stretched tail-down at the mouth of the Cave fell down—*whoosh!*—because it remembered the bargain she had made with the Cat, and when the Woman went to pick it up—lo and behold!—the Cat was sitting quite comfy inside the Cave.

"O my Enemy and Wife of my Enemy and Mother of my Enemy," said the Cat, "it is I: for you have spoken a word in my praise, and now I can sit within the Cave for always and always and always. But still I am the Cat who walks by himself, and all places are alike to me."

The Woman was very angry, and shut her lips tight and took up her spinning-wheel and began to spin.

But the Baby cried because the Cat had gone away, and the Woman could not hush it, for it struggled and kicked and grew black in the face.

"O my Enemy and Wife of my Enemy and Mother of my Enemy," said the Cat, "take a strand of the wire that you are spinning and tie it to your spinning-whorl and drag it along the floor, and I will show you a magic that shall make your Baby laugh as loudly as he is now crying."

"I will do so," said the Woman, "because I am at my wits' end; but I will not thank you for it."

She tied the thread to the little clay spindle-whorl and drew it across the floor, and the Cat ran after it and patted it with his paws and rolled head over heels, and tossed it backward over his shoulder and chased it between his hind-legs and pretended to lose it, and pounced down upon it again, till the Baby laughed as loudly as it had been crying, and scrambled after the Cat and frolicked all over the Cave till it grew tired and settled down to sleep with the Cat in its arms.

"Now," said the Cat, "I will sing the Baby a song that shall keep him asleep for an hour." And he began to purr, loud and low, low and loud, till the Baby fell fast asleep. The Woman smiled as she looked down upon the two of them and said, "That was wonderfully done. No question but you are very clever, O Cat."

That very minute and second, Best Beloved, the smoke of the fire at the back of the Cave came down in clouds from the roof—*puff!*—because it remembered the bargain she had made with the Cat, and when it had cleared away—lo and behold!—the Cat was sitting quite comfy close to the fire.

"O my Enemy and Wife of my Enemy and Mother of My Enemy," said the Cat, "it is I, for you have spoken a second word in my praise, and now I can sit by the warm fire at the back of the Cave for always and always and always. But still I am the Cat who walks by himself, and all places are alike to me."

Then the Woman was very very angry, and let down her hair and put more wood on the fire and brought out the broad blade-bone of the shoulder of mutton and began to make a Magic that should prevent her from saying a third word in praise of the Cat. It was not a Singing Magic, Best Beloved, it was a Still Magic; and by and by the Cave grew so still that a little wee-wee mouse crept out of a corner and ran across the floor.

"O my Enemy and Wife of my Enemy and Mother of my Enemy," said the Cat, "is that little mouse part of your magic?"

"Ouh! Chee! No indeed!" said the Woman, and she dropped the blade-bone and jumped upon the footstool in front of the fire and braided up her hair very quick for fear that the mouse should run up it.

"Ah," said the Cat, watching, "then the mouse will do me no harm if I eat it?"

"No," said the Woman, braiding up her hair, "eat it quickly and I will ever be grateful to you."

Cat made one jump and caught the little mouse, and the Woman said, "A hundred thanks. Even the First Friend is not quick enough to catch little mice as you have done. You must be very wise."

That very moment and second, O Best Beloved, the Milk-pot that stood by the fire cracked in two pieces—*ffft*—because it remembered the bargain she had made with the Cat, and when the Woman jumped down from the footstool—lo and behold!—the Cat was lapping up the warm white milk that lay in one of the broken pieces.

"O my Enemy and Wife of my Enemy and Mother of my Enemy," said the Cat, "it is I; for you have spoken three words in my praise, and now I can drink the warm white milk three times a day for always and always and always. But *still* I am the Cat who walks by himself, and all places are alike to me."

Then the Woman laughed and set the Cat a bowl of the warm white milk and said, "O Cat, you are as clever as a man, but remember that your bargain was not made with the Man or the Dog, and I do not know what they will do when they come home."

"What is that to me?" said the Cat. "If I have my place in the Cave by the fire and my warm white milk three times a day I do not care what the Man or the Dog can do."

That evening when the Man and the Dog came into the Cave, the Woman told them all the story of the bargain while the Cat sat by the fire and smiled. Then the Man said, "Yes, but he has not made a bargain with *me* or with all proper Men after me." Then he took off his two leather boots and he took up his little stone axe (that makes three) and he fetched a piece of wood and a hatchet (that is five altogether), and he set them out in a row and he said, "Now we will make *our* bargain. If you do not catch mice when you are in the Cave for always and always and always, I will throw these five things at you whenever I see you, and so shall all proper Men do after me."

"Ah," said the Woman, listening, "this is a very clever Cat, but he is not so clever as my Man."

The Cat counted the five things (and they looked very knobby) and he said, "I will catch mice when I am in the Cave for always and always and always; but *still* I am the Cat who walks by himself, and all places are alike to me."

"Not when I am near," said the Man. "If you had not said that last I would have put all these things away for always and always and always; but I am now going to throw my two boots and my little stone axe (that makes three) at you whenever I meet you. And so shall all proper Men do after me!"

Then the Dog said, "Wait a minute. He has not made a bargain with *me* or with all proper Dogs after me." And he showed his teeth and said, "If you are not kind to the Baby while I am in the Cave for always and always and always, I will hunt you till I catch you, and when I catch you I will bite you. And so shall all proper Dogs do after me."

"Ah," said the Woman, listening, "this is a very clever Cat, but he is not so clever as the Dog."

Cat counted the Dog's teeth (and they looked very pointed) and he said, "I will be kind to the Baby while I am in the Cave, as long as he does not pull my tail too hard, for always and always and always. But *still* I am the Cat that walks by himself, and all places are alike to me."

"Not when I am near," said the Dog. "If you had not said that last I would have shut my mouth for always and always and always; but *now* I am going to hunt you up a tree whenever I meet you. And so shall all proper Dogs do after me."

Then the Man threw his two boots and his little stone axe (that makes three) at the Cat, and the Cat ran out of the Cave and the Dog chased him up a tree; and from that day to this, Best Beloved, three proper Men out of five will always throw things at a Cat whenever they meet him, and all proper Dogs will chase him up a tree. But the Cat keeps his side of the bargain too. He will kill mice and he will be kind to Babies when he is in the house, just as long as they do not pull his tail too hard. But when he has done that, and between times, and when the moon gets up and night comes, he is the Cat that walks by himself, and all places are alike to him. Then he goes out to the Wet Wild Woods or up the Wet Wild Trees or on the Wet Wild Roofs, waving his wild tail and walking by his wild lone.

Pussy can sit by the fire and sing,
    Pussy can climb a tree,
Or play with a silly old cork and string
    To 'muse herself, not me.
But I like *Binkie* my dog, because
    He knows how to behave;
So, *Binkie's* the same as the First Friend was,
    And I am the Man in the Cave.

Pussy will play man-Friday till
    It's time to wet her paw
And make her walk on the window-sill
    (For the footprint Crusoe saw);
Then she fluffles her tail and mews,
    And scratches and won't attend.
But *Binkie* will play whatever I choose,
    And he is my true First Friend.

Pussy will rub my knees with her head
    Pretending she loves me hard;
But the very minute I go to my bed
    Pussy runs out in the yard,
And there she stays till the morning-light;
    So I know it is only pretend;
But *Binkie,* he snores at my feet all night,
    And he is my Firstest Friend!

It was related to me by Mr. Robert Dane, who was at one time a tenant of No. — Lower Seedley Road, Seedley. I quote it as nearly as possible in his words, thus:—

"When we—my wife and I—took No. — Lower Seedley Road, no possibility of the place being haunted crossed our minds. Indeed ghosts were the very last things we reckoned on, as neither of us had the slightest belief in them. Like the generality of solicitors, I am stodgy and unimaginative, whilst my wife is the most practical and matter-of-fact little woman you would meet in a day's march. Nor was there anything about the house that in any way suggested the superphysical. It was airy and light—no dark corners nor sinister staircases—and equipped throughout with all modern conveniences. We began our lease in June—the hottest June I remember—and nothing occurred to disturb us till October.

"It happened then in this wise. I will quote from my diary:—

"*Monday, October 11th.*—Dick—that is my brother-in-law—and I, at 11 p.m., were sitting smoking and chatting together in the study. All the rest of the household had gone to bed. We had no light in the room—as Dick had a headache—save the fire, and that had burned so low that its feeble glimmering scarcely enabled us to see each other's face. After a space of sudden and thoughtful silence, Dick took the stump of a cigar from his lips and threw it in the grate, where for a few moments it lay glowing in the gloom.

"'Jack,' he said, 'you will think me mad, but there is something deuced queer about this room to-night—something in the atmosphere I cannot define, but which I have never felt here—or indeed anywhere—before. Look at that cigar-end—look!'

"I did so, and received a shock. What I saw was certainly not the stump Dick had had in his mouth, but an eye—a large, red and lurid eye—that looked up at us with an expression of the utmost hate.

"Dick raised the shovel and struck at it, but without effect—it still glared at us. A great horror then seized us, and unable to remove our gaze from the hellish thing, we sat glued to our chairs staring at it. This state of affairs lasted till the clock in the hall outside struck twelve, when the eye suddenly vanished, and we both felt as if some intensely evil influence had been suddenly removed.

"Dick did not like the idea of sleeping alone, and asked if he might keep the electric light on in his room all night. Tremendous extravagance, but under the circumstances excusable. I confess I devoutly wished it was morning.

"*Tuesday, October 12th.*—I was awakened at 11.30 p.m. by Delia saying to me, 'Oh, Edward, there have been such dreadful noises on the landing, just as if a cat were being worried to death by dogs. Hark! there it is again.' And as she spoke, from apparently just outside the door, came a series of loud screeches, accompanied by savage growls and snarls.

"Not knowing what to make of it, as we had no animals of our own in the house, but concluding that a door or window having been left open, a dog and cat had got in from outside, I lit a candle, and opened the bedroom door. Instantly the sounds ceased and there was dead silence, and although I searched everywhere, not a vestige of any animal was to be seen. Moreover all the doors leading into the garden were shut and locked, and the windows closed. Not wishing to frighten Delia, I laughingly assured her the cat—a black Tom—was all right, that it was sitting on the roof of the summer-house, looking none the worse for its treatment, and that I had sent the dog—a terrier—flying out of the gate with a well-deserved kick. I explained it was my fault about the front door being left open—my brain had been a bit overstrained through excessive work—and asked her on no account to blame the servants. I grow alarmed at times when I realize how easy lawyering makes lying.

"*Friday, October 21st.*—On my way to bed last night I encountered a rush of icy cold air at the first bend of the staircase. The candle flared up, a bright blue flame, and went out. Something—an animal of sorts—came tearing down the stairs past me, and on peering over the banisters, I saw, looking up at me from the well of darkness beneath, two big red eyes, the counterparts of the one Dick and I had seen on October 11th. I threw a matchbox at them, but without effect. It was only when I switched on the electric light that they disappeared. I searched the house most carefully, but there were no signs of any animal. Joined Delia, feeling nervous and henpecky.

"*Monday, November 7th.*—Tom and Mable came running into Delia's room in a great state of excitement after tea to-day. 'Mother!' they cried, 'Mother! Do come! Some horrid dog has got a cat in the spare room and is tearing it to pieces.' Delia, who was mending my socks at the time, flung them anywhere, and springing to her feet, flew to the spare room. The door was shut, but proceeding from within was the most appalling pandemonium of screeches and snarls, just as if some dog had got hold of a cat by the neck and was shaking it to death. Delia swung open the door and rushed in. The room was empty—not a trace of a cat or dog anywhere—and the sounds ceased! On my return home Delia met me in the garden. 'Jack!' she said, 'I have probed the mystery at last. The house is haunted! We must leave.'

"*Saturday, November 12th.*—Sublet house to James Barstow, retired oil merchant, to-day. He comes in on the 30th. Hope he'll like it!

"*Tuesday, November 15th.*—Cook left to-day. 'I've no fault to find with you, mum,' she condescendingly explained to Delia.

'It's not you, nor the children, nor the food. It's the noises at night—screeches outside my door, which sound like a cat, but which I know can't be a cat, as there is no cat in the house. This morning, mum, shortly after the clock struck two, things came to a climax. Hearing something in the corner and wondering if it was a mouse—I ain't a bit afraid of mice, mum—I sat up in bed and was getting ready to strike a light—the matchbox was in my hand—when something heavy sprang right on the top of me and gave a loud growl in my ear. That finished me, mum—I fainted. When I came to myself, I was too frightened to stir, but lay with my head under the blankets till it was time to get up. I then searched everywhere, but there was no sign of any dog, and as the door was locked there was no possibility of any dog having got in during the night. Mum, I wouldn't go through what I suffered again for fifty pounds; I've got palpitations even now; and I would rather go without my month's wages than sleep in that room another night.' Delia paid her up to date, and she went directly after tea.

"*Friday, November 18th.*—As I was coming out of the bathroom at 11 p.m. something fell into the bath with a loud splash. I turned to see what it was—there was nothing there. I ran up the stairs to bed, three steps at a time!

"*Sunday, November 20th.*—Went to church in the morning and heard the usual Oxford drawl. On the way back I was pondering over the sermon and wishing I could contort the Law as successfully as parsons contort the Scriptures, when Dot—she is six to-day—came running up to me with a very scared expression in her eyes. 'Father,' she cried, plucking me by the sleeve, 'do hurry up. Mother is very ill.' Full of dreadful anticipations, I tore home, and on arriving found Delia lying on the sofa in a violent fit of hysterics. It was fully an hour before she recovered sufficiently to tell me what had happened. Her account runs thus:—

"'After you went to church,' she began, 'I made the custard pudding, jelly and blancmange for dinner, heard the children their collects, and had just sat down with the intention of writing a letter to mother, when I heard a very pathetic mew coming, so I thought, from under the sofa. Thinking it was some stray cat that had got in through one of the windows, I tried to entice it out, by calling "Puss, puss," and making the usual silly noise people do on such occasions. No cat coming out and the mewing still continuing, I knelt down and peered under the sofa. There was no cat there. Had it been night I should have been very much afraid, but I could scarcely reconcile myself to the idea of ghosts with the room filled with sunshine. Resuming my seat I went on with my writing, but not for long. The mewing grew nearer. I distinctly heard something crawl out from under the sofa; there was then a pause, during which you could have heard the proverbial pin fall, and then something sprang upon me and dug its claws in my knees. I looked down, and to my horror and distress, perceived, standing on its hind-legs, pawing my clothes, a large tabby cat, without a head—the neck terminating in a mangled stump. The sight so appalled me that I don't know what happened, but nurse and the children came in and found me lying on the floor in hysterics. Can't we leave the house at once?'

"*Wednesday, November 30th.*—Left No. — Lower Seedley Road at 2 p.m. Had an awful scurry to get things packed in time, and dread opening certain of the packing-cases lest we shall find all the crockery smashed. Just as we were starting Delia cried out that she had left her reticule behind, and I was despatched in search of it. I searched everywhere—till I was worn out, for I know what Delia is—and was leaving the premises in full anticipation of being sent back again, when there was a loud commotion in the hall, just as if a dog had suddenly pounced on a cat, and the next moment a large tabby, with the head hewn away as Delia had described, rushed up to me and tried to spring on to my shoulders. At this juncture one of the servants cautiously opened the hall door from without, and informed me I was wanted. The cat instantly vanished, and, on my reaching the carriage in a state of breathless haste and trepidation, Delia told me she had found her reticule—she had been sitting on it all the time!"

In a subsequent note in his diary a year or so later Mr. Dane says: "After innumerable enquiries *re* the history of No. — Lower Seedley Road prior to our inhabiting it, I have at length elicited the fact that twelve years ago a Mr. and Mrs. Barlowe lived there. They had one son, Arthur, whom they spoilt in the most outrageous fashion, even to the extent of encouraging him in acts of cruelty. To afford him amusement they used to buy rats for his dog—a fox-terrier—to worry, and on one occasion procured a stray cat, which the servants afterwards declared was mangled in the most shocking manner before being finally destroyed by Arthur. Here, then, in my opinion, is a very feasible explanation for the hauntings—the phenomenon seen was the phantasm of the poor, tortured cat. For if human tragedies are re-enacted by ghosts, why not animal tragedies too? It is absurd to suppose man has the monopoly of soul or spirit."

Ghost Bats

Jason C. Eckhardt

Came with the house."

"Sorry?"

Guy and Reg sat holding their beers, seated in Guy's living room and looking at the long orange beast stretched upon the couch, the one decent piece of furniture in the room. With their identical shaggy brown hair, pale skin, and slouch, the tow could have been mistaken for brothers. They were, in fact.

"What," said Reg, "the cat?"

"That's right," said Guy, and took a pull on his beer. "Wild Bill. Came with the house. Last owner left him behind, poor blighter."

"Is that what happened to his ears, then?"

"Yeah. When they opened the house after the old lady died, they found him half-starved and frostbitten on the ears. The vet trimmed them back like that."

As if conscious of their attention given him, the cat opened its eyes half-mast in that way that cats have; a look that simultaneously expresses interest, indifference, love and contempt. As the two men watched, though, Wild Bill's demeanor changed. His eyes opened wide and round, the irises bloomed black, and he stared stock-still at a point on the ceiling.

"Didn't affect his hearing, I can see," said Reg. "Whatever he's hearing, I can't hear it. Same for whatever he's seeing."

"'Ghost bats,' we call 'em," said Guy. "Give you the willies, the way he tracks them, just as if they were real."

As if to demonstrate, Wild Bill unlimbered himself from

the couch and stalked across the living room floor, his gaze never leaving the ceiling. Halfway across the room he stopped and began making a stuttering, chittering noise. Guy leaned forward.

"What do you see, Bill?"

Reg leaned forward also and said, "What d'you suppose makes them do that?"

"Chemical in their brain, I've read. Natural hallucinogen."

Reg snorted a laugh.

"Come in handy of a weekend, that."

They sat and drank and watched Wild Bill as he looked this way and that, his tail twitching in excitement and baffled rage. Guy treasured moments like this. Until two weeks previously, he, Allison, and baby Miles had been living in a flat in Peckham. Handy to his job in the City, but obscenely overpriced and too small for the newly expanded family. The house in Kentish Town had been a godsend. Their neighbor was Allison's Aunt Sarah, so when the house's former tenant had died without heirs, the aunt immediately informed Allison and Guy of the opportunity. The bank that held the title to the house was more than happy to be rid of it to a clerk at a good firm in London, who was not likely to miss a mortgage payment. Even the burden of a mortgage was less than what Guy and Allison had been paying before, and the Underground ran close enough to make the commute tolerable. The house had needed work, but Guy and Allison were young. To them it was a game that only got better as the house improved under their care.

The front door closed and Allison's "Hi, love, I'm home" woke Guy from his reverie.

"Well," said Reg with exaggerated emphasis. "Guess that's my cue to shove off. Hello, Allison, hello, baby. Cheers!"

Allison blew a lazy strand of dirty blond hair out of her face and set Miles in his baby-seat at the kitchen table. Guy met her halfway in the hall. They hugged briefly and kissed.

"I see the Red Prince has been entertaining the peasants again," said Allison.

"Aye," said Guy. "He graced us with his presence, demonstrated his hunting technique on ghost bats."

"Speaking of which, our Bill left us another 'present' on the walk."

"What is it this time?"

"Some pitiful, small rodent, a vole or something."

"Right, I'll clear it away."

The pair watched the feline stalking slowly across the floor, eyes fixed upon the empty ceiling.

"Wonder just what he sees," mused Allison.

"Probably that old bat who used to live here."

Allison and Guy looked at each other and said simultaneously, "Ghost bats!" and laughed.

"Come along then," said Allison, leading Guy into the kitchen, "and help us make dinner."

"Ooh, a fearful old harridan that one was."

Allison and her aunt were leaning on the brick wall that separated their properties, sharing tea and the quiet morning.

"Up all hours," continued Aunt Sarah, "never a 'good day' for a neighbor. And that music!"

"Music?" said Allison. "What kind of music, Auntie?"

"Oh, well, you know—music. I don't know these modern groups." She sighed. "Not like real groups like the Clash or Murderers' Row."

Allison hid a smile behind a sip of tea.

"All very avant garde, I'm sure," said Aunt Sarah reflectively. "Orchestras, strings, and choruses that couldn't hold a tune. Used to drive our Gary bonkers, God rest him." Allison nodded in sympathy over the memory of her dead uncle. A year later it still was a shock. Fifty-eight years old, going for his annual checkup, and stage-four intestinal cancer. Nothing they could do. Dead in a week. "He went over there once or twice," continued Aunt Sarah, "tried to ask her nicely to turn it down. She just stared at him and shut the door in his face! Can you imagine? The old bitch."

This time the laugh burst out of Allison in a spray of tea. Aunt Sarah allowed herself a smile—a small one. When Allison had wiped her face clean, she said, "Why didn't you call the police?"

"Oh, but we did, dear, for all the good it did. They'd knock on her door and she'd answer it in some ratty old shawl, all hunched over and pathetic—oh, dear, oh dear, she had no idea her little songs were bothering anyone, yes, officer, I will be sure to keep it down, thank you, sir, sorry to bother you." Sarah shook her head. "Blimey, but she was an actress, and no mistake. She even somehow looked smaller when the coppers came! How she managed that, I'm sure I don't know. We'd watch the whole show from the front step, and just as soon as the police had gone, it was strike up the band." She sipped her tea.

"Good riddance, I say."

"And our gain, Auntie," smiled Allison. "Having you next door is a treat. Speaking of which, can you watch Miles this afternoon? I have errands to run in the City."

Sarah pursed her lips.

"Well, I don't know. Mind that charming little gentleman over there? It's an awful lot you ask."

Allison play-punched her in the shoulder.

"You're quite the actress yourself. See you at noon, then?"

"On the dot, love."

"Auntie, I'm home."

Allison set her bags on the kitchen counter. Aunt Sarah came out of the living room with Miles on her hip.

"There's my little lord!" said Allison, and took the baby out of her aunt's arms. "Were you a good lad for your Auntie?"

"Oh, yes," said Aunt Sarah. "Good as gold and none better."

Allison caught the off-note in her aunt's voice and looked

at her. The older woman's face was tense with worry. "What is it, Aunt Sarah?"

"Hmm? Oh, nothing dear. An old woman's peculiarities. Noisy old place, isn't it?"

"Noisy? In what way?"

"Well, it must just be settling. Scuttling noises, like, in the walls, and up along the ceiling."

Allison hugged the baby to her.

"Really? Where was this?"

"Here and there." Aunt Sarah pointed vaguely upwards. "Most rooms. The bedrooms more, perhaps."

"That's disturbing. Can't be the house settling—it's nearly two hundred years old. Any settling it was going to do it would have done by now. Rodents, do you suppose?"

"Might be. Funny thing, though. That cat of yours caught on to it immediately, and acted as if he could see whatever it was, flitting around the room!" She shivered.

"Well, I'll have to tell Guy about that. Can't have any more critters than are already here." She dug her fingers into Miles's tummy and the baby squealed with laughter.

"Rats?"

Guy stopped with his fork halfway to his mouth. It was dinner time, and Miles was merrily destroying a banana in his seat by his parents.

"Well," said Allison, wiping at her mouth with a napkin, "perhaps not rats. Auntie didn't actually see anything. Though she said Wild Bill did."

"It would have to be a very brave or very foolish rat that came within a mile of this house. Isn't that so, Bill?" Guy turned to the chair beside him at the table, where Wild Bill himself sprawled in all his rusty splendor. He favored Guy with a glance, a blink, and sat up on the chair. One long, white paw on a striped arm inched over the edge of the table and toward the chicken on Guy's plate. "No you don't, you ruffian," said Guy and moved the plate back.

Allison smiled at the pair.

"I'm sure Bill does his best. Can't say as I especially like the dead 'gifts' he leaves us on the stoop. They are, no doubt, given with love. But his hunting seems to stop at the front door, and I don't relish the idea of things living in our walls, especially now that baby's here."

"Understood," said Guy. "I'll call an exterminator tomorrow. Oy, Bill—get out of it, you mangy sod!"

The scream cut through Guy's sleep like a chainsaw.

"*. . . bloodiell . . .*"

He threw off the covers and swung his feet to the floor; but Allison was already out of the room and running down the hall. Guy, still grinding sleep out of his eyes, stumbled after her. The baby's cries—howls, really—filled the midnight rooms. The light went on in Miles's room as Allison rushed in, saying, "What is it, baby, what *is* it?" At the same moment Wild Bill tore out of the baby's room. He skidded sideways along the hardwood floor before getting his footing and charging past Guy's feet.

When Guy got to Miles's room, the baby had ceased his howling and was drawing air into his lungs for a wail of biblical proportions. Allison yanked away the blankets from her child, reached for him, and stopped.

"What is it, love?" said Guy as he came up beside her. It was then that Miles unleashed his voice in terror, rage, and pain. Allison reached again for him and gently picked him up. She held him at arm's length.

"Oh, God," she whispered. "The blood—his face—"

Guy leaned forward and saw that his son's normally cherubic face was smeared with blood. More of it still pulsed out of a wound in his right cheek, and another stain was growing on the child's left arm.

"Dear God," he breathed, and Allison, pulling the screaming child to her breast said, "My baby, my baby."

When they had calmed the child and washed his face and

arm, they discovered a circular wound on his cheek made of many small punctures.

"That's a bite," said Allison in a voice somewhere between wonder and terror. "That's a bite!"

"Yeah, so's the one on his arm." Guy wiped his son's flesh gently with a cotton swab.

"What would bite him, Guy?" Allison's face pleaded with him. "What on earth"—the grief on her face broke in revelation. "Bill," she said quietly. "Wild Bill. That cat was in here, Guy!"

"Now, Allie, wait—"

"No," she said, and bundled the baby up in her arms. "No, Guy, no waiting. That cat has got to go." And she strode out of the bathroom and back into the baby's room.

Guy sighed. As he walked toward the master bedroom, he passed Wild Bill. The cat sat at the edge of the hall, looking at Guy with expectation in his wide green eyes. Guy leaned down to pat Bill's head.

"Sorry, old son," said Guy. "'Fraid it's the nick for you."

Wild Bill was confined to the cellar until further arrangements could be made. His yowls of protest rose up into the house, but Allison was adamant. Guy took the morning off to accompany Allison and the baby to the pediatrician's office. Dr. Chandraputra was tall, dark, and gentle. He tugged up his white lab coat and squatted in front of Allison and Miles. Miles sat on his mother's lap with an expression of Churchill at his darkest hour.

"Well, hello, Miles," said the doctor. "That's quite an ouch you've got on your cheek. May I look at it, please?" He cupped Miles's chin in his long hand and turned the baby's right cheek toward him. "Hmm. Nasty."

"It's that wicked old cat," said Allison. "I suppose we'll have to worry about rabies now, too. I knew we should have gotten rid of him, but—"

"Mm, no, missus," said Chandraputra, frowning. "This wasn't a cat."

"Not a cat? But—I don't understand."

"You see, missus, a cat has a certain dentition. As a carnivore, he shares with dogs, wolves, and bears prominent canine teeth"—he pointed to the canines in his own mouth—"with which to hold prey. In front are grooming-teeth and behind are molars for grinding food. This bite has none of those features."

"A rat, then?" said Guy.

"No, not a rat, either. That would have the dash-like impressions of its incisors. This bite is unlike that of either a carnivore or rodent. This ring of punctures, all the same, as if made by needles . . . I'm no zoologist, of course, but I know of no such animal that could make such a wound. I should speak to an exterminator."

"Our next stop," said Guy.

"Will it leave a scar?" said Allison.

Doctor Chandraputra smiled.

"No, missus. Children are wonderfully recuperative. He should neither remember nor bear a scar from this ordeal. The wounds, though ugly, are shallow. Whatever attacked your child was interrupted in its work before it could do much harm."

Allison and Guy looked at each other.

Wild Bill was released from his confinement immediately upon the couple's return to their house. He bounded out of the cellar stairway with a litany of purrs, trills, and meows of joy and indignation. While Guy and Allison put the baby in his chair and shed their coats, the cat, tail held high, began a rigorous patrol of his domain. Allison took Guy's hand.

"I'm sorry I doubted our Bill," she said. "I knew it would have hurt you to lose him."

Guy nodded, watching the cat's fluffy behind disappear around a corner.

"That it would. I'm just glad that it wasn't he that hurt baby."

"Then what did?"

"Time to find out." Guy took his cellphone out of his pocket.

"Naw," said the exterminator as he stumped down the steps. "Nought here I can find. House's cleaner'n most I see. I expect it's due to this fine mouser here." He held his hand out and scratched Wild Bill behind the ears. Bill graced him with a comrade's smile.

"Then what could it be?" said Guy. He was leaning over the table, writing the man a check, and didn't see his puzzled expression.

"Search me," said the exterminator. "I checked this house top to bottom, walls, floors, an' ceilings, and it's clean. I'd stake my reputation on it. No droppings, no nests. From that bite on your child's face, it must've been somethink good-size, like the size of a cat or marten. But anything that big leaves traces. There just aren't any."

"Well, I thank you for your time," said Guy, and handed him the check. The exterminator considered the paper in his hands, and his thick brows pulled together. He handed the check back to Guy.

"I didn't do anythin' but tell you what you already know," he said. "There's nothing here, sir. This place is so clean it's scary. Usually there's something, but not this time. Your cat can take credit for some of that, but honestly, it doesn't look as if any vermin have been her in over a hundred years. Unnatural, it is."

"Well, that's good news, isn't it?"

Allison and Guy and the baby sat on the front steps of their house. The adults held sweating bottles of ale; baby Miles gripped and sucked at a bottle of milk as if it were the last one in the world. Guy took a drink and shrugged.

"'Tis good, love. But it still leaves us with the question of what attacked baby."

The pair held their ales and looked out across the brief front enclosure toward the street, as if the answer lay there. Evening sunlight painted the row of houses opposite in shades of ochre. They glowed like tarnished gold against a purpling front of clouds. The effect was startlingly pretty, yet ominous.

"Weather coming," Guy observed.

"So's our Bill."

The cat came swaggering up the front walk as though on military parade, exactly up the center of the pavement. When he got to within a couple feet of the stoop, Bill halted, set the dead creature before them on the walk, and sat down to await their praise.

"Oh, God, Bill." Allison wrinkled her nose.

Guy said, "Now, Allie, Wild Bill's brought us a present, haven't you, lad?" He pushed up from the step and approached cat and victim. Wild Bill looked up at him—*Well? Aren't you going to thank me?*

Guy gingerly picked up the mouse by the tail.

"Very nice, Bill," he said. "Ta very much. At ease." He carried the creature around the side of the house to the trash bin while Bill set about cleaning his paws.

The front arrived early that evening and broke with a pent-up fury over London. Rain dashed down and slapped like handfuls of gravel against the windows. Wild winds carried it down the streets in walls, and over it all was the drumming of the downpour on the roof. Guy and Allison had moved Miles's crib to their own room until the creature that had attacked him could be identified and gotten rid of, and they were thankful that the baby seemed unconcerned about the storm roaring without. He slept like a stone. The couple read in bed for a time, then kissed and put out the light.

"Did you hear that?"

Allison sat up and peered into the darkness. She felt Guy sit up beside her.

"Yeah, I did." He glanced at the alarm clock on the bedside table—3:18 a.m. Around them the storm rampaged unabated; but behind it was something more. A snarling, a high screeching, sounds of things striking the walls.

"Bill," said Guy, and stepped out of bed. He walked into the hall and was halfway towards Miles's former room when he tripped on something in the dark.

"Bugger." He reached down and felt a small body on the floor. His first thought was for his cat. But Wild Bill had long fur, and this did not. It had, in fact, no fur at all, and was cold and clammy as a dead fish.

Guy swallowed his nausea. His curiosity overcame revulsion long enough for his fingertips to find webbed wings and a mouth full of needle-like teeth. Then he jerked his hand back and stared back down toward the baby's old room, where a battle was still being waged. Slowly he approached the cacophony of howls, spits, and shrieks, steeling himself against what awaited him. But just as he reached the door to the room, all went still. Beyond the walls the storm thumped and growled in sullen defeat, but all within was quiet. Guy reached around the corner of the doorway and snapped on the overhead light.

The room was a shambles. The wallpaper up to the height of Guy's knees was shredded in many places, the throw-rug on the floor pushed in a rumpled heap in a corner, and the baby chair and toy-bin were overturned. Stuffed animals and plastic toys lay staring in stupefied rigidity at the ceiling. And in the midst of the wreck, like a triumphant general upon the field of battle, was Wild Bill. His fur was ruffled in spots and Guy could see some bloody places that would need attending to. But with his cool, mint gaze, blazing white bib fluffed out like an ascot, and erect posture, it was clear who was the victor of this fight.

And what of the vanquished? Wild Bill's pose was the same he used when presenting dead prey to Guy, but there was nothing there this time. The floor in front of Wild Bill was bare boards.

Still the cat looked to Guy, expecting the usual approval. Guy approached the cat and stretched his hand toward the empty floor before it. Several inches before he reached it, he felt cold, dank flesh again. He squinted and he looked this way and that, but there was nothing there. Yet there was. He felt along the invisible creature's length, the taut, torn webbed wings, the horrid mouth full of teeth. He straightened up and wiped his hand on his pajama pants. Reaching forward again, he scratched Bill under the chin.

"Good lad," he said, and Bill purred his gratitude into his hand.

Allison was up with the baby by the time Guy returned to the bedroom. He reassured them that all was well, then went to the lavatory closet and retrieved the dustpan and broom. He left the hall light off—what was the use of a light?—and found the first dead thing by probing with the broom. He pushed it into the pan and returned to Miles's old room, where Wild Bill still stood guard. Guy pushed the second creature into the pan, blinking in disbelief at what he was not seeing, but feeling the weight of it in the pan. He searched the rest of the room with the tip of the broom and found two more the dead things. Then, carefully so that they wouldn't fall from the dustpan, he carried them downstairs and out the kitchen door to the bin behind the house. He didn't bother with the outside light, either. The little bodies bumped and slithered into the bin, and Guy dropped the dustpan and broom in after them.

"What was it?" said Allison when Guy had tramped his weary way back upstairs.

"Bats," he said, and gave her a thin smile. "Go to bed, love. They won't bother us anymore."

And they didn't. But some days, when the wind was high and the people were distracted with their television or their reading, Wild Bill would wake from his drowse, open his long eyes, and watch the empty ceiling.

The Cat

M. P. Shiel

Today I saw a mousie cower,
    Her baleful hour
    She could not flee,
Nailed by an Eye, a ray, a power:
Ah me! can such things be?

One murdered hind-leg kicks and thrills,
    Her fur all frills
    With horrid wo,
Her little leer black Doomsday fills:
O my! Who made it so?

My whole soul shrieked! That soul-less sphinx
    Feigns listless, slinks
    Away a wee,
Feigns change of whim, the gory minx:
But, Christ, such things should be!

Limp, panting heart! He gives her rope,
    Pernicious scope:
    He lets her go:
Darts!—massacres her shrieking Hope!
Great God! Thou mad'st it so.

And I myself am caught in ruth,
    Wheels, wheels uncouth,
    That grind me, run:
And Earth and Heaven seem fang and tooth:
Well, God, Thy will be done.

The Cat-hood of Maurice

E. Nesbit

To have your hair cut is not painful, nor does it hurt to have your whiskers trimmed. But round wooden shoes, shaped like bowls, are not comfortable wear, however much it may amuse the onlooker to see you try to walk in them. If you have a nice fur coat like a company promoter's, it is most annoying to be made to swim in it. And if you had a tail, surely it would be solely your own affair; that any one should tie a tin can to it would strike you as an unwarrantable impertinence—to say the least.

Yet it is difficult for an outsider to see these things from the point of view of both the persons concerned. To Maurice, scissors in hand, alive and earnest to snip, it seemed the most natural thing in the world to shorten the stiff whiskers of Lord Hugh Cecil by a generous inch. He did not understand how useful those whiskers were to Lord Hugh, both in sport and in the more serious business of getting a living. Also it amused Maurice to throw Lord Hugh into ponds, though Lord Hugh only once permitted this liberty. To put walnuts on Lord Hugh's feet and then to watch him walk on ice was, in Maurice's opinion, as good as a play. Lord Hugh was a very favourite cat, but Maurice was discreet, and Lord Hugh, except under violent suffering, was at that time anyhow, dumb.

But the empty sardine-tin attached to Lord Hugh's tail and hind legs—this had a voice, and, rattling against stairs, banisters, and the legs of stricken furniture, it cried aloud for vengeance. Lord Hugh, suffering violently, added his voice, and this time the family heard. There was a chase, a chorus of "Poor pussy!" and

"Pussy, then!" and the tail and the tin and Lord Hugh were caught under Jane's bed. The tail and the tin acquiesced in their rescue. Lord Hugh did not. He fought, scratched, and bit. Jane carried the scars of that rescue for many a long week.

When all was calm Maurice was sought and, after some little natural delay, found—in the boot-cupboard.

"Oh, Maurice!" his mother almost sobbed, "how *can* you? What will your father say?"

Maurice thought he knew what his father would do.

"Don't you know," the mother went on, "how wrong it is to be cruel?"

"I didn't mean to be cruel," Maurice said. And, what is more, he spoke the truth. All the unwelcome attentions he had showered on Lord Hugh had not been exactly intended to hurt that stout veteran—only it was interesting to see what a cat would do if you threw it in the water, or cut its whiskers, or tied things to its tail.

"Oh, but you must have meant to be cruel," said mother, "and you will have to be punished."

"I wish I hadn't," said Maurice, from the heart.

"So do I," said his mother, with a sigh; "but it isn't the first time; you know you tied Lord Hugh up in a bag with the hedgehog only last Tuesday week. You'd better go to your room and think it over. I shall have to tell your father directly he comes home."

Maurice went to his room and thought it over. And the more he thought the more he hated Lord Hugh. Why couldn't the beastly cat have held his tongue and sat still? That, at the time would have been a disappointment, but now Maurice wished it had happened. He sat on the edge of his bed and savagely kicked the edge of the green Kidderminster carpet, and hated the cat.

He hadn't meant to be cruel; he was sure he hadn't; he wouldn't have pinched the cat's feet or squeezed its tail in the door, or pulled its whiskers, or poured hot water on it. He felt himself ill-used, and knew that he would feel still more so after the inevitable interview with his father.

But that interview did not take the immediately painful form expected by Maurice. His father did *not* say, "Now I will show you what it feels like to be hurt." Maurice had braced himself for that, and was looking beyond it to the calm of forgiveness which should follow the storm in which he should so unwillingly take part. No; his father was already calm and reasonable—with a dreadful calm, a terrifying reason.

"Look here, my boy," he said. "This cruelty to dumb animals must be checked—severely checked."

"I didn't mean to be cruel," said Maurice.

"Evil," said Mr. Basingstoke, for such was Maurice's surname, "is wrought by want of thought as well as want of heart. What about your putting the hen in the oven?"

"You know," said Maurice, pale but determined, "you *know* I only wanted to help her to get her eggs hatched quickly. It says in 'Fowls for Food and Fancy' that heat hatches eggs."

"But she hadn't any eggs," said Mr. Basingstoke.

"But she soon would have," urged Maurice. "I thought a stitch in time—"

"That," said his father, "is the sort of thing that you must learn not to think."

"I'll try," said Maurice, miserably hoping for the best.

"I intend that you shall," said Mr. Basingstoke. "This afternoon you go to Dr. Strongitharm's for the remaining week of term. If I find any more cruelty taking place during the holidays you will go there permanently. You can go and get ready."

"Oh, father, *please* not," was all Maurice found to say.

"I'm sorry, my boy," said his father, much more kindly; "it's all for your own good, and it's as painful to me as it is to you—remember that. The cab will be here at four. Go and put your things together, and Jane shall pack for you."

So the box was packed. Mabel, Maurice's kiddy sister, cried over everything as it was put in. It was a very wet day.

"If it had been any school but old Strong's," she sobbed.

She and her brother knew that school well: its windows, dulled with wire blinds, its big alarm bell, the high walls of its grounds, bristling with spikes, the iron gates, always locked, through which gloomy boys, imprisoned, scowled on a free world. Dr. Strongitharm's was a school "for backward and difficult boys." Need I say more?

Well, there was no help for it. The box was packed, the cab was at the door. The farewells had been said. Maurice determined that he wouldn't cry and he didn't, which gave him the one touch of pride and joy that such a scene could yield. Then at the last moment, just as father had one leg in the cab, the Taxes called. Father went back into the house to write a cheque. Mother and Mabel had retired in tears. Maurice used the reprieve to go back after his postage-stamp album. Already he was planning how to impress the other boys at old Strong's, and his was really a very fair collection. He ran up into the schoolroom, expecting to find it empty. But some one was there: Lord Hugh, in the very middle of the ink-stained table-cloth.

"You brute," said Maurice; "you know jolly well I'm going away, or you wouldn't be here." And, indeed, the room had never, somehow, been a favourite of Lord Hugh's.

"Meaow," said Lord Hugh.

"Mew!" said Maurice, with scorn. "That's what you always say. All that fuss about a jolly little sardine-tin. Any one would have thought you'd be only too glad to have it to play with. I wonder how you'd like being a boy? Lickings, and lessons, and impots, and sent back from breakfast to wash your ears. You wash yours anywhere—I wonder what they'd say to me if I washed my ears on the drawing-room hearthrug?"

"Meaow," said Lord Hugh, and washed an ear, as though he were showing off.

"Mew," said Maurice again; `that's all you can say."

"Oh, no, it isn't," said Lord Hugh, and stopped his ear-washing.

"I say!" said Maurice in awestruck tones.

"If you think cats have such a jolly time," said Lord Hugh, "why not *be* a cat?"

"I would if I could," said Maurice, "and fight you—"

"Thank you," said Lord Hugh.

"But I can't," said Maurice.

"Oh, yes, you can," said Lord Hugh. "You've only got to say the word."

"What word?"

Lord Hugh told him the word; but I will not tell you, for fear you should say it by accident and then be sorry.

"And if I say that, I shall turn into a cat?"

"Of course," said the cat.

"Oh, yes, I see," said Maurice. "But I'm not taking any, thanks. I don't want to be a cat for always."

"You needn't," said Lord Hugh. "You've only got to get some one to say to you, 'Please leave off being a cat and be Maurice again,' and there you are."

Maurice thought of Dr. Strongitharm's. He also thought of the horror of his father when he should find Maurice gone, vanished, not to be traced. "He'll be sorry, then," Maurice told himself, and to the cat he said, suddenly:—

"Right—I'll do it. What's the word, again?"

"———," said the cat.

"———," said Maurice; and suddenly the table shot up to the height of a house, the walls to the height of tenement buildings, the pattern on the carpet became enormous, and Maurice found himself on all fours. He tried to stand up on his feet, but his shoulders were oddly heavy. He could only rear himself upright for a moment, and then fell heavily on his hands. He looked down at them; they seemed to have grown shorter and fatter, and were encased in black fur gloves. He felt a desire to walk on all fours—tried it—did it. It was very odd—the movement of the arms straight from the shoulder, more like the movement of the piston of an engine than anything Maurice could think of at that moment.

"I am asleep," said Maurice—"I am dreaming this. I am

dreaming I am a cat. I hope I dreamed that about the sardine-tin and Lord Hugh's tail, and Dr. Strong's."

"You didn't," said a voice he knew and yet didn't know, "and you aren't dreaming this."

"Yes, I am," said Maurice; "and now I'm going to dream that I fight that beastly black cat, and give him the best licking he ever had in his life. Come on, Lord Hugh."

A loud laugh answered him.

"Excuse my smiling," said the voice he knew and didn't know, "but don't you see—you *are* Lord Hugh!"

A great hand picked Maurice up from the floor and held him in the air. He felt the position to be not only undignified but unsafe, and gave himself a shake of mingled relief and resentment when the hand set him down on the inky table-cloth.

"You are Lord Hugh now, my dear Maurice," said the voice, and a huge face came quite close to his. It was his own face, as it would have seemed through a magnifying glass. And the voice—oh, horror!—the voice was his own voice—Maurice Basingstoke's voice. Maurice shrank from the voice, and he would have liked to claw the face, but he had had no practice.

"You are Lord Hugh," the voice repeated, "and I am Maurice. I like being Maurice. I am so large and strong. I could drown you in the water-butt, my poor cat—oh, so easily. No, don't spit and swear. It's bad manners—even in a cat."

"Maurice!" shouted Mr. Basingstoke from between the door and the cab.

Maurice, from habit, leaped towards the door.

"It's no use *your* going," said the thing that looked like a giant reflection of Maurice; "it's *me* he wants."

"But I didn't agree to your being me."

"That's poetry, even if it isn't grammar," said the thing that looked like Maurice. "Why, my good cat, don't you see that if you are I, I must be you? Otherwise we should interfere with time and space, upset the balance of power, and as likely as not destroy the solar system. Oh, yes—I'm you, right enough, and shall be, till some one tells you to change from Lord Hugh into Maurice. And now you've got to find some one to do it."

("Maurice!" thundered the voice of Mr. Basingstoke.)

"That'll be easy enough," said Maurice.

"Think so?" said the other.

"But I sha'n't try yet. I want to have some fun first. I shall catch heaps of mice!"

"Think so? You forget that your whiskers are cut off—Maurice cut them. Without whiskers, how can you judge of the width of the places you go through? Take care you don't get stuck in a hole that you can't get out of or go in through, my good cat."

"Don't call me a cat," said Maurice, and felt that his tail was growing thick and angry.

"You *are* a cat, you know—and that little bit of temper that I see in your tail reminds me—"

Maurice felt himself gripped round the middle, abruptly lifted, and carried swiftly through the air. The quickness of the movement made him giddy. The light went so quickly past him that it might as well have been darkness. He saw nothing, felt nothing, except a sort of long sea-sickness, and then suddenly he was not being moved. He could see now. He could feel. He was being held tight in a sort of vice—a vice covered with chequered cloth. It looked like the pattern, very much exaggerated, of his school knickerbockers. It *was*. He was being held between the hard, relentless knees of that creature that had once been Lord Hugh, and to whose tail he had tied a sardine-tin. Now *he* was Lord Hugh, and something was being tied to *his* tail. Something mysterious, terrible. Very well, he would show that he was not afraid of anything that could be attached to tails. The string rubbed his fur the wrong way—it was that that annoyed him, not the string itself; and as for what was at the end of the string, what *could* that matter to any sensible cat? Maurice was quite decided that he was—and would keep on being—a sensible cat.

The string, however, and the uncomfortable, tight position between those chequered knees—something or other was getting on his nerves.

"Maurice!" shouted his father below, and the be-catted Maurice bounded between the knees of the creature that wore his clothes and his looks.

"Coming, father," this thing called, and sped away, leaving Maurice on the servant's bed—under which Lord Hugh had taken refuge, with his tin-can, so short and yet so long a time ago. The stairs re-echoed to the loud boots which Maurice had never before thought loud; he had often, indeed, wondered that anyone could object to them. He wondered now no longer.

He heard the front door slam. That thing had gone to Dr. Strongitharm's. That was one comfort. Lord Hugh was a boy now; he would know what it was to be a boy. He, Maurice, was a cat, and he meant to taste fully all catty pleasures, from milk to mice. Meanwhile he was without mice or milk, and, unaccustomed as he was to a tail, he could not but feel that all was not right with his own. There was a feeling of weight, a feeling of discomfort, of positive terror. If he should move, what would that thing that was tied to his tail do? Rattle, of course. Oh, but he could not bear it if that thing rattled. Nonsense; it was only a sardine-tin. Yes, Maurice knew that. But all the same— if it did rattle! He moved his tail the least little soft inch. No sound. Perhaps really there wasn't anything tied to his tail. But he couldn't be sure unless he moved. But if he moved the thing would rattle, and if it rattled Maurice felt sure that he would expire or go mad. A mad cat. What a dreadful thing to be! Yet he couldn't sit on that bed for ever, waiting, waiting, waiting for the dreadful thing to happen.

"Oh, dear," sighed Maurice the cat. "I never knew what people meant by 'afraid' before."

His cat-heart was beating heavily against his furry side. His limbs were getting cramped—he must move. He did. And instantly the awful thing happened. The sardine-tin touched the iron of the bed-foot. It rattled.

"Oh, I can't bear it, I can't," cried poor Maurice, in a heart-rending meaow that echoed through the house. He leaped from the bed and tore through the door and down the stairs, and behind him came the most terrible thing in the world. People might call it a sardine-tin, but he knew better. It was the soul of all the fear that ever had been or ever could be. *It rattled.*

Maurice who was a cat flew down the stairs; down, down—the rattling horror followed. Oh, horrible! Down, down! At the foot of the stairs the horror, caught by something—a banister—a stair-rod—stopped. The string on Maurice's tail tightened, his tail was jerked, he was stopped. But the noise had stopped too. Maurice lay only just alive at the foot of the stairs.

It was Mabel who untied the string and soothed his terrors with strokings and tender love-words. Maurice was surprised to find what a nice little girl his sister really was.

"I'll never tease you again," he tried to say, softly—but that was not what he said. What he said was "Purrrr."

"Dear pussy, nice poor pussy, then," said Mabel, and she hid away the sardine-tin and did not tell any one. This seemed unjust to Maurice until he remembered that, of course, Mabel thought that he was really Lord Hugh, and that the person who had tied the tin to his tail was her brother Maurice. Then he was half grateful. She carried him down, in soft, safe arms, to the kitchen, and asked cook to give him some milk.

"Tell me to change back into Maurice," said Maurice who was quite worn out by his cattish experiences. But no one heard him. What they heard was, "Meaow—Meaow—Meeeaow!"

Then Maurice saw how he had been tricked. He could be changed back into a boy as soon as any one said to him, "Leave off being a cat and be Maurice again," but his tongue had no longer the power to ask any one to say it.

He did not sleep well that night. For one thing he was not

accustomed to sleeping on the kitchen hearthrug, and the black-beetles were too many and too cordial. He was glad when cook came down and turned him out into the garden, where the October frost still lay white on the yellowed stalks of sunflowers and nasturtiums. He took a walk, climbed a tree, failed to catch a bird, and felt better. He began also to feel hungry. A delicious scent came stealing out of the back kitchen door. Oh, joy, there were to be herrings for breakfast! Maurice hastened in and took his place on his usual chair.

His mother said, "Down, puss," and gently tilted the chair so that Maurice fell off it. Then the family had herrings. Maurice said, "You might give me some," and he said it so often that his father, who, of course, heard only mewings, said:—

"For goodness' sake put that cat out of the room."

Maurice breakfasted later, in the dust-bin, on herring heads.

But he kept himself up with a new and splendid idea. They would give him milk presently, and then they should see.

He spent the afternoon sitting on the sofa in the dining-room, listening to the conversation of his father and mother. It is said that listeners never hear any good of themselves. Maurice heard so much that he was surprised and humbled. He heard his father say that he was a fine, plucky little chap, but he needed a severe lesson, and Dr. Strongitharm was the man to give it to him. He heard his mother say things that made his heart throb in his throat and the tears prick behind those green cat-eyes of his. He had always thought his parents a little bit unjust. Now they did him so much more than justice that he felt quite small and mean inside his cat-skin.

"He's a dear, good, affectionate boy," said mother. "It's only his high spirits. Don't you think, darling, perhaps you were a little hard on him?"

"It was for his own good," said father.

"Of course," said mother; "but I can't bear to think of him at that dreadful school."

"Well—," father was beginning, when Jane came in with the tea-things on a clattering tray, whose sound made Maurice tremble in every leg. Father and mother began to talk about the weather.

Maurice felt very affectionately to both his parents. The natural way of showing this was to jump on to the sideboard and thence on to his father's shoulders. He landed there on his four padded feet, light as a feather, but father was not pleased.

"Bother the cat!" he cried. "Jane, put it out of the room."

Maurice was put out. His great idea, which was to be carried out with milk, would certainly not be carried out in the dining-room. He sought the kitchen, and, seeing a milk-can on the window-ledge, jumped up beside the can and patted it as he had seen Lord Hugh do.

"My!" said a friend of Jane's who happened to be there, "ain't that cat clever—a perfect moral, I call her."

"He's nothing to boast of this time," said cook. "I will say for Lord Hugh he's not often taken in with a empty can."

This was naturally mortifying for Maurice, but he pretended not to hear, and jumped from the window to the tea-table and patted the milk jug.

"Come," said the cook, "that's more like it," and she poured him out a full saucer and set it on the floor.

Now was the chance Maurice had longed for. Now he could carry out that idea of his. He was very thirsty, for he had had nothing since that delicious breakfast in the dust-bin. But not for worlds would he have drunk the milk. No. He carefully dipped his right paw in it, for his idea was to make letters with it on the kitchen oil-cloth. He meant to write "Please tell me to leave off being a cat and be Maurice again," but he found his paw a very clumsy pen, and he had to rub out the first "P" because it only looked like an accident. Then he tried again and actually did make a "P" that any fair-minded person could have read quite easily.

"I wish they'd notice," he said, and before he got the "l" written they did notice.

"Drat the cat," said cook; "look how he's messing the floor up." And she took away the milk.

Maurice put pride aside and mewed to have the milk put down again. But he did not get it.

Very weary, very thirsty, and very tired of being Lord Hugh, he presently found his way to the schoolroom, where Mabel with patient toil was doing her home-lessons. She took him on her lap and stroked him while she learned her French verb. He felt that he was growing very fond of her. People were quite right to be kind to dumb animals. Presently she had to stop stroking him and do a map. And after that she kissed him and put him down and went away. All the time she had been doing the map, Maurice had had but one thought: *Ink!*

The moment the door had closed behind her—how sensible people were who closed doors gently—he stood up in her chair with one paw on the map and the other on the ink. Unfortunately, the inkstand top was made to dip pens in, and not to dip paws. But Maurice was desperate. He deliberately upset the ink—most of it rolled over the table-cloth and fell pattering on the carpet, but with what was left he wrote quite plainly, across the map:—

> "Please tell Lord Hugh
> to stop being
> a cat and be Mau
> rice again."

"There!" he said; "they can't make any mistake about that." They didn't. But they made a mistake about who had done it, and Mabel was deprived of jam with her supper bread.

Her assurance that some naughty boy must have come through the window and done it while she was not there convinced nobody, and, indeed, the window was shut and bolted.

Maurice, wild with indignation, did not mend matters by seizing the opportunity of a few minutes' solitude to write:—

"It was not Mabel
it was Maur
ice I mean Lord Hugh,"

because when that was seen Mabel was instantly sent to bed.

"It's not fair!" cried Maurice.

"My dear," said Maurice's father, "if that cat goes on mewing to this extent you'll have to get rid of it."

Maurice said not another word. It was bad enough to be a cat, but to be a cat that was "got rid of"! He knew how people got rid of cats. In a stricken silence he left the room and slunk up the stairs—he dared not mew again, even at the door of Mabel's room. But when Jane went in to put Mabel's light out Maurice crept in too, and in the dark tried with stifled mews and purrs to explain to Mabel how sorry he was. Mabel stroked him and he went to sleep, his last waking thought amazement at the blindness that had once made him call her a silly little kid.

If you have ever been a cat you will understand something of what Maurice endured during the dreadful days that followed. If you have not, I can never make you understand fully. There was the affair of the fishmonger's tray balanced on the wall by the back door—the delicious curled-up whiting; Maurice knew as well as you do that one mustn't steal fish out of other people's trays, but the cat that he was didn't know. There was an inward struggle— and Maurice was beaten by the cat-nature. Later he was beaten by the cook.

Then there was that very painful incident with the butcher's dog, the flight across gardens, the safety of the plum tree gained only just in time.

And, worst of all, despair took hold of him, for he saw that nothing he could do would make any one say those simple words that would release him. He had hoped that Mabel might at last be made to understand, but the ink had failed him; she did not understand his subdued mewings, and when he got the cardboard letters and made the same sentence with them Mabel only thought it was that naughty boy who came through locked windows. Somehow he could not spell before any one—his nerves were not what they had been. His brain now gave him no new ideas. He felt that he was really growing like a cat in his mind. His interest in his meals grew beyond even what it had been when they were a schoolboy's meals. He hunted mice with growing enthusiasm, though the loss of his whiskers to measure narrow places with made hunting difficult.

He grew expert in bird-stalking, and often got quite near to a bird before it flew away, laughing at him. But all the time, in his heart, he was very, very miserable. And so the week went by.

Maurice in his cat shape dreaded more and more the time when Lord Hugh in the boy shape should come back from Dr. Strongitharm's. He knew—who better?—exactly the kind of things boys do to cats, and he trembled to the end of his handsome half-Persian tail.

And then the boy came home from Dr. Strongitharm's, and at the first sound of his boots in the hall Maurice in the cat's body fled with silent haste to hide in the boot-cupboard.

Here, ten minutes later, the boy that had come back from Dr. Strongitharm's found him.

Maurice fluffed up his tail and unsheathed his claws. Whatever this boy was going to do to him Maurice meant to resist, and his resistance should hurt the boy as much as possible. I am sorry to say Maurice swore softly among the boots, but cat-swearing is not really wrong.

"Come out, you old duffer," said Lord Hugh in the boy shape of Maurice. "I'm not going to hurt you."

"I'll see to that," said Maurice, backing into the corner, all teeth and claws.

"Oh, I've had such a time!" said Lord Hugh. "It's no use, you know, old chap; I can see where you are by your green eyes. My word, they do shine. I've been caned and shut up in a dark room and given thousands of lines to write out."

"I've been beaten, too, if you come to that," mewed Maurice. "Besides the butcher's dog."

It was an intense relief to speak to some one who could understand his mews.

"Well, I suppose it's Pax for the future," said Lord Hugh; "if you won't come out, you won't. Please leave off being a cat and be Maurice again."

And instantly Maurice, amid a heap of goloshes and old tennis bats, felt with a swelling heart that he was no longer a cat. No more of those undignified four legs, those tiresome pointed ears, so difficult to wash, that furry coat, that contemptible tail, and that terrible inability to express all one's feelings in two words—"mew" and "purr."

He scrambled out of the cupboard, and the boots and galoshes fell off him like spray off a bather.

He stood upright in those very chequered knickerbockers that were so terrible when their knees held one vice-like, while things were tied to one's tail. He was face to face with another boy, exactly like himself.

"*You* haven't changed, then—but there can't be two Maurices."

"There sha'n't be; not if I know it," said the other boy; "a boy's life a dog's life. Quick, before any one comes."

"Quick what?" asked Maurice.

"Why tell me to leave off being a boy, and to be Lord Hugh Cecil again."

Maurice told him at once. And at once the boy was gone, and there was Lord Hugh in his own shape, purring politely, yet with a watchful eye on Maurice's movements.

"Oh, you needn't be afraid, old chap. It's Pax right enough," Maurice murmured in the ear of Lord Hugh. And Lord Hugh, arching his back under Maurice's stroking hand, replied with a purrrr-meaow that spoke volumes.

"Oh, Maurice, here you are. It *is* nice of you to be nice to Lord Hugh, when it was because of him you—"

"He's a good old chap," said Maurice, carelessly. "And your not half a bad old girl. See?"

Mabel almost wept for joy at this magnificent compliment, and Lord Hugh himself took on a more happy and confident air.

Please dismiss any fears which you may entertain that after this Maurice became a model boy. He didn't. But he was much nicer than before. The conversation which he overheard when he was a cat makes him more patient with his father and mother. And he is almost always nice to Mabel, for he cannot forget all that she was to him when he wore the shape of Lord Hugh. His father attributes all the improvement in his son's character to that week at Dr. Strongitharm's—which, as you know, Maurice never had. Lord Hugh's character is unchanged. Cats learn slowly and with difficulty.

Only Maurice and Lord Hugh know the truth—Maurice has never told it to any one except me, and Lord Hugh is a very reserved cat. He never at any time had that free flow of mew which distinguished and endangered the cat-hood of Maurice.

The Cats

H. P. Lovecraft

Babels of blocks to the high heavens tow'ring,
    Flames of futility swirling below;
Poisonous fungi in brick and stone flow'ring,
    Lanterns that shudder and death-lights that glow.

Black monstrous bridges across oily rivers,
    Cobwebs of cable by nameless things spun;
Catacomb deeps whose dank chaos delivers
    Streams of live foetor, that rots in the sun.

Colour and splendour, disease and decaying,
    Shrieking and ringing and scrambling insane,
Rabbles exotic to stranger-gods praying,
    Jumbles of odour that stifle the brain.

Legions of cats from the alleys nocturnal,
    Howling and lean in the glare of the moon,
Screaming the future with mouthings infernal,
    Yelling the burden of Pluto's red rune.

Tall tow'rs and pyramids ivy'd and crumbling,
    Bats that swoop low in the weed-cumber'd streets;
Bleak broken bridges o'er rivers whose rumbling
    Joins with no voice as the thick tide retreats.

Belfries that blackly against the moon totter,
    Caverns whose mouths are by mosses effac'd,
And living to answer the wind and the water,
    Only the lean cats that howl in the waste!

The Brazilian Cat

Sir Arthur Conan Doyle

It is hard luck on a young fellow to have expensive tastes, great expectations, aristocratic connections, but no actual money in his pocket, and no profession by which he may earn any. The fact was that my father, a good, sanguine, easy-going man, had such confidence in the wealth and benevolence of his bachelor elder brother, Lord Southerton, that he took it for granted that I, his only son, would never be called upon to earn a living for myself. He imagined that if there were not a vacancy for me on the great Southerton Estates, at least there would be found some post in that diplomatic service which still remains the special preserve of our privileged classes. He died too early to realise how false his calculations had been. Neither my uncle nor the State took the slightest notice of me, or showed any interest in my career. An occasional brace of pheasants, or basket of hares, was all that ever reached me to remind me that I was heir to Otwell House and one of the richest estates in the country. In the meantime, I found myself a bachelor and man about town, living in a suite of apartments in Grosvenor Mansions, with no occupation save that of pigeon-shooting and polo-playing at Hurlingham. Month by month I realised that it was more and more difficult to get the brokers to renew my bills, or to cash any further post-obits upon an unentailed property. Ruin lay right across my path, and every day I saw it clearer, nearer, and more absolutely unavoidable.

What made me feel my own poverty the more was that, apart from the great wealth of Lord Southerton, all my other relations were fairly well-to-do. The nearest of these was Everard King, my father's nephew and my own first cousin, who had spent an adventurous life in Brazil, and had now returned to this country to settle down on his fortune. We never knew how he made his money, but he appeared to have plenty of it, for he bought the estate of Greylands, near Clipton-on-the-Marsh, in Suffolk. For the first year of his residence in England he took no more notice of me than my miserly uncle; but at last one summer morning, to my very great relief and joy, I received a letter asking me to come down that very day and spend a short visit at Greylands Court. I was expecting a rather long visit to Bankruptcy Court at the time, and this interruption seemed almost providential. If I could only get on terms with this unknown relative of mine, I might pull through yet. For the family credit he could not let me go entirely to the wall. I ordered my valet to pack my valise, and I set off the same evening for Clipton-on-the-Marsh.

After changing at Ipswich, a little local train deposited me at a small, deserted station lying amidst a rolling grassy country, with a sluggish and winding river curving in and out amidst the valleys, between high, silted banks, which showed that we were within reach of the tide. No carriage was awaiting me (I found afterwards that my telegram had been delayed), so I hired a dog-cart at the local inn. The driver, an excellent fellow, was full of my relative's praises, and I learned from him that Mr. Everard King was already a name to conjure with in that part of the country. He had entertained the school-children, he had thrown his grounds open to visitors, he had subscribed to charities—in short, his benevolence had been so universal that my driver could only account for it on the supposition that he had Parliamentary ambitions.

My attention was drawn away from my driver's panegyric by the appearance of a very beautiful bird which settled on a tele-graph-post beside the road. At first I thought that it was a jay, but it was larger, with a brighter plumage. The driver accounted for its presence at once by saying that it belonged to the very man whom we were about to visit. It seems that the acclimatisation of foreign creatures was one of his hobbies, and that he had brought with him from Brazil a number of birds and beasts which he was endeavouring to rear in England. When once we had passed the gates of Grevlands Park we had ample evidence of this taste of his. Some small spotted deer, a curious wild pig known, I believe, as a peccary, a gorgeously feathered oriole, some sort of armadillo, and a singular lumbering intoed beast like a very fat badger, were among the creatures which I observed as we drove along the winding avenue.

Mr. Everard King, my unknown cousin, was standing in person upon the steps of his, house, for he had seen us in the distance, and guessed that it was I. His appearance was very homely and benevolent, short and stout, forty-five years old perhaps, with a round, good-humoured face, burned brown with the tropical sun, and shot with a thousand wrinkles. He wore white linen clothes, in true planter style, with a cigar between his lips, and a large Panama hat upon the back of his head. It was such a figure as one associates with a verandahed bungalow, and it looked curiously out of place in front of this broad, stone English mansion, with its solid wings and its Palladio pillars before the doorway.

"My dear!" he cried, glancing over his shoulder; "my dear, here is our guest! Welcome, welcome to Greylands! I am delighted to make your acquaintance, Cousin Marshall, and I take it as a great compliment that you should honour this sleepy little country place with your presence."

Nothing could be more hearty than his manner, and he set me at my ease in an instant. But it needed all his cordiality to atone for the frigidity and even rudeness of his wife, a tall, haggard woman, who came forward at his summons. She was, I believe, of Brazilian extraction, though she spoke excellent English, and I excused her manners on the score of her ignorance of our customs. She did not attempt to conceal, however, either then or afterwards, that I was no very welcome visitor at Greylands Court. Her actual words were, as a rule, courteous, but she was the possessor of a pair of particularly expressive dark eyes, and I read in them very clearly from the first that she heartily wished me back in London once more.

However, my debts were too pressing and my designs upon my wealthy relative were too vital for me to allow them to be upset by the ill-temper of his wife, so I disregarded her coldness and reciprocated the extreme cordiality of his welcome. No pains had been spared by him to make me comfortable. My room was a charming one. He implored me to tell him anything which could add to my happiness. It was on the tip of my tongue to inform him that a blank cheque would materially help towards that end, but I felt that it might be premature in the present state of our acquaintance. The dinner was excellent, and as we sat together afterwards over his Havanas and coffee, which later he told me was specially prepared upon his own plantation, it seemed to me that all my driver's eulogies were justified, and that I had never met a more large-hearted and hospitable man.

But, in spite of his cheery good nature, he was a man with a strong will and a fiery temper of his own. Of this I had an example upon the following morning. The curious aversion which Mrs. Everard King had conceived towards me was so strong, that her manner at breakfast was almost offensive. But her meaning became unmistakable when her husband had quitted the room.

"The best train in the day is at twelve-fifteen," said she.

"But I was not thinking of going today," I answered, frankly—perhaps even defiantly, for I was determined not to be driven out by this woman.

"Oh, if it rests with you—" said she, and stopped with a most insolent expression in her eyes.

"I am sure," I answered, "that Mr. Everard King would tell me if I were outstaying my welcome."

"What's this? What's this?" said a voice, and there he was in the room. He had overheard my last words, and a glance at our faces had told him the rest. In an instant his chubby, cheery face set into an expression of absolute ferocity.

"Might I trouble you to walk outside, Marshall," said he. (I may mention that my own name is Marshall King.)

He closed the door behind me, and then, for an instant, I heard him talking in a low voice of concentrated passion to his wife. This gross breach of hospitality had evidently hit upon his tenderest point. I am no eavesdropper, so I walked out on to the lawn. Presently I heard a hurried step behind me, and there was the lady, her face pale with excitement, and her eyes red with tears.

"My husband has asked me to apologise to you, Mr. Marshall King," said she, standing with downcast eyes before me.

"Please do not say another word, Mrs. King."

Her dark eyes suddenly blazed out at me.

"You fool!" she hissed, with frantic vehemence, and turning on her heel swept back to the house.

The insult was so outrageous, so insufferable, that I could only stand staring after her in bewilderment. I was still there when my host joined me. He was his cheery, chubby self once more.

"I hope that my wife has apologised for her foolish remarks," said he.

"Oh, yes—yes, certainly!"

He put his hand through my arm and walked with me up and down the lawn.

"You must not take it seriously," said he. "It would grieve me inexpressibly if you curtailed your visit by one hour. The fact is—there is no reason why there should be any concealment between relatives—that my poor dear wife is incredibly jealous. She hates that anyone—male or female—should for an instant come between us. Her ideal is a desert island and an eternal *tete-à-tete*. That gives you the clue to her actions, which are, I confess, upon this particular point, not very far removed from mania. Tell me that you will think no more of it."

'No, no; certainly not."

"Then light this cigar and come round with me and see my little menagerie."

The whole afternoon was occupied by this inspection, which included all the birds, beasts, and even reptiles which he had imported. Some were free, some in cages, a few actually in the house. He spoke with enthusiasm of his successes and his failures, his births and his deaths, and he would cry out in his delight, like a schoolboy, when, as we walked, some gaudy bird would flutter up from the grass, or some curious beast slink into the cover. Finally he led me down a corridor which extended from one wing of the house. At the end of this there was a heavy door with a sliding shutter in it, and beside it there projected from the wall an iron handle attached to a wheel and a drum. A line of stout bars extended across the passage.

"I am about to show you the jewel of my collection," said he. "There is only one other specimen in Europe, now that the Rotterdam cub is dead. It is a Brazilian cat."

"But how does that differ from any other cat?"

"You will soon see that," said he, laughing. "Will you kindly draw that shutter and look through?"

I did so, and found that I was gazing into a large, empty room, with stone flags, and small, barred windows upon the farther wall.

In the centre of this room, lying in the middle of a golden patch of sunlight, there was stretched a huge creature, as large as a tiger, but as black and sleek as ebony. It was simply a very enormous and very well-kept black cat, and it cuddled up and basked in that yellow pool of light exactly as a cat would do. It was so graceful, so sinewy, and so gently and smoothly diabolical, that I could not take my eyes from the opening.

"Isn't he splendid?" said my host, enthusiastically.

"Glorious! I never saw such a noble creature."

"Some people call it a black puma, but really it is not a puma at all. That fellow is nearly eleven feet from tail to tip. Four years ago he was a little ball of back fluff, with two yellow eyes staring out of it. He was sold me as a new-born cub up in the wild country at the head-waters of the Rio Negro. They speared his mother to death after she had killed a dozen of them."

"They are ferocious, then?"

"The most absolutely treacherous and bloodthirsty creatures upon earth. You talk about a Brazilian cat to an up-country Indian, and see him get the jumps. They prefer humans to game. This fellow has never tasted living blood yet, but when he does he will be a terror. At present he won't stand anyone but me in his den. Even Baldwin, the groom, dare not go near him. As to me, I am his mother and father in one."

As he spoke he suddenly, to my astonishment, opened the door and slipped in, closing it instantly behind him. At the sound of his voice the huge, lithe creature rose, yawned and rubbed its round, black head affectionately against his side, while he patted and fondled it.

"Now, Tommy, into your cage!" said he.

The monstrous cat walked over to one side of the room and coiled itself up under a grating. Everard King came out, and taking the iron handle which I have mentioned, he began to turn it. As he did so the line of bars in the corridor began to pass through a slot in the wall and closed up the front of this grating, so as to make an effective cage. When it was in position he opened the door once more and invited me into the room, which was heavy with the pungent, musty smell peculiar to the great carnivora.

"That's how we work it," said he. "We give him the run of the room for exercise, and then at night we put him in his cage. You can let him out by turning the handle from the passage, or you can, as you have seen, coop him up in the same way. No, no, you should not do that!"

I had put my hand between the bars to pat the glossy, heaving flank. He pulled it back, with a serious face.

"I assure you that he is not safe. Don't imagine that because I can take liberties with him anyone else can. He is very exclusive in his friends—aren't you, Tommy? Ah, he hears his lunch coming to him! Don't you, boy?"

A step sounded in the stone-flagged passage, and the creature had sprung to his feet, and was pacing up and down the narrow cage, his yellow eyes gleaming, and his scarlet tongue rippling and quivering over the white line of his jagged teeth. A groom entered with a coarse joint upon a tray, and thrust it through the bars to him. He pounced lightly upon it, carried it off to the corner, and there, holding it between his paws, tore and wrenched at it, raising his bloody muzzle every now and then to look at us. It was a malignant and yet fascinating sight.

"You can't wonder that I am fond of him, can you?" said my host, as we left the room, "especially when you consider that I have had the rearing of him. It was no joke bringing him over from the centre of South America; but here he is safe and sound—and, as I have said, far the most perfect specimen in Europe. The people at the Zoo are dying to have him, but I really can't part with him. Now, I think that I have inflicted my hobby upon you long enough, so we cannot do better than follow Tommy's example, and go to our lunch."

My South American relative was so engrossed by his grounds and their curious occupants, that I hardly gave him credit at first for having any interests outside them. That he had some, and pressing ones, was soon borne in upon me by the number of telegrams which he received. They arrived at all hours, and were always opened by him with the utmost eagerness and anxiety upon his face. Sometimes I imagined that it must be the Turf, and sometimes the Stock Exchange, but certainly he had some very urgent business going forwards which was not transacted upon the Downs of Suffolk. During the six days of my visit he had never fewer than three or four telegrams a day, and sometimes as many as seven or eight.

I had occupied these six days so well, that by the end of them I had succeeded in getting upon the most cordial terms with my cousin. Every night we had sat up late in the billiard-room, he telling me the most extraordinary stories of his adventures in America—stories so desperate and reckless, that I could hardly associate them with the brown, little, chubby man before me. In return, I ventured upon some of my own reminiscences of London life, which interested him so much that he vowed he would come up to Grosvenor Mansions and stay with me. He was anxious to see the faster side of city life, and certainly, though I say it, he could not have chosen a more competent guide. It was not until the last day of my visit that I ventured to approach that which was on my mind. I told him frankly about my pecuniary difficulties and my impending ruin, and I asked his advice—though I hoped for something more solid. He listened attentively, puffing hard at his cigar.

"But surely," said he, "you are the heir of our relative, Lord Southerton?"

"I have every reason to believe so, but he would never make me any allowance."

"No, no, I have heard of his miserly ways. My poor Marshall, your position has been a very hard one. By the way, have you heard any news of Lord Southerton's health lately?"

"He has always been in a critical condition ever since my childhood."

"Exactly—a creaking hinge, if ever there was one. Your inheritance may be a long way off. Dear me, how awkwardly situated you are!"

"I had some hopes, sir, that you, knowing all the facts, might be inclined to advance—"

"Don't say another word, my dear boy," he cried, with the utmost cordiality; "we shall talk it over to-night, and I give you my word that whatever is in my power shall be done."

I was not sorry that my visit was drawing to a close, for it is unpleasant to feel that there is one person in the house who eagerly desires your departure. Mrs. King's sallow face and forbidding eyes had become more and more hateful to me. She was no longer actively rude—her fear of her husband prevented her—but she pushed her insane jealousy to the extent of ignoring me, never addressing me, and in every way making my stay at Greylands as uncomfortable as she could. So offensive was her manner during that last day, that I should certainly have left had it not been for that interview with my host in the evening which would, I hoped, retrieve my broken fortunes.

It was very late when it occurred, for my relative, who had been receiving even more telegrams than usual during the day, went off to his study after dinner, and only emerged when the household had retired to bed. I heard him go round locking the doors, as custom was of a night, and finally he joined me in the billiard-room. His stout figure was wrapped in a dressing-gown, and he wore a pair of red Turkish slippers without any heels. Settling down into an arm-chair, he brewed himself a glass of grog, in which I could not help noticing that the whisky considerably predominated over the water.

"My word!" said he, "what a night!"

It was, indeed. The wind was howling and screaming round the house, and the latticed windows rattled and shook as if they were coming in. The glow of the yellow lamps and the flavour of our cigars seemed the brighter and more fragrant for the contrast.

"Now, my boy," said my host, "we have the house and the night to ourselves. Let me have an idea of how your affairs stand, and I will see what can be done to set them in order. I wish to hear every detail."

Thus encouraged, I entered into a long exposition, in which all my tradesmen and creditors, from my landlord to my valet, figured in turn. I had notes in my pocket-book, and I marshalled my facts, and gave, I flatter myself, a very business-like statement of my own unbusiness-like ways and lamentable position. I was depressed, however, to notice that my companion's eyes were vacant and his attention elsewhere. When he did occasionally throw out a remark it was so entirely perfunctory and pointless, that I was sure he had not in the least followed my remarks. Every now and then he roused himself and put on some show of interest, asking me to repeat or to explain more fully, but it was always to sink once more into the same brown study. At last he rose and threw the end of his cigar into the grate.

"I'll tell you what, my boy," said he. "I never had a head for figures, so you will excuse me. You must jot it all down upon paper, and let me have a note of the amount. I'll understand it when I see it in black and white."

The proposal was encouraging. I promised to do so.

"And now it's time we were in bed. By Jove, there's one o'clock striking in the hall."

The tingling of the chiming clock broke through the deep roar of the gale. The wind was sweeping past with the rush of a great river.

"I must see my cat before I go to bed," said my host. "A high wind excites him. Will you come?"

"Certainly," said I.

"Then tread softly and don't speak, for everyone is asleep."

We passed quietly down the lamp-lit Persian-rugged hall, and through the door at the farther end. All was dark in the stone corridor, but a stable lantern hung on a hook, and my host took it down and lit it. There was no grating visible in the passage, so I knew that the beast was in its cage.

"Come in!" said my relative, and opened the door.

A deep growling as we entered showed that the storm had really excited the creature. In the flickering light of the lantern, we saw it, a huge black mass coiled in the corner of its den and throwing a squat, uncouth shadow upon the whitewashed wall. Its tail switched angrily among the straw.

"Poor Tommy is not in the best of tempers," said Everard King, holding up the lantern and looking in at him. "What a black devil he looks, doesn't he? I must give him a little supper to put him in a better humour. Would you mind holding the lantern for a moment?"

I took it from his hand and he stepped to the door.

"His larder is just outside here," said he. "You will excuse me for an instant, won't you?" He passed out, and the door shut with a sharp metallic click behind him.

That hard crisp sound made my heart stand still. A sudden wave of terror passed over me. A vague perception of some monstrous treachery turned me cold. I sprang to the door, but there was no handle upon the inner side.

"Here!" I cried. "Let me out!"

"All right! Don't make a row!" said my host from the passage. "You've got the light all right."

"Yes, but I don't care about being locked in alone like this."

"Don't you?" I heard his hearty, chuckling laugh. "You won't be alone long."

"Let me out, sir!" I repeated angrily. "I tell you I don't allow practical jokes of this sort."

"Practical is the word," said he, with another hateful chuckle. And then suddenly I heard, amidst the roar of the storm, the creak and whine of the winch-handle turning, and the rattle of the grating as it passed through the slot. Great God, he was letting loose the Brazilian cat!

In the light of the lantern I saw the bars sliding slowly before me. Already there was an opening a foot wide at the farther end. With a scream I seized the last bar with my hands and pulled with the strength of a madman. I *was* a madman with rage and horror. For a minute or more I held the thing motionless. I knew that he was straining with all his force upon the handle, and that the leverage was sure to overcome me. I gave inch by inch, my feet sliding along the stones, and all the time I begged and prayed this inhuman monster to save me from this horrible death. I conjured him by his kinship. I reminded him that I was his guest; I begged to know what harm I had ever done him. His only answers were the tugs and jerks upon the handle, each of which, in spite of all my struggles, pulled another bar through the opening. Clinging and clutching, I was dragged across the whole front of the cage, until at last, with aching wrists and lacerated fingers, I gave up the hopeless struggle. The grating clanged back as I released it, and an instant later I heard the shuffle of the Turkish slippers in the passage, and the slam of the distant door. Then everything was silent.

The creature had never moved during this time. He lay still in the corner, and his tail had ceased switching. This apparition of a man adhering to his bars and dragged screaming across him had apparently filled him with amazement. I saw his great eyes staring steadily at me. I had dropped the lantern when I seized the bars, but it still burned upon the floor, and I made a movement to grasp it, with some idea that its light might protect me. But the instant I moved, the beast gave a deep and menacing growl. I stopped and stood still, quivering with fear in every limb. The cat (if one may call so fearful a creature by so homely a name) was not more than ten feet from me. The eyes glimmered like two discs of phosphorus in the darkness. They appalled and yet fascinated me. I could not take my own eyes from them. Nature plays strange tricks with us at such moments of intensity, and those glimmering lights waxed and waned with a steady rise and fall. Sometimes they seemed to be tiny points of extreme brilliancy—little electric sparks in the black obscurity—then they would widen and widen until all that corner of the room was filled with their shifting and sinister light. And then suddenly they went out altogether.

The beast had closed its eyes. I do not know whether there may be any truth in the old idea of the dominance of the human gaze, or whether the huge cat was simply drowsy, but the fact remains that, far from showing any symptom of attacking me, it simply rested its sleek, black head upon its huge forepaws and seemed to sleep. I stood, fearing to move lest I should rouse it into malignant life once more. But at least I was able to think clearly now that the baleful eves were off me, Here I was shut up for the night with the ferocious beast. My own instincts, to say nothing of the words of the plausible villain who laid this trap for me, warned me that the animal was as savage as its master. How could I stave it off until morning? The door was hopeless, and so were the narrow, barred

71

windows. There was no shelter anywhere in the bare, stone-flagged room. To cry for assistance was absurd. I knew that this den was an outhouse, and that the corridor which connected it with the house was at least a hundred feet long. Besides, with the gale thundering outside, my cries were not likely to be heard. I had only my own courage and my own wits to trust to.

And then, with a fresh wave of horror, my eyes fell upon the lantern. The candle had burned low, and was already beginning to gutter. In ten minutes it would be out. I had only ten minutes then in which to do something, for I felt that if I were once left in the dark with that fearful beast I should be incapable of action. The very thought of it paralysed me. I cast my despairing eyes round this chamber of death, and they rested upon one spot which seemed to promise I will not say safety, but less immediate and imminent danger than the open floor.

I have said that the cage had a top as well as a front, and this top was left standing when the front was wound through the slot in the wall. It consisted of bars at a few inches' interval, with stout wire netting between, and it rested upon a strong stanchion at each end. It stood now as a great barred canopy over the crouching figure in the corner. The space between this iron shelf and the roof may have been from two or three feet. If I could only get up there, squeezed in between bars and ceiling, I should have only one vulnerable side. I should be safe from below, from behind, and from each side. Only on the open face of it could I be attacked. There, it is true, I had no protection whatever; but at least, I should be out of the brute's path when he began to pace about his den. He would have to come out of his way to reach me. It was now or never, for if once the light were out it would be impossible. With a gulp in my throat I sprang up, seized the iron edge of the top, and swung myself panting on to it. I writhed in face downwards, and found myself looking straight into the terrible eyes and yawning jaws of the cat. Its fetid breath came up into my face like the steam from some foul pot.

It appeared, however, to be rather curious than angry. With a sleek ripple of its long, black back it rose, stretched itself, and then rearing itself on its hind legs, with one forepaw against the wall, it raised the other, and drew its claws across the wire meshes beneath me. One sharp, white hook tore through my trousers—for I may mention that I was still in evening-dress—and dug a furrow in my knee. It was not meant as an attack, but rather as an experiment, for upon my giving a sharp cry of pain he dropped down again, and springing lightly into the room, he began walking swiftly round it, looking up every now and again in my direction. For my part I shuffled backwards until I lay with my back against the wall, screwing myself into the smallest space possible. The farther I got the more difficult it was for him to attack me.

He seemed more excited now that he had begun to move about, and he ran swiftly and noiselessly round and round the den, passing continually underneath the iron couch upon which I lay. It was wonderful to see so great a bulk passing like a shadow, with hardly the softest thudding of velvety pads. The candle was burning low—so low that I could hardly see the creature. And then, with a last flare and splutter it went out altogether. I was alone with the cat in the dark!

It helps one to face a danger when one knows that one has done all that possibly can be done. There is nothing for it then but to quietly await the result. In this case, there was no chance of safety anywhere except the precise spot where I was. I stretched myself out, therefore, and lay silently, almost breathlessly, hoping that the beast might forget my presence if I did nothing to remind him. I reckoned that it must already be two o'clock. At four it would be full dawn. I had not more than two hours to wait for daylight.

Outside, the storm was still raging, and the rain lashed continually against the little windows. Inside, the poisonous and fetid air was overpowering. I could neither hear nor see the cat. I tried to think about other things—but only one had power enough to draw my mind from my terrible position. That was the contemplation of my cousin's villainy, his unparalleled hypocrisy, his malignant hatred of me. Beneath that cheerful face there lurked the spirit of a mediæval assassin. And as I thought of it I saw more clearly how cunningly the thing had been arranged. He had apparently gone to bed with the others. No doubt he had his witness to prove it. Then, unknown to them, he had slipped down, had lured me into his den and abandoned me. His story would be so simple. He had left me to finish my cigar in the billiard-room. I had gone down on my own account to have a last look at the cat. I had entered the room without observing that the cage was opened, and I had been caught. How could such a crime he brought home to him? Suspicion, perhaps—but proof, never!

How slowly those dreadful two hours went by! Once I heard a low, rasping sound, which I took to be the creature licking its own fur, Several times those greenish eyes gleamed at me through the darkness, but never in a fixed stare, and my hopes grew stronger that my presence had been forgotten or ignored. At last the least faint glimmer of light came through the windows—I first dimly saw them as two grey squares upon the black wall, then grey turned to white, and I could see my terrible companion once more. And he, alas, could see me!

It was evident to me at once that he was in a much more dangerous and aggressive mood than when I had seen him last. The cold of the morning had irritated him, and he was hungry as well. With a continual growl he paced swiftly up and down the side of the room which was farthest from my refuge, his whiskers bristling angrily, and his tail switching and lashing. As he turned at the corners his savage eyes always looked upwards at me with a dreadful menace. I knew then that he meant to kill me. Yet I found myself even at that moment admiring the sinuous grace of the devilish thing, its long, undulating, rippling movements, the gloss of its beautiful flanks, the vivid, palpitating scarlet of the glistening tongue which hung from the jet-black muzzle. And all the time that deep, threatening growl was rising and rising in an unbroken crescendo. I knew that the crisis was at hand.

It was a miserable hour to meet such a death—so cold, so comfortless, shivering in my light dress clothes upon this gridiron of toment upon which I was stretched. I tried to brace myself to it, to raise my soul above it, and at the same time, with the lucidity which comes to a perfectly desperate man, I cast round for some possible means of escape. One thing was clear to me. If that front of the cage was only back in its position once more, I could find a sure refuge behind it. Could I possibly pull it back? I hardly dared to move for fear of bringing the creature upon me. Slowly, very slowly, I put my hand forward until it grasped the edge of the front, the final bar which protruded through the wall. To my surprise it came quite easily to my jerk. Of course the difficulty of drawing it out arose from the fact that I was clinging to it. I pulled again, and three inches of it came through. It ran apparently on wheels. I pulled again . . . and then the cat sprang!

It was so quick, so sudden, that I never saw it happen. I simply heard the savage snarl, and in an instant afterwards the blazing yellow eyes, the flattened black head with its red tongue and flashing teeth, were within reach of me. The impact of the creature shook the bars upon which I lay, until I thought (as far as I could think of anything at such a moment) that they were coming down. The cat swayed there for an instant, the head and front paws quite close to me, the hind paws clawing to find a grip upon the edge of the grating. I heard the claws rasping as they clung to the wire netting, and the breath of the beast made me sick. But its bound had been miscalculated. It could not retain its position. Slowly, grinning with rage, and scratching madly at the bars, it swung backwards and dropped heavily upon the floor. With a growl it instantly faced round to me and crouched for another spring.

I knew that the next few moments would decide my fate. The creature had learned by experience. It would not miscalculate again. I must act promptly, fearlessly, if I were to have a chance for life. In an instant I had formed my plan. Pulling off my dress-coat, I threw it down over the head of the beast. At the same moment I dropped over the edge, seized the end of the front grating, and pulled it frantically out of the wall.

It came more easily than I could have expected. I rushed across the room, bearing it with me; but, as I rushed, the accident of my position put me upon the outer side. Had it been the other way, I might have come off scathless. As it was, there was a moment's pause as I stopped it and tried to pass in through the opening which I had left. That moment was enough to give time to the creature to toss off the coat with which I had blinded him and to spring upon me. I hurled myself through the gap and pulled the rails to behind me, but he seized my leg before I could entirely withdraw it. One stroke of that huge paw tore off my calf as a shaving of wood curls off before a plane. The next moment, bleeding and fainting, I was lying among the foul straw with a line of friendly bars between me and the creature which ramped so frantically against them.

Too wounded to move, and too faint to be conscious of fear, I could only lie, more dead than alive, and watch it. It pressed its broad, black chest against the bars and angled for me with its crooked paws as I have seen a kitten do before a mouse-trap. It ripped my clothes, but, stretch as it would, it could not quite reach me. I have heard of the curious numbing effect produced by wounds from the great carnivora, and now I was destined to experience it, for I had lost all sense of personality, and was as interested in the cat's failure or success as if it were some game which I was watching. And then gradually my mind drifted away into strange vague dreams, always with that black face and red tongue coming back into them, and so I lost myself in the nirvana of delirium, the blessed relief of those who are too sorely tried.

Tracing the course of events afterwards, I conclude that I must have been insensible for about two hours. What roused me to consciousness once more was that sharp metallic click which had been the precursor of my terrible experience. It was the shooting back of the spring lock. Then, before my senses were clear enough to entirely apprehend what they saw, I was aware of the round, benevolent face of my cousin peering in through the opened door. What he saw evidently amazed him. There was the cat crouching on the floor. I was stretched upon my back in my shirt-sleeves within the cage, my trousers torn to ribbons and a great pool of blood all round me. I can see his amazed face now, with the morning sunlight upon it. He peered at me, and peered again. Then he closed the door behind him, and advanced to the cage to see if I were really dead.

I cannot undertake to say what happened. I was not in a fit state to witness or to chronicle such events. I can only say that I was suddenly conscious that his face was away from me—that he was looking towards the animal.

"Good old Tommy!" he cried. "Good old Tommy!"

Then he came near the bars, with his back still towards me.

"Down, you stupid beast!" he roared. "Down, sir! Don't you know your master?"

Suddenly even in my bemuddled brain a remembrance came of those words of his when he had said that the taste of blood would turn the cat into a fiend. My blood had done it, but he was to pay the price.

"Get away!" he screamed. "Get away, you devil! Baldwin! Baldwin! Oh, my God!"

And then I heard him fall, and rise, and fall again, with a sound like the ripping of sacking. His screams grew fainter until they were lost in the worrying snarl. And then, after I thought that he was dead, I saw, as in a nightmare, a blinded, tattered, blood-soaked figure running wildy round the room—and that was the last glimpse which I had of him before I fainted once again.

I was many months in my recovery—in fact, I cannot say that I have ever recovered, for to the end of my days I shall carry a stick as a sign of my night with the Brazilian cat. Baldwin, the groom, and the other servants could not tell what had occurred when, drawn by the death cries of their master, they found me behind the bars, and his remains—or what they afterwards discovered to be his remains—in the clutch of the creature which he had reared. They stalled him off with hot irons, and afterwards shot him through the loophole of the door before they could finally extricate me. I was carried to my bedroom, and there, under the roof of my would-be murderer, I remained between life and death for several weeks. They had sent for a surgeon from Clipton and a nurse from London, and in a month I was able to be carried to the station, and so conveyed back once more to Grosvenor Mansions.

I have one remembrance of that illness, which might have been part of the ever-changing panorama conjured up by a delirious brain were it not so definitely fixed in my memory. One night, when the nurse was absent, the door of my chamber opened, and a tall woman in blackest mourning slipped into the room. She came across to me, and as she bent her sallow face I saw by the faint gleam of the night-light that it was the Brazilian woman whom my cousin had married. She stared intently into my face, and her expression was more kindly than I had ever seen it.

"Are you conscious?" she asked.

I feebly nodded—for I was still very weak.

"Well, then, I only wished to say to you that you have yourself to blame. Did I not do all I could for you? From the beginning I tried to drive you from the house. By every means, short of betraying my husband, I tried to save you from him. I knew that he had a reason for bringing you here. I knew that he would never let you get away again. No one knew him as I knew him, who had suffered from him so often. I did not dare to tell you all this. He would have killed me. But I did my best for you. As things have turned out, you have been the best friend that I have ever had. You have set me free, and I fancied that nothing but death would do that. I am sorry if you are hurt, but I cannot reproach myself.

I told you that you were a fool—and a fool you have been." She crept out of the room, the bitter, singular woman, and I was never destined to see her again. With what remained from her husband's property she went back to her native land, and I have heard that she afterwards took the veil at Pernambuco.

It was not until I had been back in London for some time that the doctors pronounced me to be well enough to do business. It was not a very welcome permission to me, for I feared that it would be the signal for an inrush of creditors; but it was Summers, my lawyer, who first took advantage of it.

"I am very glad to see that your lordship is so much better," said he. "I have been waiting a long time to offer my congratulations."

"What do you mean, Summers? This is no time for joking."

"I mean what I say," he answered. "You have been Lord Southerton for the last six weeks, but we feared that it would retard your recovery if you were to learn it."

Lord Southerton! One of the richest peers in England! I could not believe my ears. And then suddenly I thought of the time which had elapsed, and how it coincided with my injuries.

"Then Lord Southerton must have died about the same time that I was hurt?"

"His death occurred upon that very day." Summers looked hard at me as I spoke, and I am convinced—for he was a very shrewd fellow—that he had guessed the true state of the case. He paused for a moment as if awaiting a confidence from me, but I could not see what was to be gained by exposing such a family scandal.

"Yes, a very curious coincidence," he continued, with the same knowing look. "Of course, you are aware that your cousin Everard King was the next heir to the estates. Now, if it had been you instead of him who had been torn to pieces by this tiger, or whatever it was, then of course he would have been Lord Southerton at the present moment."

"No doubt," said I.

"And he took such an interest in it," said Summers. "I happen to know that the late Lord Southerton's valet was in his pay, and that he used to have telegrams from him every few hours to tell him how he was getting on. That would be about the time when you were down there. Was it not strange that he should wish to be so well informed, since he knew that he was not the direct heir?"

"Very strange," said I. "And now, Summers, if you will bring me my bills and a new cheque-book, we will begin to get things into order."

Talmir and Threstenios

Manuel Pérez-Campos

And Talmir the beggar whispered under the night skies of autumn to the desert that swallowed cities and whose company had been forbidden: "Take me and do with me as you will, O desert, for the one who comforted me in my old age with his short tufted ears and controlled adventurousness and terrifying claws, Threstenios the glorious cat, is gone to I know not whither. And though I have called out to him in many a winding lane he has not answered, and the lads and lasses who will one day be given positions of power in the cities for their expertise in perpetrating atrocities on such as he have mocked me. A merchant of olives has told me that Threstenios drowned trying to cross a river to escape from their stoning. I have no reason to disbelieve him. There is only sorrow now for me to look forward to and no one to feed from my hand and so justify my existence."

So the desert came to him like an ogre and tore off his ragged clothes and wrapped him in a mantle of sand instead, and swept him long and savagely throughout its phantasmal depths.

For thirty years Talmir existed in a dream, not knowing at any given moment if he was crawling out of the dunes after being interred by the simoom or if a whirlwind had just lifted him into its haze and he was being borne like a mote across their incessant sinuous slopes. In his dream, Talmir sought Threstenios all over the desert. Although he grew discouraged many times over, he always found cause in his heart not to give up, not for a moment, lest he lose the thread of his great love for Threstenios. It was this thread he followed, and which he hoped would lead him to his friend. Throughout this ordeal, the desert, not wanting the grand entertainment it had found in thrashing him to come to an end on occasion blew dead birds and water all around him that he might subsist.

Eventually however, the desert wearied of him, and abandoned him to his own devices. Talmir made new clothes for himself in an oasis from debris scattered by a caravan that had been detained there, and a knapsack which he filled with subpar victuals from the same source to avail him until the next oasis. After journeyings that were erased by sunset from his intellectual grasp even as all yesterdays are erased by the wind from the desert, Talmir came across an isolated plinth and standing on it looking with infinite boredom at infinity the gigantic statue of a winged king. To his amazement, the statue seemed familiar and spoke to him: "I am Vormazouf, the deity you built in your youth when you had yet to learn as you have with Threstenios, to sacrifice yourself for another and whom you promptly forgot a twelvemonth later."

"O Vormazouf, if it be within your granting, tell me the whereabouts of Threstenios, that we may be reunited."

"Fool, the one you seek you cannot get to without the help of one like me, for he is a citizen of another eternity."

"Then help me, for I created you. Surely you are obligated to me for that reason."

"I am, yet I too have my pride. If you want my help, you must become my worshipper again."

"What must I do to become your worshipper?"

"You must do penance for abandoning me." In the mighty silence that came after these words, a sword materialized on the sand by the sandalled feet of Talmir.

Talmir did not hesitate. Taking up the sword, he cut off his right arm and offered it to Vormasouf. No sooner had Vormazouf accepted it with a nod and a grunt and indicated for him to set it down before the plinth. There the right arm turned to ashes.

"What next, O venerable one?"

"Take all you need from the nearest oasis and build around me a temple seven cubits high."

And when after a lustrum Vormazouf was housed inside a temple, Talmir asked "What next, O venerable one?"

But Vormazouf gloated. "Stone by stone you shall raise a mountain; mountain by mountain you shall raise a land mass; land mass by land mass you shall raise a world; world by world you shall raise a vastness; vastness by vastness you shall raise a universe; universe by universe you shall raise an age; age by age you shall raise an eternity, and it is this which you shall then endeavor to lay at the foot of my throne. And when you have done this, I shall reunite you with Threstenios."

"Now I remember why we parted ways. It was because I eventually discovered you were simply an excuse I made to prevent me from experiencing the sacred feeling of pity. This time I shall make sure that you are a temptation no more to my psyche."

And Talmir took the sword, and brought it down on the head of Vormazouf with such uncanny strength and resolve that a long jagged crack developed lengthwise and the statue separated presently into two halves that fell apart into the sand. And so without a cry Vormazouf ceased to exist.

But lo, out of each half of the statue a mist emerged, and as Talmir wondered at this unusual occurrence, the two pieces of mist joined up and solidified as Threstenios, who ran toward him as if in a hurry. Rejoicing, Talmir knelt down and picked him up and held him against his face. Talmir wept. "The next time we are disjoined, Threstenios, it shall be because oblivion has decreed so, not because those who lack pity have decreed so. Somehow I have faith that this is how it shall be."

And the desert took pity on Talmir, and did not wake him from his new dream.

Le Chat Noir, La Femme Vieille

Alan Dean Foster

The snow was pure white and as soft as an eiderdown quilt, but unlike a comforter it was not warm. Crossing her slender arms over her chest and squeezing tightly, Jeanette tugged the heavy old coat as snug as she could against her torso. She could feel the deep chill of the stone wall against her back even through the dense fabric. Years of leaning back against the dark unyielding stone had worn thin the material of the coat where it rubbed against her spine. At least the thick woolen blanket, doubled over and spread out on the sidewalk, kept her backside from the worst of the cold. Having spent so many years sitting in the same spot, she had grown accustomed to the seated position. But by the end of a winter's day she was stiff and sore and inexorably numbed, the chill seeping through her body like cold sweat soaking an old mattress.

It was unusually frigid tonight. Extravagant clouds muffled the moon. And though she sat under the dark green canvas overhang that both protected and advertised the store behind her, when the wind picked up, blowing snow still found her and had to be brushed off lest its icy damp be added to the coldness of the air.

Tonight the snow seemed to be falling in slow motion. Big, fat, white flakes. Little slices of arctic, silent and sparkling. Across the street from where she huddled the lights of the Opéra Garnier blazed bright as usual, defying the night and the snow while illuminating the massive structure's stone columns and carvings, its magnificent decorative statuary, and especially the giant, dazzlingly gilded statues of Harmony and Poetry that beckoned from the corners. It was one of the most beautiful buildings in all Paris, and therefore automatically one of the most beautiful buildings in all the world.

As a young woman she had been inside several times. The wonder of its grand, ornate, gold-and-mirrored interior remained etched in her memory. Those sublime visits, like all the good things in her life, had taken place a long while ago. It had been some time since she had been young. Since then all good things had fallen away from her, like the crumbling slate shingles slowly sliding off the roof of an abandoned old house. Cracked and gray, as was she.

She did not complain. Living on the street wasn't so bad, provided the street was the Rue Auber, directly across from the Opéra. Sometimes on a slow night when traffic was sparse, traces of Rameau and Puccini, of Verdi and Saint-Saëns, would drift across to where she sat. Her familiar spot on the sidewalk was flanked by a bank and a restaurant, both long since shuttered at this hour. In front of her extended legs a wooden box roughly half a meter square and half again as tall rested on the sidewalk at her feet. Piled into a mound atop the box was a small whirlpool of colorful strips of cloth salvaged from nearby trash bins: tutti-frutti scraps. In its center dozed a cat, coiled up and asleep, its eyes closed against the strollers and the cold. Tonight the box's feline occupant happened to be a tabby. Tomorrow, perhaps a calico. Another day, a manx. All strays, all temporary visitors, and all comfortable in her presence. Somehow the cats of Paris knew that the box was always there, warm with memories of human acquaintances gone by.

Jeanette's favorite visitor was a lean, muscular black moggie. One of her regulars. Though its pedigree was conjectural, its fur was always sleek and clean, its eyes as intensely yellow as vintage street lamps. It looked remarkably like the ebon cat that stared out from the famous Art Nouveau poster by Théophile Steinlen, a piece of nineteenth-century advertising that had somehow become as celebrated an image of the City of Light as the Eiffel Tower or the Arc de Triomphe. Whenever the moggie lay in the makeshift bedding atop the wooden box, or even better, sat up, its handsome, lean muscularity and striking yellow stare invariably drew more than the usual attention from passersby—and therefore more than the typical number of coins to the small cast-iron pot that sat beside the box.

Propped up against front of the makeshift cat bed stood a piece of salvaged cardboard on which with a borrowed marker she had written her polite request for a little money, a little help. For her and for her cat. Though they were never "her" cats. She owned none of them. Not the tabbies, not the Nebelung, not the occasional Chartreux or the distinctive black male with the unsettling stare. The strays visited her for the warmth of the bed, the regular petting, and for the food she always set out. She was never sure whether the coins and occasional bill that were placed in the old pot nearby were for her, for the cat du joir, or both.

Of one thing she *was* certain. The occasional comment from a passerby of "Oh, how cute!" or "Isn't she precious?" were always for the cat, never for her. She did not mind. She kept her once attractive face and her waterfall of loosely curled gray hair as clean as her limited resources and circumstances would allow, and did not make the mistake common to many older women of putting on too much blush. Not that she could afford even cheap makeup anyway. From time to time, when the air grew truly brutal and the wind coming down the Rue bit at her scalp, she would don the old knit cap she kept close at hand. She didn't like to wear it. Though she could no longer afford fashion, she strove to look fashionable. But in winter, warmth was more important than appearance.

On the pavement on the other side of the box were two small bowls: one holding water, the other dry cat food. From time to time she would push the water dish under the blanket and against her thigh to keep it from freezing. No matter what life dealt her that day, no matter how dire her personal circumstances, she fought to keep both bowls full. A kindly clerk at the nearby Franprix market on the Rue Godoy de Mauroy would slip her small bags of expired cat food whenever management was not watching. She would have preferred to set out canned food, but in weather like this it too would freeze.

A shiver ran through her, shaking her torso like a baby's rattle. Near her left hip stood a battered metal thermos, now empty. It had been filled earlier that day with hot tea, and she had emptied it too quickly. Now she had none. It was very late indeed. Certainly well after midnight, and snowing harder now. She realized it had been some time since anyone, tourist or local, had passed by. She had to find shelter. The Rue Auber was too exposed to weather that was quickly turning evil. There were several Métro stations nearby that she would frequent when circumstances grew desperate. She tried to rotate her visits between them. It made the police less likely to roust her back out into the weather. They would not arrest her, but they would insist she "move on." Although given the really miserable weather tonight, it might not be a bad time to be arrested. At least it would be warm in jail.

A glance up and then down the Rue Auber showed nothing moving. That was the trouble with winter in Paris for someone like herself. It was neither the cold nor, in the case of tonight, the snow. In the absence of a steady flow of tourists paying homage to the Opéra, her meager income diminished proportionately. She always fared much better in the spring, she knew as she sat shivering. Summer was best of all and autumn would be tolerable. But winter—winter she hated. Not for the first time she envied the cats who were her only companions. At least they had fur and could squeeze themselves into small, snuggly spaces. She was a clumsy old woman with no fat left on her to keep her warm.

It struck her that she could not continue to sit there contemplating her surroundings. She knew she had to move. Had to get up. The street was mostly dark now, the commercial buildings surrounding the Opéra looming like cold canyon walls. Only the Opéra itself seemed alive, permanently illuminated at night, defying the weather as forcefully as it did the ages. Rubbing her gloved palms against each other to warm her hands, she gently urged the slumbering tabby off the box. Reluctantly hopping down onto the snow-covered pavement, it looked back at her and uttered a single quizzical *meow* before turning to trot off down the street. It would seek out a protected place in an alley somewhere. She might see it tomorrow or she might not. If it failed to show, another of its streetwise relations would take up residence for the duration of the evening in the pile of assorted cloth scraps atop the box.

Grunting softly she started to get up, only to discover she could not move. Her legs were numb. It was not the first time. Reaching down under the blanket, she rubbed her unresponsive limbs, her palms sliding back and forth along the tops of her thighs. Despite the gloves she realized was starting to lose sensation in her fingers, too. The weak attempt at massage only tired her out and did nothing for her legs. She was cold, cold. And still the snow continued to fall, hushed and aloof, enveloping her with an uncaring chill.

Blinking away the snowflakes that kept invading her eyes, she looked up and down the street. It remained deserted, as one would expect at this time of night in weather like this. Squinting, she looked for one of the other, more physically active beggars who like her haunted the immediate environs of the Opéra. She could see no one in any of the usual locations on the other side of the street; not behind the iron fence, not on the steps. By now they were all most likely to be holed up in their own alley somewhere, or huddled below in the heated Métro trying to keep one step ahead of the gendarmerie.

It was a struggle simply to turn to her left, but she succeeded. Pushing down against the pavement with her left hand, she tried to get her hips off the ground. But there was no strength in her arm and no energy in her body. Exhausted from the effort, she slumped back against the wall. A pharmacy fronted the street only meters from where she sat, but it had closed at nine. Everything near the Opéra Garnier was closed now, shut up against the storm. No one was out in this weather. Rendered carefree by youth, the most determined lovers would be found cuddling against the snow on one of the bridges over the Seine; not here. She had been one of those lovers once. Her husband had died fifteen years ago, leaving her only with fading remembrances.

Unable to rise or even to muster enough energy to brush off the snow that had rapidly begun to accumulate on her legs and lower body, she drifted into memory. Of warm days in July, of picnics at Point Aragon on the Île Saint-Louis watching the boats ply the Seine. Of the tang of cold fruit sorbet and the crush of his strong embrace. Good thoughts, good food, good times. They warmed her soul.

But not her body.

It was very quiet inside the Pharmacie Perrault. Centimeters of snow were beginning to accumulate outside. The streets were deserted. Even Doublemard's grand statue of Marshal Maréchal Moncey that dominated the center of Place Clichy was losing its martial pose beneath a homogenizing blanket of white.

It was ten minutes past 3 a.m. Having little to do, the night manager had wandered to the front of the establishment to check for the tenth time on the depth of the snow. In lieu of a genuine emergency, even the late-night regulars who frequented the twenty-four-hour pharmacy were unlikely to emerge from their cozy apartments to brave the storm simply for a bottle of aspirin or a packet of flavored lozenges.

As Jules reached the front of the store he heard a thump at the door. It was loud, heavy, and unmissable. Strange, he thought. The door was unlocked and anyone could simply walk in, so why the *thump?* Frowning, he shifted his attention to make a cautious check of the portal. Crazy kids out throwing snowballs, most likely. He could not think of another possible explanation. What he saw slumped against outside of the door caused his eyes to widen.

"Abdou, Clement! Come quick, hurry!"

As soon as they opened the door the insensate, snow-covered body of the old woman fell inside. Reaching down, Jules first touched the back of his hand to her forehead. The wrinkled skin felt like a wet washrag. Quickly taking her hand, he pressed the tips of his fingers against her wrist and counted. It was slow and weak, but there was definitely a pulse. Rising, he crisply gave orders to the other employees.

"Clement—ready some coffee in the back. With sugar. She needs all the energy we can get into her." He nodded at the remaining employee as their companion vanished toward the rear of the pharmacy. "Help me get her on a cot in back, Abdou."

She was not heavy. Most of the weight seemed to come from the snow that had frozen to her face and clothing and could not easily be brushed off. Once they had her safely on the cot in the room at the rear of the store, Abdou slid two pillows beneath the gray hair that fanned out behind her head. Careful not to tear the worn fabric of her dress, Jules gently but swiftly opened the buttons. From a storage shelf he grabbed a long rectangular cardboard box, tore off one end, and removed the brand new electric blanket it contained. Shaking out the folds, he placed it against her now bared torso. Working deftly, he plugged the control unit into the blanket, the power cord into the nearest socket, and turned it to high.

Moments later Clement appeared holding a mug of steaming coffee. Resisting the urge to sip from the cup, he continued to hold it as the three of them waited. More moments passed in silence until her eyes fluttered and her breathing strengthened. While Abdou held her head up, Clement fed her the heavily sweetened coffee one small swallow at a time. Increasingly optimistic, Jules looked on.

"You are very, very lucky, Madame. Fortunate that pharmacists in France are trained in emergency care, fortunate that you found us. There are not many twenty-four-hour pharmacies in this part of the city."

She nodded weakly as she continued to sip at the coffee. Abdou looked up at the night manager.

"I think she will live. But if she had been another hour outside in this …" He gestured meaningfully toward the front of the establishment and the storm that continued to intensify outside.

Jules nodded grimly. "We'll keep her here until morning. Let her sleep and recover some strength. Then I'll call the hospital and we'll have her transferred." Peering down at the venerable, petite form, he was suddenly uncertain. "I think I may know this woman." In response to Clement and Abdou's expressions of puzzlement, he explained. "Down by the Opéra Garnier. She sits on the Rue Auber and begs. I imagine she must be there every night. The police must be sympathetic to let her stay there."

Clement's heavy brow furrowed. "Do you think she walked all the way up here from the Opéra? In this weather?"

"I don't know." Jules looked toward the front of the pharmacy. He was tall, wiry, and confused. "I didn't see a taxi outside, a car, or anyone else." He started out of the rear room. "Keep feeding her that coffee, if she'll take it. No solid food yet. I'll be right back."

Halting at the front door, he shielded his eyes with his right hand and peered out into the softly lit traffic circle that was rapidly filling with snow. There was no one standing outside the pharmacy, no one waiting in the street. A glance downward showed no footprints in the snow; nothing to indicate that the woman had been given help to reach her destination. But then, he told himself, by now the falling snow might have covered any tracks, any footprints. He started to turn away when movement caught his eye. A cat.

And a second cat, and a third. Suddenly there seemed to be an unusual amount of activity out in the traffic circle and on the sidewalk. The source of it was a commotion of cats, though he could not tell how many. For just a second he thought there might have been a hundred or more, but that absurd estimation was gone in the blink of an eye. And now he saw footprints—or rather, pawprints. Why he had not noticed them before he did not know. He shrugged. A trick of the night and the light and the falling snow.

The presence of some wandering felines was not a surprise. They would be drawn to the bright lights of the all-night pharmacy and to the suggestion of warmth. Well, he had a poor woman in back who had nearly frozen to death and needed attending to. He had no time for strays, however many.

He sensed a presence nearby. It was Abdou. He looked excited. He also needed a shave. Jules made a mental note to remind him. Appearances were important in any business.

"I was checking her pockets for some kind of identification. Look what I found!" He held up a fistful of banknotes. They were dirty and wrinkled and ranged in denominations from twenty to a hundred. "There must be over a thousand euros here!"

Though every bit as quietly shocked by this discovery as his co-worker, Jules maintained his calm. "That's as marvelous as it is unexpected. It means she can pay for whatever care the state does not. Transportation, food—anything." He pursed his lips. "I wonder why, with that kind of money, she is so thin? It is as if she doesn't want to eat. Or sleep in a room with heat." Baffled by the contradiction, he could only shrug. "Maybe she will have time to explain it to us before the ambulance comes for her." A smile creased his face. "She should not be carrying that kind of money loose in a pocket. Put it in one of the small purses from the side counter. Something compact enough to fit in her coat. On my responsibility."

Clement started to grin. Then his face wrinkled up in disgust as he held the money away from his body. "Pfagh! It all stinks." He forced himself to take a deep whiff of the money before drawing back in disgust. "It smells like fish!"

"Here, let me see," Jules asked. In response, Clement passed him a couple of twenties. The wary night manager inhaled of first one.

"You're wrong. Sour milk." He sniffed cautiously of the other. "Worse still. Something dead. A mouse perhaps, or a rat." With a slight shudder he passed both bills back to the other man. "Spray it all with disinfectant. The purse, too. She must have found the money in the garbage."

Clement eyed his boss doubtfully. "A thousand euros?"

"So she was lucky. Even a beggar gets lucky sometimes."

Nodding, the other man rushed to fumigate the clutch of foul-smelling currency.

A impulsive notion took hold of the night manager. Fish. Cats like fish. Sour milk. Cats like milk. Dead rodents. Cats like …

He hastily discarded the nonsensical notion. What cats surely did not care for was cash. They knew nothing of money or what it might be used for. It was very late and he was starting to think stupid thoughts.

He was about to turn and head to the back of the pharmacy to rejoin his companions when something new drew his attention and caused him to pause. But it was only one more cat outside. Oddly, the snow did not seem to cling to its jet black fur. It sat on its haunches, self-possessed and a bit haughty. As it moved its head its eyes caught the light from the pharmacy sign above the entrance. In its present regal pose it looked quite exactly like that black cat that the artist Steinlen had painted and that now adorned seemingly half the touristy posters and knickknacks in Paris. Of course it couldn't be the same cat. Steinlen's feline model had been painted from life in 1883, and to the best of the night manager's knowledge there were no hundred-and-forty-year-old cats in Paris.

It really was very late, he reminded himself, and therefore not surprising that fatigue, snow, reflections, and night should play tricks on a man.

For an instant a fiery yellow light was reflected in what seemed to be unnaturally large cat's eyes. Then it turned away, vanishing into the darkness and the snow. Had Jules cared to look further into the night he would have seen that it left behind no pawprints. As it was, he retained nothing more than a momentary impression of an intense feline essence the memory of which remained with him well into the next day.

The Cat with Wings

Robert W. Service

You never saw a cat with wings,
I'll bet a dollar—well, I did;
'Twas one of those fantastic things
One runs across in old Madrid.
A walloping big tom it was,
(Maybe of the Angora line),
With silken ears and velvet paws,
And silver hair, superbly fine.

It sprawled upon a crimson mat,
Yet though crowds came to gaze on it,
It was a supercilious cat,

And didn't seem to mind a bit.
It looked at us with dim disdain,
And indolently seemed to sigh:
"There's not another cat in Spain
One half so marvelous as I."

Its owner gently stroked its head,
And tickled it with fingers light.
"Ah no, it cannot fly," he said;
"But see—it has the wings all right."
Then tenderly from off its back
He raised, despite its feline fears,

Appendages that seemed to lack
Vitality—like rabbit's ears.

And then the vision that I had
Of Tabbie soaring through the night,
Quick vanished, and I felt so sad
For that poor pussy's piteous plight.
For though frustration has it stings,
Its mockeries in Hope's despite,
The hell of hells is to have wings
Yet be denied the bliss of flight.

Cat and Mouse

Ramsey Campbell

You couldn't say the house crouched. Yet as we came off the roundabout on whose edge the house stood, and stooped beneath the trees that hung glistening over the garden, I had an impression of stealth. It couldn't be related to anything; not the summer glare nor the white house within the garden—but silence settled on us, and the circling cars hushed. And although the sunlight glittered on the last raindrops dripping from the leaves, a waiting shadow touched us and the quiet in the garden seemed poised to leap.

I had to struggle with the key in the unfamiliar lock; my wife Hazel laughed, annoying me a little. I'd wanted to throw the door wide and carry her in, enjoying my triumph; God knows I'd gone through enough to buy the house. At least I enjoyed her delight once I managed to open the door.

We'd seen the house before, of course, when we were furnishing the rooms, but now we both felt a shock of unfamiliarity. The white telephone amazed us; so did the stairs, a construction of treads like the tail of a kite, which was the major addition we owed to the previous tenants. Hazel's was the reaction I could have predicted; she rushed through the downstairs rooms and then clattered upstairs, eager to own the rest of the house. As I watched her run up the open stairs I felt a dull surge of desire. But when I made my own tour of the pale green living-room, the white kitchen cold as a hospital, the bathroom with its abstract blocks of colour and its pink pedestal, I felt imprisoned. The air smelled slightly dank, like fur. Of course Hazel had been wearing her sheepskin coat, but it seemed odd that the entire ground floor should smell of wet fur, a smell that trailed with me like a cloak. I began to open windows. Perhaps, since we'd lived on a third floor for years, I simply needed time to adjust to entering a house whose windows weren't open.

I found Hazel within a maze of double-jointed lights and drawing-board and cartons of books, in the room we'd decided to use as an attic. The smell was stronger here. "Come down and I'll make some tea," she said.

"Just let me tidy up a little."

"You've done enough for a while, love."

"You mean selling myself?" I said, thinking of my ideas and my art, which I'd battered against the advertising agency where I worked until they had been pounded half out of shape.

"No, I mean selling your talent," Hazel said, and with an edge of doubt "You do like our house, don't you?"

"Of course I do. That's why I worked to buy it," I said and stopped, peering down at the windowsill. We had liked the rough wood of that sill and had left it unpainted. Now, trying to peer closer without appearing to do so, I saw that the sill looked chewed. Or clawed. The former owners must have had a cat or a dog. That was the explanation, yet I was disturbed to think that they had locked it in here, for nothing else could have driven it to such a frenzy that it would have left its claw-marks on the sill and even in the putty round the windowpane.

"I'm sure you'll sleep now we're here," Hazel said, and I started. "What are you looking so worried about?" she said.

I was thinking how, when I'd stripped the attic to paint it, I had noticed claw-marks tearing through the wallpaper without realising until now what they were, but I didn't want to upset her; besides, I wished she wouldn't probe me so often, even though it was out of love she did so. "I'm wondering where the stereo is," I said.

"It must be on its way," she said. "They'll take care of it. They can see how expensive it is."

"Yes, well," I told her, faintly annoyed that I should feel bound to explain this point again, "it's the most sensitive. You have to pay for sensitivity."

"I know you do," she said smiling, and I realised she'd found another meaning, a personal meaning she wanted to share with me. Sometimes her insistence on puns infuriated me; often it made me love her more. I coaxed my gaze away from the patch on the wall where the paper had been clawed. "I wouldn't mind dinner," I said.

The stereo arrived after dinner, halfway through my third cup of coffee. The workmen were clearly annoyed that I should supervise them, as if I were showing them how to do their job. But it was only a job to them; to me it was perfection in jeopardy. When they'd left I played *Ein Heldenleben* at full volume, caring nothing for the neighbours, since they were beyond the garden. Hazel listened quietly, more in order not to disturb me than out of a genuine response to the music. Somehow I felt trapped; the Strauss surged against Hazel's tranquil uncommunicative face, against the padded silence of the room, and never broke. I crossed to the windows and flung them high, and the feeling streamed out into the dark garden, where its remnants clung to the trees.

That night I could neither make love nor sleep. Outside the bedroom window cars whirred lingeringly by, like a sound by Stockhausen passing across speakers. My wife slept buried in the pillow, frowning, her thumb in her mouth. The tip of my cigarette glowed and reddened the landing; it opened in the gloss of the doors like a crimson eye, watching from the attic and from the other bedroom whose purpose was beginning to seem increasingly futile. I had meant to go downstairs, but down there or in my ears lay a faint ominous hiss, quite unlike the threshing of the leaves above the garden. I listened for a few minutes, and then I scraped my cigarette on the ashtray by the bed and pulled the covers up.

Hazel woke me at noon. I gathered she'd awoken only recently herself. I unstuck myself from sleep and followed her downstairs. I must have looked disgruntled, judging by Hazel's glances at me.

I felt she'd woken me up merely for company. When we reached the living-room she said "Darling, listen."

I heard only the words, which were the formula she used when she wasn't sure that I would agree. Of course her tone implied another meaning, but I wasn't awake enough to notice. "What is it?" I demanded.

"No, listen."

That was the second half of the formula. I often spent an hour before sleep juggling ideas and an hour after breakfast waking up; nothing angers me more than to be called upon to make a decision before I'm awake. "Look," I said, "for Christ's sake, now that you've dragged me out of bed—"

Then I saw that she had been gazing at the stereo. From its speakers came a sound like the hiss of a hostile audience. "You see, it moves back and forth," Hazel said. "The stereo must have been on all night. Will it have gone wrong?"

"I take it you've left it on to make sure it will?" I couldn't tell her that I wasn't shouting at her but at something else, because I didn't care to admit it to myself. As I pulled out *Ein Heldenleben* and almost ripped it with the stylus I felt the movement of the hiss, felt it loom like a lurking predator, an actual dark physical presence, as it crept from one speaker to another. Then the Strauss rushed richly out. It sounded perfect, but aside from that it meant nothing. I took it off, scowled at Hazel and stumped back to bed.

I was running upstairs, and the stairs tilted steeply like a ladder. Suddenly sliding gates clanged shut at both ends of the staircase, and something groped hugely through the wall and felt around the trap for me. I awoke struggling. The blanket lay heavy and fluid on my body like a cat, and my skin prickled with what felt like the memory of claws. I threw off the blanket and sat up.

For a moment I was lost; I stared at the blue walls, the grey wall, the impossible silence. I struggled to my feet and listened. It was five o'clock, and there should have been more sound; Hazel should have been audible; the silence seemed charged, alert, on tiptoe. I made my way downstairs, padding carefully. I didn't know what I might find.

Hazel was sitting in the living-room, a book in her hand. I couldn't tell whether she'd been crying; her face looked scrubbed as it would have if she had wept, but I was confused by the thought that this might be the impression she had contrived for me. More disturbingly, I felt that something had happened to change the silence while I had been asleep. She came to the end of a chapter and inserted a bookmark. "I like to sleep too, you know," she said.

"No doubt," I said, and that was that. Through dinner we didn't speak, we hardly looked at each other. It was less that each of us was waiting for the other to speak than as if the silence itself was poised to pounce on the first to succumb. Several times I was almost frightened enough to speak, so that at least my fears might be defined; but each time I determined that it was up to Hazel to begin.

I don't know what music I played after dinner; I recall only visualising fists of sound crudely battling the blankets of silence. I looked at Hazel, who was trying to read against the barrage of noise, which for the moment had lost all meaning. I felt grief for what I might be beginning to destroy. "I'm sorry," I said. "Maybe I'm starting to crack up."

Sometimes Hazel would dodge around the bedroom and I, having pinned her to the bed, would rape her; we seemed to need this more and more often. Tonight we waltzed gently over each other, exploring delicately, until I was too deep in her to need ornamentations. "You're a deep one," I said.

"What, love?" she gasped, laughing.

I could never offer her puns more than once, and now less than ever, for my body had stiffened and chilled. Perhaps, despite her reassurances, I was cracking up. I knew that at that moment I was being watched. I peered down into Hazel's eyes and tried to gaze through them, and as I felt her nails move on my back I remembered the sensations of claws at the end of my dream.

101

The next day, Monday, I came home tired by a lunch one of our clients had bought me; my constant smile had felt more like a death-grin, and certainly had expressed as little emotion. Returning to the agency I'd walked through shafts of envy that had penetrated even my six whiskies. Our house should have offered peace, but all I felt as I opened the front door was the taut snap of tension. I felt awaited, and not only by Hazel.

In the early evening cars passed with a muffled undulating hum, but soon faded. I remembered that back at our flat we could always hear the plop of a tap like a dropper or the echoing cries of children in the public baths across the road. Here in the house the silence seemed worse than ever, threatening to drown us, and our speech was waterlogged. Yet it wasn't the silence I found most disturbing. Over dinner and afterwards, as we sat reading, I glimpsed an odd expression several times on Hazel's face. It wasn't fear, exactly; I should have described it as closer to doubt. What upset me most was that each time she caught me watching her, she quickly smiled.

I couldn't stop thinking that something had happened while I had been at work. "How was our house today?" I asked.

"It was fine," she said. "Oh, while I was out shopping—"

I wouldn't let her escape. "Do you like our house, then?" I asked. "What do you think?"

I was certain now that she was hiding something from me, but I didn't know how to find it. She could elude my questions by any number of wiles, by weeping if necessary. Frowning, I desisted and put Britten's *Curlew River* on the stereo. Of all Britten's work I love the church parables more than any; their sureness and astringency can make me forget my crumpled colleagues at the agency and their clumsy machinations. I thought *Curlew River* might help me define my thoughts, but I didn't get as far as the second side, with its angelic resolution. Peter Pears' eerie vocal glissandi in the part of the madwoman chilled me like the howls of a sad cat; the church which the stereo recreated seemed longer and more hollow, like a tunnel gaping invisibly before me in the air, and the calm silences with which Britten punctuates his parables seemed no longer calm. They seemed to pounce closer and to grow as they approached. Determined to respond to the music, I closed my eyes. At once I felt a dark stealthy shape leap at me between the music. My eyes started open, and I glanced to Hazel for some kind of support. The room was empty.

And it was dark. On the wall opposite me the wallpaper hung clawed into strips. It was not the living-room. Perhaps I cried out, for I heard Hazel call "Don't worry, you're all right," and something else inaudible. I saw that the wallpaper was after all not clawed, that it was merely shadows that had made it seem so. Then Hazel came in with a tray. "What did you say?" I demanded.

"Nothing. I crept out to make some coffee."

"Just now, I mean. When you called out."

"I haven't said a word for ten minutes."

After Hazel had gone to bed I stayed downstairs for an hour of last cigarettes and fragments of slogans. The month looked slack at the agency, but I couldn't stop thinking, and I preferred not to think about the house. Eventually, of course, the house overtook my thoughts. All right, I argued in mute fury, if I was moved by Britten's melodious angels then I might as well admit to a lurking belief in the supernatural. So the house was haunted by the presence of a dog or, as I sensed intuitively, a cat: so what? It didn't worry me, and Hazel hadn't even noticed. But if my grudging belief was the latest fashion in enlightenment, the retreat from scepticism, it didn't seem to be helping me. Spectral cats could have nothing to do with my hearing Hazel's voice when she hadn't spoken. I felt that my mind was beginning to fray.

A paroxysm of dry coughs persuaded me to stub out my cigarette. I threw the scribbled scraps of paper into the fireplace and came out into the hall. As I turned out the light in the living-room, a shadow leapt from the hall to the landing with a single bound.

Of course I wasn't sure, and I tried to be less so. I crept upstairs, feeling my heels hang over the open treads of the staircase. For a moment my nightmare returned, and I was heaving myself up a tilted ladder that grew steeper as the gaps between the treads widened. Halfway up I could hear myself panting with exhaustion, perhaps from lack of sleep. At the top the shadows crowded indistinguishably. On tiptoe, I opened the bedroom door. I had drawn it back only inches when a fluid shadow rippled through the crack into the room.

I threw the door open, and Hazel jumped. I was certain she had, although it might have been the bedroom light jarring her blanketed shape into focus. As I undressed I watched her, and after a minute or two she shifted a little. Now I was convinced that she hadn't been asleep when I entered, and was still only pretending. I didn't try to make sure, but it took me some time to turn out the light and slip into bed. For minutes I stood staring at Hazel's obscured body, wondering where the shadow had gone.

I awoke feeling lightened. The room gave out its colours brilliantly; beyond the window waves of leaves sprang up glowing in the sun. It was only as sleep began to peel back a little that I wondered whether Hazel's absence had lightened me.

Once downstairs I didn't go to her. Instead I walked dully into the dark living-room and slumped on the settee. I began to wonder whether I was afraid of Hazel. Certainly I couldn't talk to her about last night. My eyes began to close, and the living-room darkened further. Shadows striped the wall again; in a moment the wallpaper might peel. Or a claw might tear through— The door gushed light and Hazel came in, carrying plates of breakfast. She smiled when I leapt to my feet, but I wasn't greeting her. The living-room was bright, as it had been since I'd entered. I had realised who I might see. After all, the house was his responsibility. "How do you feel?" I said, staring into my coffee and then glancing up at her.

"All right, love. Don't start worrying about me. I should try and have a rest today if I were you."

I didn't know whether the shadow was speaking; in any case, I resented the implication that I looked incapable. "I'm going to take a couple of hours off this morning," I said. "If you want to come—I mean, if you want to get away from the house for a while—"

"Silly," she said. "You'd be upset if dinner wasn't ready."

My suspicions were confirmed. I couldn't believe that she wouldn't take the chance to escape the house unless it had infected her somehow. I was glad I hadn't told her where I was going. I managed to kiss her, forgetting to notice whether the feel of her had changed, and hurried round the corner to the car. Muffled thunder hung in the air. For a moment I regretted leaving Hazel alone, but I was afraid to return to the house. Besides, perhaps she was past rescuing. I drove blindly around the roundabout, not looking at the house, and was at the estate agent's within half an hour.

I'd forgotten the office wouldn't be open. I had a cup of coffee and a few cigarettes in a café across the road, and by the time the estate agent arrived I'd perfected my smile and my story. A faint astringent scent clung to him, and he pulled at his silver moustache more often than when first I'd met him. I convinced him I'd merely been passing, but still he drew his rings nervously from his fingers and paced behind his desk. At last I fastened on the shrill garrulous couple who had been leaving as I entered, and guided the conversation to them. "Yes, abominable," he agreed. "I suppose I dislike people. I decided to live with cats a long time ago. People and dogs can be led where cats can't. You'd never train a cat to salivate at your whim."

"Were there cats in our house?"

"Have you been dreaming?" he demanded.

"Just a feeling."

"You're right, of course," he said. "To me, you know, the most frightful act is to kill or maim a cat. Don't offer me Auschwitz. People aren't beautiful. Auschwitz was unforgivable, but there's nothing worse than a man who destroys beauty."

"What happened?" I said, trying to be casual.

"I shan't go into detail. Briefly, your predecessors were

obsessed with pests. One mouse and they were convinced the house was overrun. There are none there now, of course. People and cats have one thing in common: they can lose themselves in their own internal drives to the exclusion of morality, or reality for that matter."

"Go on."

"These people left five cats in the house without food while they went away on holiday. Starve a cat to kill a mouse, you see—as stupid and vile as that. Somehow the attic door closed and trapped the cats. When our friends returned they opened the front door and one cat ran out, never to be seen again. The others were in pieces in the attic. Cannibalism."

"And no doubt," I said, "if someone exceptionally sensitive were to take the house—"

"Yourself, you mean?"

"Perhaps. Or if you left some piece of sensitive electrical equipment running—"

"I don't pretend to know," he said, but there was despair around his eyes. "Ghosts of cats? I'll tell you this. People under-rate the intelligence of cats simply because they refuse to be taught tricks. I think the ghosts of cats would play with their victims for a while, as revenge. Sometimes I wonder what I'm doing in this job," he said. "You can see I don't care."

When I left I drove slowly through the city, thinking. The lunchtime crowds eddied about me; eventually the thickening sky above the roofs was split by lightning, and grey rain leapt from the pavements, washing away the crowds. I drove on as the rain smashed at the windscreen. "Playing with their victims"—there was something to which this was the key. If I were to believe in ghosts, however absurd it seemed beneath the tic of traffic lights, I might as well accept the idea of possession. Was the house playing us as hunter and victim? I couldn't altogether believe that one's personality could be ousted; I could imagine a framework within which this might be logical, but I wasn't sure that I felt it to be real. Yet I noticed that here, caged in by ropes of rain, I still felt more free than recently: free of the house's influence.

Suddenly I wanted to be with Hazel. If I had to I would drag her out, whatever was within her, however dangerous she might be. I could telephone my agency when I arrived at the house. I turned my car and it coursed through the pools of the city.

Along the carriageways out of the city the trees looked bedraggled and broken. Occasionally I passed torn cars, steaming where they'd skidded in mud. I was hardly surprised, when I reached the house, to see that the telephone wire had snapped and was sagging between the roof and the trees in the garden. As I drove past the roundabout it occurred to me that if Hazel was a victim she was trapped now. She would have to admit she was as vulnerable as me. No longer would I have to suffer the entire burden of disquiet.

I think it wasn't until I got out of the car that I perceived what I had been thinking. I felt a chill of horror at myself. I loved her hands on my back, yet for a while I had turned them into claws. All along Hazel had been frightened but had tried to hide her fear from me. That was the doubt I'd seen in her eyes. At once I knew what had blinded me, what had sought to destroy her. The rain dwindled and the sun blazed out; a rainbow lifted above the carriageway. I rushed through the garden, lashed by wet leaves, and dragged open the door to the house.

The house was dark—darker than it should have been now that the sun had returned. It was dim with stealth and silence. There was no sound of Hazel. I hurried through the ground floor, stumbled upstairs and searched the bedrooms, but the house seemed empty. I gazed down from the landing and saw that the front door was still open. I was ready to run out and wait for Hazel outside, yet I couldn't rid myself of the impression that the staircase was far longer and steeper than I remembered. Trying to control my fears, I started down. I was halfway down when a shadow crept across the carpet in the living-room.

For a moment I thought it was Hazel's, but not only did

its shape relate to something else entirely—it was far too large. I stood on the edge of the stairs. If I ran now, whatever was moving in the dim room might misjudge its leap. I wavered, fell down two stairs and jumped clumsily into the hall. At that moment the telephone rang.

In my terror I could see it only as an ally. I backed up the stairs, reached down and caught up the receiver. I muttered incoherently, and then I heard Hazel's voice. "I've got out," she said. "I hoped I might catch you before you came home. Is the door open?"

"Yes," I said. "Listen, love—don't come back in. I'm sorry. I didn't understand what was going on. I blamed you."

"If the door's open you can make it," she said. "Just run as fast as you can"—and then I remembered that the telephone wire was down, remembered the voice that had called to me from the other room.

As I dropped the receiver the air came alive with hissing. It was the sound the stereo had trapped, but worse now, overpowering. I launched myself from the stairs and came down in the middle of the hall. One more leap and I would be outside—but before I regained my balance I saw the front door was closed.

I might have wasted my strength in trying to wrench it open. But although I didn't understand the rules of what was happening, I felt that if the house had tried to convince me Hazel was safe this meant she was still inside somewhere. Behind me the hall spat. I clutched at the front door. I told myself that I was only using it for support, and turned.

It took me some time to determine where I was. In the dimness the hall seemed a good deal smaller. I told myself I could see the stairs; the walls weren't closing like a trap; the shadows hadn't massed into a poised shape, ready to sink its claws into my back. My mind began to scream and scrabble at itself, and I concentrated on the stairs. Eventually, after some hours, the hall imperceptibly altered and seemed stretched to dim infinity. The stairs were miles away. It wasn't worth making for them. There was an acre of open space to be crossed, and I knew I had no chance. I cried out for Hazel, and from somewhere above she answered my cry.

That cry I knew wasn't faked. It was scarcely coherent, pulled out of shape by terror; it was scarcely Hazel, and in some way I knew that guaranteed its truth. I ran to the stairs, counting my footsteps. Two, and I was on the stairs. I had control of the situation for a moment. I should have kept going blindly; I shouldn't have looked around—but I couldn't help glancing into the living-room.

The doorway was dark, and in the darkness a face appeared, flashed and was gone, like the momentary luminous spectres in a ghost train. I glimpsed an enormous black head, glowing green eyes, a red mouth barred with white teeth. Then I tore my gaze away and looked up to the landing, and I saw that the stairs had become a towering ladder, a succession of great treads separated by yawning gaps which I could never cross. The air hissed behind me, and I could go neither up nor down.

Then Hazel cried out again. There was only one way to conquer myself, and my mind was so numbed that I managed it. I shut my eyes tight and crawled upwards, grasping each higher stair and dragging myself painfully over space. Beneath me I felt the stairs tremble. I wondered whether they would throw me off, until I realised something was climbing up behind me. I tightened every muscle of my face to keep my brain from bursting out, and heaved myself upwards. I felt a purring breath on my neck, and then I was on the landing.

I stumbled to my feet and opened my eyes. Unless the house was able to blot Hazel from my gaze, she could only be in the one room I hadn't searched, the attic. As I ran across the landing, a huge face flashed at the top of the stairs. Its eyes gleamed with bottomless hatred, and for a second it seemed to fill with teeth. Then I had reached the attic and slammed the door.

I slumped. The attic was so crowded with lamps and cartons that nobody could have hidden there. The objects massed, suffocated and strung together by cords of dust; I didn't see how

I could even make my way between them. I might be trapped in the maze and cut off from Hazel, if indeed she was in the room. I knocked one of the looming cartons to the floor in an attempt to clear the view, and on the thud of the carton I heard breath hiss in muffled terror.

At once the room rearranged itself, and I saw Hazel. She was crouched in a corner, her knees drawn up to her chin, her arms pressed tight over her face. She was sobbing. I moved gently towards her, loving her, bullying the fear from my mind. My feet tangled in wire. I looked down and saw the cord for the lamps. I knew where the socket was; I plugged in the lamps and let them blind the door. Then I went to Hazel. "Come on, love," I said. "Come on, Hazel. We're going now. Come on, love."

Her arms drew back from her face. She looked up at me; then she shrank into the corner and her eyes gaped in horror. I fell back. But her lips moved. She was trying to speak to me. She wasn't frightened of me. I looked behind me, towards the door.

The door had opened, and the doorway was half filled by an enormous face. Its mouth yawned wide and a tongue sprang dripping across its teeth. I grabbed the lamps and shone them into its eyes, but they didn't blink. Its face began to bulge in through the doorway, and behind it others leapt across the landing to hover grinning above the first. With a surge of pure energy and terror I hurled the lamps at the faces.

What happened I don't know. I never heard the lamps strike the floor, but the surge of energy carried me across the room to heave the window open. I ran to Hazel and pulled her to her feet, although she shrank sobbing into the corner. I threw her across my shoulder and staggered with her to the window. I glanced back into the room, where faces with gleaming eyes capered in the air and flew at us in a single toothed mass. Then I jumped.

I think the house must have overlooked that. Mice might fall from a window, but they aren't supposed to jump. So I spent time in hospital with a broken leg, while Hazel was furious enough by the end of the week to visit the estate agent's. Once she had made him admit that he wouldn't spend a night in the house, the rest was easy. "I have no time for horror," he told her. My leg soon improved. Not so Hazel's insomnia; and yet when we lie awake together talking through the uneasy hours, I think there are times when we're grateful. Somehow we could never talk that way before.

The Black Cat

Rainer Maria Rilke

A ghost, though invisible, still is like a place
your sight can knock on, echoing; but here
within this thick black pelt, your strongest gaze
will be absorbed and utterly disappear:

just as a raving madman, when nothing else
can ease him, charges into his dark night
howling, pounds on the padded wall, and feels
the rage being taken in and pacified.

She seems to hide all looks that have ever fallen
into her, so that, like an audience,
she can look them over, menacing and sullen,
and curl to sleep with them. But all at once

as if awakened, she turns her face to yours;
and with a shock, you see yourself, tiny,
inside the golden amber of her eyeballs
suspended, like a prehistoric fly.

A Cargo of Cat

Ambrose Bierce

On the 16th day of June, 1874, the ship *Mary Jane* sailed from Malta, heavily laden with cat. This cargo gave us a good deal of trouble. It was not in bales, but had been dumped into the hold loose. Captain Doble, who had once commanded a ship that carried coals, said he had found that plan the best. When the hold was full of cat the hatch was battened down and we felt good. Unfortunately the mate, thinking the cats would be thirsty, introduced a hose into one of the hatches and pumped in a considerable quantity of water, and the cats of the lower levels were all drowned.

You have seen a dead cat in a pond: you remember its circumference at the waist. Water multiplies the magnitude of a dead cat by ten. On the first day out, it was observed that the ship was much strained. She was three feet wider than usual and as much as ten feet shorter. The convexity of her deck was visibly augmented fore and aft, but she turned up at both ends. Her rudder was clean out of water and she would answer the helm only when running directly against a strong breeze: the rudder, when perverted to one side, would rub against the wind and slew her around; and then she wouldn't steer any more. Owing to the curvature of the keel, the masts came together at the top, and a sailor who had gone up the foremast got bewildered, came down the mizzenmast, looked out over the stern at the receding shores of Malta and shouted: "Land, ho!" The ship's fastenings were all giving way; the water on each side was lashed into foam by the tempest of flying bolts that she shed at every pulsation of the cargo. She was quietly wrecking

115

herself without assistance from wind or wave, by the sheer internal energy of feline expansion.

I went to the skipper about it. He was in his favorite position, sitting on the deck, supporting his back against the binnacle, making a V of his legs, and smoking.

"Captain Doble," I said, respectfully touching my hat, which was really not worthy of respect, "this floating palace is afflicted with curvature of the spine and is likewise greatly swollen."

Without raising his eyes he courteously acknowledged my presence by knocking the ashes from his pipe.

"Permit me, Captain," I said, with simple dignity, "to repeat that this ship is much swollen."

"If that is true," said the gallant mariner, reaching for his tobacco pouch, "I think it would be as well to swab her down with liniment. There's a bottle of it in my cabin. Better suggest it to the mate."

"But, Captain, there is no time for empirical treatment; some of the planks at the water line have started."

The skipper rose and looked out over the stern, toward the land; he fixed his eyes on the foaming wake; he gazed into the water to starboard and to port. Then he said:

"My friend, the whole darned thing has started."

Sadly and silently I turned from that obdurate man and walked forward. Suddenly "there was a burst of thunder sound!" The hatch that had held down the cargo was flung whirling into space and sailed in the air like a blown leaf. Pushing upward through the hatchway was a smooth, square column of cat. Grandly and impressively it grew—slowly, serenely, majestically it rose toward the welkin, the relaxing keel parting the mast heads to give it a fair chance. I have stood at Naples and seen Vesuvius painting the town red—from Catania have marked afar, upon the flanks of Ætna, the lava's awful pursuit of the astonished rooster and the despairing pig. The fiery flow from Kilauea's crater, thrusting itself into the forests and licking the entire country clean, is as familiar to me as my mother-tongue. I have seen glaciers, a thousand years old and quite bald, heading for a valley full of tourists at the rate of an inch a month. I have seen a saturated solution of mining camp going down a mountain river, to make a sociable call on the valley farmers. I have stood behind a tree on the battle-field and seen a compact square mile of armed men moving with irresistible momentum to the rear. Whenever anything grand in magnitude or motion is billed to appear I commonly manage to beat my way into the show, and in reporting it I am a man of unscrupulous veracity; but I have seldom observed anything like that solid gray column of Maltese cat!

It is unnecessary to explain, I suppose, that each individual grimalkin in the outfit, with that readiness of resource which distinguishes the species, had grappled with tooth and nail as many others as it could hook on to. This preserved the formation. It made the column so stiff that when the ship rolled (and the *Mary Jane* was a devil to roll) it swayed from side to side like a mast, and the mate said if it grew much taller he would have to order it cut away or it would capsize us.

Some of the sailors went to work at the pumps, but these discharged nothing but fur. Captain Doble raised his eyes from his toes and shouted: "Let go the anchor!" but being assured that nobody was touching it, apologized and resumed his revery. The chaplain said if there were no objections he would like to offer up a prayer, and a gambler from Chicago, producing a pack of cards, proposed to throw round for the first jack. The parson's plan was adopted, and as he uttered the final "amen," the cats struck up a hymn.

All the living ones were now above deck, and every mother's son of them sang. Each had a pretty fair voice, but no ear. Nearly all their notes in the upper register were more or less cracked and disobedient. The remarkable thing about the voices was their range. In that crowd were cats of seventeen octaves, and the average could not have been less than twelve.

Number of cats, as per invoice 127,000
Estimated number dead swellers...................... <u>6,000</u>
Total songsters 121,000
Average number octaves per cat.......................... <u>12</u>
Total octaves 1,452,000

It was a great concert. It lasted three days and nights, or, counting each night as seven days, twenty-four days altogether, and we could not go below for provisions. At the end of that time the cook came for'd shaking up some beans in a hat, and holding a large knife.

"Shipmates," said he, "we have done all that mortals can do. Let us now draw lots."

We were blindfolded in turn, and drew, but just as the cook was forcing the fatal black bean upon the fattest man, the concert closed with a suddenness that waked the man on the lookout. A moment later every grimalkin relaxed his hold on his neighbors, the column lost its cohesion and, with 121,000 dull, sickening thuds that beat as one, the whole business fell to the deck. Then with a wild farewell wail that feline host sprang spitting into the sea and struck out southward for the African shore!

The southern extension of Italy, as every schoolboy knows, resembles in shape an enormous boot. We had drifted within sight of it. The cats in the fabric had spied it, and their alert imaginations were instantly affected with a lively sense of the size, weight and probable momentum of its flung bootjack.

The Witch of the Dark Woods

Katherine Kerestman

Once upon a time there were a little girl and a little boy who loved to read books, and were nice to animals and other people, and therefore they were picked on. They talked to the cats who lived in the barn across the meadow from their humble cottage about their problem, and the cats told them they should run away with them to the gentle kingdom. The cats said they needed a king and queen in the kingdom who were good and kind, and the children had the very qualifications for the positions. The cats told them that there was a little problem, though. The big fluffy white cat stepped forward, and he explained that there was a mean witch in the dark forest, which they must cross to get where they wanted to go, and that she would try to stop them.

"How do we get past her?" asked the little boy named Charlie.

"King Carol—that is the white cat's name—will help us," answered Sarah, the little girl. She pulled some cheese from the little basket she was carrying and gave some little treats to the cats.

"I will show you the way to the Scholomance," answered King Carol. "There you will learn everything you need to know." Then the little kittens, black, gray, striped, and spotted, trotted and scampered, the head of one kit running into the rump of another, the littlest black kitten rolling right over on its little paws in a somersault, as they gathered around King Carol. The King began to groom the kits, holding one down with his left front paw, and another down with his right front paw, while he went to work with his rough pink tongue, scrubbing the dirt off the fluffy little kittens.

The little kittens were giggling and purring, a little embarrassed at being bathed in front of strangers.

The little boy and the little girl each held an armful of kittens and were busy kissing their little faces and asking them their names. They were having so much fun they almost forgot they had to go to the school in the forest.

"It's time now to start our journey to the Scholomance," proclaimed King Carol, standing erect upon a fallen log. "Mother and father cats, gather your little kits and follow me through the forest to the Scholomance, for our little friends' sake."

The little group of pilgrims put one foot or paw in front of the other and began their march into the forest. Once they were inside the forest of tangled trees, the bright yellow sunshine went away and the forest became darker and darker as they moved on. The leaves were worm-eaten and crumbly, and the ground was damp and moldy. The birds that had sung on the outside were nowhere to be seen. The newborn kittens were mewing, and they had to take rest stops so the mothers could give them milk, and when they were tired the fathers would carry them in their mouths, careful not to hurt them with their teeth. Eventually they decided they all needed dinner, and Charlie and Sarah ate apples and berries from the trees, while the cats went hunting for mice. After they ate, all the cats gathered around the children, and even on top of their laps and their heads, and they waited for direction from King Carol.

The air grew cold, and the little girl was shivering. Charlie gave her his coat. The wind grew strong, and the sound of cannons shook the ground. Lightning began to flash. Leaves began to swirl. "It will rain soon," said King Carol, "therefore, we should take shelter." The party trotted to the big room beneath the huge fir tree. It was such a large tree that a grown person could stand tall and not touch the ceiling formed by its lowest branches, and the branches stretched far and wide and touched the forest floor, so that it formed a little house wherein the pilgrims could keep safe from the storm.

"Are you frightened, children?" asked the kingly white cat.

"No, Your Majesty," said Charlie. "We know we are safe in your care."

"Me, too," said Sarah.

"Then stay close by me and do as I say, for the Witch of the Dark Woods is nearby. You shall know her by her raging storms. We must be careful as we journey through the forest to the Scholomance," said King Carol.

"My whiskers are twitching, and my fur is ruffled, Your Highness," said Radar Cat, as he put his nose to the ground and his rump in the air before the King.

"That is cause for concern, Sir Radar Cat," said King Carol, and he thanked him for his faithful service. "Sir Radar Cat has given three of his lives to protect our clowder," he explained to the children. "You may scratch his head now." The children did as they were advised, and the orange tiger cat purred and rubbed their ankles; he even lay down on his back and indicated that he should like his tummy rubbed, which task Sarah was pleased to perform.

The pilgrims used their time wisely by telling tales of the never-ending war between good and evil. They spoke in story, they spoke in rhyme, and they spoke in song. They told of struggles against bullies who picked on children who were kind and liked to read books, and of the no good end to which those who did evil would come. They sang of heroes who defeated the mean ones who hurt little puppies and drowned little kittens (the mother cats wept whenever they heard this story). They spoke of knights of the gentle kingdom, whose golden armor shone in the sun and blinded the evil witch whenever she attempted a siege against the castle. Then stepped forward Remember Cat, a tabby with three white paws and one black, and a stub where a tail had been, a tail tall and proud until it was cut off by a man who was hurting a woman: Remember Cat had clawed at the man's legs to save the woman, and the man had turned on Remember Cat. Remember Cat was proud that his tail would remind people to protect the ones they loved. King Carol had appointed him the historian cat of the clowder, to prevent the good people and cats from forgetting what was important. Sarah told how she threw her books at a boy who had cornered Charlie on the playground. King Carol gave her a medal of valor.

At last the storm ended, and King Carol said it was time to be going. Every minute in the dark forest was risky. The children needed to be taken to the Scholomance, where they would learn what they needed to know in order to reach the gentle kingdom. The strong young tomcats led the way, and the weaker cats followed behind them. By this time it was very dark, and it was a good thing that cats have good night vision. They also have good hearing, and their ears pricked up, and they turned their heads, and the King gave the command: "Take cover at once!"

The children and cats were well hidden by the time the troop of deputies of the Black Sheriff came pounding by on their big black horses, whipping the shrubbery to flush out the runaways. The children were afraid, but they didn't cry, for they knew that not only their own lives but those of the cats were at stake. The men on the horses kept on going, right past their hiding place, and Charlie and Sarah and the clowder kept close for a good while. When they thought the danger had passed, they crept out of their holes and burrows and convened around King Carol, who issued a Declaration of War: "The Clowder of Cats hereby declares war against the Black Sheriff and his Mean Men, for they have engaged in acts of aggression against little ones and defenseless animals." He did not blame the horses, who were captives of the men. He said they must resume their journey immediately, and recommended everyone eat and drink and ready themselves for travel. They resumed their journey, and Charlie asked the King to tell him about the Scholomance.

The Scholomance, said King Carol, is a school of black magic run by the devil. Pupils were taught the languages of animals and other magical things. The devil took as his price a pupil for his own—but no worry, said the King: the devil always chose the pupil who was the most evil one of the lot and who would end up going to the devil anyway. Sarah said it was a frightening kind of school, but Charlie said there were a lot of devils in the place they were running away from, too. King Carol agreed: there are devils almost everywhere, and good and gentle folk needed to be aware of them and learn to protect themselves, and that was one of the things they would learn in the Scholomance. Sarah told the King that she and Charlie liked to learn things, and that they learned many things from books. The King told them they would be great scholars and wise rulers when they grew up, and that the world certainly needed those.

A very large and very loud screeching owl swooped from the reaching branches of a gnarled tree, and the King made a great leap and avoided him. Charlie spun around to see what had whooshed past, and the owl circled around and toward Sarah, who was nuzzling a little white kitten and not looking up. Charlie grabbed a log and swung it like a baseball bat to scare the owl off, and Sarah put the kitten in her pocket for safe-keeping. The tomcats, hearing the screeching of the owl and the caterwauling of the King, came bounding through the brush. Francis (the Abyssinian) scampered quickly up the trunk of a dead tree, slinked out along a branch high up, and swatted the owl as it flew past, and knocked him to the ground. While the owl lay stunned, Charlie tied him up in Sarah's apron and put him in her basket, to keep him from hurting anyone else. "Great work," said King Carol. "The owl is the servant of the Witch. She is close on our trail, and we must keep moving." The company drew bravery from their leader and began to move forward once more.

Down, down, down, down very deep, through a cave dark with drip-drip-dripping water and fluttering bat wings, and slippery floors, down a narrow-ledged cliff, past a subterranean lake, and

123

down again, far below the surface of the earth, far below the craggy snow-topped Black Mountain, very, very far below the moon and stars in the heavens, was the domain of the devil. Vast and dark chambers of ebony and black marble echoed with the squeals of rodents and the buzz of flying insects. Past a labyrinth of serpentine corridors, some of which led only to dead ends, and down a steep and narrow stairwell lit dimly by dark iron sconces holding fat smoky tallow candles was the Scholomance. Thirteen children at thirteen desks, heads bent over copy books and fingers holding pens with which they copied out spells, were monitored by the cloven-hooved professor, who snorted green vapors and passed sulfurous emissions. The students labored to learn all they could, so that the term of their education in the bowels of the earth would yield them some benefit on the day of their release back to the surface. No one knew who—but each pupil feared to find out who—would pay the price of the devil's tuition and be conveyed to the underworld 'til the end of time. They studied and practiced and learned to conjure and to do the devil's bidding, always remembering that at the end of seven years all but one of the Solomonari would be released to the sunshine.

Grigori Perfidius vowed not to be the one to remain in the pits. He painted the canvas of his mind with brushes dipped in bold crimsons and dark yellows, with sharp angular dashes of black, envisioning a fearsome portrait of himself wielding the power he was accumulating by toil and by wile in the cold, dank Scholomance. He leaned to the right and pulled the hair of the girl sitting next and looked at the answers on her slate, and he flicked a paper wad at the boy on the left and read the answers on his scroll. He would gain the knowledge to control the beasts and the men above ground, to make himself the dark lord and the master of the world, and what he did not learn he would steal. He picked the legs off a spider, then squashed him, and thought how he would amuse himself when he was in charge, pitting armies one against the other and coloring the earth red, burning villages to see the people run and the sky turn to flame, and taking every good thing he saw for himself. He was going to get the highest marks of all the Solomonari, and he was going to outwit the devil. Grigori was very sly and held his cards close to his vest, to all outward appearances a devoted and humble scholar, but plotting devious and deadly plans within the inky recesses of his heart. The devil said, "Two more pupils draw near, a boy and a girl."

Hell hath no fury like a young girl torn from her dollhouse, ripped from her grandmother's arms, abducted from the land of yellow sun and green grass, hurled into the abyss, imprisoned in the Scholomance, forced to learn the devil's spells, made to breathe his sulfurous miasma, compelled to feel his hot and slimy breath, to toil over spellbooks and parchments, and ne'er to see the blue sky and her china dollie for seven long years. Grief fermented into rage within the breast of the beautiful (tall and willowy now that she was grown) girl with the green eyes and the wrist-length raven hair; rage ignited the flame of wrath in the cauldron that had once been Veronica's heart. The Dark Woods Veronica claimed as her domain, banishing the light of a world that had been denied her, a world she remembered from long ago, but which was not for her. She summoned the damp and dismal, the crawling and lurking creatures. The owl she claimed as her own, the wriggling snakes and the crawling spider, the creatures shunned and abhorred by the dwellers in the sunlight: "This is our kingdom—the kingdom of the forsaken and the damned. Misery and death shall be the portion of those who dare trespass," she proclaimed. The earth quaked and the sky thundered as the evil that Veronica had endured poured forth from her black and shriveled heart into the world.

Extending the graceful form of her well-turned arm, Veronica allowed the approaching raven to roost upon it. Putting his beak down and spreading his tail, the raven made obeisance to his dark and beautiful lady: "If I may be so bold, Milady," quoth the raven, "I have news to impart."

"Very well, Raven, what intelligence have you?" replied the Witch.

"Dame, I bring news of the approach of two children on their way to the Scholomance. They travel under the protection of a clowder of cats. They travel through the dark forest, your own demesne."

"Raven, thou knowest that the miseries of hell shall be the portion of all who enter here, and death the only release," spake the Witch in all her fury, "for all who dare to trespass." The skies turned black, blacker than the darkest eclipse. Lightning crackled and flashed and split some trees, and the smell of smoke wafted through the dark forest. Howling winds blew leaves from the trees and rendered them barren. The Witch of the Dark Forest quivered with all the years of anger burning through her eyes, scorching thereupon she gazed.

The clowder, meanwhile, steadily made their way through the thick woods as the sun sank lower on the horizon and the shadows thrown by gnarled trees stretched out longer, until there was more shadow than light. King Carol ascended a stump and called to his subjects: "Look to yonder forbidding Black Mountain, my good people. In the deep recesses of the earth beneath the dread mountain is the Scholomance." The cats huddled close to the ground, and the kits snuggled next to the adults. Sarah and Charlie squeezed each other's hand, and Charlie said, "King Carol, sir, this is frightening country. Must we go to school there?"

"My boy," answered King Carol, "That is the very place the sainted Sir Bloofer Cat foretold as being the source of powerful dark knowledge, wherewith to arm the champions of good in their struggle against evil. There it is prophesied the future monarchs of the gentle kingdom shall gain the wisdom to defend and protect their citizenry. Brave and good children like yourselves will grow into noble and fearless leaders through your education in the devil's Scholomance." Sarah and Charlie, standing shoulder to shoulder and hip to hip, nodded their heads to signify they understood, albeit with reservations. "Let us hasten on, for the end of our journey is within sight," said King Carol, as he rubbed the children's ankles, and when they bent to pet him he licked their faces.

The pilgrims continued walking toward the Black Mountain, which got bigger and bigger, and rockier and craggier, as they drew nearer to it. The damp, cold leaves and mud of the forest floor began to turn white with frost, and they could now see their breaths, as the air became chill.

Radar Cat's ears went up and he began to meow; he told the King that he heard the sound of a weeping woman, and the King sent two of his tomcat scouts ahead to reconnoiter. They returned with a report of a beautiful raven-haired woman with flashing green eyes, rimmed red now with weeping, lying huddled on the ground beneath a dead elm tree. The King and the children followed the toms back to the place where they had found the woman, and they approached her.

"Dear Lady," said Carol, "what unhappiness has caused you to weep and moan so pitifully?" whereupon the dark and lovely Veronica rose to her full height and reached her arms to the skies.

"Know Ye," she thundered, "that you stand before the Witch of the Dark Woods, and that you have trespassed into her domain, forbidden to all living things who dwell in light. My wrath is great." Veronica turned toward the north, and the biting polar wind blew hard from the Black Mountain, and snow began to whirl around them.

"I call forth the black and the cold and the fanged and the clawed and the slimy, slippery and the poisonous demons and creatures of the dark realms. I command you now to destroy those who have dared invade my forlorn and forsaken domain." Black leathery-winged hairy beasts with snouts full of bared teeth and bloodshot eyes and six legs with claws circled above. Slithering green crackly-scaly serpents slipped down the tree trunks and inched toward the clowder.

The kittens made for the cover of the foliage, and King Carol drew himself up before the children, signifying that he would protect them with his nine lives, if necessary. Francis (the Abyssinian) caterwauled orders to his troops, and the young and strong cats assumed offensive and defensive positions according to his directions. Radar Cat slipped quietly away, behind enemy lines, to gather intelligence of their movements and plans. King Carol said to Veronica, "My lady of the Dark Woods, we have come in friendship. We have no intention of disturbing your peace. We are charged with taking this boy and this girl to the Scholomance, where they may prepare for their destinies as the rightful sovereigns of the gentle kingdom. I beg your pardon if we have inadvertently offended Your Ladyship."

Veronica was giving some consideration to King Carol's polite speech just when the groaning of heavy iron gates being forced open drew her attention. She knew that sound. She had heard it before. The sound of the metal groaning pulled her back to the awful past, so that she nearly forgot what was happening in the present, so strong was the effect of the groaning gates upon her ears. Veronica called to her dark creatures to follow her, and she led the way toward the horrible, rusty metal groans. King Carol called for Francis and his warrior cats to follow, and they went forward to discover what it was that drew the witch from them.

The devil climbed up the slippery, narrow stairs, crept along the tiny ledges, scaled the dripping walls, and worked his way up from the depth of the Scholomance, to the gates at the tip-top of the steep passage. He pulled open the heavy wood and iron-clad doors to reveal the dismal, dark bat-filled cave on the side of the dread mountain, which could be seen through the heavy rusted iron gates embossed with fiendish skulls and swords and cups. Rats scurried in and out of the cave entrance through the bars of the gate. Donning a rainbow-hued robe and a beard of gold to cover his pointy chin, the devil picked up a pile of beautiful blue and green and yellow silk-bound books with golden clasps and went forward to lure Charlie and Sarah into the Scholomance, where they would toil the next seven years under his tuition.

Grigori Perfidius, rushing from behind, pushed the diabolical schoolmaster out of the way just as the devil was forcing the groaning iron gates apart. The devil pulled his errant pupil's long brown locks in his fist and yanked the escapee back toward the underworld. As they struggled the heavy iron gates clanged shut, catching the scholar and crushing him to a pulpy mess, even as the devil was still gripping his lovely brown hair. Casting the handful of hair, which was all that was left of Grigori, upon the ground, the devil pushed the weighty gates apart and squeezed himself through.

The rainbow robe was caught in the gate, and the golden beard was lost in the scuffle, and the devil emerged from the Scholomance without his disguise, as Veronica and her creatures of gloom drew nigh. At the sight of her erstwhile teacher, the green-eyed witch's hardened heart cracked and splintered, purple flames bursting through the fissures, so that the witch glowed violet with the heat of hatred contained no more: "Foul fiend, author of misery, destroyer of joy, cesspool of corruption and filth, you are my true enemy, my jailer for seven long years in the sewer of the damned beneath the dread mountain. It is you who are my true nemesis. You are the rightful object of my wrath. Perish, hellish abductor of children!" She unleashed her lightning upon him, and a whiff of smoke rose from the tip of the devil's tail. The devil stung her face with his bristled tongue, which spooled out from his fanged mouth and over his cracked lips and began wrapping itself around the witch's waist.

Veronica called to her fiendish menagerie, and her flying creatures, reptilian and mammal, with claws and sharp incisors dove at the devil and drove him back. Francis (the Abyssinian)

129

led the charge of the soldier cats. The devil, his thorny tongue still wrapped around the witch, tried to cast a spell, but could not, for Remember Cat was sinking his teeth into his outstretched tongue. In fury, the devil sliced off Remember Cat's right ear with his taloned fingers, but Remember Cat maintained his hold on the devil's tongue until he bit clean through it.

Forced to retreat, the devil vanished in a puff of green smoke, and the Solomonari escaped through the open gate back into the world. Veronica smiled—her first smile since she had been torn from her grandmother's arms—at seeing the children run as fast as they could, as far as they could, from the Scholomance.

"Lady of the Dark Woods, you are bleeding. You are wounded with the stings of the devil's barbed tongue. Please accept the comfort only a cat can give," said Felicity, a long-haired cat of a patchwork of every cat color. Veronica acceded, and Felicity began to lick her wounds, and after a while curled up on the lady's lap and purred.

"Good cats and children, and slimy creatures, too," Veronica said as they all rested under the scraggly trees, "I ask forgiveness of all whom I have harmed in my own misery. I have lived a life forsaken by the light and shorn of all joy and knew no better in my pain. You have come to my rescue, and have helped soften my hard heart, and I wish to make amends."

"Please, lady, join our pilgrimage to the gentle kingdom," King Carol answered, "for you have rejected vengeance and will henceforth be the good and gentle creature you were born to be." And to the pilgrims he called, "Let us be on our way, for I see shining through the trees the sunshine of the gentle kingdom. We are almost arrived." The kittens and cats trotted and pranced, pleased as pudding, and Charlie and Sarah skipped and ran through the edge of the forest into the light of day.

The citizens of the gentle kingdom, cats and horses, garter snakes and shopkeepers, bunny rabbits and farmers, bluebirds and dogs big and little, artisans and duchesses and dukes, came running to the green meadow to welcome the ragged troop approaching from the Dark Woods. King Carol gave thanks for their hospitality and Remember Cat told of the adventures of Sarah and Charlie on their way to the Scholomance, where they had been going to prepare themselves to reign in the gentle kingdom, and how they would be perfect for that job after they had grown a little. He told how the devil was routed and the Solomonari were freed, and of how the Witch of the Dark Woods repented and wished to make amends.

The citizens excused themselves and held a council, after which they reported to King Carol that they were very glad to welcome the adventurers into their kingdom. They asked Veronica to accept the position of High Minister of Good Magic, to which she agreed. They offered Remember Cat the job of Minister of Education, and they sent him to the veterinarian to have his ear attended to. As per King Carol's recommendation, they offered the golden throne to Charlie and Sarah, to be their own good and gentle rulers. King Carol they asked to be regent until the sovereigns reached their fifteenth birthdays. Carol agreed and appointed Francis (the Abyssinian) the Defender of the Good and Protector of the Little, in recognition of his meritorious service. As the years passed, Remember Cat would educate the people of the surrounding countries about the fate of the devil and of the Scholomance, and the devil's old school would fall into oblivion and become a legend for want of pupils. Henceforth, the devil would have to go somewhere else to make trouble.

Gray

M. F. Webb

'Tis quiet as the morning hours descend
And fog obscures the rain-abandoned street
Heavy yet the sodden branches bend
With tumbling drops, as soft as padded feet

Faintly now the sullen darkness lifts,
A gentle premonition of the day
From out the shadows, measured colors sift
The daisies and nasturtiums ease from gray

And here, a shadow seems to have a place
Upon a cushion lately occupied
It turns and moves with newly founded grace
Beside the rose where late it would abide

Then raises up and softly passes by
A brush of whisker, glint of golden eye.

Protectors, Psychopomps, and Other Cats in Weird Fiction

Brandon R. Grafius

Cats and the Weird

Anyone who has ever owned a cat knows, beyond a doubt, that they are weird creatures. Their motives are inscrutable, they have their own sense of time, and their moods seem to be governed by no force that humans can discern. But above all, they seem to know something about the world that we don't. And that's what makes them such natural fits for weird fiction.

I live with two cats: a senior citizen Tuxedo named Felix and a younger Calico named Tazey. (It's short for Tazerface—we'd taken the kids to see *Guardians of the Galaxy 2* right before we adopted her.) Tazey, in particular, is prone to standing in a random corner of the house, *Blair Witch*-style, transfixed by something that, to pedestrian human eyes, doesn't seem to be there. I don't know what she sees—but it's something. She's practicing something those of us who live with cats recognize as a pretty common feline pastime: seeing the sights of some kind of different plane, some level of existence that human perception can't enter into. I've often wondered if being a cat wouldn't be like living in Crawford Tillinghast's machine from Lovecraft's "From Beyond" all the time, and having direct access to the creatures that float among and through us.

I've known many people who think they know what their cats are staring at, even if it's something that humans can't see. Over the years, more than a couple of friends have confided in me that they're pretty sure a ghost lives in their house, and that their cat is the only living creature who can see it. Mind you, these are well-grounded, generally rational people, not prone to throwing seances or hunting for Bigfoot. They're just pretty certain that their cat knows some deep, mystical truth that they can't access. It seems weird, but who am I to say that they're wrong?

If we understand the weird tale as did Lovecraft, as that which gives "the reader a profound sense of dread, and of contact with unknown spheres and powers" (*Annotated* 28), cats seem like a perfect emissary for the weird. The weird tale, at its heart, is a tale of the universe being a different place from what we imagined it, one in which we are nowhere near as important or as safe as we've spent our lives believing. Reality is so much larger than we had ever imagined, and the rules that seem to govern it are comforting fictions humans have invented to help ourselves sleep at night. The weird tale opens its readers up to these possibilities, this disquieting expanse of the possible. With every movement they make in the world, cats seem to demonstrate that they have always known what is outside the known universe. They might not be the ones scratching on its outer rim, but they know whose claws we are hearing when we read a tale of cosmic horror.

While cats can serve many functions in fiction—they can be a witch's familiar, they can be Bukowskian metaphors for untrustworthy women, they can be fickle companions—their strongest contribution to weird fiction is this ability to see a world beyond the world that most of us can access. In pre-Lovecraftian tales of the Gothic and supernatural, we sometimes see this ability in nascent form, expressed as depictions of cats who understand something about the human characters in the story that others don't, and can draw this out—whether it's an uncanny ability to sense death or some deep insight into what lurks in the hearts of people. We see this aspect of cats explored by several of the authors mentioned by Lovecraft in *Supernatural Horror in Literature,* including Poe, Chambers, and Hawthorne. But as the weird tale develops as a genre, more and more we see cats who have insight that goes beyond knowledge of the depths of the human heart, and instead possess knowledge about the nature of reality that goes beyond what we are able to see. In many of the most haunting stories featuring cats, the cat is the emissary who brings this knowledge to us. Even if we can't see what they see, sometimes we can see that *they* see something beyond our knowledge. And in this knowledge, chilling possibilities can unfold.

Cats in the Pre-Lovecraftian Weird

Of the authors discussed by Lovecraft in *Supernatural Horror in Literature,* none features cats as prominently as does Algernon Blackwood in his short story "Ancient Sorceries." However, this is one of Blackwood's tales that seems more in line with the mundanely horrifying, not one that enters into cosmic dread as does a tale such as "The Willows." In "Ancient Sorceries," an entire village seems to be comprised of shapeshifters, townsfolk who transform into cats at night and celebrate a Witches' Sabbath. There are strange corners of the world where dark rituals are practiced, but it doesn't rattle the foundations of reality in the way that a weird tale would.

But as we move closer toward the realm of the truly weird, we begin to find cats that challenge our understanding of reality—or at least of the nature of our individual selves. Poe's short story "The Black Cat" is perhaps the most obvious example of this. While it seems close to the category of Poe's stories that Lovecraft refers to as those dealing with "abnormal psychology and monomania," expressing "terror but not weirdness" (*Annotated* 57), there are enough hints of the supernatural and cosmic justice to place the story at least on the edge of the weird. This grim tale begins, as Poe's stories often do, with a narrator asserting his sanity on the day before he is to be executed for the murder of his wife. We learn that among the narrator's many pets was a black cat named Pluto, his "favorite pet and playmate" (193). At least, until the narrator returns home drunk one night and Pluto takes a nip at him; the narrator responds by cutting out one of the cat's eyes. Soon afterwards, he decides to kill the cat, to "continue and finally to consummate the injury" (194) for no real reason other he can articulate other than "perverseness." But shortly after Pluto's death, another black cat ingratiates himself to the narrator—"closely resembling [Pluto] in every respect" (196) except for a white patch on its breast. This new (?) cat has an intense affection for the narrator, which drives the narrator to try and kill this cat as well. When his wife intervenes, he kills her instead and decides that the best course of action is to brick her up behind his basement wall. When the police arrive to investigate, they are alerted to the corpse's presence by a cry coming from behind the wall, which turns out to be the cat, bricked up as well.

Poe's cat embodies many weird characteristics. We might wonder if these are two cats, related through some uncanny means, but the singular title of the story seems to tell us that they are only one; this is a cat who, through whatever means, has escaped death and returned to torment the narrator. And the cat seems to have a close link with death in other ways as well, with its unexplained presence behind the wall serving to alert the authorities to the murderous crime. At the conclusion the cat is able to reveal the true nature of the narrator. But in other ways the cat has been relating this narrator's character all along: it has drawn out the narrator's sadism, his "perverseness," and served as a focal point for all the horror that dwells within this profoundly disturbed character. Without the cat's presence to pull this forth, one might wonder if it would have found other ways to express itself or remained latent throughout the narrator's life.

Nathaniel Hawthorne's novels and short stories are usually thought of as romances, with a slight shading of Gothic, but Lovecraft felt moved enough by his work to include a discussion of the author in *Supernatural Horror in Literature* as a having crafted body of work that borders on the weird. Hawthorne writes of a cat who has an unsettling relationship with the dead in his novel *The House of the Seven Gables*, a cat whom Lovecraft has dubbed "the psychopomp of primeval myth, fitted and adapted with infinite deftness to its latter-day setting" (*Annotated* 65). In Lovecraft's reading, Hawthorne's cat serves this mythic role of escort of souls in a manner similar to that of Poe's Pluto. Lovecraft pulls this out of a rather brief remark of Hawthorne's: "It is the visage of grimalkin, outside of the window, where he appears to have posted himself for a deliberate watch . . . Is it a cat watching for a mouse, or the devil for a human soul?" (253). Though only appearing for a few lines, this feline's appearance at such a key juncture in the novel is certainly unsettling.

Another deeply weird cat of this period appears in Robert W. Chambers's 1895 short story collection *The King in Yellow*, a collection that Lovecraft referred to as achieving "notable heights of cosmic fear in spite of uneven interest" (*Annotated* 69). The first four stories of this volume are the most famous, all containing references to a play called *The King in Yellow* that makes its readers go mad. The story that leads off the collection, "The Repairer of Reputations," features an extremely malevolent cat whose relationship to the title character is deeply unsettling. Mr. Wilde is the repairer, a shadowy puppeteer of a businessman who seems to be at the heart of a plot to blackmail and manipulate his way to control over the nation. (At least, if any of these events are occurring in reality, as opposed to being in the warped imagination of the deeply disturbed narrator.) But he lives with an unnamed cat, with whom he seems to have some kind of sadistic relationship. When we first meet Mr. Wilde, "[h]alf a dozen new scratches covered his nose and cheeks" (11), and we can only wonder if his lack of ears and fingers on his left hand is also due to the creature he lives with. The narrator remembers a previous visit when the cat attacked Mr. Wilde: "Howling and foaming they rolled over and over on the floor, scratching and clawing, until the cat screamed and fled under the cabinet, and Mr. Wilde turned over on his back, his limbs contracting and curling up like the legs of a dying spider" (11). Somehow, Mr. Wilde continues to live with this beast, at least until the end of the story when the narrator returns to visit him again, only to find him "on the floor with his throat torn open" (23). Throughout the story this narrator is portrayed as clearly unreliable; it is left open whether this cat is truly as murderous as she has been depicted or if the narrator is actually responsible for Mr. Wilde's murder. As in Poe's tale, the cat becomes a means of drawing out the madness in the people around her, revealing what lies under the surface. It is another in the line of cats who can understand humans better than they can understand themselves—or, at least, better than they will admit to understanding themselves.

Lovecraft, the Cats of Ulthar, and their modern descendants

The best-known of Lovecraft's cats might be the narrator's companion in "The Rats in the Walls," given the name of an ugly racial slur. This cat, one of nine that the narrator owns, is one of the main impetuses that spurs the narrator to uncover the ghastly secrets of his newly acquired ancestral home. The cat is seen "scratching at the new panels which overlaid the ancient stone" ("Rats" 96) and follows the narrator into the depths of the mansion. While the narrator is just being indoctrinated into the horrors that lie beneath the known world, this cat seems to have known about them all along.

But for truly weird cats, we turn to Lovecraft's story "The Cats of Ulthar." From its opening paragraph, Lovecraft makes clear that this tale will be a paean to the wonderful weirdness of cats: "the cat is cryptic, and close to strange things which men cannot see . . . The Sphinx is his cousin, and he speaks her language; but he is more ancient than the Sphinx, and remembers that which she hath forgotten" (19). We have moved away from the cats of Poe and

Chambers, who understand the human soul, and into the realm of cats who understand the innermost workings of the universe.

The story is etiological in nature, setting itself up as an explanation for why the village of Ulthar has a law against killing cats. This law finds its origin in "an old cotter and his wife" (19), who took pleasure in killing the local cats. But when a group of "strange wanderers from the South" (20) come to town and lose one of their cats to this sadistic couple, their prayers have a strange effect on the local cats. In the middle of the night the village cats band together and descend upon the cat-killers, leaving behind only a pile of picked-clean bones. How they were roused to band together to protect themselves in such a fashion, or the manner in which they did the deed, is left up to the reader's imaginations. But the connection between this feline uprising and the prayer leads us to believe that their act of self-defense is somehow linked to supernatural realms that remain largely closed off to humanity.

The cats of Ulthar show up again in *The Dream-Quest of Unknown Kadath,* when they save Randolph Carter from the servants of Nyarlathotep. These cats are clearly kin to the cats of Ulthar that we have encountered before; Lovecraft writes that there are "cryptical realms known only to cats," and that it is "to the moon's dark side that they go to leap and gambol on the hills and converse with ancient shadows" (170). These are cats who are confident travelers between the worlds, and they seem comfortable with this knowledge of realities that goes far beyond what humans are able to understand.

As the weird tale develops further in Lovecraft's wake, it is this understanding of cats as liminal figures, possessing knowledge of the deep structures of the cosmos, that will come to dominate. The role of cats as guardians standing between humanity and these cosmic forces will also be developed further.

Cats are everywhere in Neil Gaiman's stories. Perhaps best-known is the nameless cat of *Coraline,* who explains its lack of a name to the book's protagonist: "Now you people have names.

That's because you don't know who you are. We know who we are, so we don't need names" (37). This cat serves as a (mostly) faithful companion to Coraline, helping to guide her between the two worlds she inhabits and keep her safe from the malevolent Other Mother, a walker-between-worlds like Lovecraft's cats of Ulthar. But the cat's essential weirdness is summed up with this introductory self-description. The cat proposes that human's lack of knowledge about the world extends to their very own selves: we not only don't understand the ancient beings who rule the universe or our cosmic insignificance, but we fundamentally have no conception of our own identity. The knowledge that cats can access, but to which humans are denied, is the basic knowledge of self. As such, this cat is in a similar lineage to those of Poe and Chambers, though it seems less interested in revealing what humans are unwilling to understand about themselves, and more content to be secure in its own self-knowledge.

But this is far from the only Gaiman cat who holds knowledge that humans cannot grasp. Perhaps most intriguing are the cats from his stories "The Price," originally published in the chapbook *On Cats & Dogs,* and "Dream of a Thousand Cats," originally published as issue #18 of *The Sandman.* In both of these stories cats provide insight into a world that exists around us all the time, but which is usually inaccessible to us. Cats, however, can either walk seamlessly between the two worlds or exist in both at the same time. And they can either serve to protect us from this other world—or work to leverage its power against that of humanity.

The center of "A Dream of a Thousand Cats" is an unnamed cat who has traveled through the dreaming, met the Lord of Dreams (referred to in this tale as "The Dream Cat"), and received a revelation regarding the nature of reality, and the power of dreams to reshape it. The Dream Cat tells her that "many, many seasons ago" (15) cats were the dominant species on the planet, and tiny humans existed only to serve the needs of their feline masters. But eventually a human started speaking of a new world where humans are the "kings and the queens, and the gods" (17), and eventually enough humans dreamed of this to remake the world according to this vision. "They dreamed the world so it always was the way it is now" (19), the Dream Cat says.

As a result of this meeting with the Dream Cat, the unnamed cat becomes an evangelist for reshaping the world yet again. It is not that humans have forgotten the previous world; that world has never existed. So now, through her revelation from the Dream Cat, this cat has a knowledge of another world, a knowledge denied to humanity. She promises that "if a bare thousand" cats dream of the world being "the way it truly is" (20, 22), they will have the power to change it back. (Of course, Gaiman makes a joke about the impossibility of a thousand cats doing anything together.) This cat sees far beyond what humans are able to comprehend, seeing even a world that has been dreamed out of existence.

One of Gaiman's cats sees another world and seems to be the only thing standing in between the malevolence of this other world and us. In his short story "The Price," the narrator (who seems a lot like Gaiman himself) takes in an injured stray cat, who is referred to only as the Black Cat. It always seems to have new injuries, the narrator presumes from nighttime fighting. He takes the Black Cat to his basement office to recuperate, and during the days the cat is resting things start to go poorly for the narrator and his family. Small things go wrong, such as writing deals falling through, his daughter being unhappy at summer camp, and his wife hitting a deer with her car. When the cat has recovered enough to go outside again, things start to turn around, and the problems that had crept into the narrator's life over the last few days all resolve themselves.

Rather than keeping the cat indoors at night, the narrator resolves to do some surveillance and determine what kind of animal it has been fighting. He is shocked when, late one night, he sees the devil come out of the woods and approach his house, and the Black Cat fight it off. These scratches, bites, and gouges are all the result of the Black Cat keeping the devil away from the narrator's family, at great cost to itself. It is hard to imagine a story with higher praise for cats—or one that imagines a thinner line between our everyday existence and the malevolent forces that truly govern the universe, and are always seeking to do us harm.

Recent years have seen cats continue to serve as important characters in weird fiction, many of whom maintain the role of walker-between-worlds imagined by Lovecraft, and even the role of protector of our world described by Gaiman. In Kij Johnson's fictional foray into Lovecraft's world, the novella *The Dream-Quest of Vellitt Boe*, the protagonist is tracking a student who escaped from the dream world into the waking world; her on this quest companion ("which had accompanied her for its own inscrutable reasons" [56]) is an unnamed black cat who serves as spirit guide and protector. The novella's narrator informs us that "Cats move fearlessly between the dream lands, the moon, and the waking world—and to other, unknowable places" (42–43). This cat, as we understand is common for its kind, knows shortcuts into the waking world, but unfortunately "it's not possible for men of the dream lands to travel thus" (109). So Vellitt is forced to take the more arduous route, through the land of the ghouls. While walking between worlds is a dangerous task for humans, it seems to come naturally to cats.

The core of weird fiction is about providing a glimpse of a reality that lies just beneath what we think we know of the world, however fleeting or sideways the glimpse might be. In the best weird tales these glimpses linger long after the book has been closed, causing us to rethink how we view sunlight, how we feel the warmth of the breeze around us, and every step we take in the world. Cats are a perfect conduit for this glimpse, because our lived experience with them seems to imply that they see this world around them all the time and that they have grown uncannily comfortable with living in it. Those of us who live with cats are always reminded of their inherent weirdness, whether it's their entirely baffling agendas or their ability to see things that seem forbidden to humans. This fundamental weirdness makes them a natural companion for weird fiction, as they can serve as spirit guides for the characters who are just learning about this unseen world; and, if we're lucky, they might serve to protect us from the malevolent forces that dwell within that unseen world. At least, if we continue to feed them and give them enough pets to make us worth keeping around.

Works Cited

Blackwood, Algernon. "Ancient Sorceries." In *Ancient Sorceries and Other Strange Tales*. Ed. S. T. Joshi. New York: Penguin, 2002. 87–130.

Chambers, Robert W. "The Repairer of Reputations." In *The King in Yellow*. n.p.: Arcadia Press, 2017. 7–23.

Gaiman, Neil. *Coraline.* New York: HarperCollins, 2002.

———. *A Dream of a Thousand Cats. The Sandman.* No. 18 (1990).

———. "The Price." In *Tails of Wonder and Imagination.* ed. Ellen Datlow. 2010. San Francisco: Night Shade Books, 2022. 17–21.

Hawthorne, Nathaniel. *The House of the Seven Gables.* New York: Signet Classics, 1961.

Johnson, Kij. *The Dream-Quest of Vellitt Boe.* New York: TOR, 2016.

Lovecraft, H. P. *The Annotated Supernatural Horror in Literature.* Ed. S. T. Joshi. Rev. ed. New York: Hippocampus Press, 2012.

———. "The Cats of Ulthar." In *The Dreams in the With House and Other Weird Stories.* Ed. S. T. Joshi. New York: Penguin, 2004. 19–22.

———. *The Dream-Quest of Unknown Kadath.* In *The Dreams in the Witch House and Other Weird Stories.* Ed. S. T. Joshi. New York: Penguin, 2004. 155–251.

———. "The Rats in the Walls." In *The Call of Cthulhu and*

Other Weird Stories. Ed. S. T. Joshi. New York: Penguin, 1999. 89–108.

    Poe, Edgar Allan. "The Black Cat." In *The Portable Edgar Allan Poe*. Ed. J. Gerald Kennedy. New York: Penguin, 2006. 191–201.

The Cats of River Street (1925)

Caitlin R. Kiernan

1

Essie Babson lies awake, listening to the soft, soft murmur of the Manuxet flowing by, on its way down to the harbor and the sea beyond. Unable to find sleep, or unable to be found by sleep, she listens to the voice of the river and thinks about the long trip the waters have made, all the way from the confluence of the Pemigewasset and the Winnipesaukee, and before that, the headwaters at Franconia Notch and faraway Profile Lake in the White Mountains of New Hampshire. The waters have traveled hundreds of miles just to keep her company in the stillness of this too-warm last night of July. Or so she briefly chooses to pretend. Of course, the waters of the river, like all the rest of the wide world, neither know nor care about this sleepless spinster woman, but it's a pretty thought, all the same, and she holds tightly to it.

Some insomniacs count sheep; Essie traces the courses of rivers.

"You're still awake?" asks her sister, Emiline.

I thought you were asleep," Essie sighs and turns over onto her right side, rolling over to face Emiline.

"No, no, it's too hot to sleep," Emiline replies. "I'm so tired, but it's really much too hot. I'm sweating on my sheets. They're soaked right through with sweat."

"Me, too," says Essie. "Mine, too."

There's only a single window in the second-story bedroom,

and both storm shutters are open and the sash is raised. But the night is so still there's no breeze to bring relief, to stir the stagnant air trapped inside the room with the two women.

"Think about the river," Essie tells her sister. "Shut your eyes and think about the river and how cool it must be, out there in the night. Think about the harbor and the bay."

"No, I won't do that," Emiline says. "You know I won't do that. Why would you even suggest such a thing, when you know I won't."

Essie shuts her eyes. The room smells of perspiration and dust, talcum powder, tea rose perfume, and the potpourri they order from a shop in Boston. The latter sits in a bowl on the chifforobe: a salmagundi of allspice, marjoram leaves, rose hips, lavender, juniper and cinnamon bark, with a little mugwort thrown in to help keep the moths at bay. Emiline insists on having a bowl of the potpourri in every room in the high old house on River Street. She dislikes the smell of the Manuxet and the fishy, low-tide smells of the bay, whenever the wind blows from the east, and also the muddy odor of the salt-marshes, whenever the wind blows from the west or south or north. Essie has never minded these smells, and sometimes they even comfort her, the way the sound of the river sometimes comforts her. But she also rarely minds the scent of the potpourri. Tonight, though, the potpourri is cloying and unwelcome, and it almost seems as if it could smother her, as if it means to seep up her nostrils and drown her.

Emiline is deathly afraid of drowning, which, of course, is why it was foolishness to suggest that thinking on the river might help her to sleep.

Essie rolls onto her back once more, and the box springs squeak like a bucket of angry mice.

"I'm going to buy a new mattress," she says.

And, again, Emiline says, "It's much too hot to sleep." Then she adds, "It's very silly, lying here, not sleeping, when there's work to be done."

"Yes, in the autumn, I think I will definitely buy a new mattress."

"There's really nothing wrong with the mattress you have," says Emiline.

"You don't know," Essie replies. "You don't have to sleep on it. Sometimes I think there are stones sewn up inside it."

"I should get up," whispers Emiline, and Essie isn't sure if her sister is speaking to her or speaking to herself. "I could get some baking done. A pie, some biscuits. It'll be too hot to bake after sunrise."

"Em, it's too hot to bake now. Try to sleep."

Then the door creaks open, just enough to admit their striped ginger tom Horace to the bedroom, and Essie listens to the not-quite inaudible padding of velvet paws against the white-pine floorboards. Horace reaches the space between the women's beds, and he pauses there a moment, deciding which sister he's in the mood to curl up with. The moonlight coming in through the open window is bright, and Essie can plainly see the cat, sitting back on its haunches, watching her.

"Well, where have you been?" she asks the ginger tom. "Making certain we're safe from marauding rodents?"

The cat glances her way, then turns its head towards Emiline. Emiline calls Horace their "tough old gentleman." His ears are tattered, and there are ugly scars crisscrossing his broad nose and marring his flanks and shoulders, souvenirs of the battles he's won and lost. The sisters have had him for almost seventeen years now, since he was a tiny kitten, since they were both still young women. They found him one afternoon in the alley out back of the Gilman House, hiding behind an empty produce crate, and Emiline named him Horace, after Horace Greeley. It seemed an odd choice to Essie, but she's never asked her sister to explain herself. It isn't a bad name for a cat, and the kitten seemed to grow into it.

"Well, make up your mind," Essie says. "Don't take all night."

"Don't rush him," Emiline tells her. "What's the hurry. It's not as if we're going anywhere."

Downstairs, the grandfather clock in the front parlor chimes midnight.

And then Horace chooses Emiline. He jumps—a little stiffly—up onto her bed and, after sniffing about the quilt and sheets for a bit, lies down near her knees. Essie feels slightly disappointed, but then the cat has always preferred her sister. She sighs and stares up at the fine cracks in the ceiling plaster, concentrating once again on the soft, wet sound of the Manuxet flowing between River and Paine streets. Across from her, Horace purrs himself and Emiline to sleep. After another hour or so, Essie also drifts off to sleep, and she dreams of tall ships and the sea.

2

The brass bell hung over the shop door jingles, and Bertrand Cowlishaw—proprietor of River Street Grocery and Dry Goods—looks up from his newspaper just long enough to note that it's the elder Miss Babson whose come in. He nods to the woman as she eases the door shut behind her. Though the shades are drawn against the noonday heat, and despite the slowly spinning electric ceiling fan, it's stifling inside the dusty, dimly-lit shop.

"And how are you today, Miss Babson," he says, then turns his attention back to the front page of a two-week old edition of the *Gloucester Daily Times*. Bertrand remembers when it wasn't so hard to get newspapers from Gloucester and Newburyport, and even as far away as Boston, in a timely fashion. He's old enough to remember when the offices of the Innsmouth Courier were still in business, and also he remembers when it quietly folded amid rumors of threats from elders of the Esoteric Order, of which it had frequently been openly critical.

"A bit out of sorts, Bert," she replies. "Emiline and me, we're having trouble sleeping again. It's the heat, I suppose. You'd think it would rain, wouldn't you? I can't recall such a dry summer." And then she picks up a can of peaches in heavy syrup and stares at the label a moment before setting in back on the shelf.

"Hot as Hades," Bertrand agrees, "and dry as a bone, to boot. You got a list there, Miss Babson?"

She tells him yes, she certainly does, and takes her neatly-penned grocery list from a pocket of her gingham dress. It's written on the back of a letter from a cousin who moved away to Gary, Indiana several years ago. Essie goes to the counter, stepping around a barrel of apples piled so high it's a marvel they haven't spilled out across the floor, and she gives the envelope to Bertrand.

"I confess, we haven't had much of an appetite," she tells the grocer. "And neither of us wants to cook, the house being as terribly hot as it is."

While Bertrand examines the list, Essie steals a glance at his newspaper, reading it upside down. The headline declares: SCOPES FOUND GUILTY OF TEACHING EVOLUTION and there's a photograph of William Jennings Bryan, smug and smiling for the press. Farther down the page, there's an article on a coal strike in West Virginia and another on the great-grandnephew of Napoleon Bonaparte. Essie Babson tends to avoid news of the world outside of Innsmouth, as it never seems to be anything but unpleasant. In all her forty years, she's not traveled farther from home than Ipswich and Hamilton, neither more than six miles away, as the crow flies.

"Let's see," says Bertrand, as he gathers the items from her shopping list and places them in a cardboard box. "Condensed milk, icing sugar, one can of lime juice, baking powder, raspberry jam, a dozen eggs, a can of lima beans. We do have some nice fresh blueberries, as it happens, if you and—"

"No, no," she tells him. "Just what's on the list, please."

"Very well, Miss Babson. Just thought I'd mention the blue-berries. They're quite nice, for baking and canning."

"It's really much too hot for either."

"Can't argue with you there."

"You'd think," she says, glancing again at the July 22nd *Gloucester Daily Times,* "people would want to be properly educated, in this day and age. Even in Tennessee, you'd think people wouldn't put up such a ridiculous fuss over a man just trying to teach his students science."

"Folks can be peculiar," he says, reaching for a box of elbow macaroni. "And when it comes down to religion, people get pigheaded and don't seem to mind how ignorant they might look to the rest of the world. Five cans of sardines, yes?"

"Yes, five cans. Emiline and I enjoy them for our luncheon. And soda crackers, please. Mother and Father, they were Presbyterians, you know. But they prided themselves on being enlightened people."

"Folks can be very peculiar," he says again, adding an orange tin of Y & S licorice wafers to the cardboard box. "And we are talking about Tennessee, after all."

"Still," says Essie Babson.

Just then, Bertrand Cowlishaw's fat calico cat—whose name is Terrapin—leaps from the shadows onto the counter, landing silently next to the cash register. Terrapin isn't as old as Horace, but she isn't a youngster, either. Bertrand has been known to boast that she's the best mouser in all of Essex County. Whether or not that's strictly true, there's no denying she's a fine cat.

"And what about you, Turtle," says Essie Babson. "Has the weather got you out of sorts, as well?" She always calls the cat Turtle, because she can never remember its name is actually Terrapin.

The cat crosses the counter to Essie, walking over Bertrand's paper and the smug newsprint portrait of William Jennings Bryan. Terrapin purrs loudly and gently butts Essie in the arm with its head.

"Well, then I'm glad to see you, too."

"Molasses? I don't see it on the list, bu—"

"Oh, yes please. I must have forgotten to write it down."

Essie scratches behind Terrapin's ears, and the cat purrs even louder. Then, apparently tired of the woman's affection, she retreats to the register and begins washing her front paws.

"Horace," says Essie, "has been acting a little odd."

"Maybe it's the full moon coming on," replies Bertrand. "The Hay Moon's tonight.

The tide'll be high."

"Maybe."

"Animals, you know, they're more sensitive to the moon and the tides and whatnot than we are."

"Maybe," Essie says again, watching the cat as it fastidiously grooms itself.

"Well, I'm pretty sure I have everything you needed. If you're absolutely certain Ican't interest you in a pint or two of these blueberries."

"No, that's all, thank you."

Bertrand Cowlishaw brings the box to the counter, and Essie checks it over, checking it against her list to be certain nothing's been overlooked. The cat meows at Bertrand, and he strokes its back and waits patiently until Essie is satisfied.

"I'll have Matthew bring these around to you just as soon as he gets back," the grocer tells her. "He had a delivery over on Lafayette, but he shouldn't be long."

Matthew Cowlishaw is Bertrand's only son. Next year, he goes away to college in Arkham to study mathematics, astronomy, and physics, which has always been the boy's dream and Bertrand has reluctantly given up his own dream that Matthew would one day take over the store when his father retired. His son is much too bright, Bertrand knows, to spend his life selling groceries in a withering North Shore seaport.

"When it's cooler," Essie Babson says, "I'll bake some sugar cookies and bring some around to you. I will, or I'll have Emiline do it. She needs to get out more often. But it's much too hot to bake in this heat. It surely won't last much longer."

"One can only hope not," replies Bertrand. He licks the tip

of his pencil, tallies up her bill, and writes it down in his ledger book. He rarely ever uses the fancy new nickel-plated machine he bought last year from the National Cash Register Company in Dayton, Ohio. It's noisy, and the keys make his fingers ache.

Essie gives Terrapin a parting scratch beneath the chin, and the cat shuts its eyes and looks as content as any cat ever has.

"You take care," says Bertrand Cowlishaw.

"Just hope we get a break in this weather," she says, then leaves the shop, and the brass bell jingles as the door opens and swings shut behind her. Bertrand goes back to his newspaper, and Terrapin, having gotten her fill of humans for the time being, leaps off the counter to prowl among the aisles and barrels and bushel baskets.

3

Frank Buckles sits in his rocking chair on the front porch of his narrow yellow house on River Street, sweating and smoking hand-rolled cigarettes and drinking the bootlegged Canadian whiskey he buys down on the docks near the jetty. He stares at the green-black river flowing between the grey granite-and-mortar quay walls built half a century ago to contain it and keep the water flowing straight down to the harbor, a bulwark against spring floods. The river glistens brightly beneath the summer sun. He dislikes the river and often thinks of selling the house his grandfather built and getting a place set farther back from the Manuxet. Or, better yet, moving away from Innsmouth altogether, maybe all the way up to Portland or Bangor. Sometimes, he thinks he wouldn't stop until he was safely in the Maritimes, where no one had ever heard of Innsmouth or Obed Marsh or the Esoteric fucking Order of Dagon. But he isn't going anywhere, because he lacks the resolve, and what few tenuous roots he has, they're here, in this rotting town the outside world has done an admirable job of forgetting.

Lucky them, thinks Frank Buckles, as he shakes out a fresh line of Prince Albert, then licks the paper and twists it closed. He lights the cigarette with a kitchen match struck on the side of his chair, and for a few merciful seconds the smell of sulfur masks the musky stink of the river. It isn't so bad up above the falls, back in the marshes towards Choate and Corn and Dilly islands, where the waters are broad and still. When he was young, he and his brother Joe would often spend their days in those marshes, digging for quahogs and fishing for white perch, steelhead, and shad. Back there, away from the sewers that spill into the Manuxet below the falls, it was easy to pretend Innsmouth was only a bad dream.

In April of '18, both he and his brother were drafted, and they were sent off to the French trenches to fight the Huns. Joe died less than five months later in the Meuse-Argonne Offensive, blown limb from limb by a mortar round. The very next week, at the Battle of Blanc Mont Ridge, Frank lost his left foot and his right eye, and they shipped what was left of him back home to Massachusetts. Joe's remains were buried in Lorraine, in the American cemetery at Romagne-sous-Montfaucon, in a grave that Frank has never seen and never expects to see. That his brother was killed and he was mangled only weeks before the end of the war to end all wars is a horrible irony that isn't lost on Frank. And now, seven years have gone by, and both his mother and father have passed, and Frank spends his days sitting on the porch, drinking himself numb, watching the filthy river roll by. He spends his nights tossing and turning, lying awake or dreaming of murdered men tangled in barbed wire and of skies burning red as blood and roses. Sometimes, he sits with a shotgun pressed to his forehead or his mouth around the muzzle, pretending that he'll pull the trigger. But he hasn't got that much courage left anywhere in him. He wonders if there would be time to smell the cordite before his soul winked out, if he would taste it, how much pain there would be in the split second before this brains were sprayed across the wall. He has a stingy inheritance that might or might not be enough to see him through however many years he's left to suffer, and he has the narrow yellow house on River Street. Sometimes, he sobers up enough to do odd jobs about town.

Frank exhales a steel-grey cloud of smoke, and the breeze off the river immediately picks it apart. The breeze smells oily, of dead fish and human waste; it smells of rot.

This is Hell, he thinks. *I'm alive, and this is Hell.* It's an old thought, worn smooth as the cobbles along the breakwater.

> *"Is it better to be a living coward,*
> *Or thrice a hero dead?"*
> *"It's better to go to sleep, my lad,"*
> *The Colour Sergeant said.*

One of the three tortoiseshell kittens—two female, one male—that have recently taken up residence beneath his porch scrambles clumsily up the steps and mews at him. It can't be more than a couple or three months old. He has no idea where the kittens came from, whether they were abandoned by their mother, or if the mother were killed. She might have gotten a belly full of poison left out for the rats. She might have perished under the wheels of an automobile. It could have been a hungry dog, or she might have run afoul of the tribes of half-feral boys who roam the streets and alleys and the wharves, happy for any opportunity to do mischief or cruelty that comes their way. It might simply have been her time. But it hardly matters. Now, the kittens live beneath the porch of his narrow yellow house.

The first is followed by a second, and then the third, the brother, comes scrambling up. The trio is thin and crawling with fleas. The little tom has already lost an eye to some infection or parasite. To Frank, that makes him a sort of comrade in the great shitstorm of the world. Frank has been told that a male tortoiseshell is a rare thing.

"What's it you three want, eh?" he asks them, and they loudly mewl in tandem. "That so?" he replies. "Well, people in Hell want ice water, or so I've heard."

One of the tortoiseshell girls parks herself between his boots, and she begins playing with the tattered laces. When the kittens first showed up, he seriously considered herding them all into an empty burlap potato sack from the pantry, putting a few stones in there to keep them company and weight it down, then dropping the sack into the river. It's what his father would have done with the strays. But the thought passed almost as soo as it had come. Frank Buckles knows he's a sorry son of a bitch, but he's not so heartless that he'd send anything to its death in those foul waters.

He scratches at the stubble on the chin he hasn't bothered to shave in days and stares down at the kitten. Ash falls from his cigarette, but it misses the cat.

"Yeah, okay," he says. "How about you moochers just give me a goddamn minute."

Then he gets up and goes inside the dark house. The kittens all line up at the screen door, waiting and watching for Frank's return. After only five minutes or so he comes back with a third of a tin of Holly-brand canned salmon and a chipped china saucer. He empties what's left into the dish and gives it to the hungry kittens. They fall upon it with as much ferocity as any cat has ever shown a fish, living or dead. In only a few moments the saucer is licked clean.

"Greedy little shits," Frank mutters, tossing the empty tin at the Manuxet before sitting back down in the rocker. The chair was built by his paternal grandfather, as a gift to his grandmother, before he signed up with the 8th Massachusetts Volunteer Militia, left his pregnant wife behind, and marched off to die at the hands of a pro-succession mob in Baltimore, on the 19th day of April, 1861. His great grandfather made many chairs and cabinets and tables, and sometimes Frank Buckle wonders where they've all gone, how many have survived the sixty-four years since the man's untimely death.

The kittens, their hunger sated for the time being, have all disappeared back beneath the porch, to the cool shadows below.

"Yeah," Frank mutters, "beat it. The lot of you. Stuff your

faces and leave me here holding an empty can. Lotta gratitude that is, you bums."

Lithe and supple lads they were
Marching merrily away–
Was it only yesterday?

Frank Buckle, he sips his illegal whiskey, and he rocks in his grandmother's chair, and he watches the demon sun shining bright as diamonds off the greasy river. He reminds himself that there's always the shotgun he keeps beside his bed, and he tries not to think about where that burning river leads.

4

She was only fourteen years of age when Annie Phelps took a keen interest in the things that wash up along the sands and shingle beaches of Innsmouth Harbor, the breakwater, and the marshy shorelines to the north and south of the port. The strandings and junk, the flotsam and jetsam of commerce and mishap, the remains of dead and dying creatures, fronds and branches of the kelp and algae forests that grow below the waves. As a child, her parents didn't exactly encourage her boyish fascinations, but neither did they *discourage* them. When she was eighteen, she would have gone away to study natural history and anatomy and chemistry at a university in Arkham, maybe, or Boston, or even Providence. But there wasn't the money for her tuition. So, she stayed at home, instead, and cared for her ailing mother and father.

Annie didn't marry, preferring always the company of women to that of men. There is talk that she enjoys much more than their *platonic* company. However, in a shadowed and ill-starred place like Innsmouth, there are always far darker rumors than whispers of Sapphic passion to provide the grist for clothesline gossips. She was twenty-eight years when the influenza of '18 claimed Charles and Beulah Phelps, and afterwards she sold their listing

Georgian house on Hancock Street and took up residence in three adjoining rooms in Hephzibah Peabody's boarding house on River Street. Her study and bedroom both have excellent views of the gurgling Manuxet.

Annie Phelps makes a modest living as a seamstress and a typist, keeping back most of the income from the sales of the house on Hancock for that proverbial rainy day. But her passion has remained for those treasures she finds on the shore, and hardly three days pass that she doesn't find time to make her way down to the fish markets or past the waterfront, where few women dare to venture alone, to see what the boats or the tides or a fortuitous storm have hauled in to arouse her curiosity. Most of the fishermen and fishmongers, the sailors, boatwrights, deckhands, and dockworkers, know her by sight and leave her be.

This day, this sweltering late Monday afternoon in July, she sits at her father's old roll-top desk, in her study, a small room lined with shelves loaded down with books and jars of biological specimens she's pickled in solutions of formaldehyde. There are squid and sea cucumbers, eels and baby dogfish. Among the books and jars, there are also the bones of whales and dolphins, the jaws of a Great White shark, the skull and shell of a loggerhead sea turtle. There are also fossils and minerals sent to her by correspondents—of which she has many—from as far away as Montana, California, and Mexico. The pride of her collection is an enormous petrified whale vertebra from the Eocene of Alabama, fully two feet long. She pays Mrs. Peabody a little extra to allow her to keep this cabinet of oddities, but that doesn't prevent the old woman from regularly grousing about Annie's peculiar collection or the unpleasant odors that sometimes leak from beneath her door.

Annie Phelps has four cats: a black-and-white tom she's named Huxley; a fat grey tom with one yellow eye and one blue eye, whom she's named Darwin; a perpetually thin calico lady, Mary

159

Anning; and, finally, the skittish young girl she christened Rowena after a Saxon woman in *Ivanhoe*. When she's not entertaining a friend or a lover, the cats are all the companionship she needs, even if the apartment is rather too small for all five of them, and even though they claw her mother's already threadbare heirlooms and leave the rooms smelling of piss. The cats are another thing she pays Mrs. Peabody extra to overlook. Were it not for the fact that it's getting harder and harder to find lodgers, the land lady likely would not be willing to make these concessions to Annie's eccentricities.

On this afternoon, she sits drinking a lukewarm glass of lemonade, spiked with a dash of Jamaican ginger, the jake she gets from a pharmacist over on Federal. Annie is very careful how often she imbibes, because she's well aware of the cases of paralysis, and even death that have resulted from excessive use of the extract.

Darwin and Huxley are both perched on the back of the roll-top. Darwin has scaled a stack of monographs on malacology and the hydromedusae of coastal New England. Meanwhile, Huxley has wedged himself between one of her compound microscopes and a copy of Lyell's *Geological Evidences of the Antiquity of Man*. Both are cats are purring loudly and watching as she composes a letter to Dr. Osborn at the American Museum. Occasionally, she'll send him a few of her more intriguing specimens and is proud that some have become permanent additions to the museum's collections in Manhattan.

"What will he think of this piece, Mr. Darwin?" she asks the cat. "Frankly, I think it may be the most fascinating and curious object I've sent him yet."

Darwin shuts his yellow-green eyes.

"Yes, well, what do you know, you chubby old fool?"

Annie stops writing and stares at the jawbone in its cardboard box, cradled in wads of excelsior. It's a bit worn from having been rolled about in the surf, but is unbroken and still has all its teeth. At first glance, she took it for the jaw of a man or woman, some unfortunate soul drowned in the harbor or the cold sea beyond the Water Street jetty. But that impression was fleeting, lasting hardly longer than the time it took her to pick the bone up off the sand. It's much too elongate and slender to be the jaw of any normal human being, and both the condyle and the coronoid process are all but absent. The mental protuberance of the mandibular symphysis is almost blade-like. But the teeth are the strangest of all the strange jawbone's features. Instead of the normal adult human compliment of four incisors, two canines, and eight molars, the teeth are homodont—completely undifferentiated—and more closely resemble the fangs of a garpike than those of any mammal.

Standing at the edge of the murky harbor, low waves sloshing insistently against the shore, Annie Phelps was briefly gripped by an almost irresistible urge to toss the strange bone away from her, to give it back to the sea from whence it had come. To be rid of it. She squinted through the mist, out past the lines of ruined and decaying wharves, at the low dark line of rock that the people of Innsmouth call Devil Reef. Growing up, she heard all the tales about the reef, yarns of pirate gold, sirens, and sea demons, and she knows, too, of the locals who compete in swimming races out to the granite ridge on moonlit nights, a sport sponsored by the Esoteric Order, a religious sect who long ago took over the Masonic Hall at New Church Green.

But she didn't throw the bone away. She carefully wrapped it in newspaper and added it to her basket with the other day's finds.

Annie Phelps is a rational woman of the twentieth century, a woman of science and reason, even if her circumstances mean that she will never be more than an amateur naturalist. She is not bound by the fearful, superstitious ways of so many of the people of the town, all those citizens of Innsmouth who mistake the effects of inbreeding, disease, and poor nutrition among the Marshes, Eliots, Gilmans, Waites, and other old families of the town for some metaphysical transformation brought about by the secretive rites and rituals of the Order of Dagon—as certainly a witch-cult as any described in the scholarly works of Margaret Murray. Growing up, she heard all that bushwa, and she sometimes feels anger and embarrassment at the way so many of her neighbors live in terror of whatever goes on inside the dilapidated, pillared hall.

"It certainly isn't a fossil," she says to Huxley, ignoring the less-than-useful Mr. Darwin. "There's no sign whatsoever of per-mineralization. It's no sort of reptile, and I don't believe it's a fish, neither cartilaginous or osteichthyan. But I can't believe it's a mammal, either."

If the cat has an opinion, he keeps it to himself.

Annie writes a few more lines of her letter—

I am very grateful for the copy of your description of Hespero-pithicus, *though I must confess it still looks to me very like a pig's tooth.*

—and then she glances at the jawbone again.

"The water gets deep out past the reef," she says to Huxley and Darwin, "and who knows what might be swimming around out there."

The cats purr, and Huxley begins vigorously cleaning his ears.

The enclosed specimen has entirely confounded all my best attempts at classification. Beyond the self-evident fact that it resides somewhere within the Vertebrata, I'm entirely at a loss.

Sometimes, Annie dares to imagine she will one day find something entirely new to science, and Dr. Osborn—or someone else—will name the new animal or plant after her. She stares at the jaw and considers a number of appropriate Latin binomina, if it should prove to be something novel, finally settling on *Deinog-nathus phelpsae,* Phelps' terrible jaw. She likes that. She likes that very much.

But then she feels the prickling at the back of her neck and along her forearms, and the sinking, anxious feeling she first expe-rienced the day she found the bone, and she quickly looks away and tries to focus on finishing the day's correspondence:

. . . and at any rate, I hope this letter finds you well.

Outside, there's a sudden commotion, a loud splashing from

the river, and Annie sets her pen aside and goes to the window to see what it might have been. But there's nothing, just the waters of the Manuxet swirling past the boarding house, dark and secret as the coming night.

"Someday," she says to the cats, "I'm gonna pack up and leave this place. You just watch me. Someday, we're gonna get out of here."

5

Ephraim Asher Peaslee closes his wrinkled eyelids, sixty-one years old and thin as vellum paper, sinking into the sweet rush and warm folds of the heroin coursing through his veins. All the world bleeds to white, and he could well be staring into the noonday sun, patiently waiting to go mercifully blind, so bright does the darkness around him blaze. But it doesn't blind him. It doesn't ever blind him, and neither does it burn him. He lies cradled in the worn cranberry velvet of the chaise lounge in the parlor of his house at the corner of River and Fish streets, directly across from the shattered arch of the Fish Street Bridge. The heavy drapes are drawn, like his eyelids, against the last dregs of twilight, against the rising Hay Moon, Corn Moon, Red Moon, goddamn Grain Moon, whichever folk name suits your fancy. None suit his. The moon is a cruel cyclopean eye, lidless, watchful, prying, and this night it will drag the sea far inland, swelling the harbor and tidal river all the way back to the lower falls. It won't be the kindly, obscuring white of his opiate high, but will lie orange and bloated, low on the horizon. It will scrape its cratered belly against the sea, hemorrhaging for all the bloodthirsty mouths that lie in wait, always, just below the waves. Oh, Ephraim Asher Peaslee has seen so many of those slithering, spiny things, has drowned again and again in their serpent coils. He's been kissed by every undertow and riptide, dragged down screaming to bear witness to abyssal lands no human man ever was meant to see. Right now, this evening, he pushes back against those thoughts, awakened by the rising moon. He tries to cling to nothing but the heroin, the forever white expanse laid out before him after the needle kiss. The radio's on, "I'll Build a Stairway to Paradise," and the music makes love to his waking alabaster dream. *It's madness to be always sitting around in sadness, when you could be learning the steps of gladness.* He folds his bony hands in supplication, in prayer to St. Gershwin and the ghost of Guglielmo Marconi and the Crosley Model 51 that they have graced him with this balm, a sacred ward against the memories and the nightmares and the long hours to come before dawn. God bless, and take your choice of gods, but surely, please, bless the pharmaceutical manufacturers in faraway eastern Europe, in Turkey and Bulgaria, god bless the Chinese farmers and poppy fields, where moralizing tyrants have not yet obliterated his ragged soul's deliverance from the abominations of Innsmouth. Pray a rosary for the white powder that ferries him away to Arctic wastes, Antarctic plains, where water is stone and nothing can swim through those crystalline rivers. *I won't open my eyes*, thinks Ephraim Asher Peaslee. *I won't open my eyes until morning, and maybe not even then. Maybe I will never again open my eyes, but fall eternally, perpetually, into the saving grace of the heroin light.* Then he hears the rising moon, a sound like the sky being torn open, like steam engines and furnaces, and he turns his face into a brocade pillow, wishing he were able to smother himself, but knowing better. He's a failed suicide, several times over; a coward with straight razor and noose. And trying not to hear the moon or the sluice of the rising tide, trying only to drown in white and ancient snow and the fissured glaciers that course down the basalt flanks of Erebus, there is another sound, past the radio—*Dance with Maud the countess, or just plain Lizzy. Dance until you're blue in the face and dizzy. When you've learn'd to dance in your sleep, you're sure to win out*—past crooning and tinny strings, there is the thunder, earthquake, sundering purr of Bill Bailey, his gigantic Maine Coon, twenty-five pounds if he's an ounce. Bill Bailey, raised up from a kitten, and now he comes heroic, thinks the heroin addict hopefully, *to pull my sledge up the crags of a dead and* frozen volcano in the South Polar climes, Mr. Poe's Mount Yaanek, where the filthy, unhallowed Manuxet never, never will do them mischief on this hot August night. Risking so many things—his shredded sanity not the least of all—Ephraim Asher Peaslee opens his eyes, letting the world back in, releasing his desperate hold on the white. He rolls over, and Bill Bailey stands not far from the cranberry chaise, watching him, waiting cat-patient, those amber eyes secret filled. "You hear it, too, don't you? We ought to have run. We ought to have packed our bags and taken that rattletrap bus away to Newburyport. They'd have let us go. They have no use for the likes of us. They be *glad* to be rid of us." The cat merely blinks, then sets about licking its shaggy chocolate coat, grooming paws and chest. "You *do* hear it, I *know* you do." And then, close to tears and disappointed by the cat's apparent lack of concern, by Bill Baily's usual pacific demeanor, the old man once more turns away and presses his face into the cushion. Sure, what has a cat to fear from the evils of an encroaching, salty sea? A holy temple child of Ubaste, privy to immemorial knowledge forever set beyond the kin of loping ape's fallen from African trees and the grace of Jehovah. Bill Bailey purrs and bathes and does not move from his appointed station by the chaise. And Ephraim Asher Peaslee tries to give himself back to the white place, but finds that, in the scant handful of seconds it took him to converse with the cat, the luminous White Lands have deserted him. Left him to his own meager devices, none of which are a match for the monsters the mad and unholy men and women of the Esoteric Order see fit to call forth on nights when the moon sprawls so obscenely large in the Massachusetts heavens. Their oblations and devotions that rot and gradually discard their human forms, sending those lost souls tumbling backwards, descending the rungs of the evolutionary ladder towards steamy Devonian and Carboniferous yesteryears, muddy swamp pools, silty lagoons, dim memories held in bone and blood and cells of morphologies devised and then abandoned two-hundred and fifty, three hundred million ago. Ephraim Asher

Peaslee of No. 7 River Street shuts his eyes more tightly than, he would say, he ever has shut his eyes before, skating his hypodermic fix down, down, down, but not down to the sanctuary of his alabaster realms. Some door slammed and bolted shut against him, and, instead, he has only clamoring, fish- stinking recollections of the waterfront, the docks where beings no longer human cast suspicious, swollen eyes towards interlopers. Grotesque faces half glimpsed in doorways and peering out windows. Shadows and murmurs. The squirming green-black mass he once caught a fleeting sight of before it slipped over the edge of a pier and, with a plop, was swallowed up by the bay. The chanting and hullabaloo that pours from the old Masonic Hall.

All of this and a hundred other images, sounds, and smells burned indelibly into his mind's eye. Shuffling hulks. Naked dancers on New Church Green, seen on stormy, starless nights, whirling devil dervishes. *All you preachers who delight in panning the dancing teachers, let me tell you there are a lot of features of the dance that carry you through the gates of Heaven!* So many other citizens might turn their heads and convince themselves they've seen nothing, and anyway, what business is it of theirs, the pagan rites of the debased followers of Father Dagon and Mother Hydra? Oh, old Ephraim Asher Peaslee, he knows those names, because he can't seem to shut out the voices that ride between the crests and troughs. Out there, as night comes on and the last scrap of sunset fades, he prays to his own heathen deities, the narcotic molecules in his veins, the radio, to keep him insensible for all the hours between now and dawn. And Bill Bailey stands guard, and listens, and waits.

6

When even the solar system was young, a fledgling, Pre-Archean Earth was kissed by errant Theia, daughter of Selene, and four and a half billion years ago all the cooling crust of the world became once more a molten hell. In that mighty collision, Theia was obliterated for her reckless show of affection and reborn as a cold, dead sphere damned always to orbit her intended paramour; she a planet no more, but only a satellite never again permitted to touch the Earth. And so it is that the moon, spurned, scarred, diminished, has always haunted the sky, gazing spitefully across more than a million miles of vacuum, hating silently—but not entirely powerless.

She has the tides.

A dance for three—sun, moon, and earth.

She can pull the seas, twice daily, and twice monthly her pull is vicious.

And so she has formed an alliance with those things within the briny waters of the world that would gain a greater foothold upon the land or would merely reach out and take what the ocean desires as her own.

For the ocean, like the moon, is a wicked, jealous thing.

Hold that thought.

Cats, too, have secrets rooted in antiquity and spanning worlds, secret histories known to very few living men and women, most of whom have only read books or heard tales in dreams and nightmares; far fewer have for themselves beheld the truth of the lives of cats, whether in the present day or in times so long past there are only crumbling monuments to mark the passage of those ages. The Pharaoh Hedjkheperre Setepenre Shoshenq's city of Bubastis, dedicated to the Cult of Bast and Sekhmet, where holy cats swarmed the temples and were mummified, as attested by the writings of Herodotus. And the reverence for the *Tamra Maew* shown by Buddhist monks, the breeds sacred to the Courts of Siam, the *Wichien-maat, Sisawat, Suphalak, Khaomanee*, and *Ninlarat*. In the Dream Lands, the celebrated cats of Ulthar, whom no man may kill on pain of death, and, too, the great battle the cats fought against the loathsome, rodent-like zoogs on the dark side of the moon.

Cats upon the moon.

Star-eyed guardians whose power and glory has been for-gotten, by and large, by humanity, which has come to look upon them as nothing more than pets.

The stage has been set.

Here's the scene:

All the cats of Innsmouth have assembled on this muggy night, coming together at a designated place within the shadowed, dying seaport at the mouth of Essex Bay, south of

Plum Island Sound, and west of the winking lighthouses of Cape Ann. The sun is finally down, and that swollen moon has cleared the Atlantic horizon to shine so bright and violent over the harbor and the wharves, over fishing boats, the meeting hall of the Esoteric Order of Dagon, and over all the gabels, balustrades, hipped Georgian and slate-shingled gambrel rooftops, the cupolas and chimneys and widow's walks, the high steeples of shuttered churches. The cats takes their positions along the low stone arch of Banker's Bridge, connecting River Street with Paine Street, just below the lower falls of the Manuxet. They've slipped out through windows left open, through attic crannies and basement crevices, all the egresses known to cats whose "owners" believe they control the comings and goings of their feline charges.

The cats of Innsmouth town have come together to hold the line. They've come, as they've done twice monthly since the sailing ships of Captain Obed Marsh returned a hundred years ago with his strange cargoes from the islands of New Guinea, Sumatra, and Malaysia. Strange cargoes and stranger rituals that set the seaport on a new and terrible path, as the converts to Marsh's transplanted South Sea's cult of Cthulhu called out to the inhabitants of the drowned cities beyond Devil Reef and far out beyond the wide plateau of Essex Bay. They sang for the deep ones and all the other abominations of that unplumbed submarine canyon and the halls of Yha-nthlei and Yoharneth-Lahai. And their songs were answered. Their blasphemies and blood sacrifices were rewarded.

Evolution spun backwards for those who chose that road.

And even as the faithful went down, so did the deep ones rise.

On these nights, when the spiteful moon hefts the sea to cover the cobble beaches and slop against the edges of the tallest piers, threatening to overtop the Water Street jetty, on these nights do the beings called forth by the rites of the Esoteric Order seek the slip past the falls and gain the wetlands and the rivers beyond Innsmouth, to spread inland like a contagion. On these nights, the Manuxet swells and, usually, is contained by the quays erected when the city was still young. But during especially strong spring tides, such as this one of the first night of August 1925, the comingled sea and river may flood the streets flanking the Manuxet. And things may crawl out.

But the cats have come to hold the line.

None among them—not even the very young or the infirm or the very old—shirk this duty.

Essie and Emiline Babson's tom Horace is here, as is shopkeeper Bertrand Cowlishaw's plump calico Terrapin. The three tortoiseshell kittens have scrambled out from beneath Frank Buckle's front porch to join the ranks. All four of Annie Phelps' cats—Darwin and Huxley, Mary Anning and Rowena—are here, and a place of honor has been accorded Mister Bill Bailey, the heroin addict Ephraim Asher Peaslee's enormous Maine Coon. Bill Bailey has led the cats of Innsmouth since his seventh year and will lead them until his death, when the burden will pass to another. All these have come to the bridge, and five score more, besides. The pampered and the stray, the beloved and the neglected and forgotten.

By the whim of gravity, the three celestial bodies have aligned, sun, moon, and earth all caught now in the invisible tension of syzygy, and within an hour the Manuxet writhes with scaled and slimy shapes eager and hopeful that this is the eventide that will see them spill out into the wider world of men. The waters froth and splash as the deep ones, hideous frog-fish parodies of human beings, clamber over the squirming mass of great eels long as Swampscott dories and the arms of giant squid and cuttlefish that might easily crush a man in their grip. There are sharks and toothsome fish no ichthyologist has ever seen, and there are armored placoderms with razor jaws and lobe-finned sarcopterygians, believed by science to have vanished from the world aeons ago. Other Paleozoic anachronisms, neither quite fish nor quite amphibians, beat at the quay with stubby, half-formed limbs.

The conspiring moon is lost briefly behind a sliver of cloud, but then that obstructing cataract passes from her eye and pale, borrowed light spills down and across the Belgian-block paving running the length of River and Paine, across all those rooftops and trickling down into alleyways. And there are those few, in this hour, who dare to peek between curtains pulled shut against the dark, and among them is Annie Phelps, distracted from her reading by some noise or another. She sees nothing more than the water growing perilously high between the quays, and she's grateful she has nothing of value stored in the basement, not after the flood of '18, when she lost her entire collection of snails and mermaids' purses, which she'd unwisely stored below street level. But she sees nothing more than the possibility of a flood, and she reminds herself again how she should move to some village where there would be crews with sandbags out on nights like this. She closes the curtain and goes back to her books.

Two doors down, Mr. Buckles sits near the bottom of the stairs, his 12-gauge, pump-action Browning across his lap. He carried the gun in France, and if it was good enough to kill Huns in the muddy trenches it ought to do just damn fine against anything slithering out of the muck to come calling at his door. The shotgun is cocked, both barrels loaded; he drinks from his bottle of whisky and keeps his eyes open. Even in the house he can smell the stench from the river, worse times ten than it ever is during even the hottest, stillest days.

On Banker's Bridge, Bill Bailey glares with amber eyes at the interlopers, as they surge forward, borne by the tide.

Farther up the street, Essie Babson looks down at the river, and she sees nothing at all out of the ordinary, despite what she plainly hears.

"Come back to bed," says Emiline.

"You didn't hear that?" she asks her sister.

"I didn't hear anything at all. Come back to bed. You're keeping me awake."

"The heat's keeping you awake," mutters Essie.

"Have you seen Horace?" Emiline wants to know. "I couldn't find him. He didn't come for his dinner."

"No, Emiline. I haven't seen Horace," says Essie, and she squints into the night.

"I'm sure he'll be along later."

Bill Bailey's ears are flat against the side of his head. The eyes of all the other cats of Innsmouth are, in this moment, upon him.

Above his store, Bertrand Cowlishaw lies in his bed, exhausted from a long, hot afternoon in the shop, by all the orders filled and the shelves he restocked himself because Matthew was in and out all day, making deliveries. Bertrand drifts uneasily in that liminal space between waking and sleep. And he half dreams about a city beneath the sea, and he half hears the clamor below the arch of Banker's Bridge.

Bill Bailey tenses, and all the other cats follow his lead.

Something hulking and only resembling a woman in the vaguest of ways lurches free of the roiling, slippery horde, rising to her full height, coming eye to eye with the chocolate Maine Coon.

Its eyes are black as holes punched in a midnight sky.

Ephraim Asher Peaslee floats, coddled in the gentle, protective arms of Madame héroïne; after a long hour of pleading, he's been permitted to reenter the White Lands, where neither the sea nor the moon nor their demons may ever come. He isn't aware that Bill Bailey no longer sits near the cranberry velvet chaise lounge. And the radio is like wind through the branches of distant trees, wind through a forest in a place he but half recalls. He is blissfully ignorant of the rising river and the tide and the coming of the deep ones and all their retinue.

The scaled thing with bottomless pits for eyes opens its mouth, revealing teeth that Annie Phelps would no doubt recognize from the jaw she found on the shingle. Dripping with ooze and kelp fronds, its hide scabbed with barnacles and sea lice, the monster howls and rushes the bridge.

And the cats of Innsmouth town do what they have always done.

They hold the line.

They cheat the bitter moon, with claws and teeth, with the indomitable will of all cats, with iridescent eyeshine and with a perfect hatred for the invaders. Some of them are slain, dragged down and swallowed whole, or crushed between fangs and gnashing beaks, or borne down the riverbed and drowned. But most of them will live to fight at the next battle during New Moon spring tide.

Bill Bailey opens the throat of the black-eyed beast that once was a woman who lived in the town and cared for cats of her own.

Mary Anning is devoured, and Annie Phelps will spend a week searching for her.

One of the kittens from beneath Frank Buckles' front porch is crushed, its small body broken by flailing tentacles.

But there have been worse fights, and there will be worse fights again.

And when it is done and the soldiers of Yha-nthlei and Dagon and Mother Hydra have all been routed, retreating to the depths beyond the harbor, beyond the bay, when the cats have won, the survivors carry away the fallen and lay them is the reeds along the shore of Choate Island.

When the sun rises, there is left hardly any sign of the invasion, or of the bravery and sacrifice of the cats. Some will note dying crabs and drying strands of seaweed washed up along River and Paine streets, but most will not even see that much.

The day is hot again, but by evening rain clouds sweep in

from the west, and from the windows of the Old Masonic lodge on New Church Green the watchers watch and curse. They say their prayers to forgotten gods, and they bide their time, patient as any cat.

Old Man

H. P. Lovecraft

So I *hadn't* spoken about "Old Man" & my dreams of him! Well—he was a great fellow. He belonged to a market at the foot of Thomas Street—the hill street mentioned in "Cthulhu" as the abode of the young artist—& could usually (in later life) be found asleep on the sill of a low window almost touching the ground. Occasionally he would stroll up the hill as far as the Art Club, seating himself at the entrance to one of those old- fashioned courtyard archways (formerly common everywhere) for which Providence is so noted. At night, when the electric lights made the street bright, the space within the abyss, or the gateway of some nameless dimension. And there, as if stationed as a guardian of the unfathomed mysteries beyond, would crouch the sphinxlike, jet-black, yellow-eyed, & incredibly ancient form of Old Man. I first knew him as a youngish cat in 1906, when my elder aunt lived in Benefit St. nearby, & Thomas St. lay on my route downtown from her place. I used to pet him & remark what a fine boy he was. I was 16 then. The years went by, & I continued to see him off & on. He grew mature—then elderly—& finally cryptically ancient. After about 10 years—when I was grown up & had a grey hair or two myself—I began calling him "Old Man". He knew me well, & would always purr & rub around my ankles, & greet me with a kind of friendly conversational "e-ew" which finally became hoarse with age. I came to regard him as an indispensable acquaintance, & would often go considerably out of my way to pass his habitual territory, on the chance that I might find him visible. Good Old

175

Man! In fancy I pictured him as an hierophant of the mysteries behind the black archway, & wondered if he would ever invite me *through* it some midnight . . . wondered, too, if I could ever come back to earth alive after accepting such an invitation. Well—more years slipped away. My Brooklyn period came & went; & in 1926, a middle-aged relique of 36, with a goodly sprinkling of white in my thatch, I took up my abode in Barnes Street—whence my habitual downtown route led straight down Thomas St. hill. And there by the ancient archway Old Man still lingered! He was not very active now, & spent most of his time sleeping—but he still knew his fellow-elder, & never failed to give his hoarse, friendly "e-ew" when he chanced to be awake. About 1927 he took on a sort of final second youth & began to be awake more. He had been sticking rather close to the market, but now I met him farther & farther up the hill, & very often at the old archway. Good Old Man! In 1928 he seemed a trifle feeble, but his purring friendliness was unabated. Not long before my 38th birthday I saw him—him whom I had known at 16. Then in August I began to miss him. Always when turning the corner on to the hill I used to look down ahead & see if I could discern a familiar lump of black by the archway or at the market. Now I failed to see the graceful old furry lump. I feared the worst—but scarcely dared to enquire at the market. At last—in September—I did enquire & found that my fears were all too well founded. After more than two decades Old Man had gone through the archway at last, & dissolved into that eternal night of which he was a true fragment—that eternal night which had sent him up to earth as a tiny black atom of sportive kittenhood so long ago! Assuredly, I felt desolate enough without my old friend—without any black lump to look for on the ancient hill. I had dreamed of him—& the mysteries of the archway— before; but I now began to do so with redoubled vividness. He would greet me in sleep on a spectral Thomas Street hill, & gaze with aged yellow eyes that spoke secrets older than Ægyptus or Atlantis. And he would mew an invitation for me to follow him through the archway—beyond which lay (as saith Dunsany) "the unreverberate darkness of the abyss." In no dream up to now have I actually followed him through—but I have often wondered what will happen if ever I do . . . whether, in such an event, I shall ever again awake in this tri-dimensional world? When I mentioned these dreams to Dwyer he wanted to make a story about Old Man, but he has not yet done so. If he doesn't, I may myself some day. Good Old Man! But I am sure that no world he would lead me to would be a world of horror. He is too old & true a friend for that! When little Sam Perkins appeared on the scene last summer I decided that he must be a great-great-great- great-great-grandson of Old Man—perhaps a messenger despatched from the Abyss by my old friend. As soon as his great violet eyes began to turn yellow, I occasionally addressed him as Old Man, & fancied I could sense a spark of recognition! Perhaps he was my friend himself in a new body! But, alas, he did not remain long. He, too, returned to that eternal Night of which he & all his kind are inalienable fragments! Thanks, by the way, for immortalising little Sam in the name of your character. The Kappa Alpha Tau is investigating the hostile influence which seems to hover over the felidae this year; & as soon as we discover the daemon responsible for it, we shall call forth some very strange force through monstrous midnight incantations! All hands, by the way, send their sincerest regards to Crom, & express the hope that his indisposed paw may soon regain its pristine vigour.

Nimbus

Stephen Mark Rainey

On the chilly Saturday that Henry Stewart turned twelve years old, it rained and rained, as it had for a solid week. He felt lonely and a little stir-crazy, so that afternoon he decided to don his raincoat and galoshes and go wandering. His mother disliked the idea of him venturing out and getting soaked, but being cooped up made him so morose, and it was, after all, his birthday. So she told him not to stay out long, and—for the love of heaven!—to keep away from the Miskatonic's riverbanks, for the water had risen dramatically since the deluge began. He gave her a perfunctory "Yes, ma'am," although he now considered himself mature enough to determine where he could go and when.

Tomorrow was Halloween, but heavy rain remained in the forecast for several more days. As non-consolations went, his father told him that a boy his age should have already left such childish nonsense behind (which obviously meant he was old enough to make his own decisions about going outside). Regardless, Halloween still excited him. Spooky decorations filled the town, and on such a dark afternoon they might even be lit up. The best of them lay across the river on Peabody Street, so he set out walking in that direction.

The downpour had dwindled to a drizzle, so he barely got wet as he made his way southward. He encountered only a handful of cars and no other pedestrians. But when he reached the bridge, a surge of surprise and apprehension froze him where he stood. The river—which usually crested well below the bridge—now raged all the way up to its rails. On either side turbulent water roiled up the steep banks with the sound of continuous thunder.

As he pondered the prospect of crossing, to his left, something emerged from beneath the bridge: a small, dark shape, barely visible, thrashing and struggling in the powerful current.

A *kitten!*

A little black kitten, helpless in the rushing water.

His heart skipped a beat before becoming a hammering piston. Without pausing to think, he went sprinting along the riverbank, his sharp eyes locked on the figure in the water. Ahead, along the banks where the river curved northward, the water swirled and groped its way into a broad, shallower inlet. The current was sweeping the kitten toward it. His feet slipped and slid in the seemingly endless mud, but he forced himself onward and gradually gained ground.

As soon as he reached the inlet, heedless of his own safety, Henry plunged into the water. The current immediately grabbed him and tugged him toward the river's violent center. Still, with a few desperate strokes and kicks, he propelled himself close enough to reach for the kitten. Frigid water bucked and slapped at him, but with heroic determination he closed his hand around the small, wriggling body. He drew it to his chest and into the shelter of his raincoat.

Oh, thank you, God!

But now, how to get himself out of this? If the current dragged him farther, he might end up riding the river all the way to the Atlantic, many miles distant.

There! A couple of hundred feet downriver: a huge, fallen tree, its roots tenaciously clinging to the bank, its branches protruding from the water like the legs of a giant, dead spider.

Choppy swells pummeled the bare limbs, causing them to sway and shudder.

Still, if he could somehow maneuver toward the tree, he might yet avoid discovering the Atlantic.

He didn't even have to try.

The next thing he knew, ragged branches seemed to reach for him at lightning speed. Black, skeletal hands seized him and held him fast. Icy water battered his exposed face, but by now his body had gone nearly numb. He kept a firm hold on the little bundle beneath his coat as he used his free arm and both legs to hook branches, one after another, and drag himself toward the cluster of roots at the river's edge.

The effort exhausted him. His right arm *wanted* to release the kitten so he could keep fighting his way to safety. But he *couldn't* let the kitten drown! So on and on he fought.

His mind only grasped what had happened—what he'd done—when found himself lying on solid earth with cold drops from the sky splashing into his eyes. For a time he couldn't move— not until he felt something stirring beneath his raincoat. With that, his blood turned to magma and his muscles came alive again. With delicate fingers he drew the front of his coat open.

A wet, black, fuzzy face lay against his chest. Its drooping little ears, both limned with white, flipped a few times, spraying water. A pair of emerald eyes squinted blankly at him. Then, with a few sharp *hacking* sounds, the kitten shook its head and expelled a glob of water and mucus from its mouth and nose. Again and again it did this until it once again lay still. But the green eyes brightened a little, and when Henry touched its throat he felt a very faint purring.

Then he was sitting upright, cradling the kitten, stroking water from its body, and crying harder than he had ever cried in his life.

At Halloween, certain idiotic, horrible fools were known to kill black cats. Henry didn't know whether someone had thrown this kitten into the river on purpose, but he knew exactly why he'd risked his life to save it.

When he was nine, two of the neighborhood's worst

bullies—Garth Worden and Luke Corey—had found a black cat and forced him to watch while they bashed it to death with a rock. Screaming and cursing, he'd struggled with herculean effort to stop them, but he could not. After the cat was dead, they'd punched Henry over and over before throwing him to the ground beside the little body and running off, laughing.

Laughing!

At that young age, he'd sworn he would never permit such horror to happen again. Not if it cost him everything. He would *never* allow an innocent animal to suffer.

Never!

Henry's ordeal in the river paled beside the resulting storm with his parents. But their shock and anger over what he had done shifted toward comprehension and compassion as he nursed the little cat—which he named Nimbus—back to health with unwavering devotion. In the way of cats, Nimbus recovered with no discernible complications. He ate a lot. He tended to be quite vocal, even conversational. And he had the most endearing way of squinting at Henry, which meant "I won't rip your arms off if you feed me when I want you to and you don't touch me except when I want you to and even that is no guarantee."

Love, more or less.

And so, Nimbus became a bona fide family member. Henry loved him, and even his parents more than once quipped that, for a cat, he was not altogether terrible.

Three Years Later

When Henry started high school, hardly to his (or anyone's) dismay, Garth Corey and Luke Worden turned up absent. The boys hadn't moved away or died or anything; during the summer, people simply encountered them with ever-decreasing frequency, until one day it seemed they had just plain *gone*. Their families remained in Arkham, but they never talked, and no one ever asked. Henry cared only to the extent that, before the two bullies faded from collective memory, their repulsive faces served to remind him of his pledge.

Not that he would ever forget it.

Henry liked high school, inasmuch as anyone could really like school. He was studious and earned good grades, especially in math and science. While not antisocial, he considered only a handful of his peers "friends," and he rarely attended any of the school's extracurricular functions—other than varsity football games, which he did enjoy.

The Stewarts lived in an aging three-story brownstone, tucked tight among several others along Halsey Street, at the edge of the old warehouse district in Arkham's northeastern corner. Mr. Stewart's study/home office had long occupied the one finished room on the upper floor, but shortly after the start of the school year he decided to move downstairs to spare his aging knees a daily battle with the long, steep staircase. So, with much enthusiasm and his dad's blessing, Henry moved his bedroom to the larger and far more private space.

The room's single window overlooked the entrance of a dim alley between a row of long-abandoned commercial establishments, above which a stone arch rose like the gateway to a medieval castle. If anything about the view displeased him, it was that the mostly effaced lettering on the arch once read "Worden & Corey Curio Co."

Nimbus clearly enjoyed his new primary living space, for he spent most of his wakey time perched on the windowsill survey-ing his kingdom (which he was *not* permitted to wander through, since the higher powers had relegated him to indoors). Once in a while, however—particularly at night—he would stare into the dark spaces beyond the window and perform the chattery teeth thing typically reserved for fussing at birds.

One late autumn evening while doing his homework, Henry

noticed that Nimbus appeared especially agitated. He left his desk and crouched next to the chattery cat, expecting to see, amid a sea of darkness, only an empty island of light beneath the lone streetlight above the alley entrance.

But no.

In the center of the golden circle a very tall, very dark figure, apparently clad in an overcoat and fedora, stood like an onyx statue. To Henry's astonishment, the light from above failed to illuminate any portion of the figure. A solid black silhouette, it seemed; a two- dimensional cutout. Or, maybe more aptly, a figure *excised* from three-dimensional space, its contours revealing only a lightless abyss beyond.

The figure took a few steps toward the alley entrance and extended its arms at its sides. To Henry's further disbelief—and Nimbus's increased disquiet—the figure's feet rose from the ground, its body angling up and back until its legs stretched out behind it. Then, very slowly, it glided into the alley until it merged with the darkness and vanished.

I did NOT see that!

He debated with himself for only a few seconds before bolting down the stairs, into the kitchen, and out the back door, which opened to their little gated courtyard. He rushed through the gate and into the narrow back street, where he stood facing the entrance of the alley. The streetlight's glow extended only a short distance past the stone archway. Beyond that, the darkness became one with the star-filled sky.

Henry had been back here countless times, though almost always in daylight. Now, his mind reeled and his nerves tingled, but he somehow kept fear behind him. As he took several steps into the alley, darkness closed around him like a vast black gauntlet. Even as his eyes adjusted, he could make out little more than the featureless shapes of buildings rising into the starlit sky. The faint murmur of distant traffic waxed and waned, and a light breeze sighed through the alley.

Nothing out of the ordinary.

Until, somewhere ahead, he heard a creak, then a clatter, and a pair of molten gold eyes flared into existence. Another noise, and a second, identical pair of eyes appeared across the alley from the first.

Now he felt the cold tickle of fear in his gut.

From somewhere out there, a low, rising moan became the distinctive angry cry of a cat.

Another joined in harmony, and then another. Henry stumbled backward, spun, and broke into a sprint toward his house. When he reached the courtyard gate, heart pounding, he paused to peer back into the alley.

The golden eyes had vanished. But he could still hear, faintly now, the angry feline yowling. He hurried through the gate, slammed it shut, and locked it. Glancing up at his warmly lit window, he saw Nimbus's green eyes gleaming down at him. Somehow his fear retreated—at least a little—and he made his way back inside.

His mom stood in the kitchen, pouring a mug of hot tea. She glanced at him in surprise. "Where have you been?"

"Needed a break from homework. Just stepped out for a little air."

"What's the matter?"

"Huh?"

"The last time you looked this upset, Garth Worden and Luke Corey had chased you around the block." Her gaze sharpened. "They're not out there, are they?"

"Nope." He drew a deep breath, hoping to steady his nerves. "I guess I'd better get back to work."

His mom gave him a last thoughtful look as he headed for the stairs but said nothing more. As soon as he opened his bedroom door, Nimbus hopped down from the window, rushed to him, and wrapped himself happily around Henry's legs, purring noisily.

Never had he been so happy to see his little friend.

Henry found the Stairway to Nowhere on one of his increasingly frequent expeditions into the always-empty alley.

Strange he hadn't happened upon it before. When he was a little kid, he wandered here often enough, sometimes alone, though usually with his friends Dave and Anthony (both of whom, sadly, had moved away). They probably just hadn't slipped into the right alcove, as there were lots to explore.

Since he'd seen that floating black figure, the alley seemed to draw him, especially at night, but he would venture into its shadowy depths only in daylight. Today, though, he'd left late enough that it was already getting dark. Still, this discovery fascinated him, and he could not bring himself to head home yet. A few hundred feet in, he'd noticed an alley within an alley: a narrow strip of darkness between two ancient buildings. Inside this near-lightless corridor he spied a square of denser black in the floor, which closer examination revealed to be a stairwell. There, a flight of stone stairs led deeper into the earth than his eyes could follow.

Perched on the edge of the uppermost stair, he leaned forward and listened, thinking his ears might perceive something his eyes could not. But no; he detected only the hollow ambiance of deep, empty space. He designated this the "Stairway to Nowhere," though he knew it must lead *somewhere.*

Behind him, the setting sun sent a few feeble rays into the alley. On the wall to his right, a sickly puddle of pinkish light revealed something chiseled into the brick. Leaning closer, he found it was a weathered inscription:

D. M. WORDEN—J. T. COREY
DESCENDED 29 NOVEMBER 1928

Forty years ago. Garth and Luke's grandparents? If he remembered right, they had owned the curio company advertised on the arch above the alley. Did this inscription mean they had descended these stairs? Why commemorate *that?*

It was almost dark, but something prevented him from tearing himself away and hurrying home. Before he realized what was happening, his feet were carrying him down the stairs into the inscrutable darkness.

No! He could *not* be doing this! He'd brought no light, not even a match!

The stairs had no railing, no landings, did not spiral downward; they continued straight on, growing dimmer with every step. Yet he wasn't completely blind. The pale mortar between the bricks on either side seemed weirdly luminous, just enough to highlight each stair ahead.

He didn't count his steps—or the minutes—but it seemed ages before he reached the bottom. And here, the staircase simply ended at a featureless brick wall, no different from the walls that lined the stairwell.

His heart stuttered when he saw movement in the brick. As if the wall had become a translucent curtain, images began to take shape: vague, towering trees against a pale violet sky; great, rounded humps that might have been mountains. Other shapes shuffled and slunk back and forth, shapes that *might* have been people—except something about their proportions appeared *off*.

Their limbs were far too long and spindly.

Unable to do otherwise, he reached out to touch the wall. Instead of brick, his fingers felt something like warm water, and his hand passed through the bulwark. He jerked it back, his brain refusing to process this incongruity. A moment later some dark form, a weird silhouette, took shape in the heart of this staggering tableau and slowly moved toward him.

A second dark figure followed the first.

The first drew up before him and leaned forward. Henry's breath caught in his lungs, for a black, bulbous head now seemed to *push* its way through the brick barrier. As it emerged, a pair of hot, golden eyes appeared in the featureless face.

Run! Turn and run like hell back up those stairs!

187

But Henry's legs had become stone, his blood ice. He was a statue. One that quivered and huffed in terror, but that otherwise might have been chiseled from granite.

The protruding face now acquired features as if an invisible hand were etching them on as he watched. Little by little, the face became recognizable.

It belonged to Garth Worden—but it was an adult face, the features aged but clearly those of the bully who had tormented him so many times.

No! This face belonged to D. M. Worden—Garth's grandfather!

Seconds later he knew he'd hit on the truth, for a second visage forced its way through the translucent brick. And this one was Garth Worden—or whatever hellish thing that young man had become.

Or always had been.

He could guess the identities of the other two approaching figures.

Then a piercing feline cry rang from beyond the skin that separated that insane world from this one. The pair of two-dimensional figures withdrew to the other side, though their golden eyes blazed at him for some time before finally fading away.

Henry now saw only dull, solid brick. Touching it, he felt a cold, hard surface.

He spun and bounded up the stairs, two, three at a time. Then four and five. He realized his feet no longer met the stone. And when he looked down, his arms and legs seemed to be darkening. Flattening.

Becoming a silhouette. Like them!

Panic—freezing, scorching, roiling panic—surged through his body. But then, as swiftly as it had gripped him, the panic dissipated, leaving his body and mind stunned. Numb.

Detached.

He stopped moving. His feet, such as they were, again rested on stone. But then, of their volition, his arms extended at his sides. His brain re-engaged, and with a single thought he brought his legs up to float behind him. With a push of his mind he began to drift up the stairs, a paper doll carried by an invisible hand toward the starry sky high above.

It was exhilarating.

Horrifying.

From behind him came a chorus of distant, angry yowling.

Twelve Years Later

Early on, Henry had learned that, if he kept his distance from the alley, his body remained *his,* as he had always known it, the way it was meant to be. Yet something about that staircase, the insane world beyond it, maintained a hold on him, refused his every effort to deny it or venture far from its influence. Somehow, over time, he made his peace with this. As a youth he'd never foreseen remaining a resident of Arkham, but after high school, rather than seek advanced education and a new life elsewhere, he'd attended Miskatonic University, obtained degrees sufficient to become *Doctor* Stewart, and taken a position on the faculty as professor of physics.

All the while seeking—and so far failing—to understand the *physics* of that inexplicable dimension that existed here, so close to home.

But never venturing back there.

Three years ago Henry's father had died, far too young, of heart disease. Subsequently his mother, also too young, suffered a rapid decline into dementia and now occupied a relatively comfortable space in a memory care unit in Boston. The family home, now legally Henry's, he made comfortably his own.

His, and Nimbus's.

The little cat, though aging, still enjoyed good health. As

foolish as it might seem, Henry didn't have the heart to uproot his best friend and settle in a new location, even here in Arkham.

Although he had moved his bedroom to the downstairs master, he kept the upstairs room for his study, and Nimbus continued to occupy his traditional place on the windowsill, as if to guard against any threat from outside.

Or *beyond* outside.

For Henry, clues to certain mysteries had fallen into place, at least loosely. By way of various individuals in town and at the university, he had determined that the "curios" from the shop once owned by D. M. Worden and J. T. Corey indeed came from the *other* side of the wall at the base of the Stairway to Nowhere. The owners of these *objets*—abstract sculptures, ornaments of metal and crystal, weirdly nonfunctional furnishings and devices—claimed they'd found the pieces too compelling to resist.

One such item, gifted to him by Errick Harrison, Miskatonic's resident professor of fine art, now rested on the desk in Henry's study. About ten inches tall, it resembled a flower with a tall, scaly stem, whiplike tendrils in place of sepals, and a bulbous base that sprouted an array of spiderlike legs.

Nimbus hated the thing. Mostly he shied away from it, but on occasion, from his place on the windowsill, he'd stare at it and growl in the pit of his throat. Henry considered removing it, but this prospect made him feel so uncomfortable, as if the inanimate object might somehow resent it—dangerously so—that he left the damned thing in place.

He now believed that the towering shadows he had once taken for trees in that other place must actually resemble this thing.

Long ago, when Worden and Corey, the elders, had descended those stairs, they became part of that other world. Those men's grandsons had also crossed over. Why the intermediate generation had not, Henry could scarcely guess. Maybe they served as some kind of anchor for those families in this world. Maybe they simply chose different paths. Perhaps they remained altogether ignorant of such an unthinkable realm.

God only knew.

But because of those families—or the world they had led him to discover—Henry traveled a solitary path through this life. Well, solitary but for Nimbus, his true best friend. He knew, though, that his cat was getting older, and Henry would almost certainly outlive him. Beyond that . . .

God only knew.

A late Friday evening in early November, Henry sat at his desk grading student papers while Nimbus lazed on his windowsill. Even here, upstairs, the air felt chilly, the silence almost uncanny. At once Nimbus came alert. His eyes locked on something outside the window, and a growl rose in his throat.

Henry moved to peer outside, and though he'd *almost* expected such a sight, shock jolted him when two black silhouettes drifted, as if on a carpet of air, from the dark alley into the pool of light beneath the streetlamp. Two pairs of golden eyes flashed into existence and scanned the darkness before settling on Henry's window.

Unnerved, he backed away. Yet an inexplicable tugging, like an arcane magnet, drew him toward the outdoors. Down the stairs, to the kitchen, and then to the back door.

He *knew* those silhouettes out there belonged to Garth Worden and Luke Corey. The bullies who had tormented him in his youth. Who had killed a cat in front of his eyes. Who, like their grandparents, now existed as something *other*—and sought to drag him to that *other* place. Whether to end his existence or prolong it in a state of unimaginable horror, he had no idea. Years ago that realm had already touched him; for a brief time its dark light rendered him a silhouette.

The moment he set foot onto the concrete stoop, the tugging grew stronger. And before he could draw the door closed, to his horror, a little black shape slipped past his legs, raced through the courtyard, and wriggled through the iron gate, out to the narrow backstreet.

"No!" he cried. "Nimbus, come back!"

Panic for his cat spurred him forward. He tore open the gate and leaped into the street, caring little whether a pair of baleful shades waited for him there. He saw no sign of them—or Nimbus. The streetlight above the alley entrance beckoned him, and nauseating fear gripped him when he realized Nimbus must have run that way.

He peered into the near-endless darkness, praying to glimpse movement or hear his cat's familiar meow.

Nothing.

He crept forward, immersed in almost perfect silence. His footsteps made no sound. He couldn't even hear his own breathing. Then a distant train whistle blew, so faint it might have echoed from a remote, unknown world. A forlorn sound, and he realized he had never felt so isolated and vulnerable.

Ahead, two figures appeared, infinitely blacker than the surrounding darkness, blazing gold eyes focused on him. Malevolence, like an electrical charge, crackled through the space between them. Frigid fingers seemed to close around his body, and all his weight— his entire mass—evaporated. When he looked down, his feet—now mere silhouettes—had left the ground.

He began to drift toward the figures.

Yet the space between them barely diminished, and he realized that they too were drifting through the alley, toward the Stairway to Nowhere. His attempts to tear free of their power felt like struggling against quicksand.

Into the alcove they glided and then into the stairwell. Fury and resignation warred in Henry's mind, his fear for Nimbus dominating all. Where could his cat be? His sole consolation was that these once-human things did not appear to have him.

Deeper and deeper they went, the darkness broken only by the faint, luminous outlines of the bricks. At last, somewhere below, he heard a faint scrabbling and then a soft, familiar meow.

His heart leaped, yet his terror intensified. Just ahead, at the base of the stairs, lay the seemingly solid brick wall.

No sign of Nimbus.

The two silhouettes halted and turned to face him, their eyes burning like lasers. Pure *thought,* rather than words, as if transmitted directly into his brain, imparted the chaos—the insanity—that seethed within these beings, that defined everything they were. Whatever once drew these people here, it had subjugated their humanity, and for Henry's part in thwarting their unfathomable designs—his rescuing Nimbus all those years ago—they intended to take him away.

To make him into something *else.*

The wall lost its solidity until it revealed a vista of tall, spindly shadows—yes, like the thing on his desk!—that swayed either in a breeze or of their own accord. A chorus of chirps and clicks crept from some inconceivable distance. And the pair of silhouettes began to dissolve into the translucent brick, drawing him along behind them.

A second before he would pass through, above those subtle sounds, a harsh growl erupted.

And a new, very different silhouette materialized beyond the wall.

The growl became a deafening roar. Now, the two silhouettes re-emerged on this side of the brick, and the *other* shape burst through like a black tsunami: a giant, panther-like silhouette with blazing green eyes.

And ridges of white that limned its ears.

A massive paw that sprouted long, curved claws shot forward and shredded one of the silhouettes like a rake ripping through black paper. The golden eyes flickered and went dark. An instant later, its featureless shape came apart like so much black confetti cast in the wind.

Henry realized his weight had returned only when he found

himself trying to pull his body, now as heavy as a boulder, up from the cold stone floor. He felt a rush of wind as those claws swished above his head and the ghostly feline ripped into the second silhouette. Banshee cries rang through the stairwell, whether from the beast, the doomed once-human, or both, he had no idea.

On the far side, two new silhouettes appeared. With absolute certainty Henry identified them as D. M. Worden and J. T. Corey—or whatever they had become in that world. But as the raging beast reduced its remaining victim to ghostly black shards, which whirled away and vanished, those two silhouettes turned and as quickly disappeared.

The next thing Henry knew, he was fleeing up the stairs—up, up, and up—seemingly without end. He had no recollection of racing back to his house and to his study as if a raging devil snarled at his heels.

Breathless, he collapsed on the hardwood floor, only to spy a small, black shape lying just beneath the window.

"Oh, no."

Nimbus's eyes were closed as if he were asleep. He looked comfortable, peaceful. But he wasn't breathing.

How? Henry had seen Nimbus run outside! He had scurried into the dark alley and down the Stairway to Nowhere.

Hadn't he?

That massive, incredible black cat—for cat he knew it was—had ears limned with white. Just like his best friend.

His mind awhirl with confusion, he recognized only one reality: Nimbus was gone.

Gently he gathered the little body, cradled it to his chest, and bawled like a baby.

Present Day

Henry often missed teaching at the university. It had given him direction, provided the ideal channel for his energies, his passions. Even after retiring, a decade ago, he continued to frequent the old halls, to visit with his peers, many of whom had become friends. He published, he blogged, he spoke at events. His personal studies brought him rare satisfaction. And understanding.

Yet only partial understanding.

How could anyone fully comprehend a state of nature that transcended the boundaries of any conceivable science? Something that both sprang from and extended into the realm of pure dream?

Or nightmare?

These years later, more than the capacity to understand, he desired—required—the capacity to accept. He had trained himself to think beyond, or disregard, conventional concepts of cause and effect, time and space, or even metaphysical abstraction.

In these, his twilight years, he kept cats. He adopted strays, housed rescues, fed those feral ones who refused to accept human contact. Many of his little housemates became best friends.

In this, he felt fulfilled.

Justified.

Yes, out there in that alley, the Stairway to Nowhere still existed—sometimes; not always. He could determine no pattern or schedule for its manifestation; no correlation with any terrestrial or astronomical event or phenomenon.

It just was.

He knew mortal danger lay within the realm beyond those stairs. Maybe also great wonder.

Maybe incredible beauty. In the end he had *accepted* that something there offered only death or worse. Something there had taken four human beings and made them *other*. It was Henry's conviction that those four had chosen their paths and embraced a dark and terrible *other*.

Two of the four still existed, for on occasion he spied their lurking silhouettes, their molten gold eyes blazing from the deepest shadows.

The yowling of cats almost always accompanied their appearance.

First from outside, and then from his friends *inside*.

The *others'* presence had always upset the local feline population. And clearly, the dark beings hated cats; they had tried to drown Nimbus as a kitten. Henry accepted this as indisputable fact. The Wordens and the Coreys had probably been responsible for killing far too many cats in this world.

In the *other* realm, however, cats were of altogether different stature. And they remained opposed to the darkness that those evil men embraced.

On that one terrible night, so many years ago, Nimbus had in some fashion crossed over—to save him. It was the last act that little body had left in it.

Yes, when Henry saw the signs of that dark *other* here, Henry knew fear. Deepest fear. At the same time he inevitably saw, perched outside his study window, a small, dark shape with gleaming emerald eyes that squinted at him. And a pair of triangular ears whose crests were limned with white.

It was always a brief, reassuring appearance, but in those moments he knew the warmth and love he had always shared with his longtime best friend.

Henry knew that, for the rest of his days, he would be safe.

The Only Thing a Cat Can Do

Christina Sng

I watch Papa from between
The narrow gap of my eyelids,
Pretending to be asleep,
Pretending not to see anything.

He holds Momma by her neck again,
Lifting her up against the wall
While she feebly kicks.
She weeps when he lets go.

He says incomprehensible words
That make her eyes widen and
She rushes to the children's room,
Turning the lock with a soft click.

He does not see me.
I am not witness to his cruelty.
No one would believe me
Even if I could speak.

Fearful he will kick me again,
I hide in the darkness,
Fearful he will once again
Break my bones.

When the outside is bright,
When he is gone, I sit on
Momma's lap, letting her hold me
As she watches the children play.

Pain emanates from her skin
Like waves of grief
Flooding the air like fog.
I stay with her till it is dark.

Years pass and I find myself
Slowing down and tiring faster.
Momma does too, while
The children are now tall as trees.

Papa turns meaner. There is
Perpetual fear in Momma's face,
The exhaustion, yet
A glint in her eyes.

She smiles when she hides
Suitcases outside. One night
I hear her and the children
Move quietly in the dark.

Papa hears them too.
He storms out, knife in hand.
Seeing them by the front door,
He bellows rage at them

And they freeze in terror
As they have been trained to do
All these years.
But I haven't.

I dive between his feet
While he races down the stairs.
I watch him roll and tumble
Like ping pong balls.

A loud crack tears through
The silence when he stops
At the bottom, body bent
And limbs twisted.

Momma rushes to me,
Picks me up and hugs me,
One bag of old bones
Embracing the other.

We leave the house, driving
Until it is bright and the sea
Close enough to touch.
Far in the distance

I see a new adventure for us.
Momma turns back to look at me.
For the first time in forever,
She is smiling.

The Boy Who Drew Cats

Lafcadio Hearn

A long, long time ago, in a small country-village in Japan, there lived a poor farmer and his wife, who were very good people. They had a number of children, and found it very hard to feed them all. The elder son was strong enough when only fourteen years old to help his father; and the little girls learned to help their mother almost as soon as they could walk.

But the youngest child, a little boy, did not seem to be fit for hard work. He was very clever,—cleverer than all his brothers and sisters; but he was quite weak and small, and people said he could never grow very big. So his parents thought it would be better for him to become a priest than to become a fanner. They took him with them to the village-temple one day, and asked the good old priest who lived there, if he would have their little boy for his acolyte, and teach him all that a priest ought to know.

The old man spoke kindly to the lad, and asked him some hard questions. So clever were the answers that the priest agreed to take the little fellow into the temple as an acolyte, and to educate him for the priesthood.

The boy learned quickly what the old priest taught him, and was very obedient in most things. But he had one fault. He liked to draw cats during study-hours, and to draw cats even where cats ought not to have been drawn at all.

Whenever he found himself alone, he drew cats. He drew them on the margins of the priest's books, and on all the screens of the temple, and on the walls, and on the pillars. Several times the priest told him this was not right; but he did not stop drawing cats. He drew them because he could not really help it. He had what is called "the genius of an *artist*," and just for that reason he was not quite fit to be an acolyte;—a good acolyte should study books.

One day after he had drawn some very clever pictures of cats upon a paper screen, the old priest said to him severely: "My boy, you must go away from this temple at once.

You will never make a good priest, but perhaps you will become a great artist. Now let me give you a last piece of advice, and be sure you never forget it. *Avoid large places at night;—keep to small!*"

The boy did not know what the priest meant by saying, "*Avoid large places;—keep to small.*" He thought and thought, while he was tying up his little bundle of clothes to go away; but he could not understand those words, and he was afraid to speak to the priest any more, except to say good-by.

He left the temple very sorrowfully, and began to wonder what he should do. If he went straight home he felt sure his father would punish him for having been disobedient to the priest: so he was afraid to go home. All at once he remembered that at the next village, twelve miles away, there was a very big temple. He had heard there were several priests at that temple; and he made up his mind to go to them and ask them to take him for their acolyte.

Now that big temple was closed up but the boy did not know this fact. The reason it had been closed up was that a goblin had frightened the priests away, and had taken possession of the place. Some brave warriors had afterward gone to the temple at night to kill the goblin; but they had never been seen alive again. Nobody had ever told these things to the boy;—so he walked all the way to the village hoping to be kindly treated by the priests.

When he got to the village it was already dark, and all the people were in bed; but he saw the big temple on a hill at the other end of the principal street, and he saw there was a light in the temple. People who tell the story say the goblin used to make that light, in order to tempt lonely travelers to ask for shelter. The boy went at once to the temple, and knocked. There was no sound inside. He knocked and knocked again; but still nobody came. At last he pushed gently at the door, and was quite glad to find that it had not been fastened. So he went in, and saw a lamp burning,—but no priest. He thought some priest would be sure to come very soon, and he sat down and waited. Then he noticed that everything in the temple was gray with dust, and thickly spun over with cobwebs. So he thought to himself that the priests would certainly like to have an acolyte, to keep the place clean. He wondered why they had allowed everything to get so dusty. What most pleased him, however, were some big white screens, good to paint cats upon. Though he was tired, he looked at once for a writing-box, and found one, and ground some ink, and began to paint cats.

He painted a great many cats upon the screens; and then he began to feel very, very sleepy. He was just on the point of lying down to sleep beside one of the screens, when he suddenly remembered the words, *"Avoid large places;—keep to small!"*

The temple was very large; he was all alone; and as he thought of these words,—though he could not quite understand them—he began to feel for the first time a little afraid; and he resolved to look for a *small plac*e in which to sleep. He found a little cabinet, with a sliding door, and went into it, and shut himself up. Then he lay down and fell fast asleep.

Very late in the night he was awakened by a most terrible noise,—a noise of fighting and screaming. It was so dreadful that he was afraid even to look through a chink of the little cabinet: he lay very still, holding his breath for fright.

The light that had been in the temple went out; but the awful sounds continued, and became more awful, and all the temple shook. After a long time silence came; but the boy was still afraid to move. He did not move until the light of the morning sun shone into the cabinet through the chinks of the little door.

Then he got out of his hiding-place very cautiously, and looked about. The first thing he saw was that all the floor of the temple was covered with blood. And then he saw, lying dead in the middle of it, an enormous, monstrous rat,—a goblin-rat,—bigger than a cow!

But who or what could have killed it? There was no man or other creature to be seen. Suddenly the boy observed that the mouths of all the cats he had drawn the night before, were red and wet with blood. Then he knew that the goblin had been killed by the cats which he had drawn. And then also, for the first time, he understood why the wise old priest had said to him, *Avoid large places at night;—keep to small.*" Afterward that boy became a very famous artist. Some of the cats which he drew are still shown to travelers in Japan.

The Crimson Curse

Tony LaMalfa

"What a man does for pay is of little significance. What he is, as a sensitive instrument responsive to the world's beauty, is everything!"

~H. P. Lovecraft

As a well-respected civil engineer in the good graces of officials responsible for the development of Providence, I fervently supported any expansion of the city's infrastructure. The advent of the automobile simultaneously marked an eclipsing of public transit, and if I were to stay ahead of the proverbial curve, it was in my best interest to arduously defend any reigning technology of the foreseeable future. As such, I relished the daily drive in my premium green Cadillac Series 341B from our family home on College Hill to my office at City Hall.

My usual route to work brought me past the Rhode Island State House, whose glorious marble dome—topped with its bronze statue of The Independent Man—gleamed in the morning sun, a testament to the liberty and order around which my reality was constructed. Upon making the return trip down Dorrance and Dyre Streets, across the Point Street Bridge and then back north along Benefit Street, I never failed to be impressed at how Providence Harbor represented an unadulterated blend of bustling cityscape with healthy maritime commerce.

Thus I drove, day after day, leaving for home in the mid-afternoon—stopping by the post office if necessary—and smiling at the ever-expanding campus of my alma mater, Brown University.

With our two adult children off starting families of their own, I had resolved to purchase the Cadillac as an early retirement gift, with no small amount of disapproval from my loving wife, Sarah. However, a recent accident involving the unceremonious dashing of a stray animal in front of my vehicle resulted in regrettable damage to its front left wheel.

After an exceptionally long and tiresome day at the office, I was admiring the late July sunset over Prospect Terrace before approaching my turnoff at the corner of Congdon Street and Lloyd Lane. As I started to execute the right-hand turn, a pesky stray suddenly darted out from the passenger side, and I veered left to avoid hitting the creature—though still doing so, despite my efforts. The bumper and driver's side fender penetrated the tire wall upon impact with a fire hydrant, which began spouting water and would need to be seen to by public works immediately.

All told, the vehicle could be repaired in short order; but regardless, I would report the incident to my younger brother, a local police officer who—under the right pressure—would withhold the mishap from the newspapers to protect my career. Yet before stumbling home to make that particular call, I inspected the road for the remains of the blasted stray and was amazed to find only a small pool of blood where I had struck the animal. More than anything, I was disturbed by the fact that the crimson liquid emitted a putrid stench so offensive I could not help but gag several times over.

It was on Tuesday, the day following that ill-fated accident involving my prized Cadillac, when a series of unsettling events began to unfold. Departing a full hour earlier than usual, I begrudgingly walked the distance to City Hall. Sleep had not come easily, as I was in the throes of preparing for an important meeting on Wednesday with Governor Case and his staff, during which I would deliver a proposal suggesting a complete renovation of the area between

Fox Point and the Washington Street Bridge. This neighborhood had fallen by the wayside, in my opinion, having degenerated to cheap tracts of land upon which impoverished immigrants and their mangy pets congregated over the past decade—making it prime real estate for future road development!

Not long into my morning trek, I became turned around at what was undoubtedly the west end of Lloyd Lane, where the accident had occurred. On the ground lay a gruesome sight of horrific description: a tabby's corpse decorated the pavement, its face shorn clear off from a traumatic blow. Dried blood was pooled in a spot not far from where I had found fresh blood the night before, but again, I recalled having seen no carcass to speak of.

I covered my nose with a handkerchief to reduce exposure to a familiar, repugnant odor emanating from the creature's lifeless body and noticed a tiny charm fastened around the dead animal's neck. But before I might investigate further, I was rendered lightheaded by that morbid scene splayed across the cement. Turning to head what I believed to be north—or was it south?—I hurried onward, taking comfort at the sight of the replacement fire hydrant . . . at least public works was still dependable.

Checking my Rolex Oyster Perpetual, I was relieved to see there was still plenty of time for me to arrive at least a quarter of an hour early to my office. However, after nearly thirty minutes of wandering the streets, I grew discouraged by my lack of progress. Even the magnificent dome of the State House—usually a reliable landmark—eluded me in those moments. I was not accustomed to being lost in Providence and eventually found my way, albeit bewildered by the path I had purportedly taken.

With only a minute to spare, I breached the entrance to City Hall and quickly ascended the stairs—unkempt, perspiring, and out of breath. A steady day of work ensued as I recovered my faculties and continued preparing my proposal, with my secretary, Miss Lillibridge, asking minimal questions as to the disagreeable state in which I had arrived.

Around eleven o'clock, my wife telephoned the office to suggest we meet for a late afternoon picnic at Tockwotton Park, anticipated to be a moment of relaxation before the stress of tomorrow's meeting with the governor. Sarah would bring a basket filled with a sumptuous feast while I, in turn, would present her with a fresh bouquet of white Asiatic lilies: her favorite flower. There was a florist on Brook Street, Barney Bros., from whom we always purchased, and I agreed that if my preparations were completed, I would call her to confirm our picnic engagement.

The only other notable interruption came as a self-imposed break to peruse Sanborn insurance maps of Providence, an attempt to rationalize my confusing trip from Lloyd Lane to City Hall. But alas, I could not locate the road, nor any specific intersection, from which my intended course had deviated. *Perhaps,* I reasoned, *age was finally catching up with me . . .*

Later that day I experienced a deep satisfaction upon delivering the finishing touches to my proposal yet became more than a little dismayed when I could not raise Sarah at home. Three times I telephoned her, and three times I received no answer. Assuming she was already en route to our picnic rendezvous, I bid my secretary good day, obtained the conciliatory bouquet of lilies, and made for Tockwotton Park.

It was down a side street perpendicular to Hope, in the heart of that very neighborhood in which my proposal would restore decency, where I again lost my way. The brushing of a stray black cat against my pant leg—combined with a strange pungency from the flowers, which I knew to hold no fragrance—evoked an inexplicable sense of mounting dread. This feeling was further intensified by a light breeze that stirred a nearby set of wind chimes and foretold of angry clouds visibly gathering in the south.

At the park, I became truly concerned when I found Sarah's gingham blanket unattended, with her lacy handkerchief discarded next to our wicker basket. All of a sudden, from somewhere to the southeast, beyond India Point, I heard her voice softly calling my name: "Daniel . . . *Daniel* . . ."

It sounded as if she were on the move, so I followed, leaving the park and stopping only once at the railroad yard to pick up her cream-colored hat from the dirty tracks. Turning the accessory over with apprehension, I recoiled in terror at the bloodstains soaked into its inner fabric.

Before this, I had imagined Sarah playfully luring me to her like Odysseus and his crew to the Sirens, but I now traversed the train bridge over the Seekonk River in sheer panic, chasing a voice that began to scream urgently for me from a place southwest of Fort Hill. The sky, a dull mixture of pale pink and sickly yellow hues, was all but blotted out by dark clouds silhouetted against increasingly frequent strikes of silent lightning. The humid air positively thrummed, bearing the unbridled power of nature and carrying with it a scent of wet, heavy malignancy indicative of a mighty storm . . . yet no rain fell.

Screeching seagulls made landfall above me as my aching body raced in the opposite direction, bound for the Wilkes Barre Pier, underneath that turbulent weather rolling in off Narragansett Bay. However, when I reached the end of the pier—shaking with adrenaline—my beloved Sarah was nowhere to be found, and her frantic voice no longer guided me forward.

Instead, I was met with a hideous trauma. Looking down into the rough waves, I saw her beautiful face: white as porcelain and wearing the tranquility of a death mask, despite the wild flashes of lightning and howling wind around us!

And still, no rain fell . . .

I dropped to the ground, heedless of pain as my careworn knees struck the pier with a loud crack. But before I could mourn the apparent loss of my wife, I was startled from that haze of disbelief by the gentle mewing of a cat behind me. I spun around as the first crash of thunder came down from the heavens, ominously punctuating the entrance of a lone tabby. It tiptoed toward me as if to provide comfort. Unsure of its intentions, I did not touch its gray fur but noticed a charm dangling from its fragile neck, on which the word "Ulthar" was carved.

As the peculiar name left my lips, a second rumbling of thunder brought about the start of a rain shower. The cool precipitation would have been welcome had its fat drops not begun to burn my skin upon contact! The tabby wailed in agony as acidic, crimson rain poured down upon us. Insanity overtook me when the fur-covered flesh of the cat's face and dilated eyes melted to the ground, revealing that same grisly carnage I had witnessed at Lloyd Lane, concerning the animal I most assuredly ran over with my Cadillac the night before.

I cried in never-ending torment and lost my mind when a sizable group of cats approached from the open end of the pier. At this, I took flight—desperate to escape their feline fury—and dove headlong into the bloody waters of the harbor below!

"Mr. Monahan . . . *Mr. Monahan.*"

My head snapped up, nearly striking Miss Lillibridge as I came to. Apparently I had dozed off at my desk, and the secretary was rousing me so I might receive a telephone call.

"It's *Mrs.* Monahan," she said, with a tone of criticism at my falling asleep on the job.

In as few words as possible, I rejected Sarah's offer to meet for a picnic. Hanging up the phone, I left City Hall early and rode the trolley past Tockwotton Park to the station nearest our house, where I savored a home-cooked meal with my wife—grateful for her safety.

That evening I contacted the road commissioner and postponed my meeting with the governor . . . indefinitely. The final shock that drove me to such drastic measures was this: after taking out the trash, I spied a snow-white cat—illuminated and waiting—under a nearby street lamp. In its delicate maw it carried a single crimson flower . . . a blood-red Asiatic lily.

The Sphinx at Gizeh

Lord Dunsany

I saw the other day the Sphinx's painted face.

She had painted her face in order to ogle Time.

And he has spared no other painted face in all the world but hers.

Delilah was younger than she, and Delilah is dust.

Time hath loved nothing but this worthless painted face.

I do not care that she is ugly, nor that she has painted her face, so that she only lure his secret from Time.

Time dallies like a fool at her feet when he should be smiting cities.

Time never wearies of her silly smile.

There are temples all about her that he has forgotten to spoil.

I saw an old man go by and Time never touched him.

Time that has carried away the seven gates of Thebes!

She has tried to bind him with ropes of eternal sand, she had hoped to oppress him with the Pyramids.

He lies there in the sun with his foolish hair all spread about her paws.

If she ever learns his secret we will put out his eyes, so that he shall find no more our beautiful things—there are lovely gates in Florence that I fear he will carry away.

We have tried to bind him with song and with old customs, but they only held him for a little while, and he has always smitten us and mocked us.

When he is blind he shall dance to us and make sport.

Great clumsy Time shall stumble and dance, who liked to kill little children and can hurt even the daisies no longer.

Then shall our children laugh at him who slew Babylon's winged bulls and smote great numbers of the elves and fairies, when he is shorn of his hours and his years.

We will shut him up in the Pyramid of Cheops, in the great chamber where the sarcophagus is. Thence we will lead him out when we give our feasts. He shall ripen our corn for us and do menial work.

We will kiss thy painted face, O Sphinx, if thou wilt betray to us Time.

And yet I fear that in his ultimate anguish he may take hold blindly of the world and the moon and slowly pull down upon him the House of Man.

The King of Cats

Adam Bolivar

In a wicked wood,   where witches meet,
And ravens roost   in rowan trees,
I came across   an uncanny scene
In remote ruins,   rotted by ages:
A cavalcade of cats,   a coffin on their backs,
A crown resting   on the casket's lid,
Strode by stately,   the strangest sight.
Raving, I ran   rapidly homeward,
Where my wife wondered   at my worried looks.
I told my tale,   and Tin, my cat,
Who was sleeping soundly   by the snapping fire,
Jumped up jubilantly   and jigged on hind-legs.
"Then I am King of Cats!"   he cried with glee.
And vaulted up the chimney   to vanish evermore.

In the Valley of the Sorceress
Sax Rohmer

1

Condor wrote to me three times before the end (said Neville, Assistant-Inspector of Antiquities, staring vaguely from his open window at a squad drilling before the Kasr-en-Nîl Barracks). He dated his letters from the camp at Deir-el-Bahari. Judging from these, success appeared to be almost within his grasp. He shared my theories, of course, respecting Queen Hatasu, and was devoting the whole of his energies to the task of clearing up the great mystery of Ancient Egypt which centres around that queen.

For him, as for me, there was a strange fascination about those defaced walls and roughly obliterated inscriptions. That the queen under whom Egyptian art came to the apogee of perfection should thus have been treated by her successors; that no perfect figure of the wise, famous, and beautiful Hatasu should have been spared to posterity; that her very cartouche should have been ruthlessly removed from every inscription upon which it appeared, presented to Condor's mind a problem only second in interest to the immortal riddle of Gîzeh.

You know my own views upon the matter? My monograph, "Hatasu, the Sorceress," embodies my opinion. In short, upon certain evidences, some adduced by Theodore Davis, some by poor Condor, and some resulting from my own inquiries, I have come to the conclusion that the source—real or imaginary—of this queen's power was an intimate acquaintance with what nowadays we term, vaguely, magic. Pursuing her studies beyond the limit which is lawful, she met with a certain end, not uncommon, if the old writings are to be believed, in the case of those who penetrate too far into the realms of the Borderland.

For this reason—the practice of black magic—her statues were dishonored, and her name erased from the monuments. Now, I do not propose to enter into any discussion respecting the reality of such practices; in my monograph I have merely endeavored to show that, according to contemporary belief, the queen was a sorceress. Condor was seeking to prove the same thing; and when I took up the inquiry, it was in the hope of completing his interrupted work.

He wrote to me early in the winter of 1908, from his camp by the Rock Temple. Davis's tomb, at Bibân el-Mulûk, with its long, narrow passage, apparently had little interest for him; he was at work on the high ground behind the temple, at a point one hundred yards or so due west of the upper platform. He had an idea that he should find there the mummies of Hatasu—and another; the latter, a certain Sen-Mût, who appears in the inscriptions of the reign as an architect high in the queen's favor. The archæological points of the letter do not concern us in the least, but there was one odd little paragraph which I had cause to remember afterwards.

"A girl belonging to some Arab tribe," wrote Condor, "came racing to the camp two nights ago to claim my protection. What crime she had committed, and what punishment she feared, were far from clear; but she clung to me, trembling like a leaf, and positively refused to depart. It was a difficult situation, for a camp of fifty native excavators, and one highly respectable European enthusiast, affords no suitable quarters for an Arab girl—and a very personable Arab girl. At any rate, she is still here; I have had a sort of lean-to rigged up in a little valley east of my own tent, but it is very embarrassing."

Nearly a month passed before I heard from Condor again; then came a second letter, with the news that on the eve of a great discovery—as he believed—his entire native staff—the whole fifty—had deserted one night in a body! "Two days' work," he wrote, "would have seen the tomb opened—for I am more than ever certain that my plans are accurate. Then I woke up one morning to find every man Jack of my fellows missing! I went down into the village where a lot of them live, in a towering rage, but not one of the brutes was to be found, and their relations professed entire ignorance respecting their whereabouts. What caused me almost as much anxiety as the check in my work was the fact that Mahâra—the Arab girl—had vanished also. I am wondering if the thing has any sinister significance."

Condor finished with the statement that he was making tremendous efforts to secure a new gang. "But," said he, "I shall finish the excavation, if I have to do it with my own hands."

His third and last letter contained even stranger matters than the two preceding it. He had succeeded in borrowing a few men from the British Archæological camp in the Fáyûm. Then, just as the work was restarting, the Arab girl, Mahâra, turned up again, and entreated him to bring her down the Nile, "at least as far as Dendera. For the vengeance of her tribesmen," stated Condor, "otherwise would result not only in her own death, but in mine! At the moment of writing I am in two minds what to do. If Mahâra is to go upon this journey, I do not feel justified in sending her alone, and there is no one here who could perform the duty," etc.

I began to wonder, of course; and I had it in mind to take the train to Luxor merely in order to see this Arab maiden, who seemed to occupy so prominent a place in Condor's mind. However, Fate would have it otherwise; and the next thing I heard was that Condor had been brought into Cairo, and was at the English hospital.

He had been bitten by a cat—presumably from the neighboring village; and although the doctor at Luxor dealt with the bite at once, traveled down with him, and placed him in the hand of the Pasteur man at the hospital, he died, as you remember, in the night of his arrival, raving mad; the Pasteur treatment failed entirely.

I never saw him before the end, but they told me that his

howls were horribly like those of a cat. His eyes changed in some way, too, I understand; and, with his fingers all contracted, he tried to scratch everyone and everything within reach.

They had to strap the poor beggar down, and even then he tore the sheets into ribbons.

Well, as soon as possible, I made the necessary arrangements to finish Condor's inquiry. I had access to his papers, plans, etc., and in the spring of the same year I took up my quarters near Deir-el-Bahari, roped off the approaches to the camp, stuck up the usual notices, and prepared to finish the excavation, which, I gathered, was in a fairly advanced state.

My first surprise came very soon after my arrival, for when, with the plan before me, I started out to find the shaft, I found it, certainly, but only with great difficulty.

It had been filled in again with sand and loose rock right to the very top!

2

All my inquiries availed me nothing. With what object the excavation had been thus closed I was unable to conjecture. That Condor had not reclosed it I was quite certain, for at the time of his mishap he had actually been at work at the bottom of the shaft, as inquiries from a native of Suefee, in the Fáyûm, who was his only companion at the time, had revealed.

In his eagerness to complete the inquiry, Condor, by lantern light, had been engaged upon a solitary night-shift below, and the rabid cat had apparently fallen into the pit; probably in a frenzy of fear, it had attacked Condor, after which it had escaped.

Only this one man was with him, and he, for some reason that I could not make out, had apparently been sleeping in the temple—quite a considerable distance from Condor's camp. The poor fellow's cries had aroused him, and he had met Condor running down the path and away from the shaft.

This, however, was good evidence of the existence of the shaft at the time, and as I stood contemplating the tightly packed rubble which alone marked its site, I grew more and more mystified, for this task of reclosing the cutting represented much hard labor.

Beyond perfecting my plans in one or two particulars, I did little on the day of my arrival. I had only a handful of men with me, all of whom I knew, having worked with them before, and beyond clearing Condor's shaft I did not intend to excavate further.

Hatasu's Temple presents a lively enough scene in the daytime during the winter and early spring months, with the streams of tourists constantly passing from the white causeway to Cook's Rest House on the edge of the desert. There had been a goodly number of visitors that day to the temple below, and one or two of the more curious and venturesome had scrambled up the steep path to the little plateau which was the scene of my operations. None had penetrated beyond the notice boards, however, and now, with the evening sky passing through those innumerable shades which defy palette and brush, which can only be distinguished by the trained eye, but which, from palest blue melt into exquisite pink, and by some magical combination form that deep violet which does not exist to perfection elsewhere than in the skies of Egypt, I found myself in the silence and the solitude of "the Holy Valley."

I stood at the edge of the plateau, looking out at the rosy belt which marked the course of the distant Nile, with the Arabian hills vaguely sketched beyond. The rocks stood up against that prospect as great black smudges, and what I could see of the causeway looked like a gray smear upon a drab canvas. Beneath me were the chambers of the Rock Temple, with those wall paintings depicting events in the reign of Hatasu which rank among the wonders of Egypt.

Not a sound disturbed my reverie, save a faint clatter of cooking utensils from the camp behind me—a desecration of that sacred solitude. Then a dog began to howl in the neighboring village. The dog ceased, and faintly to my ears came the note of a reed pipe. The breeze died away, and with it the piping.

I turned back to the camp, and, having partaken of a frugal supper, turned in upon my campaigner's bed, thoroughly enjoying my freedom from the routine of official life in Cairo, and looking forward to the morrow's work pleasurably.

Under such circumstances a man sleeps well; and when, in an uncanny gray half-light, which probably heralded the dawn, I awoke with a start, I knew that something of an unusual nature alone could have disturbed my slumbers.

Firstly, then, I identified this with a concerted howling of the village dogs. They seemed to have conspired to make night hideous; I have never heard such an eerie din in my life. Then it gradually began to die away, and I realized, secondly, that the howling of the dogs and my own awakening might be due to some common cause. This idea grew upon me, and as the howling subsided, a sort of disquiet possessed me, and, despite my efforts to shake it off, grew more urgent with the passing of every moment.

In short, I fancied that the thing which had alarmed or enraged the dogs was passing from the village through the Holy Valley, upward to the Temple, upward to the plateau, and was approaching me.

I have never experienced an identical sensation since, but I seemed to be audient of a sort of psychic patrol, which, from a remote *pianissimo*, swelled *fortissimo*, to an intimate but silent clamor, which beat in some way upon my brain, but not through the faculty of hearing, for now the night was deathly still.

Yet I was persuaded of some *approach*—of the coming of something sinister, and the suspense of waiting had become almost insupportable, so that I began to accuse my Spartan supper of having given me nightmare, when the tent-flap was suddenly raised, and, outlined against the paling blue of the sky, with a sort of reflected elfin light playing upon her face, I saw an Arab girl looking in at me!

By dint of exerting all my self-control I managed to restrain the cry and upward start which this apparition prompted. Quite still, with my fists tightly clenched, I lay and looked into the eyes which were looking into mine.

The style of literary work which it has been my lot to cultivate fails me in describing that beautiful and evil face. The features were severely classical and small, something of the Bisharîn type, with a cruel little mouth and a rounded chin, firm to hardness. In the eyes alone lay the languor of the Orient; they were exceedingly—indeed, excessively—long and narrow. The ordinary ragged, picturesque finery of a desert girl bedecked this midnight visitant, who, motionless, stood there watching me.

I once read a work by Pierre de l'Ancre, dealing with the Black Sabbaths of the Middle Ages, and now the evil beauty of this Arab face threw my memory back to those singular pages, for, perhaps owing to the reflected light which I have mentioned, although the explanation scarcely seemed adequate, those long, narrow eyes shone catlike in the gloom.

Suddenly I made up my mind. Throwing the blanket from me, I leapt to the ground, and in a flash had gripped the girl by the wrists. Confuting some lingering doubts, she proved to be substantial enough. My electric torch lay upon a box at the foot of the bed, and, stooping, I caught it up and turned its searching rays upon the face of my captive.

She fell back from me, panting like a wild creature trapped, then dropped upon her knees and began to plead—began to plead in a voice and with a manner which touched some chord of consciousness that I could swear had never spoken before, and has never spoken since.

She spoke in Arabic, of course, but the words fell from her lips as liquid music in which lay all the beauty and all the deviltry of the "Siren's Song." Fully opening her astonishing eyes, she looked up at me, and, with her free hand pressed to her bosom, told me how she had fled from an unwelcome marriage; how, an outcast and a pariah, she had hidden in the desert places for three days and three nights, sustaining life only by means of a few dates which she had brought with her, and quenching her thirst with stolen water-melons.

"I can bear it no longer, *effendim*. Another night out in the desert, with the cruel moon beating, beating, beating upon my brain, with creeping things coming out from the rocks, wriggling, wriggling, their many feet making whisperings in the sand—ah, it will kill me! And I am for ever outcast from my tribe, from my people. No tent of all the Arabs, though I fly to the gates of Damascus, is open to me, save I enter in shame, as a slave, as a plaything, as a toy. My heart"—furiously she beat upon her breast—"is empty and desolate, *effendim*. I am meaner than the lowliest thing that creeps upon the sand; yet the God that made that creeping thing made me also—and you, you, who are merciful and strong, would not crush any creature because it was weak and helpless."

I had released her wrist now, and was looking down at her in a sort of stupor. The evil which at first I had seemed to perceive in her was effaced, wiped out as an artist wipes out an error in his drawing. Her dark beauty was speaking to me in a language of its own; a strange language, yet one so intelligible that I struggled in vain to disregard it. And her voice, her gestures, and the witch-fire of her eyes were whipping up my blood to a fever heat of passionate sorrow—of despair. Yes, incredible as it sounds, despair!

In short, as I see it now, this siren of the wilderness was playing upon me as an accomplished musician might play upon a harp, striking this string and that at will, and sounding each with such full notes as they had rarely, if ever, emitted before.

Most damnable anomaly of all, I—Edward Neville, archæologist, most prosy and matter-of-fact man in Cairo, perhaps—*knew* that this nomad who had burst into my tent, upon whom I had set eyes for the first time scarce three minutes before, held me enthralled; and yet, with her wondrous eyes upon me, I could summon up no resentment, and could offer but poor resistance.

"In the Little Oasis, *effendim,* I have a sister who will admit me into her household, if only as a servant. There I can be safe, there I can rest. O *Inglîsi,* at home in England you have a sister of your own! Would you see her pursued, a hunted thing from rock to rock, crouching for shelter in the lair of some jackal, stealing that she might live—and flying always, never resting, her heart leaping for fear, flying, flying, with nothing but dishonor before her?"

She shuddered and clasped my left hand in both her own convulsively, pulling it down to her bosom.

"There can be only one thing, *effendim,*" she whispered. "Do you not see the white bones bleaching in the sun?"

Throwing all my resolution into the act, I released my hand from her clasp, and, turning aside, sat down upon the box which served me as chair and table, too.

A thought had come to my assistance, had strengthened me in the moment of my greatest weakness; it was the thought of that Arab girl mentioned in Condor's letters. And a scheme of things, an incredible scheme, that embraced and explained some, if not all, of the horrible circumstances attendant upon his death, began to form in my brain.

Bizarre it was, stretching out beyond the realm of things natural and proper, yet I clung to it, for there, in the solitude, with this wildly beautiful creature kneeling at my feet, and with her uncanny powers of fascination yet enveloping me like a cloak, I found it not so improbable as inevitably it must have seemed at another time.

I turned my head, and through the gloom sought to look into the long eyes. As I did so they closed and appeared as two darkly luminous slits in the perfect oval of the face.

"You are an impostor!" I said in Arabic, speaking firmly and deliberately. "To Mr. Condor"—I could have sworn that she started slightly at sound of the name—"you called yourself Mahâra. I know you, and I will have nothing to do with you."

But in saying it I had to turn my head aside, for the strangest, maddest impulses were bubbling up in my brain in response to the glances of those half-shut eyes.

I reached for my coat, which lay upon the foot of the bed, and, taking out some loose money, I placed fifty piastres in the nerveless brown hand.

"That will enable you to reach the Little Oasis, if such is your desire," I said. "It is all I can do for you, and now—you must go."

The light of the dawn was growing stronger momentarily, so that I could see my visitor quite clearly. She rose to her feet, and stood before me, a straight, slim figure, sweeping me from head to foot with such a glance of passionate contempt as I had never known or suffered.

She threw back her head magnificently, dashed the money on the ground at my feet, and, turning, leaped out of the tent.

For a moment I hesitated, doubting, questioning my humanity, testing my fears; then I took a step forward, and peered out across the plateau. Not a soul was in sight. The rocks stood up gray and eerie, and beneath lay the carpet of the desert stretching unbroken to the shadows of the Nile Valley.

3

We commenced the work of clearing the shaft at an early hour that morning. The strangest ideas were now playing in my mind, and in some way I felt myself to be in opposition to definite enmity. My excavators labored with a will, and, once we had penetrated below the first three feet or so of tightly packed stone, it became a mere matter of shoveling, for apparently the lower part of the shaft had been filled up principally with sand.

I calculated that four days' work at the outside would see the shaft clear to the base of Condor's excavation. There remained, according to his own notes, only another six feet or so; but it was solid limestone—the roof of the passage, if his plans were correct, communicating with the tomb of Hatasu.

With the approach of night, tired as I was, I felt little inclination for sleep. I lay down on my bed with a small Browning pistol under the pillow, but after an hour or so of nervous listening drifted off into slumber. As on the night before, I awoke shortly before the coming of dawn.

Again the village dogs were raising a hideous outcry, and again I was keenly conscious of some ever-nearing menace. This consciousness grew stronger as the howling of the dogs grew fainter, and the sense of *approach* assailed me as on the previous occasion.

I sat up immediately with the pistol in my hand, and, gently raising the tent flap, looked out over the darksome plateau. For a long time I could perceive nothing; then, vaguely outlined against the sky, I detected something that moved above the rocky edge.

It was so indefinite in form that for a time I was unable to identify it, but as it slowly rose higher and higher, two luminous eyes—obviously feline eyes, since they glittered greenly in the darkness—came into view. In character and in shape they were the eyes of a cat, but in point of size they were larger than the eyes of any cat I had ever seen. Nor were they jackal eyes. It occurred to me that some predatory beast from the Sûdan might conceivably have strayed thus far north.

The presence of such a creature would account for the nightly disturbance amongst the village dogs; and, dismissing the superstitious notions which had led me to associate the mysterious Arab girl with the phenomenon of the howling dogs, I seized upon this new idea with a sort of gladness.

Stepping boldly out of the tent, I strode in the direction of the gleaming eyes. Although my only weapon was the Browning pistol, it was a weapon of considerable power, and, moreover, I counted upon the well-known cowardice of nocturnal animals. I was not disappointed in the result.

The eyes dropped out of sight, and as I leaped to the edge of rock overhanging the temple a lithe shape went streaking off in the greyness beneath me. Its coloring appeared to be black, but this appearance may have been due to the bad light. Certainly it was no cat, was no jackal; and once, twice, thrice my Browning spat into the darkness.

Apparently I had not scored a hit, but the loud reports of the weapon aroused the men sleeping in the camp, and soon I was surrounded by a ring of inquiring faces.

But there I stood on the rock-edge, looking out across the desert in silence. Something in the long, luminous eyes, something in the sinuous, flying shape had spoken to me intimately, horribly.

Hassan es-Sugra, the headman, touched my arm, and I knew that I must offer some explanation.

"Jackals," I said shortly. And with no other word I walked back to my tent.

The night passed without further event, and in the morning we addressed ourselves to the work with such a will that I saw, to my satisfaction, that by noon of the following day the labor of clearing the loose sand would be completed.

During the preparation of the evening meal I became aware of a certain disquiet in the camp, and I noted a disinclination on the part of the native laborers to stray far from the tents. They hung together in a group, and whilst individually they seemed to avoid meeting my eye, collectively they watched me in a furtive fashion.

A gang of Moslem workmen calls for delicate handling, and I wondered if, inadvertently, I had transgressed in some way their iron-bound code of conduct. I called Hassan es-Sugra aside.

"What ails the men?" I asked him. "Have they some grievance?"

Hassan spread his palms eloquently.

"If they have," he replied, "they are secret about it, and I am not in their confidence. Shall I thrash three or four of them in order to learn the nature of this grievance?"

"No thanks all the same," I said, laughing at this characteristic proposal. "If they refuse to work to-morrow, there will be time enough for you to adopt those measures."

On this, the third night of my sojourn in the Holy Valley by the Temple of Hatasu, I slept soundly and uninterruptedly. I had been looking forward with the keenest zest to the morrow's work, which promised to bring me within sight of my goal, and when Hassan came to awaken me, I leaped out of bed immediately.

Hassan es-Sugra, having performed his duty, did not, as was his custom, retire; he stood there, a tall, angular figure, looking at me strangely.

"Well?" I said.

"There is trouble," was his simple reply. "Follow me, Neville Effendi."

Wondering greatly, I followed him across the plateau and down the slope to the excavation. There I pulled up short with a cry of amazement.

Condor's shaft was filled in to the very top, and presented, to my astonished gaze, much the same aspect that had greeted me upon my first arrival!

"The men—" I began.

Hassan es-Sugra spread wide his palms.

"Gone!" he replied. "Those Coptic dogs, those eaters of carrion, have fled in the night."

"And this"—I pointed to the little mound of broken granite and sand—"is their work?"

"So it would seem," was the reply; and Hassan sniffed his sublime contempt.

I stood looking bitterly at this destruction of my toils. The strangeness of the thing at the moment did not strike me, in my anger; I was only concerned with the outrageous impudence of the missing workmen, and if I could have laid hands upon one of them it had surely gone hard with him.

As for Hassan es-Sugra, I believe he would cheerfully have broken the necks of the entire gang. But he was a man of resource.

"It is so newly filled in," he said, "that you and I, in three days, or in four, can restore it to the state it had reached when those nameless dogs, who regularly prayed with their shoes on, those devourers of pork, began their dirty work."

His example was stimulating. I was not going to be beaten, either.

After a hasty breakfast, the pair of us set to work with pick and shovel and basket. We worked as those slaves must have worked whose toil was directed by the lash of the Pharaoh's overseer. My back acquired an almost permanent crook, and every muscle in my body seemed to be on fire. Not even in the midday heat did we slacken or stay our toils; and when dusk fell that night a great mound had arisen beside Condor's shaft, and we had excavated to a depth it had taken our gang double the time to reach.

When at last we threw down our tools in utter exhaustion, I held out my hand to Hassan, and wrung his brown fist enthusiastically. His eyes sparkled as he met my glance.

"Neville Effendi," he said, "you are a true Moslem!"

And only the initiated can know how high was the compliment conveyed.

That night I slept the sleep of utter weariness, yet it was not a dreamless sleep, or perhaps it was not so deep as I supposed, for blazing cat-eyes encircled me in my dreams, and a constant feline howling seemed to fill the night.

When I awoke the sun was blazing down upon the rock outside my tent, and, springing out of bed, I perceived, with amazement, that the morning was far advanced. Indeed, I could hear the distant voices of the donkey-boys and other harbingers of the coming tourists.

Why had Hassan es-Sugra not awakened me?

I stepped out of the tent and called him in a loud voice. There was no reply. I ran across the plateau to the edge of the hollow.

Condor's shaft had been reclosed to the top!

Language fails me to convey the wave of anger, amazement, incredulity, which swept over me. I looked across to the deserted camp and back to my own tent; I looked down at the mound, where but a few hours before had been a pit, and seriously I began to question whether I was mad or whether madness had seized upon all who had been with me. Then, pegged down upon the heap of broken stones, I perceived, fluttering, a small piece of paper.

Dully I walked across and picked it up. Hassan, a man of some education, clearly was the writer. It was a pencil scrawl in doubtful Arabic, and, not without difficulty, I deciphered it as follows:

"Fly, Neville Effendi! This is a haunted place!"

Standing there by the mound, I tore the scrap of paper into minute fragments, bitterly casting them from me upon the ground. It was incredible; it was insane.

The man who had written that absurd message, the man who had undone his own work, had the reputation of being fearless and honorable. He had been with me before a score of times, and had quelled petty mutinies in the camp in a manner which marked him a born overseer. I could not understand; I could scarcely believe the evidence of my own senses.

What did I do?

I suppose there are some who would have abandoned the thing at once and for always, but I take it that the national traits are strong within me. I went over to the camp and prepared my own breakfast; then, shouldering pick and shovel, I went down into the valley and set to work. What ten men could not do, what two men had failed to do, one man was determined to do.

It was about half an hour after commencing my toils, and when, I suppose, the surprise and rage occasioned by the discovery had begun to wear off, that I found myself making comparisons between my own case and that of Condor. It became more and more evident to me that events—mysterious events—were repeating themselves.

The frightful happenings attendant upon Condor's death were marshaling in my mind. The sun was blazing down upon me, and distant voices could be heard in the desert stillness. I knew that the plain below was dotted with pleasure-seeking tourists, yet nervous tremors shook me. Frankly, I dreaded the coming of the night.

Well, tenacity or pugnacity conquered, and I worked on until dusk. My supper despatched, I sat down on my bed and toyed with the Browning.

I realized already that sleep, under existing conditions, was impossible. I perceived that on the morrow I must abandon my one-man enterprise, pocket my pride, in a sense, and seek new assistants, new companions.

The fact was coming home to me conclusively that a menace, real and not mythical, hung over that valley. Although, in the morning sunlight and filled with indignation, I had thought contemptuously of Hassan es-Sugra, now, in the mysterious violet dusk so conducive to calm consideration, I was forced to admit that he was at least as brave a man as I. And he had fled! What did that night hold in keeping for me?

I will tell you what occurred, and it is the only explanation I have to give of why Condor's shaft, said to communicate with the real tomb of Hatasu, to this day remains unopened.

There, on the edge of my bed, I sat far into the night, not daring to close my eyes. But physical weariness conquered in the end, and, although I have no recollection of its coming, I must have succumbed to sleep, since I remember—can never forget—a repetition of the dream, or what I had assumed to be a dream, of the night before.

A ring of blazing green eyes surrounded me. At one point this ring was broken, and in a kind of nightmare panic I leaped at that promise of safety, and found myself outside the tent.

Lithe, slinking shapes hemmed me in—cat shapes, ghoul shapes, veritable figures of the pit. And the eyes, the shapes, although they were the eyes and shapes of cats, sometimes changed elusively, and became the wicked eyes and the sinuous, writhing shapes of women. Always the ring was incomplete, and always I retreated in the only direction by which retreat was possible. I retreated from those cat-things.

In this fashion I came at last to the shaft, and there I saw the tools which I had left at the end of my day's toil.

Looking around me, I saw also, with such a pang of horror as I cannot hope to convey to you, that the ring of green eyes was now unbroken about me.

And it was closing in.

Nameless feline creatures were crowding silently to the edge of the pit, some preparing to spring down upon me where I stood. A voice seemed to speak in my brain; it spoke of capitulation, telling me to accept defeat, lest, resisting, my fate be the fate of Condor.

Peals of shrill laughter rose upon the silence. The laughter was mine.

Filling the night with this hideous, hysterical merriment, I was working feverishly with pick and with shovel filling in the shaft.

The end? The end is that I awoke, in the morning, lying, not on my bed, but outside on the plateau, my hands torn and bleeding and every muscle in my body throbbing agonisingly. Remembering my dream—for even in that moment of awakening I thought I had dreamed—I staggered across to the valley of the excavation.

Condor's shaft was reclosed to the top.

La Gata

Lori R. Lopez

"Talk to La Gata."
I was led through a dark alley,
wondering if I'd see daylight again.
Embarked on a quest. Not fitting
in the ordinary world. Dysphoric,
at odds, I didn't wish to be human.
I wanted a tail, pointed ears.
I couldn't stand my bare skin!

There were rumors of a Cult
that welcomed those like me who
craved Metamorphosis. The M-Word.
Flesh tingling, I followed a catty
unchatty female into the shaft to
an underground realm defined by garish
graffiti, silhouettes, cat glyphs on walls.
A No Man's Land (or Woman's).

La Gata was a goddess, everything
I desired to become! The deformed
feline-feminine aspect, her smugly
intense gaze, the amber orbs and
fur-flecked complexion.
She led Cat Colony, recruiting
a wild pack to exist beyond the
parameters of Society and Norms.

"You are young." Even her accent
felt exotic, enticing. "Such change
bears a price. At an early age
the mind is not set. You would be
surprised how much you can still
transform without magick or other
means. Impressions, decisions,
experiences. You must wait."

A brusque dismissal, a gesture.
"Come back when you are truly
grown!" I struggled at the door.
"No! This is all I can think about!"
"Of course. Who doesn't want to
be something else at times?
We go through phases . . .
This isn't a game, a fantasy."

The Cat-Woman leaped toward me,
snarling, teeth grimacing, eyes
aglow. "It is a breaking of bones —
a destroying of your very nature!"
I shrank from the heat of her breath.
"You cannot switch back temporarily.
You cannot return to your old life.
You will cease to be."

Her bodyguard's grip on my arm
tightened. La Gata confronted me,
nose pressed to mine. "Understand.
The longer you are a cat, the more
uncivilized, instinctive, inhuman
you will behave. Ruthless. Savage.
Chimeric. That should not be
risked, unless absolutely certain."

I couldn't focus—eye to eye.
Was I certain? I couldn't think.
"You've heard of Werewolves
haven't you? Lycans transformed
from men. In these parts, if your
sister is bitten, she won't turn
into a dog. This is her fate!
But it is permanent. Forever."

A claw pricked my cheek.
"Full-Moon or broad daylight.
Meow!" Her fanglike teeth
exposed, threatening. A fierce
smile expanded lips. "There is
a golden aura for Gatas and silver
aura for Lobos. The two factions
battle. Arch-enemies."

Her claw stroked the base of my
chin. "Still here? I can always use
warriors. You will be trained in
the Feral Arts. Cat-Fighting."
She attacked, sinking those cusps
into my shoulder. I howled,
then contorted. An excruciating
moment. Shockingly abrupt.

Like her shift in mood, her
change of mind. Like her . . .
I had converted to a beast,
impulsive, cunning, mercurial.
Both beautiful and horrible.
She was right. I am no longer
me. I have shed my life
to serve La Gata.

Marked

Anna Taborska

*". . . thou art the Great Cat, the avenger of the gods, and
the judge of words, and the president of the sovereign chiefs,
and the governor of the holy Circle . . ."*
~From a tomb inscription in the Valley of the Kings

It had been a hard but satisfying day. The girl had fought val-
iantly for her life—particularly given her slight build and tender
age—and the very process of bagging up her body and weighing
it down with stones before depositing it into just the right spot
in the canal had been physically draining. The man took a sip of
his pint and gazed absentmindedly at the cat with the unusual
markings that had been his constant drinking companion ever
since he'd started frequenting The Organ Grinder.

The cat's coat was the light sandy brown of the desert at dusk,
with a cream throat and belly, narrow bands of dark fur around its
legs and black-tipped tail, and rings of white fur around its eyes.
The eyes themselves were the colour of sun-washed savannah,
and long pale hairs sprouted on the insides of its delicately tufted
orangey-brown ears. Its whiskers were long and white, its nose a
salmon pink, and a dark stripe ran the length of its back.

The man's thoughts turned from the cat back to the day's
events and he smiled to himself. He'd first chosen the girl—or
"marked her" as he liked to think of it—a month earlier. After
that it was simply a matter of following her home, observing her
movements, working out her daily routine, and picking the best
time and place to make his move.

As the time approached, the waiting, the watching, the antic- ipation had become almost unbearable, but in the end worth every minute—as it always was. The profound sense of calm he now felt would last for a couple of weeks—perhaps more, given the souvenir that he'd kept: a heart-shaped locket containing a photo of the smiling faces of the girl and her best friend. He'd keep the little silver-plated pendant in his secret place, and could take it out whenever he wanted to relive the day's events. When the burning need took hold of him again, the whole process would begin anew. And, thanks to the photo in the locket, he already had his next mark.

A nudge against his calf brought the man out of his reverie. He looked down at the cat, which was up to its usual trick of weaving between his legs, rubbing its flanks against his calves, but never allowing itself to be stroked. When it was done, it sat close by, staring intently up at him. The two locked eyes for a long moment.

The man finished his pint and was about to get up when the animal leapt on his lap, turned around as though it were about to lie down for a snooze, rubbing itself against the man's chest as it did so, and then was gone—jumping down before the man could react and disappearing into the darkness by the side of the bar.

Officers from the Metropolitan Police Service's Homicide and Major Crime Command had been watching the man for a while. The CCTV cameras near the school of the teenage victim had captured him several times walking on the opposite side of the road. There was no crime against walking in the street, but when the broken body of the girl was eventually found by police divers, the officer in charge of the investigation decided to take a chance and pay a visit to the man's West London home, along with his sergeant.

"Do you have any pets, sir?" asked Detective Chief Inspector Harrison, surreptitiously placing in his pocket the animal hair he'd spotted clinging to a jacket hanging over the back of a chair in the man's sitting-room.

"No." The man was genuinely surprised. "No, I don't. Why d'you ask?"

"No reason, sir. I just noticed some animal hair on your jacket there."

"Ah, I see," the man smiled, relaxing into the sofa. "It must be the cat from the pub.

It's all over me whenever I go in." DCI Harrison smiled and nodded. Reassured that there was nothing sinister behind the question, the man ventured a little joke. "Cats can tell who's good and who's bad, you know, Chief Inspector, so I must be a very good man . . . But seriously, I'm afraid I really can't help you. I hope you catch who did it, though."

"You mentioned a pub . . ." DCI Harrison wasn't going to let it go. One of the few surviving pieces of DNA evidence, given the state of decomposition of the girl's body after weeks in a bag in a canal, were a couple of sandy-coloured cat hairs that had been removed from the girl's hair and from the inside of the bag. And neither the girl's family, nor apparently anyone she knew, owned a cat with matching fur.

The man paused for moment, weighing up his options. He couldn't pretend that he'd forgotten the name of the pub because he'd already let the cat out the bag, as it were, by indicating that he'd been there more than once. If he gave the name of another pub and the police checked it out, they wouldn't find a cat in it and they'd wonder why he'd lied. If he gave them the right name, what was the worst that could happen? There was nothing linking any of the girls to the pub, and the police would see that he wasn't lying.

"The Organ Grinder," he finally said, adding casually in a bid to appear helpful: "It's just the other side of Southfield Green. Kind of a spooky old place, but quiet enough of an evening."

While waiting for the lab results to come in, DCI Harrison decided to go for a pint at The Organ Grinder. He was surprised he'd never come across the pub before. Then again, who'd want to drink in a pub painted entirely black on the exterior, and with lighting that hardly penetrated the creeping shadows inside?

"How can I help you?" the tired, sad-looking woman at the bar gazed at DCI Harrison with little enthusiasm.

"I'm DCI Harrison with the Metropolitan Police. I'd be grateful if you could take a look at this photo and tell me if you've seen this man before." He held out a photo of the man he'd recently visited.

"Yes," the woman behind the bar replied. "I first noticed him a few months ago, and since then he's become something of a regular. Has something happened to him?"

"Just routine questions, madam," said Harrison. "You must have a lot of customers.

How come you remember him so well?"

"It's a funny thing. There's a cat that hangs around the pub. I feed it sometimes, but it never lets me get anywhere near it. Or anybody else for that matter. Except for that man. Whenever he comes in, the cat's all over him."

"You mean he's the only one that can stroke it?"

"Not exactly. I mean, it follows him around everywhere, pesters him, even jumps on him. But I don't think he's ever actually managed to stroke it."

As DCI Harrison left The Organ Grinder, he thought he caught sight of a pair of green-flecked amber eyes glowing in the shadows under one of the tables. But when he looked closer, they were gone.

"*Felis silvestris lybica.* It's your African wildcat again." The forensics specialist looked distinctly pleased with himself. "This time I was prepared." The first time Harrison had brought him a couple of animal hairs—recovered from the body of the murdered girl—he'd had to consult with an American colleague and do a global database search, as the feline they came from didn't match anything native to Britain. A search of public and private zoos hadn't unearthed any missing stock, and there was no such animal listed on any veterinary database either.

"Thanks!" DCI Harrison headed swiftly for the door, convinced now that the man marked by the cat hair was the sick bastard he was after. Now he'd have to do everything by the book: get a search warrant, Miranda the man, help the Crown Prosecutor build a strong case.

"Detective Chief Inspector!" the forensics expert stopped Harrison for a moment. "You caught me by surprise last time, so I did a little reading. Most of our moggies are descended from the African wildcat, you know. But your cat is the real deal—they still live in the wild in Africa and the Middle East. In the past some of them chose to live with people because they could prey on rodents attracted by grain stores. They've been known to kills snakes and scorpions, so the Ancient Egyptians believed they could vanquish evil."

A year had passed since the successful prosecution and incarceration of the girl's killer. The cat with fur the colour of the desert, dubbed Monster by the barwoman—in revenge for the fact that it took the food she offered, but refused to come anywhere near her—continued to skulk around The Organ Grinder, startling the occasional punter with its silent footfall and soul-penetrating stare.

It was a surprisingly warm day in early March, when rays of the afternoon sun had somehow managed to invade the less gloomy corners of The Organ Grinder, and a small group of delivery boys from the local pizza parlour who had just finished their shift were playing a round of pool on the newly installed table.

The cat, which had been hiding in some spot of the pub

known only to itself, appeared suddenly by the entrance door, ears alert, and quivering from whiskers to tail. A moment later the door opened, and a tall, attractive brunette, well dressed and wearing large sunglasses, strode confidently in. Her sights were set on one of the young men playing pool; she'd singled him out for her own special brand of "cat and mouse," and she certainly wouldn't be assuming the role of *mus musculus*. She'd buy herself a drink and watch him for a while from a table that remained bathed in darkness despite the brightness of the day.

But first she had to shake the strange-looking cat that was rubbing itself against her legs and leaving pale-coloured hairs all over her black lace stockings.

The Cat and the Moon

W. B. Yeats

The cat went here and there
And the moon spun round like a top,
And the nearest kin of the moon
The creeping cat, looked up.
Black Minnaloushe stared at the moon,
For wander and wail as he would
The pure cold light in the sky
Troubled his animal blood.
Minnaloushe runs in the grass
Lifting his delicate feet.
Do you dance, Minnaloushe, do you dance?
When two close kindred meet
What better than call a dance,
Maybe the moon may learn,
Tired of that courtly fashion,
A new dance turn.
Minnaloushe creeps through the grass
From moonlit place to place,
The sacred moon overhead
Has taken a new phase.
Does Minnaloushe know that his pupils
Will pass from change to change,
And that from round to crescent,
From crescent to round they range?
Minnaloushe creeps through the grass
Alone, important and wise,

And lifts to the changing moon
His changing eyes.

The Adventure of the
Hanoverian Vampires

Darrell Schweitzer

I found it. It was mine, a pretty, shiny thing, which I found amusing to swat about on the ground for several minutes, watching the evening sunlight gleam off the polished surface. Then, of course, I lost interest and left it where it lay. But it was still mine. So when one of the "street arabs"—verminous boys—snatched it up, I yowled in protest and gave the villain a fine raking on the calf.

He yowled right back and kicked me away. I landed nimbly and hissed, ready for another round of combat.

"What have you got there, Billy?" came another voice.

"I dunno, Mr. 'Olmes."

"I'll give you a shilling for it."

The transaction was done, though the shiny object was still mine.

But now I was content, for the trouser leg I rubbed against belonged to the most perceptive of all human beings, the Great Detective himself, and the result of that encounter is the only Sherlock Holmes adventure ever narrated by a cat.

It is not possible for me to give you my name, for the true names of cats are never revealed outside our secretive tribe, and not even Sherlock Holmes may deduce them; whether the street arabs or Dr. Watson called me Fluffy or Mouser or something far less complimentary is, frankly, beneath notice. Suffice it to say that Holmes and I had a certain understanding by which we recognized and respected each other. You won't read of any of this in the chronicles penned by the doltish Watson, an altogether inferior lump of clay, who once owned a bulldog pup, probably without appreciating the crucial distinction that one owns a dog but entertains a cat. A dog is a useful object, even as, I suppose, Watson at times was useful.

But he tried to shoo me way, hissing, "Scat!" and other ridiculous imprecations, before Holmes drew his attention to the object in hand.

"It is the clue we have been seeking," said he. "Come, Watson, we have much to do this night. It would be well if you brought your revolver."

Moments later, all three of us were clattering along the rapidly darkening streets of London in a hansom. At first the driver, like the boorish Watson, objected to my presence, but Holmes gave the driver an extra coin. Watson, doglike, acquiesced. Holmes would have found it useless to explain to him that cats partake of the most ancient mysteries of the dark, and so have a proper place in any night of intrigue and adventure.

It was indeed such a night.

As we wove through the narrow, filthy streets of the East End, past increasingly disreputable denizens, Holmes held up the shiny thing—which I now conceded I had lent to Mr. Holmes.

"Deduce, Watson."

I assume this was a game for Holmes, like swatting a ball of string.

"It is a very thin locket," said Watson, "for I see that a spring-lock opens it—"

"Look out, Watson!" cried Holmes, for Watson had unthinkingly sprung open the locket, allowing a scrap of paper to flutter out. Deftly, Holmes snatched the paper out of the air.

"What is it, Holmes?"

"Momentarily, Watson. First, the locket."

"It and its chain are gold-plated."

"Not silver, Watson. Perhaps you will see the significance of that."

Obviously not. Watson continued. "On one side, is a female portrait—not an attractive one, I dare say—"

"I shall entirely trust your judgment in that department, Watson. Pray, continue."

"She wears a royal crown. The inscription is in German, and it reads: VICTORIA KAISERIN GROSS BRITANNIEN—Good God, Holmes!"

"Yes, Watson, it is the emblem of the current Hanoverian pretender, whose plottings against our king and country never cease, even after the failure—so ably chronicled by another writer—of the desperate scheme to place St. Paul's Cathedral on rollers and wheel it into the Thames, back in the days of James the Fourth."

"God save His Majesty, King James the Sixth, and all the House of Stuart!"

"A sentiment I echo, Watson, but we must hurry on and save the patriotism for our leisure. As you see, we are running out of time."

I placed my paws on the high dashboard of the hansom for a better view. We were near the London docks. A fog had settled in among the poorly lit streets. The air was thick with strange smells. Many of the passers-by were foreigners of the most unsavory sort.

"Recall, Watson," said Holmes, "that the notorious Dr. Moriarty, before he turned to crime, wrote, in addition to a curious monograph about an asteroid, a treatise on the possibility of an infinity of alternative worlds existing side by side, which may perhaps be realized by the use of certain potent objects—he actually used the word 'numinous'—which suggests all manner of fantastic combinations, such as, for example, one in which Bonny Prince Charlie was defeated at Culloden and England today is ruled by this same unhandsome Victoria of the House of Hanover—"

"Good God, Holmes!"

"You could as well imagine a world in which you, Watson, are Grand Panjandrum of Nabobistan, complete with harem. You would enjoy that, would you not?"

"I wouldn't be with you, Holmes," he said with some regret.

For an instant I almost admired Watson, though I knew his was mere doglike loyalty.

"But to conclude," said Holmes, "it was Moriarty's theory, which I believe he has passed on to his Hanoverian confederates and which will perhaps be put to the test tonight, that with the use of such an object, which has been manufactured in one of the alternative worlds and conjured into ours, all manner of what the ignorant would call supernatural beings or creatures may be imposed—"

At that moment the hansom came to a halt. We three debarked. The cab hurried off. I ran ahead of the two humans, into the gloom. The hideous smell of the river and of river rats was ahead of me.

Holmes and Watson hurried to keep pace with me, their great, clumsy feet thundering on the pavement. Dr. Watson gasped between breaths.

"This theory, Holmes, seems perfectly insane—"

"Watson, at such times it pays to be a little mad!"

"And you, the rationalist!"

Holmes made no reply to Watson's taunt, for we had come to our destination, a deserted wharf amid tumbledown warehouses. The fog was so thick it seemed a solid thing. Even I shivered.

Holmes struck a match for light. He held the paper from inside the locket up so Watson could read it.

"It is a shipping document," said Watson. "In receipt of five boxes of earth ... what would anybody want with those, Holmes?"

"Observe the crest, Watson."

"An odd one. With a bat—"

"It is the arms of a certain voivode of Transylvania, a Count Dracula, about whom many terrible things are whispered. Now all the pieces of the puzzle come together. This Dracula, in the employ of the Hanoverians, under the direction of Moriarty—"

"I don't understand, Holmes."

Impatiently, Holmes got out the locket and showed Watson the reverse.

"It's the same crest, Holmes, to be sure, but—"

I let out a screech of challenge, and at this point Holmes had no time to deal with Watson's thick-headedness. A low, flat barge drifted out of the fog toward the wharf, heavily laden with long, rectangular boxes.

"Quick, Watson! Under no circumstances must that vessel be allowed to touch land!"

The two of them ran to the end of the wharf, and with a long leap all three of us landed squarely in the middle of the approaching barge. Watson's thick head proved to be of some service at this point, I must admit, because even as we landed one of those disreputable foreigners arose from behind one of the boxes and clubbed Watson with a stout cudgel, which would have broken his skull had it not been so thick, but instead sent him tumbling back against his assailant, who was thus set off balance.

Sherlock Holmes, strikingly agile for a human, had all the advantage he needed. He dealt with the single live crewman on the barge, leaving him unconscious at his feet.

But even he could not quite grasp the true danger. I was the one who first appreciated the significance of the horrible carrion smell which wafted from the boxes, now all the more intense as the lids of those boxes creaked and rose up, opened from within.

In the struggle, Holmes dropped the gold locket. It gleamed even in the poor light.

The thing which streaked out of one of the boxes far more swiftly than the other occupant could emerge went straight for the locket, swatted it to one side, then to the other, then turned to confront me.

"Mine!" I communicated, in the secret language of cats, which no human may ever understand.

When I call it a cat, I use the term loosely, for though it had the form of a huge, black-furred tom, it was a dead thing with burning red eyes and glistening fangs. We struggled even as Holmes and his opponents did, both seeking to regain the shiny

249

locket-and-chain, while we rolled right to the edge of the barge's deck, mere inches above the noxious water.

That was when the inspiration came to me, though I paid a terrible price.

I let go of what was mine. Instantly my enemy grabbed hold of the chain with both forepaws and became entangled, and it took but a single swipe for me to knock him over the side into the water. The carrion-thing let out a hideous yowl, then exploded into steam upon contact with the water and was gone.

As was my pretty treasure.

The rest is less interesting. Holmes, seeing a variety of carrion humans emerging from the wooden boxes, heaved first the barge's anchor, then the semi-conscious Watson and the inert crewman over the side and leapt into the water himself. He stood up, awash to his shoulders. I might have been in a difficult situation had he not allowed me to ride atop his head all the way to shore, while he dragged Watson and the nautical thug.

Once on land, we watched the hideous spectacle of the carrion things stumbling about, seemingly unable to figure any way out of their present predicament.

"The vampires are rendered helpless by the running water of the good Thames," Holmes explained. "So enfeebled, they cannot even raise the anchor. Daylight will force them back into their boxes, where they are easily destroyed."

"What I don't understand," said Watson, the following morning, back in Baker Street, "is how the locket got there in the first place."

While they spoke, I lapped a well-deserved saucer of milk, despite Watson's disapproval.

"I think Count Dracula—who was not among the vampires destroyed, and has yet escaped us—was betrayed by his cat."

Holmes got out the locket and dangled it by its chain.

Watson stuttered. Even I looked up in amazement.

Holmes laughed. "When the sun rose and the tide went out, I hired one of the Irregulars to splash around in the shallow water until he found it."

The thought of a "street arab" immersing himself in the nasty element to recover my prize made me think that even boys have their uses.

"Dracula's feline," said Holmes, "must have passed from ship to shore many times, perhaps carried by a human agent, to serve as a scout. On one of those missions, it stole the crucial locket, then, losing interest, abandoned it. The object is a perfect cat-toy, don't you think?"

He dangled the beautiful thing on its chain. I watched, fascinated. But I continued with my milk. It was mine, after all, and I could play with it later.

Bad Cats

Michael Potts

To defy the laws of cat
and God is our goal.
We only pretend
to purr, we actors
of tooth and claw
sharpened, tools ready
to use at will against our human
slaves, mere fools
sucked in when we're kittens,
our cuteness a trap to capture
food, water, the great
box—and we treat our slaves
well, don't we, pay them with surprise
scratches when we're nestled
in their trusting arms, ready to give
them biting rewards from yours truly—
we, bad cats, masters
of tooth and claw.

The Cheshire Cat

Lewis Carroll

The door led right into a large kitchen, which was full of smoke from one end to the other: the Duchess was sitting on a three-legged stool in the middle, nursing a baby; the cook was leaning over the fire, stirring a large cauldron which seemed to be full of soup.

"There's certainly too much pepper in that soup!" Alice said to herself, as well as she could for sneezing.

There was certainly too much of it in the air. Even the Duchess sneezed occasionally; and as for the baby, it was sneezing and howling alternately without a moment's pause. The only two creatures in the kitchen that did not sneeze, were the cook, and a large cat which was sitting on the hearth and grinning from ear to ear.

"Please would you tell me," said Alice, a little timidly, for she was not quite sure whether it was good manners for her to speak first, "why your cat grins like that?"

"It's a Cheshire cat," said the Duchess, "and that's why. Pig!"

She said the last word with such sudden violence that Alice quite jumped; but she saw in another moment that it was addressed to the baby, and not to her, so she took courage, and went on again:—

"I didn't know that Cheshire cats always grinned; in fact, I didn't know that cats *could* grin."

"They all can," said the Duchess; "and most of 'em do."

"I don't know of any that do," Alice said very politely, feeling quite pleased to have got into a conversation.

"You don't know much," said the Duchess; "and that's a fact."

Alice did not at all like the tone of this remark, and thought it would be as well to introduce some other subject of conversation. While she was trying to fix on one, the cook took the cauldron of soup off the fire, and at once set to work throwing everything within her reach at the Duchess and the baby—the fire-irons came first; then followed a shower of saucepans, plates, and dishes. The Duchess took no notice of them even when they hit her; and the baby was howling so much already, that it was quite impossible to say whether the blows hurt it or not.

"Oh, *please* mind what you're doing!" cried Alice, jumping up and down in an agony of terror. "Oh, there goes his *precious* nose!" as an unusually large saucepan flew close by it, and very nearly carried it off.

"If everybody minded their own business," the Duchess said in a hoarse growl, "the world would go round a deal faster than it does."

"Which would *not* be an advantage," said Alice, who felt very glad to get an opportunity of showing off a little of her knowledge. "Just think of what work it would make with the day and night! You see the earth takes twenty-four hours to turn round on its axis—"

"Talking of axes," said the Duchess, "chop off her head!"

Alice glanced rather anxiously at the cook, to see if she meant to take the hint; but the cook was busily stirring the soup, and seemed not to be listening, so she went on again: "Twenty-four hours, I *think*; or is it twelve? I—"

"Oh, don't bother *me*," said the Duchess; "I never could abide figures." And with that she began nursing her child again, singing a sort of lullaby to it as she did so, and giving it a violent shake at the end of every line:—

> "Speak roughly to your little boy,
>   And beat him when he sneezes:
>   He only does it to annoy,
>   Because he knows it teases."

Chorus
(in which the cook and the baby joined):—

"Wow! wow! wow!"

While the Duchess sang the second verse of the song, she kept tossing the baby violently up and down, and the poor little thing howled so, that Alice could hardly hear the words:—

"I speak severely to my boy,
The pepper when he pleases!"

Chorus
"Wow! wow! wow!"

"Here! you may nurse it a bit, if you like!" the Duchess said to Alice, flinging the baby at her as she spoke. "I must go and get ready to play croquet with the Queen," and she hurried out of the room. The cook threw a fryingpan after her as she went out, but it just missed her.

Alice caught the baby with some difficulty, as it was a queer-shaped little creature, and held out its arms and legs in all directions, "just like a star-fish," thought Alice. The poor little thing was snorting like a steam-engine when she caught it, and kept doubling itself up and straightening itself out again, so that altogether, for the first minute or two, it was as much as she could do to hold it.

As soon as she had made out the proper way of nursing it, (which was to twist it up into a sort of knot, and then keep tight hold of its right ear and left foot, so as to prevent its undoing itself,) she carried it out into the open air. "If I don't take this child away with me," thought Alice, "they're sure to kill it in a day or two: wouldn't it be murder to leave it behind?" She said the last words out loud, and the little thing grunted in reply (it had left off sneezing by this time). "Don't grunt," said Alice; "that's not at all a proper way of expressing yourself."

The baby grunted again, and Alice looked very anxiously into its face to see what was the matter with it. There could be no doubt that it had a *very* turn-up nose, much more like a snout than a real nose; also its eyes were getting extremely small for a baby: altogether Alice did not like the look of the thing at all, "—but perhaps it was only sobbing," she thought, and looked into its eyes again, to see if there were any tears.

No, there were no tears. "If you're going to turn into a pig, my dear," said Alice, seriously, "I'll have nothing more to do with you. Mind now!" The poor little thing sobbed again, (or grunted, it was impossible to say which,) and they went on for some while in silence.

Alice was just beginning to think to herself, "Now, what am I to do with this creature when I get it home?" when it grunted again, so violently, that she looked down into its face in some alarm. This time there could be *no* mistake about it: it was neither more nor less than a pig, and she felt that it would be quite absurd for her to carry it further.

So she set the little creature down, and felt quite relieved to see it trot away quietly into the wood. "If it had grown up," she said to herself, "it would have made a dreadfully ugly child: but it makes rather a handsome pig, I think." And she began thinking over other children she knew, who might do very well as pigs, and was just saying to herself, "if one only knew the right way to change them—" when she was a little startled by seeing the Cheshire Cat sitting on a bough of a tree a few yards off.

The Cat only grinned when it saw Alice. It looked goodnatured, she thought: still it had *very* long claws and a great many teeth, so she felt that it ought to be treated with respect.

"Cheshire Puss," she began, rather timidly, as she did not at all know whether it would like the name: however, it only grinned a little wider. "Come, it's pleased so far," thought Alice, and she went on. "Would you tell me, please, which way I ought to go from here?"

"That depends a good deal on where you want to get to," said the Cat.

"I don't much care where—" said Alice.

"Then it doesn't matter which way you walk," said the Cat.

"—so long as I get *somewhere*," Alice added as an explanation.

"Oh, you're sure to do that," said the Cat, "if you only walk long enough."

Alice felt that this could not be denied, so she tried another question. "What sort of people live about here?"

"In *that* direction," the Cat said, waving its right paw round, "lives a Hatter: and in *that* direction," waving the other paw, "lives a March Hare. Visit either you like: they're both mad."

"But I don't want to go among mad people," Alice remarked.

"Oh, you can't help that," said the Cat: "we're all mad here. I'm mad. You're mad."

"How do you know I'm mad?" said Alice.

"You must be," said the Cat, "or you wouldn't have come here."

Alice didn't think that proved it at all; however, she went on: "And how do you know that you're mad?"

"To begin with," said the Cat, "a dog's not mad. You grant that?"

"I suppose so," said Alice.

"Well, then," the Cat went on, "you see, a dog growls when it's angry, and wags its tail when it's pleased. Now *I* growl when I'm pleased, and wag my tail when I'm angry. Therefore I'm mad."

"*I* call it purring, not growling," said Alice.

"Call it what you like," said the Cat. "Do you play croquet with the Queen to-day?"

"I should like it very much," said Alice, "but I haven't been invited yet."

"You'll see me there," said the Cat, and vanished.

Alice was not much surprised at this, she was getting so used to queer things happening. While she was looking at the place where it had been, it suddenly appeared again.

"By-the-bye, what became of the baby?" said the Cat. "I'd nearly forgotten to ask."

"It turned into a pig," Alice quietly said, just as if the Cat had come back in a natural way.

"I thought it would," said the Cat, and vanished again.

Alice waited a little, half expecting to see it again, but it did not appear, and after a minute or two she walked on in the direction in which the March Hare was said to live. "I've seen hatters before," she said to herself: "the March Hare will be much the most interesting, and perhaps as this is May it won't be raving mad—at least not so mad as it was in March." As she said this, she looked up, and there was the Cat again, sitting on a branch of a tree.

"Did you say pig, or fig?" said the Cat.

"I said pig," replied Alice; "and I wish you wouldn't keep appearing and vanishing so suddenly: you make one quite giddy."

"All right," said the Cat; and this time it vanished quite slowly, beginning with the end of the tail, and ending with the grin, which remained some time after the rest of it had gone.

"Well! I've often seen a cat without a grin," thought Alice; "but a grin without a cat! It's the most curious thing I ever saw in all my life!"

Nine

Hank Schwaeble

The tall older man in overalls standing up the street near the curb looked familiar, but Davis couldn't remember where he'd seen him. Straw hat, worn and baggy denim, legs straight and stiff, shoulders hunched. A peculiar sight for the suburbs, all the more due to the intense manner in which the man was staring—if not at him through his kitchen window, then at least at his house—didn't strike such an odd chord. A lot of things in the neighborhood were giving off that sort of vibe lately, contributing to a nagging sense, one he couldn't shake, that something wasn't quite right. He doubted the green feline eyes staring up at him from his front lawn had anything to do with it, but they certainly didn't help.

A tickle crawled through his nose. He set down his coffee and scanned the kitchen for a napkin, ended up using the back of his hand.

"Kendle . . . that cat is back again. Have you been feeding it?"

His wife called out for him to wait a minute, then emerged from the laundry room, robe cinched around her waist, something blue in her hand. Her red hair was frizzed and uneven.

"Sorry, I had to find Billy's Spider-Man shirt." She held it up, as if her claim needed evidence. "It was in the dryer."

Davis furrowed his brow. Come to think of it, she'd been acting a little strange lately, too.

"He's got, like, six of them."

"But he wants this one." She jutted her chin. "What were you asking about?"

"You haven't been feeding that cat, have you?"

He turned to the window. The cat hadn't moved. Same spot, same glare of intense apathy. Its gaze was locked on the glass, or perhaps on him, eyes up, an imperious cant to its head.

"I may have set out a can of tuna once or twice. Why?"

"Because it's camped outside, waiting for its next meal. You know I'm allergic."

"Poor thing must have nowhere to go. It's not like I let it inside. Was I supposed to watch it starve?"

"That's what Animal Control is for. Dander gets on clothes, even outside. I've already sneezed, like, a dozen times this morning."

"You want to send a beautiful cat like that to the pound because of some sniffles? Jeez, when did you become so callous?"

Davis sighed but didn't respond. The thing was unusual, that was for sure. Exotic, he'd probably concede. But 'beautiful' was stretching it. The animal towered over a cowering congregation of garden gnomes a few feet away, its shape and features smacking of something drawn by a talented artist who'd never seen a real one before. Its coloring stood out against the green of the grass, a base shade of bronze, coppery in some places and almost gold in others, with dark, swirling spots on its side and stripes down its back. Its coat was so short it verged on hairless, except for those extra-long white ones feathering out from the tips of its ears. And the way it opened and closed those eyes disturbed him, black slits dividing the jade of its irises like onyx spearheads. The word that came to mind as he watched it watching him was feral.

A staring contest on, he took slow sips of his coffee, eyes locked. He finished the cup a few minutes later, whispering *you win,* and stood. As he did, his wife walked their little boy to the kitchen entry.

"Will you watch Billy while I do my hair? He wants to ride his tricycle." She smoothed the boy's sandy brown hair with gentle strokes. He looked up and grinned, a finger stuck in his mouth, drool forming below his lip.

Davis glanced up the road. The tall man in the straw hat and overalls was gone.

"Sure."

"Don't let him go in the street."

"What about the cat? Aren't you worried it might scratch him or something?"

"Seriously? That poor thing doesn't bother anybody. Especially not Billy. She even let him pet her the other day."

"You allowed that? What if it has rabies?"

"What's gotten into you? If you're worried about your allergies, watch him through the window. You don't even have to get dressed. Just don't let him go in the street."

Davis grunted and refilled his mug. He heard the garage door open, saw his son hustle down the driveway on his trike, making elongated circles and figure eights, one of the back wheels leaving the ground as it swerved. He repeated the same pattern several times, with an occasional variation. The trek to the sidewalk was fast, then once there he'd end up pushing the trike with dolphin kicks back toward the garage, the incline making pedaling it too hard, and start over again.

The cat had shifted position to face the driveway but otherwise hadn't moved, its eyes now fixed on Billy.

Kendle was probably right, he thought. It's just a cat. His allergies weren't the reason he was out of sorts, and neither was some stray feline. Things had felt weird for a while now. Days at least, maybe weeks. And the feeling was progressive, a subtle itch the first time he noticed it, more recently a relentless tingle, demanding attention. He couldn't quite put his finger on it, but something was just off. And getting more off by the day.

His son raised his feet, spreading his legs forward, and coasted in a lazy S down the driveway. As he neared the sidewalk, he tried to regain his footing, but the pedals caught the back of his heels and the trike tumbled, dumping him onto the concrete. Davis planted his coffee on the table, but saw the boy sit up and glance

263

around, face contorted, mouth frozen open. After a beat he could tell Billy thought no one had seen what happened and, with no adult nearby to show fear or console him, he slid his leg out and got to his feet. The boy righted the trike with a bit of effort and climbed back on.

Davis smiled. Not bad for a four-year-old, any four-year-old, even one that wasn't what his father would have called slow. Kendle was in denial, but he knew it to be true. She clung with maternal claws to the promise of test scores described as "normal range" and pointed to the way he was potty-trained and seemed able to enjoy kicking a ball around and watching cartoons and hearing bedtime stories, but the fact was the boy consistently placed at the low end of that "normal" range, so low a stiff breeze would probably blow him off the edge. Davis figured the doctors were sugarcoating the implications to placate her. Billy recently turned four, yet rarely spoke more than a few words, hardly ever uttered a complete sentence. Why couldn't she bring herself to admit it? It did the boy no favor to pretend.

But those thoughts and their orbiting fragments disbursed as he spotted a dog padding down the road. A mastiff, perhaps, but he didn't know breeds enough to be sure. It was the size of a small horse, or at least seemed to be. A broad wrinkled skull and dark eyes, a pushed-in snout, and what looked like ropes of drool hanging from its mouth as its jowls swung back and forth with each step. There was no frolic in its gait, no playful curiosity in its gaze. It was looking in Billy's direction as if it had locked on a target and was heading right toward it. One side of its upper lip raised as it drew closer, a white canine showing.

Davis sprinted to the front of the house, stumbling in his slippers, and yanked the front door open. The dog was a few yards from Billy, loping now, almost lunging, a low growl coming from its throat. Before Davis was more than a step past the porch, something flew across his field of vision, smashing into the dog's face and attaching itself to the top of its head directly in front of the boy and his trike. There was a harsh clamor, a ferocious mix of lows and highs, before Davis realized it was the cat locked onto the dog's enormous skull, ears back, teeth sunk into the imposing animal's forehead, claws visibly digging into the canine's skin.

The dog tossed its head back and forth, bucking like a mule. Davis rushed to grab his son, scooping him up, feeling the animal's warm wet breath on his bare arms. With a violent jerk the dog flung the cat off, snarling and snapping. Davis snatched the tricycle with his free arm, ready to wield it as a weapon, bracing for an attack. But as the cat wheeled out of view, landing on the grass, the dog yowled, a piercing shriek that caused Davis to wince. It shook its head, twisting and rattling its skull in a frenzy. Blood poured from one of its eyes, or what was left of it, splashing over the concrete. It spun and bolted back in the general direction it had come, yelping as it scrambled. It smashed into a brick mailbox, yelped even more loudly, and caromed back into the road. It kept running until Davis couldn't hear it anymore, its figure shrinking and bouncing, eventually disappearing in the distance.

As his focus pulled back, Davis scanned the street. The gangly farmer-type was nowhere to be seen. Neither was anyone else. He thought about getting in his car and trying to search for the dog, thought better of it. What could he do if he found it?

"Oh my God! Is he hurt? Is Billy hurt?"

Davis turned. Kendle filled the doorway, eyes saucered, robe hanging loose and a towel around her neck, her hair slick and dark and wild. Billy was screaming, something Davis only now noticed, the boy's mouth agape, tears streaming down his cheeks.

"He's fine." Davis let go of the trike, dropping it to clank on the cement, and pulled the boy's head against his chest, patting it. "Just scared."

"What the hell happened?"

"Good question." Davis glanced over to the cat. It crouched on the grass, head low, muscles coiled, watching him with appraising eyes. "Looks like that damn stray of yours just saved the day."

Two weeks later, the note Davis found under the windshield wiper on his Prius didn't mince words:

> Your family is in danger.
> You must rid your home of that
> ABOMINATION before it is too late.
> You KNOW what I am talking about.
> RR 113 past Farmer's Branch Rd
> Find me at the end
> Do not ignore this.
> Time is running out!

He'd have tossed it—chalked it up to some clever punks hoping to find someone stupid enough to drive out to a remote location so they could bash his skull and relieve him of his car and anything else of value—if he didn't happen to know exactly what whoever left it was talking about.

Rural Route 113 was a dirt road marked by a faded metal sign, barely larger than a postcard, dangling from a bent pole. The way wound around a majestic live oak that looked as if it had seen several centuries come and go. Open acreage to each side indicated the area used to be farmland, but shrubs and clumps of wild grass dominated the stretches between stands of pine and sweetgum, all of it separated from the rutted drive by dilapidated barbed-wire fencing in various states of displacement, steadily being overtaken by the grasping fingers of green and tan tendrils that reminded Davis of tentacled creatures in old nautical sketches dragging ships into the bowels of the sea.

The road didn't end as much as dissipate, patches of it morphing into rougher and rougher terrain until it appeared to become impassable. Davis rolled his Prius to a bumpy stop, half expecting to see a pickup carrying a bunch of yahoos with pipes and bats pull up in his rearview mirror. The barbed wire had stopped a hundred yards or so back. Heavily wooded terrain lay ahead. To the left stretched tall grass prairie with thickets of large, swaying feather reeds. To his right, a dense row of tangled bushes canopied by live oak.

He had already put the car into reverse when he saw the cat.

It was black with a white patch on its chest, the dark fur on its saddle shimmering in the late afternoon sun. It sat a dozen yards or so in front of him for a moment, watching with hazel yellow eyes, then sprang to the right, sprinting behind a column of tall shrubs.

Davis studied the plants, caught sight of something out of place. He shut off the car and got out. Within the growth, a weathered curve of dull metal. He moved closer, saw it was a mailbox, overgrown with thatch and swaddled in branches and leaves. On the far side of it, a worn footpath divided the weeds, heading through a narrow gap in the tree line.

A hundred yards or so back he could make out a small house, embedded in a canopy of gnarled trees festooned with hanging moss.

The path to it was relatively straight, which he was thankful for, as the sun was low enough and the surroundings thick enough that more of the woodland floor lay in shadow than light. Footing was an issue, as were protrusions of leaning stalks and branches, the slipping of his wingtips with each step and the scrape of flora against his trousers and trenchcoat serving as constant reminders he wasn't dressed for a hike through the forest.

As best Davis could tell, the house was a Dutch Colonial, or had started out as one. Stone foundation and clapboard siding, a doghouse dormer on the forward sloping roof that flared out over a porch. One side of the porch eave was collapsing, the edge of it just a few feet from the floor. Pieces of siding were missing, as were numerous wood shingles. The entire structure hadn't seen a fresh coat of paint in decades, every part of it seeming to coalesce into a similar shade of hoary gray.

What the hell am I doing here?

He considered turning back, stood there a few beats thinking about it, but couldn't shake the contents of the note. Giving it a test first, he stepped onto the porch, cringed at the sound of the wood creaking beneath him. He hovered his fist in front of the door, inhaled deeply, and gave it three sharp raps. The door rattled in its hinges. He was about to try again when he heard a frail voice, what sounded like "Come in."

The latch handle was loose, wobbling in the wood. The door swung in with a slow whine.

The inside was dim, but not too dark to see. The place smelled of smoke and earth and decaying wood. A small fire flickered in a brick fireplace on the far side of the room. Scattered candles guttered. Dying embers of sunlight from a pair of small windows cast a twilight glow. The bulk of the house, if not all of it, seemed within view of where he stood.

In the center of the room, on a chair angled slightly toward the fire, an elderly woman sat, wrinkled and hunched, appraising him.

"Please, close the door. I was hoping you would come."

"Hard to decline an invitation like that."

"Have a seat." The woman raised a tremoring hand, vaguely gestured in the direction of another chair. "There is much to discuss. I'm sure you have questions."

Davis looked at the chair. It was antique, claw-footed with a round velvet seat and back, both covered in hairs. Just looking at it made his nose twitch. "I think I'll stand, if you don't mind."

"I would offer you something to drink, but as you can see, I'm not very mobile."

"That's quite all right." He took in his surroundings with a few glances. The parlor was cluttered, ornaments and trinkets crammed onto small surfaces in numerous locations. Above the fireplace was a portrait of a black cat seated at a cliffside window, gazing back over its shoulder at the artist, behind it a bright moon behind a stormy sea. "Who are you, if you don't mind my asking?"

"You may call me Madame Dougal." Her voice was soft and

hoarse, each syllable quavering through thin, dry lips. "Or Iona, if you prefer."

"You were the one who put the note on my car?"

"I'm the one who wrote it, yes."

"Would you mind telling me why?"

"You know why, Mr. Thorpe. What you would really like to know is whether I can offer you a solution to your problem."

Okay, he thought. *She knows my name.* He supposed that shouldn't be surprising, considering someone had to know his car and his place of work. But still.

"Yes," she added, as if sensing his unease. "I know things about you. I've spent a good deal of time learning what I can, ever since I discovered you took in that creature."

"You mean the cat."

"That thing you have brought into your house is no cat. You know that, or at least have suspected it. That is why you are here."

"Okay, I'll play. What is it then?"

"For you to know, you will have to open your mind. You'll have to rid yourself of that American tendency to scoff at everything you don't understand, stand ready to embrace things you've been taught not to accept. You'll have to see the world not merely as some physical object, but a convergence, a junction of the material, the spiritual, the transcendent. The finite and the infinite. The ephemeral and the timeless."

"No offense, but I have no idea what the heck you're talking about."

"If you are not willing to acknowledge the truth of what I have to say, I will be helpless. There is nothing I can do. If an open mind is beyond your capability, I am sorry for wasting your time. And mine."

The gray from the windows had dimmed to purple, allowing the light from the candles and the fireplace to cast a yellow glow across the room, bringing its contents into focus. The ornaments he'd noticed were mostly wood, mostly old, mostly related to cats in some way. Carvings, figurines, reliefs. Standing, sitting, curled in repose. The non-cat objects were crude, almost primitive, shapes of men and women and children, animals like horses and goats and dogs.

"Your note said my family was in danger. What did you mean?"

"You have brought into your home an entity that dates to ancient Egypt. She has been worshipped as a goddess in many cultures. Children have been sacrificed to please her. She has a cult of loyal followers to this day, people who act as her surrogates, dedicated to her protection."

"Funny, I thought we were talking about a stray my wife started feeding."

"Of course, that's how she would present herself. She needed to be welcomed, invited. The illusion of consent."

"Even if I were to believe any of this, why would such a thing show up at my house?"

"She derives her power from sacrifice, blood sacrifice. Nine of them, to be exact."

"You're saying she needs nine lives?"

"That is where the expression comes from. She needs nine to keep her from being trapped as a cat, forever. She has taken six."

"That doesn't explain why she ended up at my house."

"Nine is divisible by three, and such strong magic requires powerful symmetries. And even more importantly, it requires innocence of blood. She has taken six so far. The final sacrifice must be a child not yet five years from conception, who has yet to have had an impure thought. That sort of innocence, and accessible innocence to boot, is not as common as you may think. It requires the right set of circumstances to find the perfect soul for the taking. And, at the risk of upsetting you, the right sort of familial fractures she needs to exploit to achieve her goal."

Billy, he thought. *She's talking about Billy.* "This sounds completely insane. I mean, I may not like the damn thing, it may be strange, but an Egyptian goddess? In the twenty-first century? In my home? Even if I could get past the crazy, it makes no sense."

"It makes perfect sense. The rise of monotheistic religions cast the Old Ones aside, killing off most, sending the rest into the shadows. What used to be hailed as gods are now scorned as demons. They hide from their persecutors. They function best in secular societies, where their presence tends to go unnoticed."

"If she's so powerful, why a cat?"

"Cats, Mr. Thorpe, are mystical creatures. They exist simultaneously in multiple realms, can see through the fabric of our reality to what lies beyond. They have been worshipped and revered since ancient times due to their ethereal qualities and connections to the other side. When the sun god Ra sent his daughter Bast to earth, it was only natural he would grant her the form of a cat."

"Bast?"

"She has many names, but that is the one most commonly applied to her."

"And you're telling me she's an ancient goddess. You actually believe that?"

"I have no doubt."

"I'm sorry, but I think you need help. Professional help. It's just a cat."

"If that's the case, Mr. Thorpe, why don't you explain to me why you are standing here, talking to a crazy lady? Surely it's not because you are in the habit of following vague instructions left on your windscreen."

Davis didn't respond. His gaze drifted to the painting above the fireplace. The eyes looked down on him with cold judgment.

"I will tell you why," she continued. "Because you have already sensed the thing is far more than it seems. She cannot hide her true nature completely."

As much as he wanted to deny it, the woman was right about one thing. After saving Billy, that cat worked its way into the house. A box and blanket in the garage at first, then it darted in when he opened the door and Kendle let it eat in the kitchen. The next night, she let it in to sleep. Within another day or two, it had the run of the house. At a week, it was vaulting onto their bed when they were turning in for the night. Billy was already in the habit of sleeping there—night terrors, Kendle called it—which was bad enough. Because of his allergies, Davis told her no, that was where he drew the line. No cat in their bed. He'd lost that battle, too.

"It doesn't seem to want me around," he said, immediately regretting it.

"Of course not! You are the provider, the protector. A threat to her plan."

Provider. He wanted to laugh. He thought about telling her Kendle made more than he did, decided not to.

"She has power," Iona continued. "But she is not omnipotent. She wants to separate you from the innocent object of her design. I'm sure your family is already siding with her. Just as I'm sure you have found you cannot seem to rid yourself of her presence."

That much was true. He'd most certainly tried. He'd smuggled the cat outside several times and left it, hoping it would grow bored and roam away, only to find it sitting in the kitchen or the living room, waiting for him, as soon as he came back in. A couple of days earlier, he tried to take it to his car while Kendle was shopping, intending to drive it somewhere remote or leave it at a shelter, but it became aggressive when he approached, claws out, teeth bared, as if sensing what he had in mind.

"How do you know all this?"

"I am descended from a long line of what you might call her sworn enemies, going back to medieval Scotland. Much of my life has been consumed with determining her whereabouts. As you may imagine, she is difficult to track. She is constantly changing appearance, each set of sacrifices giving her a new body. I would know her on sight, regardless, but the world is a large place. I must rely on reports, answers to queries, others who assist me in gathering information. That, and my own instincts. Those brought me here. Ultimately, they led me to you."

He jutted his chin toward the painting above the fireplace. "Is that supposed to be her, then?"

"No. That is a portrait of a cut-sìth—a creature of Scottish folklore you needn't concern yourself with. It is nothing like her."

He stared at the picture for a few moments, thinking, *Lunacy is contagious.* He nodded and checked his watch. "Thank you for warning me. If I keep having problems, I'll contact you."

"You don't believe a word I've told you."

"I'm not sure what to believe. It's a lot to swallow."

"Have you seen the eye?"

"The what?"

"She will have adorned each room of your home with the symbol of an eye beneath a curled eyebrow. Most would be hidden, but not all. Have you seen any?"

Davis said nothing, picturing the strange scratch marks he found in odd places around the house, virtually identical to one another. He hadn't thought of them as eyes, but they certainly could have been.

"You have. What more proof do you need? It is imperative you act. I beseech you. I can give you what you need, tell you exactly what to do."

"I just need to think it over. Sleep on it."

"You don't understand, Mr. Thorpe. You don't have any time to 'think it over.' Tomorrow is the Blood Moon."

"What are you saying?"

"If you want to stop her, you must do so within the next few hours. She must complete her final sacrifice at the stroke of midnight."

"And if I don't?"

"If you want to save your child, Mr. Thorpe, that is simply not an option."

Davis white-knuckled the steering wheel the entire way home.

When he pulled into his driveway, he wasn't sure what he was going to do. Or if he would do anything at all.

He glanced at the items Madame Dougal had given him, thought of how adamant and precise her instructions had been. A coarse sack wove from goat hair. A thin, round crystal the size of a small pizza. A dagger with a long wavy blade with swirling black patterns in the silvery steel.

He left the dagger in the car. Explaining the sack and the crystal would be hard enough.

The sun had set, the sky darkening above him, purple expanding overhead from east to west like a stain. The house was still, background sounds audible in the silence. The hum of the refrigerator, the click of his heels on the floor, the faint drone of a computer fan from his study. He was about to call out when he saw a note in the foyer. He recognized his wife's familiar script.

> Long day. Totally pooped.
> Going to bed early.
> Fettuccini's in the fridge.
> XXOO

He checked his cell, saw several missed calls and a text that had a similar message. No cell reception at Madame Dougal's, apparently. He'd been so rattled by what she'd told him he hadn't thought to call Kendle and let her know he was on his way or offer an excuse for running late.

He stepped lightly, cheating to the balls of his feet, then chastised himself. Why was he so creeped out? There was a cat in his home he didn't like, that was it. He outweighed it by a hundred sixty, hundred seventy pounds, so walking around on tenterhooks was just plain stupid. Madame Looney-Toons had gotten into his head.

On the other hand, the silence reminded him of a sanctum, the reverberation of each step violating it. He made his way softly to the master bedroom. The knob clicked and the door gave a mousy squeak when he opened it. The spill of moonlight through a window cut slants of silver across the bed. He could make out two shapes, one larger than the other.

He was tempted to call out his wife's name, but then she exhaled and rolled to face the other way. His son shifted at the disturbance. Both looked normal.

No sign of the cat.

The crystal was getting heavy. He backed out of the room and eased the door closed, moved to the kitchen with gentle steps. He turned on the light and jumped back, his heart clenching, pulse pounding in his temples.

The cat sat on the island near the edge of the counter. After a long moment it meowed.

He exhaled, chuckling.

"Met a friend of yours today," he said. "Said the two of you go way back. I wouldn't exactly call her a fan, though."

The cat blinked, remained where it was, gaze locked on his.

"She gave me this." He held up the crystal lens, twisted it back and forth. "She said if I looked through it, I'd see the real you."

A few forced laughs. The cat tilted its head slightly but stayed otherwise still.

He lowered his head and swung his jaw from side to side. What the hell is wrong with me? A monster doesn't sit on a counter and mewl at you. It's a cat, bigger than normal, a bit unusual-looking, but not some demon in disguise. He couldn't believe he'd let that old bitty get into his head. Stress, he decided. It was starting to get to him.

He sighed. "Truce?"

His stomach rumbled. He remembered he hadn't eaten since lunch, and barely then. He thought about warming up some food and smiled. Kendle's fettuccini was the best.

The cat meowed again. It dawned on him why it was sitting in the kitchen.

"Did she forget to feed you? Well, you're in for a treat."

He turned on his heels and headed toward the front door. He'd hide this crap in his Prius and get rid of it tomorrow, make sure Kendle didn't see any of it. Maybe he'd leave it on the old lady's porch, not even knock. Maybe he'd just toss the lot in the nearest dumpster. Either way, he'd be glad to be rid of it.

Another meow.

"I'll be right back," he said. He glanced over shoulder as he walked, raising the glass and giving it a wiggle. "Just putting this in the ca—"

He stopped, shifted the crystal up and over a bit. He moved it to the side, then moved it back again. When he looked through it, there was a marking on the wall that wasn't there when the glass wasn't in front of it. It looked like an eye, a long slope of eyeliner swooping down from it into a curl.

Panning, he saw another on the door, then one on the foyer floor, then one in the living room. He paused. The glass trembled, but he knew it was his hand causing it. He swallowed and spun back to face the kitchen, glass out in front of him.

He let out a yelp and dropped it. Stumbled backwards, landed on his ass. The cat hadn't moved, but the crystal had passed between it and his eyes, and he saw it. Really saw it. Barely a flash of an image before his grip betrayed him, but a flash was all it took. He sat on the floor where he fell, staring at the sitting cat, his brain trying to process the visual it had just been fed. A huge, obsidian head the size of a tigress's, a gilded headdress upon it with a helmeted top and flared sides down to its shoulders. Vertical eyes glowing a hellfire shade of red. All that on the body of a full-grown woman, large and lean and angular, seated on the counter, a queen on her throne.

He rattled his skull, trying to shake the picture from his mind, but he couldn't.

Use this looking glass, the old lady had told him. She will see herself in it as she truly is, enchanting her, giving you time to catch her in the ritual sack. She will not be able to escape from it until after the moon has cycled. She is vulnerable once within it. The enchantments on it will hold her in place. That will allow you to use the dagger.

The cat watched him. He slowly gathered the bag in one hand and slid the crystal close with the other, not taking his eyes off her. He worked his fingers under the glass and got a grip. He rose to a knee, then to his feet, lifting it with care. He moved closer, one step, then another, and raised the glass when he drew near.

A chill spiked through his chest when he saw it again. It was looking right at him, or seemed to be, its face bulging with ferocity, fangs stabbing over its bottom lip, glowing eyes pulsing. Its feminine body was taut and tense, muscles rippling beneath the skin.

"Easy, now," he said. He shook the bag with his free hand, struggled to keep the glass steady as he did. The thing seemed transfixed, staring through the lens in a way he couldn't be sure wasn't at him.

This is absolute insanity, he thought. The thing was bigger than he was. How was he supposed to fit it into a sack the size of a trash bag? He looked at the hair sack, let his eyes run briefly over the symbols adorning it. The old lady had assured him it would work.

Now or never.

He lunged forward. She'd told him there would be a brief moment, a fraction of a second, when he'd have to drop the glass and slip the bag over her head. She would be the size of a cat, she'd assure him, for all purposes that mattered. But he couldn't afford a mistake. He would not get a second chance.

The glass hit the floor, shattering, and he hoisted the bag over the cat. The sack slipped off the side of its skull, missing. His heart skipped as the thing let out a hiss that rent his ears, then shot onto its hind legs, stiffening. A large paw raked across his chest, just missing his throat, claws shredding his shirt and drawing parallel lines of blood. He managed to grab the lip of the bag and yank it over the cat's head and tug the woven fabric down over it. It thrashed and shook, the strength of it stunning him as it raised him off the ground. But he didn't let go. He let his weight drag the rest of the bag down over it as he fell. The bag crashed down on top of him, cat inside, its limbs jackhammering at the cloth. He was able to cinch the end shut and held it tight, just as Madame Dougal had told him to. If he could just hold it to the count of six, it would be sealed.

If.

The savage threshing tossed him from side to side. He strained to hold the end shut, his muscles fading, his grip starting to slip. Each beat was its own lifetime as he counted.

Finally it was over. The creature inside seemed to understand it, too, its violent flails subsiding into weak prods and kicks. He pushed himself to his feet and stood over it.

You won't be able to remove it from the house until you erase the symbols. Once you do, get her out of there as quickly as possible. Drive her out as far as you're willing to go, at least ten miles away, and take her to an open field. There, you can drive that dagger into her through the weave of the sack and kill her. But make sure she is nowhere near the house at midnight. That is what matters most.

The glass spread out over the floor in several pieces and dozens of shards. He dragged a hand down his face, then checked the hallway. The bedroom door was still shut. He waited a few breaths, heard nothing. He went back into the kitchen.

The clock said it was just after nine. He spent most of the next hour wiping down the spots where the symbols were with a damp washcloth and spray cleaner, based on memory. To be sure, he scrubbed a much larger area than necessary, cleaning entire sections of wall, the whole door, and multiple other surfaces where he didn't remember seeing anything, just to be safe.

He took hold of the bag by the end and dragged it. The bag rocked and shook and deformed in various ways, its occupant making visceral noises, growls and hisses and caterwauls. He opened the door and hoisted it, holding it at arm's length, straining against the bouncing and twisting. He thumbed the key fob, popping the trunk. The cat made a few frenzied moves when he set it inside, and for a moment he thought it was going to bust out or maybe bump and jerk and spring out onto the driveway, but within a couple of seconds it quieted down. A low, muffled yowl, then nothing.

He shut the trunk, checked his watch, then let out a long breath.

An hour later, he pulled to the shoulder of a back road a few minutes off the highway and parked, the car angled sideways on a grassy slope along a drainage ditch. He shut off the car and sat, letting his eyes adjust, thinking about what he needed to do.

He yanked the bag out of the trunk, expecting a struggle, but the cat—or whatever it was—barely moved. He crossed the drainage canal, his shoes sinking in the moist earth, and carried it across an open field between the jagged moon shadows of spruce and squats of juniper.

Next to a dense fountain of tall grass, the most remote spot he could find, he set the bag down. The dagger felt hard and cold as he pulled it. The moon glistened off the waves steel, sparkling blue along the edge.

Plunge the dagger through the star near the center. Drive it home with all your might. If it goes through to the other side, you will have killed it.

The bag squirmed in the moonlight, its bright red markings now black and barely discernible. No sounds, not even that low yowling. The star was on top, riding the shifting wool like a five-pointed lily pad. He raised the dagger, held it over his head, and paused. Lowering it some, he stared at the shifting contours of the bag. Then he stretched his arm as high as he could.

He dropped his hand to his side, shaking his head. He had no idea what the thing was, but he couldn't bring himself to kill it. He slid the dagger into the pocket of his coat and pushed the bag into the burst of tall grass. After taking a moment to make sure it was obscured from view, he headed back to his car.

When he arrived home it was a few minutes before midnight. He unlocked the front door, fighting a yawn, and pushed thoughts of the cat out of his mind, focusing instead on getting a plate of food and going to bed.

As he stepped across the threshold, a man grabbed him by the arm and yanked him inside. He planted his feet and pulled back, startled and struggling. He cocked a fist, targeting the man's face. A flash of recognition made him hesitate, just as a hard punch caught him in the solar plex, followed by another. He gasped, his body folding. His shoes scraped the tile floor as the man dragged him and dropped him at the edge of the living room.

He pushed himself to his knees, cradling his abdomen, and raised his head.

Kendle lay on the floor, arms and legs bound with duct tape, a strip of it across her mouth. Her eyes welled and spilled over, her brow and cheeks clenched around them. Iona Dougal stood over her, still a woman in her eighties, possibly nineties, but erect and sturdy now, no longer the hunched, feeble geriatric he'd met hours earlier.

Behind her, Billy sat crying on the floor, a finger stuck in the side of his gaping mouth.

"You follow instructions very well," the woman said. "Though you missed one in the kitchen. Heinrich covered it before it could weaken me. Fortunately, this room is large."

Davis coughed, taking several tries before he could spit out the words. "What the hell is going on?"

"Rebirth, Mr. Thorpe! The cycle of renewal! I've used up eight of my lives, and it is time for my last to bring me full circle, back to the beginning, where I start anew! A child again! A whole new set of nine for my next hundred years!"

"I don't understand."

"Obviously. Otherwise you wouldn't have gotten rid of that pesky Bast for me. She's been my nemesis for millennia."

He glanced up at the man pinning him by his shoulder. It was the same man he'd seen in the street before the huge dog had come into his yard. Only now he had a patch over his left eye, fresh pink scars along his cheek and forehead.

"What do you want?"

"I've already told you. Your child. It's just as I explained. Only it's not Bast who is going to renew her life cycle and restore her power. It is I. And thank you for allowing it."

"No! You can't—"

"Oh, I can, and will. I've been doing it for hundreds of years. My kind, the cut-sith, perfected our craft, harnessed the power of dark magic, used the metaphysical essence of the common cat to defeat the limitations of our form. They called us witches, burned and hanged and persecuted us, but it's because of Bast, that wretched beast, that I'm the last of my line. Thanks to you, however, I can complete the ritual free of her interference, using my ninth cat life at midnight of a blood moon."

Davis tried to stand. The heavy hand on his shoulder shoved him back down.

"I don't suppose you actually killed her, did you?" the woman asked. "No, of course not. Your kind doesn't have the fortitude. No follow-through, no spine. No matter. Getting her away from here was what mattered. It is almost time."

"You sent that dog." He looked up at Heinrich, dead eyes looking down at him. "But it wasn't going after Billy. It was going after the cat."

"Once she gets into the home, she's much more difficult to deal with."

That hand clamped down hard as he tried to move. He looked at his wife, that pained expression in her eyes. He wanted to mouth words of assurance but had no idea what to say.

"She fought hard, Mr. Thorpe. Harder than you. When Heinrich picked her up, she took the opportunity to kick me several times. I can still taste the blood in my mouth, feel the bruises setting in. Don't worry. I told him to be gentle. After all, she will soon be my mother."

Two fingers and a thumb squeezed the muscles near his neck in a vise grip, causing his body to wilt. He hung his head, wondering how he could have been so stupid, doing everything she'd wanted him to, volunteering to be her puppet. The last few hours flashed through his mind, images jumping from the woman to the cat, the bag, the field in the moonlight.

The dagger.

The old woman threw up her arms and looked to the ceiling. She started to recite words Davis couldn't understand, rhythmic phrases in an alien tongue, repeating the same lines over and over. A red circle appeared in the gypsum above her, a flaming mark that expanded, a void in its center. The woman's features started to morph. Her eyes stretched and angled, her forehead flattened, her face contorted. Long, stiff hairs started to protrude from each side of her upper lip.

Davis slid his hand to his pocket. He could feel the blade's weight. He slipped his fingers in, letting his body go limp, waiting for that grip on his shoulder to relax, even a little.

The woman's face sprouted short black fuzz. Her ears dragged up her skull to the top of her head and reshaped themselves into triangles. Her gray hair began falling in clumps as black fur grew in its place.

Now.

Davis pulled the dagger from his pocket and spun his body as hard he could, driving the dagger into the man's torso. He was aiming blind, going for the high-percentage angle, assuming he would only get one shot. His fist stopped against something with a thump. He felt that large hand dig into his shoulder again, harder this time. He crumbled and let go.

Heinrich stepped back, releasing his grip, and looked down. The handle of the dagger protruded from his chest. He closed his fingers around it and pulled. A pulse of blood spurted out, followed by another, then another. He looked at Davis, leveled the dagger behind his ear, and started forward, then fell face first, his skull slamming against the floor.

A gaping hole had formed in the ceiling, dark tendrils reaching down from it. Two of them snaked around the woman, who was looking less and less like a woman each passing moment.

Billy.

Davis lunged toward his son, pulling him close. More tendrils descended, thickening into tentacles, lowering themselves closer.

He picked his son off the ground and ran. One of the tentacles whipped out and wrapped itself around his ankle, tugging him to a stop, his leg extended back. He shot glances in random directions, willing himself to think.

You missed one in the kitchen. Heinrich covered it . . .

Another tentacle wrapped itself around his waist.

Across the foyer, there was a cloth on the floor near the counter where he'd bagged the cat. He closed his eyes, asked any power that was listening, *Please give me this one thing, let this work,* and heaved his son with all the strength he could muster. The boy landed on the marble floor and slid several more feet, knocking the cloth away and coming to a stop where it had lain.

The clock struck twelve. A tremor rumbled through the house. Davis turned to see the old woman no longer there, a black cat in her place, more of those inky tentacles taking hold of her and raising her toward the void. The tentacled arms that held Davis released him and extended toward the foyer. Davis started to move, but instead of stretching toward Billy they latched onto Heinrich's body instead. They dragged it back to beneath the void, where they retracted, hoisting it, receding into the emptiness. The red flame of the perimeter brightened, then flashed, a blinding explosion of light, and Davis snapped his head away and buried his face in his hands. When he turned to look, the ceiling looked normal. There was no sign anything had happened to it.

Billy sat in the kitchen, crying in screaming fits. Davis scrambled over to his wife, tugging the tape from her mouth. The tape around her wrists was too thick to tear, so he ran to the kitchen for a knife and returned, freed her hands and feet. She raced to

Billy and swept him into her arms, pressed her face against the top of his head.

"Are you okay?"

"What the hell was that?" she said, rocking the boy as she squeezed him. "Who was that—that woman?"

"I don't really know. I met her today."

"How?"

"She left a note on my car, warning me about the—" He cut himself off. Oh my God. "Kendle, there's something I have to do."

"What? Now? You can't! We need to call the police! Figure out what's going on!"

"And tell them what? Some witch was here trying to steal our son's soul and she and some creepy hayseed she brought with her were swallowed by a giant hole she opened in our ceiling?"

He kissed her on the forehead and stroked his son's hair before hurrying to the door.

"Make sure Billy's okay. Keep him close. I'll be back as soon as I can."

"Davis! Don't leave us!"

"I'm sorry. I made a horrible mistake. I have to fix it."

He shut the door on the run, cutting off her protests.

The hour drive barely took him fifty minutes. He passed the spot initially, catching sight of tire marks off the side of the road in his headlights and skidding to a stop. He used the light on his phone and found his footprints where he crossed the ditch, hurried out to the patch of tall grass.

The bag was still there, motionless amid the stalks. He dragged it out, concerned at the feel of dead weight as he pulled it.

He tugged at the sealed end, tried to dig his fingers in and pry the weave open. It wouldn't budge. He patted his pockets.

Crap.

No knife, not even a normal car key, just a fob. He thought

about bringing it back to his car, thought better of it. He stared at the sack, running a hand through his hair and teasing it in clumps.

The enchantments on it will hold her in place.

He pulled out his phone and used the light. The symbols appeared red in the LED brightness. He doffed his coat and unbuttoned his shirt, tugging it off. He bunched part of it into a wad and spit on it, then started rubbing the large five-pointed star with the damp section. It smeared. He repeated that for each of the symbols. The final one, a long line intersected by several shorter diagonal lines, took several seconds of hard rubbing.

As soon as part of it was erased, the bag erupted in a series of jerks and bounces. A claw pushed through, followed by several more. The woven fabric tore and the creature burst out. A feline head like a huge onyx sculpture, a golden headdress adorning it above a woman's body, loomed over him. He fell back, his feet crabbing to find purchase. She had to be seven, maybe eight feet tall, her form giving off an aura like the corona of the sun.

A murderous glint of moonlight shimmered in her eyes.

Davis swallowed, trying to clear his throat. "I'm sorry."

Those eyes glared, the pouches of her mouth twitching, baring a pair of fangs. It lunged toward him, letting out a piercing screech. He curled into himself, covering his head.

A gust of wind passed over him. He raised his face after a few seconds and looked around. In the fading moonlight he could see her running, already dozens of yards away. She stopped and turned, her animal form back to what it had been before. He caught a final glisten in her eye as she looked at him, then she bounded over some shrubs and disappeared.

The small calico cat pounced onto the child's lap and wrapped its arms around his hand, much to the boy's delight. He laughed as the kitty rolled onto its back and swatted at his fingers.

"That was sweet of you to get him a kitten," Kendle said, her voice just above a whisper. "He absolutely loves that thing."

Davis put an arm around her as he watched their son, tugging her close so their hips were touching.

"I figured it might cheer him up," he said.

"Looks like you figured right."

The calico kitten, a rescue from a local shelter, was about six months old. It seemed the friendliest of the ones they had for adoption and was the only one that had eyes that particular shade of jade green.

Kendle told Billy it was time for him to get ready for bed. He pleaded for another "Figh mints! Figh mints!" and she gave in.

"Has he named her yet?" Davis asked.

"He just keeps calling her Kee-Kee. He's even got me doing it."

"Hmm. Kiki isn't bad, actually. I kind of like it."

"Whatever we call her, she sure seems to have taken to him," Kendle said. "To me, not so much. She wriggles and squirms to get away every time I pick her up as if she thinks I'm planning to make a meal out of her."

"She probably just needs time to settle in."

"Maybe. It doesn't really matter, as long as he's happy. I'm just glad something's got him smiling again."

Davis nodded. It had been a couple of weeks since the incident with Madame Dougal. After the initial trauma had started to wear off, it was obvious his son had been left confused and bereft. Though he didn't speak much, he still managed to ask Kendle about the "Kee-cah"—his way of saying "kitty cat," Davis supposed—several times a day, wanting to know where it was, when it was coming back.

"How about you? How are your allergies?"

"I'm managing. A few sniffles here and there, a sneeze every now and then, but nothing I can't handle."

Kendle eased away from her husband's side and moved toward Billy. "Okay, kiddo, your five minutes are up." To Davis she said,

"Would you mind putting her in the bathroom while I put him to bed? He'll get overtired and be cranky tomorrow if we don't separate them."

The kitten purred when Davis picked her up. He stroked her head and took her to the guest bathroom where they had a litter box set up. He poured a small cup of kibble in her bowl and gave her fresh water, crouched down and petted her while she ate. He sneezed a couple of times. He reached over and pulled a length of toilet paper to blow his nose.

Looking at the small furry creature chewing and swallowing in gulps, he couldn't help but wonder where Bast was, whether she forgave him for what he'd done to her, and whether she knew what had taken place between him and Iona Dougal. He assumed she did, hoped she did, though he had no way to be sure.

Standing, he caught sight of himself in the mirror. The skin beneath his eyes was puffy and a few shades darker than the rest. His cheeks hung in spots like an ill-fitting mask. As much as he would have liked to blame it on allergies, he couldn't. He filled his cupped hands at the sink and splashed water on his face, gently slapping it, looked up to watch it roll and drip off before patting himself dry.

Something was bothering him that he couldn't quite articulate. A lingering sense of unease that wouldn't leave. Not the same feeling he'd had leading up to recent events—this one more a sense he'd forgotten something, a mental poking, the kind that might give him pause when his brain was trying to tell him he'd left the house without his wallet or keys. He'd assumed it was something akin to PTSD at first, but now he wasn't so sure. He kept replaying Iona Dougal's words, hearing her recite them like a background track, a haunting whisper during the day, a faint echo while he tried to sleep. The more he tried not to think about it, the more his mind seemed to dwell on what she'd said.

He left the kitten in the bathroom to finish her meal, closing her in, and walked the few feet down the hallway to his son's bedroom. From the doorway he saw her place the storybook on the nightstand next to the bed. Billy was under the covers, the back of his head visible on his pillow. Davis stepped back as Kendle approached. She gently shut the door behind her, leaving it open just a crack.

"Out like a light. He closed his eyes and rolled over before I even got the book open."

Davis smiled. "I'm jealous."

"Poor dear. Still having trouble sleeping?"

"I'll be fine."

"The kitten won't yowl at night the way she has been forever. She just doesn't like being alone, poor thing. I could make her a bed in the laundry room, maybe that would be quieter. If it weren't for your allergies . . ."

"I know. It's not that. Don't worry, it'll pass."

She took his hand. "Come here. There's something I want to show you."

He followed her to the living room, where she asked him to wait. He took a seat on the couch and watched her walk through the kitchen and disappear through the back. She emerged a moment later carrying a small bag.

"I've been hiding this in the laundry room for over month," she said, placing the bag on his lap and sitting down next to him. "I had a doctor's appointment this morning. I didn't say anything, because you seemed to have enough on your mind, with all the trouble sleeping you've had."

"Are you okay?"

She squeezed his hand and nodded to the bag. He reached inside. A chill rippled over the back of his scalp as he removed a white plastic stick, flat on two sides.

He pulled in a sharp breath. The old crone's voice reverberated like fingernails across a chalkboard, her wrinkled lips vivid in his mind's eye. A child not yet five years from conception . . .

The understanding came like a hard slap. He'd been wrong—so, so wrong. He swallowed, the gulp popping his ears, and blinked his eyes wide. It wasn't Billy she'd been after. It was never about Billy.

"I can't tell if you're shocked or confused," Kendle said. "But in case you haven't figured it out yet . . ." She reached for his hand and gave it a squeeze. "I'm pregnant."

A mournful sound reached his ears, faint and barely audible, primal, like a distant wail, its embers ghosting along on the gentle night breeze. He was sure it didn't come from the bathroom.

Familiar

Frank Coffman

I wander through this world with special sight,
Doing my mistress' bidding, roaming free.
My sleek, black coat is darker than the night,
Only my mirroring eyes you'll sometimes see.
I am her favorite. !ough that crow is swift,
And toad and snake assist her in her spells.
I am the one she knows has a special gift;
A subtler magic deep within me dwells.
I prowl in stealth, spying upon Your realm.
She sees through me—though we be miles apart!
My mistress has great powers to overwhelm
Meer mortals and do magic with Dark Art.
I aid her in her witchcraft through my tricks.
I am her cat, the famed Malefelix.

The Attic

Algernon Blackwood

The forest-girdled village upon the Jura slopes slept soundly, although it was not yet many minutes after ten o'clock. The clang of the *couvre-feu* had indeed just ceased, its notes swept far into the woods by a wind that shook the mountains. This wind now rushed down the deserted street. It howled about the old rambling building called La Citadelle, whose roof towered gaunt and humped above the smaller houses—Château unfinished long ago by Lord Wemyss, the exiled Jacobite. The families who occupied the various apartments listened to the storm and felt the building tremble. "It's the mountain wind. It will bring the snow," the mother said, without looking up from her knitting. "And how sad it sounds."

But it was not the wind that brought sadness as we sat round the open fire of peat. It was the wind of memories. The lamplight slanted along the narrow room towards the table where breakfast things lay ready for the morning. The double windows were fastened. At the far end stood a door ajar, and on the other side of it the two elder children lay asleep in the big bed. But beside the window was a smaller unused bed that had been empty now a year. And to-night was the anniversary. . . .

And so the wind brought sadness and long thoughts. The little chap that used to lie there was already twelve months gone, far, far beyond the Hole where the Winds came from, as he called it; yet it seemed only yesterday that I went to tell him a tuck-up story, to stroke Riquette, the old motherly cat that cuddled against his back and laid a paw beside his pillow like a human being, and to hear his funny little earnest whisper say, "Oncle, tu sais, j'ai prié pour Petavel." For La Citadelle had its unhappy ghost—of Petavel, the usurer, who had hanged himself in the attic a century gone by, and was known to walk its dreary corridors in search of peace—and this wise Irish mother, calming the boy's fears with wisdom, had told him, "If you pray for Petavel, you'll save his soul and make him happy, and he'll only love you." And, thereafter, this little imaginative boy had done so every night. With a passionate seriousness he did it. He had wonderful, delicate ways like that. In all our hearts he made his fairy nests of wonder. In my own, I know, he lay closer than any joy imaginable, with his big blue eyes, his queer soft questionings, and his splendid child's unselfishness—a sun-kissed flower of innocence that, had he lived, might have sweetened half a world.

"Let's put more peat on," the mother said, as a handful of rain like stones came flinging against the windows; "that must be hail." And she went on tiptoe to the inner room. "They're sleeping like two puddings," she whispered, coming presently back. But it struck me she had taken longer than to notice merely that; and her face wore an odd expression that made me uncomfortable. I thought she was somehow just about to laugh or cry. By the table a second she hesitated. I caught the flash of indecision as it passed. "Pan," she said suddenly—it was a nickname, stolen from my tuck-up stories, *he* had given me—"I wonder how Riquette got in." She looked hard at me. "It wasn't you, was it?" For we never let her come at night since he had gone. It was too poignant. The beastie always went cuddling and nestling into that empty bed. But this time it was not my doing, and I offered plausible explanations. "But—she's on the bed. Pan, would you be so kind—" She left the sentence unfinished, but I easily understood, for a lump had somehow risen in my own throat too, and I remembered now that she had come out from the inner room so quickly—with a kind of hurried rush almost. I put "mère Riquette" out into the corridor. A lamp stood on the chair outside the door of another occupant further down, and I urged her gently towards it. She turned and looked at me—straight up into my face; but, instead of going down as I suggested, she went slowly in the opposite direction. She stepped softly towards a door in the wall that led up broken stairs into the attics. There she sat down and waited. And so I left her, and came back hastily to the peat fire and companionship. The wind rushed in behind me and slammed the door.

And we talked then somewhat busily of cheerful things; of the children's future, the excellence of the cheap Swiss schools, of Christmas presents, ski-ing, snow, tobogganing. I led the talk away from mournfulness; and when these subjects were exhausted I told stories of my own adventures in distant parts of the world. But "mother" listened the whole time—not to me. Her thoughts were all elsewhere. And her air of intently, secretly listening, bordered, I felt, upon the uncanny. For she often stopped her knitting and sat with her eyes fixed upon the air before her; she stared blankly at the wall, her head slightly on one side, her figure tense, attention strained—elsewhere. Or, when my talk positively demanded it, her nod was oddly mechanical and her eyes looked through and past me. The wind continued very loud and roaring; but the fire glowed, the room was warm and cosy. Yet she shivered, and when I drew attention to it, her reply, "I do feel cold, but I didn't know I shivered," was given as though she spoke across the air to someone else. But what impressed me even more uncomfortably were her repeated questions about Riquette. When a pause in my tales permitted, she would look up with "I wonder where Riquette went?" or, thinking of the inclement night, "I hope mère Riquette's not out of doors. Perhaps Madame Favre has taken her in?" I offered to go and see. Indeed I was already half-way across the room when there came the heavy bang at the door that rooted me to the ground where I stood. It was not wind. It was something alive that made it rattle. There was a second blow. A thud on the corridor boards followed, and then a high, odd voice that at first was as human as the cry of a child.

It is undeniable that we both started, and for myself I can answer truthfully that a chill ran down my spine; but what frightened me more than the sudden noise and the eerie cry was the way "mother" supplied the immediate explanation. For behind the words "It's only Riquette; she sometimes springs at the door like that; perhaps we'd better let her in," was a certain touch of uncanny quiet that made me feel she had known the cat would come, and knew also why she came. One cannot explain such impressions further. They leave their vital touch, then go their way. Into the little room, however, in that moment there came between us this uncomfortable sense that the night held other purposes than our own—and that my companion was aware of them. There was something going on far, far removed from the routine of life as we were accustomed to it. Moreover, our usual routine was the eddy, while this was the main stream. It felt big, I mean.

And so it was that the entrance of the familiar, friendly creature brought this thing both itself and "mother" *knew,* but whereof I as yet was ignorant. I held the door wide. The draught rushed through behind her, and sent a shower of sparks about the fireplace. The lamp flickered and gave a little gulp. And Riquette marched slowly past, with all the impressive dignity of her kind, towards the other door that stood ajar. Turning the comer like a shadow, she disappeared into the room where the two children slept. We heard the soft thud with which she leaped upon the bed. Then, in a lull of the wind, she came back again and sat on the oil-cloth, staring into "mother's" face. She mewed and put a paw out, drawing the black dress softly with half-opened claws. And it was all so horribly suggestive and pathetic, it revived such poignant memories, that I got up impulsively—I think I had actually said the words, "We'd better put her out, mother, after all"—when my companion rose to her feet and forestalled me. She said another thing instead. It took my breath away to hear it. "She wants us to go with her. Pan, will you come too?" The surprise on my face must have asked the question, for I do not remember saying anything. "To the attic," she said quietly.

She stood there by the table, a tall, grave figure dressed in black, and her face above the lamp-shade caught the full glare of light. Its expression positively stiffened me. She seemed so secure in her singular purpose. And her familiar appearance had so oddly given place to something wholly strange to me. She looked like another person—almost with the unwelcome transformation of the sleep-walker about her. Cold came over me as I watched her, for I remembered suddenly her Irish second-sight, her story years ago of meeting a figure on the attic stairs, the figure of Petavel. And the idea of this motherly, sedate, and wholesome woman, absorbed day and night in prosaic domestic duties, and yet "seeing" things, touched the incongruous almost to the point of alarm. It was so distressingly convincing.

Yet she knew quite well that I would come. Indeed, following the excited animal, she was already by the door, and a moment later, still without answering or protesting, I was with them in the draughty corridor. There was something inevitable in her manner that made it impossible to refuse. She took the lamp from its nail on the wall, and following our four-footed guide, who ran with obvious pleasure just in front, she opened the door into the court-yard. The wind nearly put the lamp out, but a minute later we were safe inside the passage that led up flights of creaky wooden stairs towards the world of tenantless attics overhead.

And I shall never forget the way the excited Riquette first stood up and put her paws upon the various doors, trotted ahead, turned back to watch us coming, and then finally sat down and waited on the threshold of the empty, raftered space that occu-pied the entire length of the building underneath the roof. For her manner was more that of an intelligent dog than of a cat, and sometimes more like that of a human mind than either.

We had come up without a single word. The howling of the wind as we rose higher was like the roar of artillery. There were many broken stairs, and the narrow way was full of twists and turn-ings. It was a dreadful journey. I felt eyes watching us from all the yawning spaces of the darkness, and the noise of the storm smothered footsteps everywhere. Troops of shadows kept us company. But it was on the threshold of this big, chief attic, when "mother" stopped abruptly to put down the lamp, that real fear took hold of me. For Riquette marched steadily forward into the middle of the dusty flooring, picking her way among the fallen tiles and mortar, as though she went towards—someone. She purred loudly and uttered little cries of excited pleasure. Her tail went up into the air, and she lowered her head with the unmistakable intention of being stroked. Her lips opened and shut. Her green eyes smiled. She was being stroked.

It was an unforgettable performance. I would rather have witnessed an execution or a murder than watch that mysterious creature twist and tum about in the way she did. Her magnified shadow was as large as a pony on the floor and rafters. I wanted to hide the whole thing by extinguishing the lamp. For, even before the mysterious action began, I experienced the sudden rush of conviction that others besides ourselves were in this attic—and standing very dose to us indeed. And, although there was ice in my blood, there was also a strange swelling of the heart that only love and tenderness could bring.

But, whatever it was, my human companion, still silent, knew and understood. She *saw*. And her soft whisper that ran with the wind among the rafters, "Il a prié pour Petavel et le bon Dieu l'a entendu," did not amaze me one quarter as much as the expression I then caught upon her radiant face. Tears ran down the cheeks, but they were tears of happiness. Her whole figure seemed lit up. She opened her arms—picture of great Motherhood, proud, blessed, and tender beyond words. I thought she was going to fall, for she took quick steps forward; but when I moved to catch her, she drew me aside instead with a sudden gesture that brought fear back in the place of wonder.

"Let them pass," she whispered grandly. "Pan, don't you see.. ...He's leading him into peace and safety ...by the hand!" And her joy seemed to kill the shadows and fill the entire attic with white light. Then, almost simultaneously with her words, she swayed. I was in time to catch her, but as I did so, across the very spot where we had just been standing—two figures, I swear, went past us like a flood of light.

There was a moment next of such confusion that I did not see what happened to Riquette, for the sight of my companion kneeling on the dusty boards and praying with a curious sort of passionate happiness, while tears pressed between her covering fingers—the strange wonder of this made me utterly oblivious to minor details. . . .

We were sitting round the peat lire again, and "mother" was saying to me in the gentlest, tenderest whisper I ever heard from human lips—"Pan, I think perhaps that's why God took him. . . ."

And when a little later we went in to make Riquette cosy in the empty bed, ever since kept sacred to her use, the mournfulness had lifted; and in the place of resignation was proud peace and joy that knew no longer sad or selfish questionings.

Ailurophobe

Mary Turzillo

Ailurophobe.
And yet.
This sleek gray velvet beast,
Warm like a baguette fresh from the oven.

Eat me.

It settles on her throat.
She is sleeping.
The beast, a she-cat, purrs soft, unending thunder.

The ailurophobe squirms, restive.
The beast's tail insinuates around her neck.
Its breath simmers in her mouth.

Wake up! Danger!
Moisture, a hot drug, blooms between her legs.
She moans, undulates, hypnogogically ignited.

The beast drills her eyes with its own slit pupils.
Glamorous eyes!
Spread your legs, my dear.

The beast grows longer, woman-size now,
to mimic the ailurophobe.
The beast grows breasts, firm, nipples pink as its nose.
But the beast's hands still sport claws.

And those hands caress with tiny prickles
rousing the ailurophobe to urgency.
The ailurophobe bucks against the beast.

Urgent, urgent, please let me—
And climaxes.
It is done.
The beast shrinks, says one final meow
The meow is not "I love you."
Just "Finished with you now."

The ailurophobe wakes, fully.
Sheets drenched in body-dew and vaginal oozings.

She looks at her hands. The backs begin to fur.
She is shrinking.
The size of a prey animal.
Her hands
have claws.

And starting again, the fear, the longing.

Cats and the Occult: A Canthropology

Katherine Kerestman

"Who peynted the leon, tel me who?"
~Chaucer, The Wife of Bath's Tale

Many of us know intuitively that *Felis Catus* is a different order of entity, not merely a flesh-and-blood mammalian member of earth's rich and varied zoology, but also a thoughtful and observant creature inhabiting a mental plane disparate from our own, and who is known to keep his own counsel and drive us mad with wanting to know his secrets. Then, too, the cat is a creature of paradoxes: think how a silky, soft, and pliant lap-nestling cat may at any moment transform himself into a muscular, lithe, quick-springing, sharp-clawed, and razor-toothed warrior and hunter, swatting the hand that pets him—or, alternately, defending his people by slaying the destructive rodents that threaten their well-being. A third uncanny attribute of the cat is his nocturnal nature, for a cat will venture bravely into the darkness that our kind fears, leaving us to wonder what draws him from the light. When all the world is made invisible by the cloak of night, a cat's eyes will shine weirdly from the Stygian void. The characteristic of the cat that tends to most annoy people who do not like—nay, even fear or hate—cats is their independence, for a cat neither heeds a person's orders nor hovers close to his friends, preferring solitary wandering and quiet meditation, and he will come to a person of his own accord and in his own time. Humankind's extreme reactions to these catly qualities has, over time, resulted in the exaltation of our whiskered friends—and in their cruel destruction.

When humans first began to cultivate grain, in the days of ancient Egypt, it was the cats who saved the nascent agricultural enterprise from destruction by mice, rats, and sundry rodents, who, unchecked, can consume a storehouse bursting with next year's foodstuffs faster than farmers can fill it. It was largely due to the essential aid rendered the first farmers by cats that people were able to evolve from their hunter-gathering past into their commercial and communal future. Not only the fields and the storehouses, but their own homes were well served by the cats who preyed on the rats that invaded their dwellings while humans slept at night.

The ancient Egyptians so appreciated the assistance of their feline allies that they accorded them the status of gods. Bastet, the cat-headed goddess of marriage, home, and fertility, and Sekhmet, the lion-headed goddess, a fierce huntress and healer, were the daughters of Ra, the sun god, who, cat-like, slew the Serpent of Darkness. And then there is Mafdet, the cheetah-skin-wearing goddess of judgment and justice. Deceased cats were mummified and placed in tombs, in expectancy of their awakening to an afterlife. People wore cat amulets, seeking the protection of the cat gods, and, in Bastet's temple, the priests maintained a community of cats. At the height of the cult of Bastet, it was a capital crime to kill a cat. Eventually, the ancient Greeks fused Bastet with Artemis and Hekate, who possessed a cat familiar. World-traders, the Egyptians also introduced the domesticated housecat to Europe, unwittingly doing their feline friends an ill service.

Although the Christian people of medieval Europe amassed fortunes buying and selling luxury goods brought from every heathen corner of the globe, they did not welcome the domestication of cats. For their own sake, European cats would have better remained feral, a condition in which they would have been safer from humans; for this was the time of the Inquisition, witches were identified with cats, and witches were thought to change into animals, especially cats (said to be a favorite among their menagerie of small domestic familiars). A woman could be considered a witch because she harbored a cat in her home. This identification of witches with cats did not bode well for the cats: cats were burned alive, as were witches. In 1232, the Catholic Church pronounced cats to be demonic: in a bull condemning German heretical sects (*Vox in Rama*), Pope Gregory IX said that cats were Satan incarnate; and so, although cats were usually tolerated for the service they rendered in the role of mouser, still they were the frequent object of massive hunts and exterminations. This cruel holocaust of the felines of Europe came back to bite their superstitious persecutors; for, when the Black Death came to Europe, it rode in on the backs of fleas *and mice!* And there were fewer cats around to control the population of mice.

By the eighteenth century, most people considered themselves too modern and sophisticated to believe in witches; hence they discounted as mere nonsense all the testimony given in the witch trials (which had spanned half a millennium), dismissing the confessions as the desperate words of tortured innocents who said what their accusers wanted to hear in order to receive a momentary respite from unbearable suffering. But the damage had been done, for cats, at least, who would forever bear the stigma of evil, in the eyes of many people.

The second half of the nineteenth century through the first quarter of the twentieth century was a period characterized by a widespread popular interest in the occult, with the result that many historians, theologians, and popular writers trawled the witch trials for inspiration. In 1921, in *The Witch-Cult in Western Europe,* an Egyptologist named Margaret Murray broke with the majority opinion when she took a good look at the testimonies of the accused and took them at their word; and she argued that modern witchcraft was a continuation of pre-Christian nature worship, which had never really gone extinct. Murray's theories are the foundation of many modern Wiccan and woman-centered religious beliefs. She found that a large percentage of the crimes of which the witches were accused related to reproduction:

> *The celebrated Decree of Innocent VIII, which in 1488 let loose the full force of the Church against the witches, says that "they blight the marriage bed, destroy the births of women and the increase of cattle; they blast the corn on the ground, the grapes of the vineyard, the fruits of the trees, the grass and herbs of the field." (Murray 199)*

The frequency with which Murray cites instances of charges being leveled against the accused, *that they practiced diablerie for the purpose of causing impotence,* suggests that the women were not persecuted by the Christian faithful as practitioners of Satanism, but by angry men who were incensed by the witches' impairment of their fertility:

> *Jonet Clark was tried in Edinburgh in 1590 "for giving and taking away power from sundry men's Genital-members" . . . The number of midwives who practiced witchcraft points to this fact; they claimed to be able to cause and to prevent pregnancy, to cause and to prevent an easy delivery, to cast the labour-pains, on an animal or a human being (husbands who were the victims are peculiarly incensed against these witches), and in every way to have power over the generative organs of both sexes. In short, it is possible to say that, in the sixteenth and seventeenth centuries, the better the midwife the better the witch. (Murray 200)*

The devil, who appeared at the Sabbats of the witches, according to Murray, was a man, "the chief personage of the cult" (Murray 32), who was often garbed in an animal costume, a "bull, cat, dog, goat, horse, and sheep" (Murray 66).[1] Trial testimonies yield hundreds of anecdotes of the devil appearing as a cat, as well as of witches training cats to be their familiars by feeding them with their own blood, witches turning into cats and riding in the air on their victims' backs, and witches suckling their cat familiars on their normal nipples on or on their witch teats.

Murray's chief contribution to the study of the witch trials is her assertion that not all of these stories were the hallucinations of torture-crazed victims:

> *These were women of every class and every age, from just above puberty to old women of over seventy, unmarried, married, and widows. It is unscientific to disbelieve everything, as Scot does, and it is equally unscientific to label all the phenomena as the imagination of hysterical women. . . . Such a mass of evidence cannot be ignored, and in any other subject would obtain credence at once. But the hallucination-theory, being the easiest, appears to have obsessed the minds of many writers, to the exclusion of any attempt at explanation from an unbiased point of view. (Murray 207)*

A cursory reading of *Malleus Maleficarum*, the 1486 handbook written by Jacobus Sprenger and Heinrich Kramer for the edification and guidance of witch hunters, clerics, and lawyers, on the subject of how to identify and deal with a witch, suggests that the presence of sex therapists, birth control, and Viagra would have saved the lives of more than a hundred thousand accused witches (most of whom were women)—and countless cats. For example, various chapters are entitled "How, as it were, they deprive man of his virile member" (Sprenger 90), "Remedies prescribed for those who are bewitched by the limitation of the generative power" (Sprenger 172), and "Remedies prescribed for those who by prestidigitatory art have lost their virile members or have seemingly been transformed into the shapes of beasts" (Sprenger 181).

While witches may transform themselves into the shapes of many beasts, the authors of *Malleus Maleficarum* single out the cat as the preferred animal. They tell the story of a Strasburg man who, while working, was attacked by a horde of cats, which he beat off of him, only later to be brought up on charges of beating three women, who were so badly injured that they were unable to rise from their beds and who had accused him of beating *them*.

Hearing his defense, the authorities, "understanding that it was the work of the devil, . . . released the poor man and let him go away unharmed" (Sprenger 103). The record, apparently, is silent on who did beat the women. By the Burning Times of the Inquisition and the appearance of Witch-Finder General Matthew Hopkins, the cat had already acquired a bad reputation: "an animal which is, in the Scriptures, an appropriate symbol of the perfidious . . . for cats are always setting snares for each other" (Sprenger 105).

In *The History of Witchcraft and Demonology* (1925), Montague Summers, the best-selling Roman Catholic author of many popular works on the occult, agrees with Murray that it is not good history to dismiss the entirety of the testimonies of the witch trials out of hand, simply on the ground that the confessions were obtained by intimidation and torture; he does take issue, though, with several of Murray's conclusions, primarily, her thesis that witchcraft is a resurgence of a joyous religion descended from ancient Celtic nature-worship, which had long persisted in hiding. Summers, like Murray, explores the titillating attributes of witches and witchcraft, for which contemporary readers were hungry: witches' marks, witches' teats (for suckling their familiars) the sacrifice and eating of children, utilization of "artificial penises" (Summers 98) in their rites, the Sabbat, the Satanic Kiss, the Black Mass, and demon and animal familiars; but, citing the authority of medieval theologians and more recent theorists, such as Cotton Mather and the authors of *Malleus Maleficarum,* Summers reaches the conclusion that witches are servants of Satan:

> *In some sense Witchcraft was a descendant of the old pre-Christian magic, but . . . at the advent of Christianity it was exposed and shown in its real foul essence as the worship of the Evil Principle, the Enemy of Mankind, Satan. (Summers 29)*

According to Summers, witches perpetrated their foul spells not only to render men impotent and to ruin crops, but to bring down the Church. As an example of how witches threaten Christendom, Summers cites the often-told story of King James VI (I), in which a cat is the tool of a murderous witch:

> *The most celebrated occasion when witches raised a storm was that which played so important a part in the trial of Dr. Fian and his coven, 1590-1, when the witches, in order to drown King James and Queen Anne on their voyage from Denmark, "took a Cat and christened it," and after they had bound a dismembered corpse to the animal 'in the night following the said Cat was convayed into the middest of the sea, by all these witches, sayling in their riddles or cives, . . . this done, then did arise such a tempest in the sea, as a greater hath not bene seene." (Summers 88)*

King James was so upset at the attempt on his life by witches that he wrote his own treatise on witchcraft, *Daemonologie* (1597), from which royal text Montague Summers extracted the above anecdote.

Summers concedes that the cat, to its great disadvantage, has been permanently ensconced in the collective cultural consciousness as the confederate of the witch:

> *In England particularly there is abundance of evidence concerning them, and even to-day who pictures a witch with nut-cracker jaws, steeple hat, red cloak, hobbling along on her crutch, without her big black cat beside her? (Summers 101)*

He feels sorry for the innocent women who were branded as witches simply for loving a companion animal; yet he says not all of them were innocent:

> *It is piteous to think that in many cases some miserable creature who, shunned and detested by her fellows, has sought friendship in the love of a cat or a dog, whom she has fondled and*

lovingly fed with the best tid-bits she could give, on the strength of this affection alone was dragged to the gallows or the stake. But very frequently the witch did actually keep some small animal which she nourished on a diet of milk and bread and her own blood in order that she might divine by its means. (Summers 101)

The three works discussed to this point detail hundreds anecdotes of witches in league with cats, such as this famous story:

At the trial of Elizabeth Francis, Chelmsford, 1556, the accused confessed that her familiar, given to her by her grandmother, a notorious witch, was "in the lykeness of a white spotted Catte," and her grandmother "taught her to feede the sayde Catte with breade and mylke, and she did so, also she taughte her to cal it by the name of Sattan and to kepe it in a basket. Item that euery tyme that he did any thynge for her, she sayde that he required a drop of bloude, which she gaue him by prycking herselfe, sometime in one place and then in another." (Summers 102)

As we have already noted, at the trials the accused would often speak of the devil appearing in the form of an animal. Summers describes some of the Sabbats as masquerades, with a cat costume being a preferred guise: "Francoise Secretain, who was tried in August, 1508, saw the Devil 'tantost en forme de chat.' Rolande de Vernois acknowledged 'Le Diable se presenta pour lors au Sabbat en form d'vn groz chat noir" (Summers 135).

And again: "Alexander Hunter, *alias* Hamilton, *alias* Hattaraick, a 'Warlok Cairle' who 'abused the Countrey for a long time,' was apprehended at Dunbar [and] he confessed that the Devil would meet him riding upon a black horse, or in the shape of a *corbie*, a cat, or a dog. He was burned upon Castle Hill, Edinburgh, 1631" (Summers, 135).

Another of the popular early anthropological studies of witchcraft to which Summers refers is *The Golden Bough,* a treatise on the development of religion from the dawn of humanity to the present time, initially published in 1890 by Sir James George Frazer and expanded over the next twenty-five years into a twelve-volume work. Postulating that the concept of religion began with the worship of nature by prehistoric peoples the world over and evolved in tandem with human evolution (begging the question of whether human evolution occurs in an upward, downward, or horizontal movement), discarding much of the superstition it had acquired along the way, he shook the foundations of established religions, which claimed to be divinely inspired, not merely a continuance and development of prehistoric superstitions. In his encyclopedic work, Frazer offers thousands of examples of the deification of plants, animals, men, and women by ancient societies in every corner of the globe. Additionally, he explores the fundamental characteristics that all religions possess, among these the worship of and conciliation of the deity to obtain desired outcomes; the sacrifice of animals, plants, inanimate objects, and people for said purposes; and even the sacrifice of the god himself.

Cats, as well as other animals, have a place in his discussions of sympathetic magic, in which he describes a ceremony designed to induce rain in Java, wherein a pair of cats are ritually bathed and paraded in a religious procession (Frazer 83). In his discussion of sacrifice, he tells of the frequent practice of burning cats alive:

In the midsummer fires formerly kindled on the Place de Greve at Paris it was the custom to burn a basket, barrel, or sack full of live cats, which was hung from a tall mast in the middle of a bonfire; sometimes a fox was burned. The people collected the embers and ashes of the fire and took them home, believing that they brought good luck. . . . At Metz midsummer fires were lighted with great pomp on the esplanade, and a dozen cats, enclosed in wicker cages, were burned alive in them, to the amusement of the people. Similary at Gap, in the department of the High Alps, cats used to be roasted over the midsummer bonfire. . . . In the Vosges cats were burned on Shrove Tuesday; in Alsace they were thrown into the Easter bonfire. In the department of the Ardennes the cats were flung into the bonfires kindled on the first Sunday in Lent; sometimes by a refinement of cruelty, they were hung over the fire from the end of a pole and roasted alive. . . . Thus, it appears that the sacrificial rites of the Celts of ancient Gaul can be traced in the popular festivals of modern Europe . . . [and] these rites have left the clearest traces in the customs of burning giants of wicker-work and animals enclosed in wicker-work or baskets. (Frazer 760–61)

Those of us who love cats know all too well that our furry friends continue, through no fault of their own, to inspire hatred and fear—the victims of an unfounded and unreasoned prejudice inculcated by the Catholic Church in the Middle Ages, reinforced by popular writers on the subject of witchcraft, and still held by many people—and that numerous groundless superstitions persist to this day, such as the belief that bad luck (in some societies, good luck) follows when a black cat crosses one's path. Other misconceptions, such as the conviction that black cats are in themselves unlucky, result in a more frequent incidence of abuse of felines of that color than their lighter-hued brethren. Today, many modern witches and Wiccans consider their companion animals to be their spirit guides or partners. (I have attended witchcraft seminars in Salem, Massachusetts, at which the familiars who accompanied the presenters were described as "rescued" animals.) The fact remains that a lot of people tend either to love cats or to hate them. Cats, simply by being cats, inspire strong emotions in many people, a phenomenon of "Otherness" that has resulted in both their being exalted as gods and feared as demons.

Endnotes:

[1]In *The Downfall of God: A History of Atheism in the West,* S. T. Joshi, in a passage summarizing and seeking to make sense of the witch hunt phenomenon, notes: "Nicolas Rémy (sometimes known by his Latin name Remigius), in *Daemonolatrieia* (1595), propounded the view that the Devil could appear in the shape of a black cat or a man, and in the latter role he would lead the Black Mass. He branded those who denied the existence of witches as atheists."

Works Cited

Frazer, Sir James George. *The Golden Bough: A Study in Magic and Religion.* Abridged Edition. New York: Macmillan, 1922.

Joshi, S. T. *The Downfall of God: A History of Atheism in the West.* Pitchstone Publishing, forthcoming.

Murray, Margaret Alice. *The Witch-Cult in Western Europe.* Oxford: Oxford University Press, 1921.

Sprenger, Jacobus, and Kramer, Heinrich. *Malleus Maleficarum: The Hammer of Witchcraft.* 1486. Tr. Montague Summers. Ed. Pennethorne Hughes. London: Folio Society, 1968.

Summers, Montague. *The History of Witchcraft and Demonology.* 1925. New York: Bristol Park Books, 2010.

The Editors:

S. T. Joshi is the author of *The Weird Tale* (1990), *H. P. Lovecraft: The Decline of the West* (1990), and *Unutterable Horror: A History of Supernatural Fiction* (2012). He has prepared corrected editions of H. P. Lovecraft's work for Arkham House and annotated editions of Lovecraft's stories for Penguin Classics. His exhaustive biography, *H. P. Lovecraft: A Life* (1996), was expanded as *I Am Providence: The Life and Times of H. P. Lovecraft* (2010). He has edited the anthologies *American Supernatural Tales* (Penguin, 2007), *A Mountain Walked: Great Tales of the Cthulhu Mythos* (Centipede Press, 2013), *The Madness of Cthulhu* (Titan Books, 2014), and the ongoing *Black Wings* series (PS Publishing, 2010f.). Joshi has won the World Fantasy Award, the British Fantasy Award, the Bram Stoker Award, and the International Horror Guild Award.

Katherine Kerestman is the author of *Lethal* (PsychoToxin Press, 2023) and *Creepy Cat's Macabre Travels: Prowling around Haunted Towers, Crumbling Castles, and Ghoulish Graveyards* (WordCrafts Press, 2020). Her Lovecraftian and Gothic works have been featured in *Black Wings VII*, *Penumbra*, *Journ-E*, *Spectral Realms*, and *The Little Book of Cursed Dolls* (Media Macabre, 2023). Katherine is wild about *Dark Shadows* and *Twin Peaks* and has been seen cavorting in the graveyards of Salem on Halloween. You can keep up with her at www.creepycatlair.com.

The Contributors:

Algernon Blackwood (1869–1951), English short story writer and novelist, worked extensively in the weird, with such volumes as *The Listener and Other Stories* (1907), *John Silence—Physician Extraordinary* (1908), *The Lost Valley and Other Stories* (1910), *Pan's Garden* (1912), and *Incredible Adventures* (1914). Late in life he appeared on radio and television for the BBC, reading horror tales.

William Blake (1757–1827) was a pioneering English poet of the Romantic era, with such volumes as *Songs of Innocence and Experience* (1794), *The Marriage of Heaven and Hell* (written 1790–93), *Jerusalem* (written 1804–20), many of them illustrated by himself. He also illustrated works by Mary Wollstonecraft, Edward Young, Thomas Gray, Dante, and others.

Adam Bolivar is a poet of dark fantasy, a weird fiction writer, and a playwright for marionettes with a particular interest in balladry and alliterative verse. He is the author of *The Lay of Old Hex* (Hippocampus Press, 2017), *The Ettinfell of Beacon Hill* (Jackanapes Press, 2021), *Ballads for the Witching Hour* (Hippocampus Press 2022), and *A Wheel of Ravens* (Jackanapes Press, 2023). A native of Boston, he now resides in Portland, Oregon.

The *Oxford Companion to English Literature* describes Ramsey Campbell as "Britain's most respected living horror writer," and the *Washington Post* sums up his work as "one of the monumental accomplishments of modern popular fiction." He has received the Grand Master Award of the World Horror Convention, the

Lifetime Achievement Award of the Horror Writers Association, the Living Legend Award of the International Horror Guild, and the World Fantasy Lifetime Achievement Award. In 2015 he was made an Honorary Fellow of Liverpool John Moores University for outstanding services to literature. The two volumes of *Phantasmagorical Stories* offer a sixty-year retrospective of his short fiction. *The Village Killings* collects his novellas, and *Ramsey's Rambles* his film reviews. His latest novel is *Fellstones* from Flame Tree Press, who have also recently published his *Brichester Mythos* trilogy.

Lewis Carroll was the pseudonym of Charles Luttwidge Dodgson (1832–1898), an English poet and mathematician who gained celebrity with his tales about Alice, the young girl who is featured in *Alice's Adventures in Wonderland* (1865) and *Through the Looking-Glass* (1871). His poetry appears in *Phantasmagoria and Other Poems* (1869), *The Hunting of the Snark* (1876), and other works.

Frank Coffman is a retired professor of English, Creative Writing, and Journalism. Three major collections of speculative verse—*The Coven's Hornbook & Other Poems, Black Flames & Gleaming Shadows,* and *Eclipse of the Moon*—will be followed by *What the Night Brings* [out later this year]. His poetry spanning the popular genres has appeared in many magazines, journals, and anthologies. His collection of occult detective stories, *Three Against the Dark,* was published in 2022.

Sir Arthur Conan Doyle (1859–1930), English short story writer and novelist, is best known for the creation of the consulting detective Sherlock Holmes; but his weird tales are scattered throughout his numerous short story collections. He was also a pioneer in early science fiction in such works as *The Lost World* (1912) and *The Poison Belt* (1913). He himself regarded his historical novels—*Micah Clarke* (1889), *The White Company* (1891), and others—as his greatest work.

Lord Dunsany (Edward John Moreton Drax Plunkett, 18th baron Dunsany, 1878–1957) was an Anglo-Irish short story writer, novelist, playwright, and poet who pioneered the subgenre of imaginary-world fantasy in such early volumes as *The Gods of Pegāna* (1905), *Time and the Gods* (1906), and *A Dreamer's Tales* (1910). His plays—*Five Plays* (1914), *Plays of Gods and Men* (1917), *Plays of Near and Far* (1923), and others—introduced fantasy into the drama. And his novels—*The King of Elfland's Daughter* (1924), *The Blessing of Pan* (1927), *The Curse of the Wise Woman* (1933), and others—are also highly regarded.

Jason C. Eckhardt has known many weird cats (is there any other kind?) and loved them all. His current feline companion, Laird Kenneth Swatmore, was inspiration for his contribution to this book. He lives in New Bedford, Mass., with his wife Jackie, Kenny, and dog Mike.

Born in 1946, Alan Dean Foster is the author of more than 140 books, ranging from fantasy and science fiction to westerns, mysteries, and nonfiction. A world traveler, he finds inspiration in many of the places he has visited. A nocturnal sojourn in Paris, coupled with the famous Art Nouveau poster by the Swiss artist Theophile-Alexandre Steinlen, inspired this story. Foster lives with his wife JoAnn in Prescott, Arizona. He is currently working on a new novel and, as an avid amateur composer, his seventh symphony and a symphonic poem.

Brandon R. Grafius is associate professor of biblical studies and academic dean at Ecumenical Theological Seminary, Detroit. He has published widely on the intersection of horror and religion, most recently in *Lurking under the Surface: Horror, Religion, and the Questions That Haunt Us*. His next book is scheduled to be published by Oxford University Press in 2024.

Lafcadio Hearn (1850–1904) was a writer of Greek and Anglo-Irish ancestry who emigrated to the United States in 1869. Articles written for newspapers in Cincinnati and New Orleans were collected as *Fantastics* (1914). In 1890 he moved to Japan, where he became known as Koizumi Yakumo. He probed Asian culture in such works as *Some Chinese Ghosts* (1887), *In Ghostly Japan* (1899), and *Kwaidan* (1904). He also translated weird works by Flaubert, Gautier, and others.

Caitlín R. Kiernan is a two-time winner of both the World Fantasy and Bram Stoker awards. She is also the recipient of the Locus and James Tiptree, Jr. awards. She has published ten novels, including *The Red Tree* and *The Drowning Girl: A Memoir*. Her short fiction has been collected in eighteen volumes, including *Tales of Pain and Wonder*, *The Ammonite Violin & Others*, *The Ape's Wife and Other Stories*, and, most recently, *Houses under the Sea: Mythos Tales* (Centipede Press, 2018) and *Vile Affections* (Subterranean Press, 2021). She is currently writing her next novel, *The Starkeeper*.

Rudyard Kipling (1865–1936), English short story writer, novelist, and poet, worked extensively in the realms of fantasy and horror, including such works as *The Phantom 'Rickshaw* (1888), *The Jungle Book* (1894), *The Second Jungle Book* (1896), and *Puck of Pook's Hill*

(1906). His collected weird tales can be found in *The Mark of the Beast and Other Horror Tales,* ed. S. T. Joshi (Dover, 2000).

Tony LaMalfa is at heart just a big kid from a small town who became a produced playwright a few years before joining the Horror Writers Association in 2020. His theatrical works focus on historical fiction while his horror stories are inspired by H. P. Lovecraft. He lives in Upper Michigan with his young family and is grateful to S. T. and Katherine for their kindness and professionalism. www.tonylamalfa.com.

H[oward] P[hillips] Lovecraft (1890–1937), American short story writer, essayist, poet, and epistolarian, has now become recognized as the leading weird writer of the twentieth century. Although he published extensively in *Weird Tales* and other pulp magazines in his lifetime, his book publications were mostly posthumous, beginning with *The Outsider and Others* (1939). The publication of his letters (beginning in 1965) has revealed him to be one of the world's great ailurophiles.

Author-illustrator and poet Lori R. Lopez is particularly fond of hats and cats. Stories and verse appear in *The Sirens Call, Spectral Realms, Space & Time, The Horror Zine, Weirdbook, Dreams & Nightmares, H.W.A. Poetry Showcases, JOURN-E,* Impspired, *Aphelion, Bewildering Stories, Altered Reality,* and more. Books include *The Dark Mister Snark, Odds and Ends, The Witchhunt, Leery Lane, Darkverse,* and *The Shadow Hours.* Lori has been nominated for Rhysling Awards and the Elgin Award.

E[dith] Nesbit (1858–1924) was an English writer who became

renowned for her books for and about children, many of them with fantastic elements, including *The Story of the Treasure Seekers* (1899), *Five Children and It* (1902), and *The Enchanted Castle* (1907). She wrote horror tales for adults in *Grim Tales* (1893) and *Fear* (1910). For her collected weird tales, see *From the Dead,* ed. S. T. Joshi (Hippocampus Press, 2018).

Elliott O'Donnell (1872–1965) was an English author chiefly known for purportedly true accounts of weird phenomena, including *Some Haunted Houses* (1908), *Scottish Ghost Stories* (1912), and *Ghosts, Helpful and Harmful* (1924). He also wrote two weird novels, *For Satan's Sake* (1904) and *The Unknown Depths* (1905).

Manuel Pérez-Campos of Bayamón, Puerto Rico, is a longtime poet in the tradition of the weird, with work published in several venues.

Michael Potts is the author of two horror novels, *Unpardonable Sin* and *Obedience,* and two volumes of horror poetry. He is Professor of Philosophy at Methodist University in Fayetteville, N.C. He lives with his wife, Karen, and six cats in Coats, N.C.

Stephen Mark Rainey is the author of a dozen novels, six short story collections, 200-some published works of short fiction, and the scripts to several *Dark Shadows* audio productions, which feature members of the original ABC-TV series cast. For ten years he edited the award-winning *Deathrealm* magazine and has edited four anthologies, including the upcoming *Deathrealm: Spirits* from Shortwave Publishing. Mark lives in Greensboro, N.C., with his wife, Kimberly, and a horde of unruly housecats.

Rainer Maria Rilke (1875–1926) was an Austrian poet and novelist. Among his most celebrated works are *Duineser Elegien* (1922; *Duino Elegies*) and *Sonnete an Orpheus* (1922; *Sonnets to Orpheus*). His work is characterized by mysticism and a powerful use of metaphor. Many volumes of his letters have been published.

Sax Rohmer was the pseudonym of Arthur Sarsfield Ward (1883–1959), an Anglo-Irish novelist and short story writer who gained celebrity with novels and tales about the Chinese master criminal Fu Manchu, beginning with *The Mystery of Dr. Fu Manchu* (1913). He also wrote many weird tales, along with such weird novels as *Brood of the Witch Queen* (1920). A nonfiction work, *The Romance of Sorcery* (1914), is an informal history of occultism.

Hank Schwaeble is the Bram Stoker Award–winning author of *Damnable* (Berkley/Jove), *Diabolical* (Berkley/Jove), and *The Angel of the Abyss* (re-released by Esker & Riddle in 2021). He is also the author of the horror-noir collections *American Nocturne* and *Moonless Nocturne,* which has been optioned by the producer of *The Equalizer* movies. His stories have appeared in publications such as *Weird Tales* and numerous anthologies. Hank resides in Texas with his wife, fellow writer Rhodi Hawk.

Darrell Schweitzer only became a cat person by marriage to Marilyn Mattie Brahen, but has since shared a household with a cat named Lovecraft. Otherwise he is the author of *The Mask of the Sorcerer* and three others novels, plus about 350 short stories, numerous poems, essays, etc. He co-edited *Weird Tales* magazine between 1987 and 2007 and has edited anthologies since, most recently *Shadows out of Time* from PS Publishing. The same firm issued a two-volume retrospective of his work in 2020.

Robert W[illiam] Service (1874–1958) was born in England but emigrated to Canada in 1895. His many poetry collections include *Songs of a Sourdough* (1907), *Rhymes of a Rolling Stone* (1912), and *Rhymes of a Red-Cross Man* (1916). His poems were gathered in *Collected Verse* (1930) and *More Collected Verse* (1955).

M[atthew] P[hipps] Shiel (1865–1947) was an Anglo-Irish writer who lived in the Caribbean before emigrating to England in 1885. He became a renowned weird writer with such works as the story collections *Shapes in the Fire* (1896) and *The Pale Ape and Other Pulses* (1911) and the apocalyptic novel *The Purple Cloud* (1901). His best weird tales were gathered in *The House of Sounds and Others,* ed. S. T. Joshi (Hippocampus Press, 2005).

Christina Sng is the three-time Bram Stoker Award–winning author of *A Collection of Nightmares*, *A Collection of Dreamscapes*, and *Tortured Willows: Bent. Bowed. Unbroken.* Her poetry, fiction, essays, and art appear in numerous venues worldwide, including *Interstellar Flight Magazine, New Myths, Penumbric, Southwest Review,* and the *Washington Post.*

Anna Taborska is a filmmaker, screenwriter, and British Fantasy Award- and Bram Stoker Award-nominated author of short story collections *Shadowcats* (Black Shuck Books, 2019), *Bloody Britain* (Shadow Publishing, 2020), and *For Those Who Dream Monsters* (Mortbury Press, 2013, 2020). The latter won the Dracula Society's Children of the Night Award. Anna has directed five films and worked on TV productions such as *Auschwitz: The Nazis and The Final Solution*. You can visit Anna here: http://annataborska.wixsite.com/horror.

Mary A. Turzillo won a Nebula Award ("Mars Is No Place for Children," 1999) and two Elgin awards (*Sweet Poison* [with Marge Simon], 2014, and *Lovers & Killers,* 2012). Her novel *Mars Girls* (Apex) features two young Martian women rescuing themselves from Face-on-Mars crazies. Her purrfectly delicious story collection *Cosmic Cats & Fantastic Furballs* appeared March 2022 from WordFire. As a high-rated woman épée fencer in the US in her age class, she lives with scientist-author-fencer Geoffrey Landis

M. F. Webb has been writing since childhood, but only discovered her affinity for cats when she adopted her first kitten after college—an experience that has informed her personal and professional life since then. Webb's poetry has appeared in *Spectral Realms* and her fiction in *Latchkey Tales*. Originally from Texas, she now resides a little bit north of Seattle with her husband and a clowder of rescued cats.

W[illiam] B[utler] Yeats (1865–1939) was an Irish poet and playwright who spearheaded the Irish literary renaissance with such volumes of poetry as *The Wanderings of Oisin and Other Poems* (1889) and *The Countess Kathleen* (1892) and such plays as *The Land of Heart's Desire* (1894) and *Cathleen Ní Houlihan* (1902). He published is *Autobiographies* in 1926.

Acknowledgments

"The Adventure of the Hanoverian Vampires" by Darrell Schweitzer, first published in Robert Weinberg, ed., *Crafty Cat Crimes: 100 Tiny Cat Tale Mysteries* (Barnes & Noble Books, 2000); collected in Schweitzer's *Deadly Things* (Borgo Press, 2011); copyright 2000 by Darrell Schweitzer. Reprinted by permission of the author.

"Ailurophobe" by Mary Turzillo, copyright © 2023 by Mary Turzillo. Original to this volume. Printed by permission of the author.

"The Attic" by Algernon Blackwood, first published in the *Westminster Gazette* (20 April 1912); collected in Blackwood's *Pan's Garden: A Volume of Nature Stories* (Macmillan, 1912).

"Bad Cats" by Michael Potts, copyright © 2023 by Michael Potts. Original to this volume. Printed by permission of the author.

"The Black Cat" ("Schwartze Katze") by Rainer Maria Rilke, translated by Stephen Mitchell, first published in *The Selected Poetry of Rainier Maria Rilke* (Random House, 1982).

"The Boy Who Drew Cats" by Lafcadio Hearn, first published as *The Boy Who Drew Cats* (Japanese Fairy Tales) (Hasegawa, 1898).

"The Brazilian Cat" by Sir Arthur Conan Doyle, first published in the *Strand* (December 1898); collected in Doyle's *Round the Fire Stories* (Smith, Elder, 1908).

"A Cargo of Cat" by Ambrose Bierce, first published in the *Wasp* (3 January 1885); collected in Bierce's *Collected Works*, Volume 8 (Neale Publishing Co., 1911).

"The Cat" by M. P. Shiel, first published in the *Westminster Gazette* (18 April 1901).

"Cat and Mouse" by Ramsey Campbell, first published in Michel Parry, ed., *Beware of the Cat* (Victor Gollancz, 1972); collected in Campbell's *Strange Things and Stranger Places* (Tor, 1993); copyright © 1972 by Ramsey Campbell. Reprinted by permission of the author.

"The Cat and the Moon" by W. B. Yeats, first published in Yeats's *The Wild Swans at Coole* (Macmillan, 1919).

"The Cat That Walked by Himself" by Rudyard Kipling, first published in *Just So Stories* (Doubleday, Page, 1902).

"The Cat with Wings" by Robert W. Service, first published in Service's *Lyrics of a Lowbrow* (Dodd, Mead, 1951).

"The Cat-hood of Maurice" by E. Nesbit, first published in Nesbit's *The Magic World* (Macmillan, 1912).

"The Cats" by H. P. Lovecraft (written 1925), first published in Lovecraft's *A Winter Wish*, ed. Tom Collins (Whispers Press, 1977); corrected text in Lovecraft's *The Ancient Track: Complete Poetical Works*, ed. S. T. Joshi (Night Shade, 2001; rev. ed. Hippocampus Press, 2013).

"Cats and the Occult: A Canthropology" by Katherine Kerestman, copyright © 2023 by Katherine Kerestman. Original to this volume. Printed by permission of the author.

"The Cats of River Street" by Caitlin R. Kiernan, first published in Lois H. Gresh, ed., *Innsmouith Nightmares* (PS Publishing, 2015), copyright © 2015 by Caitlín R. Kiernan. Reprinted by permission of the author.

"Le Chat Noir, La Femme Vieille" by Alan Dean Foster, copyright © 2023 by Alan Dean Foster. Original to this volume. Printed by permission of the author.

"The Cheshire Cat" by Lewis Carroll, extract from Chapter 6 of Carroll's *Alice's Adventures in Wonderland* (Macmillan, 1865).

"The Crimson Curse" by Tony LaMalfa, first published in *The Sirens Call* (Halloween 2020), copyright © 2020 by Tony LaMalfa. Reprinted by permission of the author.

"Familiar" by Frank Coffman, first published in Coffman's *The Coven's Hornbook & Other Poems* (Bold Venture Press, 2019), copyright © 2019 by Frank Coffman. Reprinted by permission of the author.

"La Gata" by Lori R. Lopez, first published in *Spectral Realms* No. 17 (Summer 2022), copyright © 2022 by Hippocampus Press. Reprinted by permission of the author.

"Ghost Bats" by Jason C. Eckhardt, copyright © 2023 by Jason C. Eckhardt. Original to this volume. Printed by permission of the author.

"Gray" by M. F. Webb, first published in *Spectral Realms* No. 12 (Winter 2020), copyright © 2020 by Hippocampus Press. Reprinted by permission of the author.

"The Headless Cat of No. — Lower Seedley Road, Seedley, Manchester" by Elliot O'Donnell, first published in O'Donnell's *Animal Ghosts* (William Rider & Son, 1913).

"In the Valley of the Sorceress" by Sax Rohmer, first published in *Premier Magazine* (January 1916); collected in Rohmer's *Tales of Secret Egypt* (Methuen, 1918).

"The King of Cats" by Adam Bolivar, first published in *Spectral Realms* No. 16 (Winter 2022), copyright © 2022 by Hippocampus Press. Reprinted by permission of the author.

"Marked" by Anna Taborska, first published in Taborska's *Shadowcats* (Black Shuck Books, 2019), copyright © 2019 by Anna Taborska. Reprinted by permission of the author.

"Nimbus" by Stephen Mark Rainey, copyright © 2023 by Stephen Mark Rainey. Original to this volume. Printed by permission of the author.

"Nine" by Hank Schwaeble, copyright © 2023 by Hank Schaweble. Original to this volume. Printed by permission of the author.

"Old Man" by H. P. Lovecraft: extract of a letter to Duane W. Rimel (22 December 1934); first published in Lovecraft's *Selected Letters V,* ed. August Derleth and James Turner (Arkham House, 1976); corrected text in Lovecraft's *Letters to F. Lee Baldwin, Duane W. Rimel, and Nils H. Frome,* ed. David E. Schultz and S. T. Joshi (Hippocampus Press, 2016).

"The Only Thing a Cat Can Do" by Christina Sng, copyright © 2023 by Christina Sng. Original to this volume. Printed by permission of the author.

"Protectors, Psychopomps, and Other Cats in Weird Fiction" by Brandon R. Grafius, copyright © 2023 by Brandon Grafius. Original to this volume. Printed by permission of the author.

"The Sphinx at Gizeh" by Lord Dunsany, first published in *Tripod* (May 1912); collected in Dunsany's *Fifty-one Tales* (Elkin Mathews, 1915).

"Talmir and Threstenios" by Manuel Pérez-Campos, copyright © 2023 by Manuel Pérez-Campos. Original to this volume. Printed by permission of the author.

"The Tyger" by William Blake, first published in *Songs of Innocence and Experience* (self-published, 1794).

"The Witch of the Dark Woods" by Katherine Kerestman, copyright © 2023 by Katherine Kerestman. Original to this volume. Printed by permission of the author.

www.ingramcontent.com/pod-product-compliance
Lightning Source LLC
Chambersburg PA
CBHW030800200726
48285CB00013B/336